ISBN

978-0-9939744-4-1 Paperback   978-0-9939744-1-0 Dust Jacket

978-0-9939744-2-7 Electronic Book Text

On a narrow stretch of desolate beach hundreds of kilometres away from the closest civilization stands an enormous, ancient, wooden barn. Inside, sixteen people of varying ages and backgrounds struggle through icy cold winters, stifling hot summers, and a feast or famine supply of the basic necessities of life, waiting to be chosen. From every surface, surveillance cameras record every moment.

There is only one rule to life in the Barn: No one can ever leave. Not willingly.

Ash, the youngest of the inhabitants, has never known a life outside of the Barn. He, like most of the others, has been trapped here for as long as he can remember. Alongside his best friend Michael, Ash leads a relatively comfortable and privileged life compared to the others. As he ages however, Ash slowly begins to realize that life in the barn isn't at all what it seems to be.

When the unthinkable happens, Ash is left with a tough choice: to either continue to lay low and stay quiet as others are taken from the barn instead of him, or to step up and volunteer himself to visit the infamous Mr. Irvine, potentially subjecting himself to a life more captive and horrific than anything he could have imagined.

The Barn

By Richard Holt

Part 1

It was our world.

For as long as I remember, the rough, hand cut, uneven boards and timbers of the old barn framed in our house. Our jail cell. Our prison. It was the only home that most of us had ever known.

There are 16 of us that live here. 'Live' is perhaps a generous term. We exist here, but not one of us feel like we are really living.

Nobody seems to remember how they got here. Some of the older people remember their lives before coming to the barn, having been brought here in their mid-teens or early twenties. Others, like me, have been here since childhood.

Each story is the same: Waking up in a small, dark, wooden room, alone, lying on a floor covered in straw. Darkness, a cloudy haze, a throbbing head and a body that just won't cooperate. A quiet click and a door swings ever so slightly open. A dirty hand grabs the knob-less door by the side and eases it open. A semi-circle of grimy, curious strangers stand silently on in a cavernous wooden room, watching the new arrival, nobody welcoming. Every face wrought with sadness and empathy.

****

Our barn is exactly that: an ancient, hand constructed wooden shell built on a thick stone foundation. Inside, the air is thick and damp, so heavy with smoke that it feels like we are perpetually blanketed by a morning fog. Soot and ash cover every surface with a fine coating that leaves our skin dry and itchy.

Many times I have counted the steps from side to side and end to end of the building. I think everyone has. From end to end it takes me one hundred and seven steps. From side to side it takes me forty three steps. The barn had clearly been divided into several rooms and levels at some point, but other than a few precariously hanging shelves and ledges where sections had long since been removed, it is one vast, open space. There are no windows.

At the one end where new arrivals are periodically discovered, a solid wall climbs from floor to ceiling, save for the small, nearly hidden door directly in the centre, which is always locked from the other side. An old ladder is built into the frame of the wall rising from ground level all the way to the peak of the roof, a full 52 rungs high, leading to a little platform hanging from the ceiling, only as long as a grown man and just about as wide. A thin strip of wood circles the platform, flimsy, but just substantial enough to act as a railing. Beside the hanging platform there is an old wooden window shutter, long since sealed shut, and a large steel wheel hanging from the ceiling. Some of the older residents have guessed that it used to be a pulley system to get supplies from the outside up to the long demolished loft. For me this strange platform is my bedroom. I share it with two others.

The floor of our home is a mixture of dirt, mud and very old hay or straw, the latter of which has been reserved in large piles by the inhabitants and used as beds. Some of the older people were resourceful enough to save a few scraps of old material to cover their sleeping areas with, protecting them slightly against the scratchiness of the hay and discouraging bites from mice and tiny bugs, though in my opinion, the thin cloth doesn't do much other than get tangled in the night.

All of the makeshift sleeping pads are set up around a small fire pit at the back half of the barn where the ground is dry and the roof is free from leaks. During the cold nights of winter, the group sleeps snuggled tightly together in two or three large nests of hay to keep warm. On hot, humid summers, we often disperse around the edges of the drafty walls hoping to catch a bit of the night breeze that seeps through the cracks in the barn boards. Few people dare to sleep alone.

There are only two interesting things about the whole barn:

Amidst all of the wood, sand, dirt and hay, not a lot stands out to catch the eye. Everything blends into the other in colour and texture, presenting a monotonous, inhospitable atmosphere. In startling contrast, dozens of white glossy cylinders brazenly attach to almost every surface available, hiding in every corner and clinging to every support beam. Each white cylinder is capped off with a dark but transparent black dome. Upon closer inspection each dome houses a rotating, non-blinking eye, always on, always following our every move. I have counted every 'eye' as we call them so many times but must occasionally miss or double count a few, as there are so many that I often forget which ones I have accounted for. The general consensus between our group is that there is about 132 little eyes hidden around the barn.

The second interesting thing about the barn is the far wall, opposite the entry door: At first sight the wall appears to be a solid, continuous structure from floor to ceiling, edge to edge. There is no mysterious entry door, no ladder, no hanging platform or ledges. Here the ground slopes at a steep downwards angle, making the wall much taller than its counterpart on the opposite side of the building. Where the ground begins to slope, mud and dirt turn to fine white sand, soft and gentle on the feet, free of any pebbles or debris. For much of the day, cold water flows between the barns boards, filling the lower area to a depth of a grown mans waist before receding back through the cracks from which it came.

What makes this area truly unique though is the wall itself. For endless days or weeks on end it is just a wall, another warden of our captivity. Sporadically though, without any warning or sign, the entire wall breaks out in a deafening cacophony of creaks, groans and bangs so loud that we all jump from surprise each and every time it happens. Slowly and gradually, by means of some unseen mechanism, the wall begins to pull outward from the base of the barn, detaching from the side walls, rising higher and higher until it comes to a groaning halt in line with the ceiling, cantilevering out over the sandy ground far below. We all stare each time this happens. The simple fact that such a large object can so quickly be altered is unnerving to those of us who have rarely seen anything move other than humans, bugs and the occasional small animal. Our eyes burn from the sudden exposure to such intense daylight, typically having only the dusty illumination of light sneaking through the narrow slits between the barn boards to light our days.

Yet we still stare. Before us, as far as we can see lays a great and vast ocean.

At first sight, natural instinct takes hold and every tissue in our bodies react like those of a trapped animal who has just discovered an escape; a natural rush of adrenaline, courage and strength driven by the possibility of escape. The ability to sprint through the open wall and into the freedom that lies beyond had been a daily fantasy and a nightly dream since the day of my arrival. The desire pulls so strongly at times that the occasional few have been known to make a run for it in absolute desperation. This has often been the case when the great door unexpectedly opens after weeks of extreme temperatures and prolonged starvation and deprivation from clean drinking water. None who have ever succumbed to this instinct have been alive for more than a few splashes into the water, brought down by a hail of small projectiles shot from unseen weapons.

There is only one rule here at the barn: No one can ever leave. At least, not willingly.

****

My name is Ash. I was given that name by the people here when I first arrived. As the story goes, I had arrived in the middle of the night during a cold wintry storm. As per the standard arrival story of all of us, my high pitched screams woke the other inhabitants of the barn and I was pulled from the darkness of the entry room into the dark barn by a young woman named Nasha. Covered in my own filth, badly bruised, my dark brown hair caked with blood, thin and very dehydrated, I was a perfect example of every person who has come through that door.

As the cold winds blew through the barn boards, I shivered uncontrollably while Nasha bathed me in the sandy, ice cold ocean water that seeped under the closed barn door during the early morning high tide. Despite our shared body heat as Nasha cuddled me in the relative warmth of her hay nest, my condition worsened as the days past and I drifted into and out of consciousness. Had it not been for her constant care, I never would have survived.

The name 'Ash' was given to me by Nasha herself several weeks after my arrival. I couldn't have been more than 2 summers old, but my speech was very delayed for my age. She had been trying to teach me to say her name, as any mother figure does with a new child, for she had quickly taken me to be her own.

As my health improved, my ramblings became incessant as I practiced making new noises and sounds. I couldn't quite say Nasha at first, childishly reducing the name down to something more like 'Asha', and subsequently began calling everyone Asha. In return, that is what everyone began calling me and the name stuck. As I aged, one of the men in the barn pointed out that in his culture, Asha was a girl's name, so the last 'a' was gradually dropped and I simply became Ash.

At this time I was the only child in the group. Nasha and the others had been here for several years by their estimate. There had been other children in the past but they had all mysteriously died or vanished by the time I arrived. Nobody has ever spoken of this time in greater detail with me.

The others in the group typically stayed away from me unless there was a time that Nasha was unable to care for me. They all seemed interested in me, but for reasons I only learned to understand later in my life, they kept as emotionally detached from me as possible. Even Nasha clearly made efforts to keep her emotions limited. She would provide me with as many of the necessities of life that she was

4

able to, ensure that I would keep myself out of harm's way, and do her best to teach me to speak and develop properly, but aside from that, I was largely left to entertain myself. I remember those rare moments of closeness so distinctly: The sweet smell of her long, soft black hair, her gentle, comforting hugs, the quiet tune she would hum as she put me to sleep each night. I yearned for her constant attention, immensely hurt when she denied me, overwhelmed with happiness in the moments when she gave in.

Going by a typical time frame, there was a relatively short period before the next occupant arrived.

Sometimes many summers and winters pass with no new arrivals. I had arrived during the bitter depths of winter, and after a quiet year surrounded by solemn adults, I became bored and temperamental. It came as no surprise to many that when the hot summer nights of my second year in the barn began to grow cool, a rustling was heard emanating from beyond the walls of the barn. I had no idea what the cause could be, but the adults all seemed to be exuding a nervous, knowing energy between them.

Long after the noises had vanished into the unknown distance, a light clinking noise broke the anxious air that hung between us and the mysterious entry door swung just slightly askew. After many moments of cautious observation, the group moved in a practiced, careful creep towards the door. In absolute silence, a young woman in the group inched her hand around the crack of the door and gently pulled it open.

Standing between the legs of Nasha and some other person who I hadn't bothered to look at, I was torn between hiding my head in fear and looking with excitement at what was about to be visible. It was the first time that I had seen this mysterious door open. I had no idea what to expect.

I gasped in shock when the door was completely opened, my reaction echoed by almost everyone else around me. There, curled up in a little ball on a bed of fresh hay, sound asleep, clad in a perfectly clean pair of shorts and a white shirt, was a small boy. The scent of his freshly cleaned hair and clothing wafted out the door tickling the senses of all of us observers. He appeared to be in better shape than any of us had been.

The woman who had opened the door stepped into the room on legs that seemed to be wobbling in fear, yet she managed to get close enough to wake the young boy, gently tapping his arm. Surprisingly, he came to quickly, almost instantly alert, standing on his own with practiced simplicity. I stood silently by, observing this miniature version of the adults around me with awe. His light brown hair, his stability and sureness of movement and his build hinted at his age being slightly older than mine, yet we were about the same height. With a huge smile on his face he scanned the faces in front of him with excitement. Clearly his delivery here had been quick and uneventful.

The moment his blue-grey eyes caught mine, his smile broadened even more. Mine quickly matched his and we ran together and embraced as if we had known each other forever. To the amazement of everyone, we immediately ran off and began playing in the sand, giggling uncontrollably, play fighting and chasing each other around the barn. The others just stared in pitied amazement.

His name was Michael. Michael could speak much better than I could and knew a lot about his life before coming to the barn.

He was 5 years old. He had a mommy and a daddy and a dog named Goose who was big and furry and liked to sleep in Michael's bed but didn't like having his tail pulled. Michael could count to twenty, knew most of his colours, and even knew how to draw letters.

I vaguely remember listening to some of his stories about home when he first arrived. He would tell me about soft beds, rooms with wheels called 'cars.' His description of 'outside' fascinated me the most: wide open spaces filled with green yards and trees, swings and slides and birds in the sky, other little kids playing together out in a park. I remember struggling to picture the scene, having trouble imagining a wide open space with no walls, covered in a green, hair-like coating, identical duplicates of Michael running around chaotically as enormous bugs circled above.

His parents, a foreign concept in itself, sounded like giants to me, as tall as the roof with hair as blonde as the straw bedding. I wondered why he only had two adults in his life when I had been surrounded by them. It was the one thing that made me feel like I had one up on him.

I had nightmares of Goose, the 'big fuzzy four legged' animal looking like an enormous version of the mice that wiggled through the barn boards on cold nights and early mornings.

Michael's simple stories fascinated me and lead me into hours of daydreams of things that I may never experience. His limited descriptions were more than I could have ever imagined on my own, having no distinct memory of life outside of the barn. I would often ask the adults around me to verify Michaels stories or share some of their own, but they would simply just nod or mumble something about it being better that I don't know about these sorts of things.

Of course I only remember these early days in the same shadowy, wispy ways that one remembers a dream moments after waking, but I have been told the stories so many times that my imagination has etched those images into my mind as clearly as any other memory I have.

****

"Do you remember anything about where you came from?" The whisper was just loud enough to wake me. With my eyes still closed and my mind still foggy from a dream already forgotten, I could tell that this was a conversation that I was not meant to hear.

"Yes," came the hushed response, the childish voice instantly recognizable as Michaels.

"Can you tell me what you remember?" The whisperer clearly a man. He sounded like one of the more senior elders, Aaron, but I couldn't be sure.

"A lady came to get me because my mommy and daddy are going away for a while and are bringing me presents soon. She brought me to the top of the big needle tower with the glass floor where people are as small as ants! We had ice cream for breakfast! Then Mr. Irvine came and brought me to his house in the big gold tower. He has a hot pool there up in the clouds and a wall of fish that are bigger than me! "

"Mr. Irvine? Did you know him before?"

"No but he said he is daddy's friend," Michael responded uncertainly.

"What else did he say to you?"

"He was gunna bring me to my new best friend and we will have animals like goats and rabbits and puppies and kitties," was the slightly more excited response.

"How did you get from the big gold house to here?" pried the male voice.

"We went in a really long black car with no seat belts and then up in the sky in a big white plane with a TV as big as the wall and I was allowed to watch movies all day!"

"Do you know where you were when the plane landed? How long it took to get from the airplane to the barn?"

Michael hesitated while he thought about his answer. With evident confusion he replied "I woke up here."

The conversation ended there as the two speakers evidently fell back to sleep. I laid there for a long time dreaming of flying inside a bird way up in the sky, of a place where people were as tiny as ants, and of a giant home made out of gold. This eavesdropped conversation would become one of my earliest, most distinct memories.

****

The first time that I ever saw the door open was at the beginning of the summer of my arrival. Winter had been bitterly cold, dark and wet. We had all become desperate for warmth and sunlight, typically spending most nights curled up in the hay with the bodies of every person in the barn pressed tightly together for warmth. On only the absolute frigid of nights did we ever have a tiny fire to lie beside and warm our numbing fingers and noses, craving a stronger flame. Our nightly ration of two small wooden boards was never enough to drive the warmth into our veins.

I didn't understand why we couldn't put more on the fire until one night when I woke to find a young woman with bright blonde hair holding one of the evenings last burning cinders from the fire against one of the barn walls. I could tell immediately that she was distressed. Uncertain of what to do, I nudged Kevin, the man lying next to me, and pointed in the woman's direction. He and the others had just begun settling in for the night but were not yet asleep. It only took a moment before the recognition of what was happening flickered through his eyes. In an instant he was at a full sprint towards the woman.

"What are you doing!?" he yelled with more force than I had ever heard in my life. Panic embraced the woman as she jumped from her place holding a short pipe forcefully in Kevin's direction, bravery and fear emanating from her at the same time.

"Stay back!" she yelled back with an intense combination of sadness and determination to her voice. "I have to get out of here! I can't do this anymore! We can set fire to this place! We can escape!"

Kevin leaped at the woman, simultaneously and skillfully disarming her and knocking her to the ground, pinning her body under his in the same movement

"You'll incinerate us!" he yelled.

"Some of us could make it out!" she cried dejectedly, struggling to escape the hold he had on her.

"And then what? We'd be shot the moment we got outside!" he yelled back

"Would that be so bad?" she whimpered, her body falling weak and defeated beneath his.

Kevin, seemingly shocked by the woman's response, seemed to crumble in understanding, staring her in the eyes for a moment before completely collapsing on her. He lowered his forehead to hers, closing his eyes as his grip on her arms relaxed.

"We will survive this," he softly replied.

Both lay together in silence as the rest of us watched in awe. As I look around me I could see that every adult had tears in their eyes. I wasn't sure if they were upset by the extremity of the event that had just taken place, sad to witness the woman's desperation, or sad because they too felt the same as her. I watched as the ember that the woman had taken lost its glow as it lay in the dirt and quickly turned black.

9

My gaze moved to the fire pit in front of me. It too was dark. An unusually cold spring wind howled through the barn boards. Tears filled my eyes as, in my young mind, all I had absorbed from the commotion was that tonight would be another desperately frigid night thanks to the woman who had just stolen our only source of warmth.

Although I knew that there must be some reason behind her actions, I drifted off to a bitter sleep soon after, hating her for every shiver and goose bump I felt.

When I awoke mid-morning, I found that everyone was still huddled together in our tight sleeping ball. I found it unusual at first, as most of us would be up with the sun on a normal day. It was only when I heard a slight whimper coming from several of the others that I realized that something other than the need for warmth and sleep had kept them all together. Something bad. It was only after I sat up and looked around that I realized what the problem was: The woman who had caused the scene last night was nowhere to be seen. In a barn so open and cavernous there wasn't a single place to hide. She simply was not in the building anymore. Nasha lay beside me, eyes open and red, tears slowly leaking down her cheek.

"Where is that woman?" I asked quietly.

Nasha choked off a sob. "She's gone."

"Where?" Fear of the answer almost prevented me from wanting to know the question.

"Don't ask that please," she replied, shaking, this time with fear.

When we found her in the entry room several weeks later, she was naked, frail, covered in bruises and open wounds and missing large chunks of her hair. Some of the other woman washed her under the cold tap, caressed her face and held her close to their bodies as they whispered gentle words to her. Not a single word came from her lips. Not that day, not for weeks. I couldn't even begin to imagine what horrors had happened to her. I felt that it was all my fault. I had been the one to point her out when she had attempted to burn the barn down.

I didn't know her name at the time, but found out later that she was called Julie. It was the day after her return to us that I saw the great barn door open for the first time.

I distinctly remember waking up that morning lying in the cold hay, tightly pressed against someone else's body, shivering with cold. I had been having nightmares all night about Julie. In my dreams, a beaten, bloody, crazy Julie chased me all around a dark room screaming 'It's all your fault!'

I could feel her cold hands and breath on me as she charged against my body and pinned me to the floor. 'We should be dead!' she yelled.

Over and over again throughout the night I would wake up after having a similar dream. Each time I forced myself to lay perfectly still in the darkness until I was sure that it was only a dream, hugging the person in front of me tightly both in effort to calm myself and conceal myself from whatever demon might be lurking in the darkness with us.

Just before sunrise I had been in a semi-slumber, beginning to fall back to sleep after another terrifying nightmare. The barn was deathly quiet; no snoring or movements from the others who slept around me, no whistling winds blowing from the outside through the barn walls. Not even the rhythmic hush from the unknown source that seemed to be constant in the background that I never really noticed until these quiet times.

Every nerve in my body was zapped to life the instant that the barn door first started to open. The fear that I had felt during my nightmares somehow transcended into reality and suddenly I was sure that I was being attacked by Julie, that the barn was on fire, that unknown monsters were smashing my world to pieces! I had no idea what was happening! I had never heard something so loud!

Not surprisingly, the sudden noise had startled everyone awake. All of the adults initially jumped in shock to the first cracks, bangs and clunks of the door beginning to move, surely as shaken by the events of the past evening as I had still was, fearing that something else bad was about to happen. Quickly though, their demeanor changed, their body language relaxed, and ignorant of the panic and fear within me, they all settled back down to their bedding, eyes wearily focused on the door.

Silence lingered between the others as we all watched the door rise. When it finally thudded into its full open position and the noises came to a groaning halt, I sat staring at the vast open space ahead of us in astonishment and confusion. The flat, calm, endless surface of the water seemed to blend synonymously with the charcoal morning sky above creating a feeling that our barn hung precariously on the edge of the world, about to fall into endless space. The thought paralyzed me as I clung tightly to others around me.

For what seemed like hours of silence may have only been seconds, silence screamed from the walls, broken finally by a solemn, resigned sigh from a woman who I knew as Mallie.

"I knew this would happen," she said under her breath, her gaze sadly shifting to look at Julie.

"At least we survived another winter," responded Aaron.

****

Daily life in the barn was always a struggle.

Usually food was scarce and we often went through long periods of famine. At other times, food was so bounteous, the water clean, and on the very rarest of occasions, both would come to us steaming with warmth. As a child I never understood why we had these extremes. It was just how things worked here. As I got older however, a clear pattern emerged.

It terrified me.

Water was almost always available to us. It came up through the ground in the centre of the barn, capped off by a rusty valve whose handle had long since corroded due to the sea's salt in the air. It took one of the elders to open and close the valve properly, as the sharp nub controlling the flow was too tough for either me or Michael to turn.

One of the older people had long ago retrieved a large plastic jug that had washed up on the beach, and though its upper half was cracked and dented, the bottom half held just enough water to last two days in the rare event that our water supply went dry.

The water was almost always ice cold, brown and smelling like dirt, but it quenched our thirst and, in those times of little or no food, would temporarily fill our bellies. It was only on particularly frigid nights in the winter, or as an occasional reward, that we would be permitted to have a few hours of warm water. To us, these precious few moments of warm water were some of the most exciting, revitalizing moments of our lives. To be able to rinse days and often weeks of grime from our skin without the sting of icy water or the dryness of salt from the ocean was almost as gratifying as a good hearty meal of meat and fruits. To be clean, warm and odour free restored our spirits, lightened our moods and made life a bit more pleasant for a few days.

I never really noticed at first, but as I aged I soon began to realize that Michael and I led a very different life than others around us. We were generally content little kids. The two of us were never at a loss for entertainment. We somehow had the ability to turn anything into a toy and play with it for hours. Michael was much better at this, as he often relied on his greater knowledge of the outside world to come up with new and amazing games. We would fill our days playing tag, burying each other in the sand and hay, throwing rocks and other small objects back and forth, laughing the whole time. Cop and robber was a daily must. We loved the part where we got shot and had to play dead. We'd often spend a whole morning repeatedly falling to the ground and laying still for as long as we could while the other would try to bring the dead person back to life.

I remember one of my favourite games was to play "Phone." Michael and I would find two similar objects, most often rocks, and, holding them to our ears, would take part in long excited conversations as if we hadn't spoken to each other just moments earlier.

"Why do we have to hold something to our ears to talk?" I remember asking the first time we played this game.

"Because we talk on phones when we are far away from each other," Michael replied with a laugh, clearly amused that this was not common sense to me.

"Why don't we just yell then?"

"Because we can be in different rooms! Or towns! Or even the other side of the world!" he responded excitedly.

I had never imagined a place where two people could be in different spaces without being able to see one another. It was a mind blowing concept for me! To imagine a place where two people could be so far apart that they wouldn't be able to walk to each other was unfathomable to me!

As I slowly grasped the concept, I began to play this game with my eyes closed, imagining myself in another barn on the other side of the ocean, or sitting in soft golden piles of hay surrounded by my interpretation of what Michael and some of the others had described as trees-- planks of long barn boards reaching to the sky, topped off with hair the colour of Nasha's green eyes--or in great houses made of stones with multiple rooms and levels. It was one of the many games that tested my imagination and helped me to learn more about the outside world. I wanted to play it more than any other game when I was younger.

****

When we first arrived here at the barn, Michael and I were watched by the others to an almost obsessive level. All eyes were on us at all times, our hands were almost always being held by an adult, always pulling us back, guiding us to sit still and be quiet. Whispering voices concealed the subject of a conversation, but glaring looks, nods and nudges in our direction always reminded Michael and I that we were under constant supervision. Fights between the elders often broke out over the care and control of us. Usually Nasha and some of the other women were arguing for a larger share of food on our behalf while one or two of the men would stand their ground, regimental in the opinion that we already got enough special treatment.

More than once I heard the argument that Michael and I should be killed for our own good. I didn't understand this statement at the time, but I have come to wonder now how things may have been better for the others if they had followed through with this idea.

****

One of our favourite activities was swimming.

At first, Michael and I were strictly forbidden to go near the water when the big door at the end of the barn was raised. Initially both Michael and I were terrified to go even close to the open side of the barn. Even Michael had never seen such a large expanse of open space before, let alone so much water.

For the first few days Nasha held tightly onto both Michael and I all throughout the day. I wasn't quite sure where her fear was based; the events from the night before Julie had disappeared, or simply her fear of the open water, but as children do, I saw her fear and made it my own. Michael reacted more with curiosity more than fear, yet the fact that the adults were so concerned worried him enough to keep his distance from the open wall as well.

As time passed, the days quickly grew warmer, as did people's attitudes. The wall had been open for thirteen full sleeps now and I spent much of my time watching the gentle pulsation of the water and the light crash of the waves on the sand. It was mesmerizing to me. Something in my mind reminded me that what I saw before me was dangerous, yet I was drawn to it in a similar way to being drawn to spoiled food after not eating for days.

Life became happier than I had ever experienced. Food arrived three to five times a week in the little entry room, abundant enough for each person to full their bellies to the brim. We ate things that I never experienced before: pre-cooked meats, breads, warm soups, brightly coloured fruits of all shapes and sizes, and even sweet treats of chocolate, nuts or chewy, jiggly worms. All were new to me and each flavour brought great waves of excitement coursing through my body. My favourite by far was the pineapple and the chewy worms.

Nasha would often have to stop Michael and I from over-eating, saying that we would get stomach aches and nightmares if we did. The few times we did this without her knowledge, we found out that she had been right.

Warm water was also very abundant at this time. Nights were still cool but come morning, the rising sun quickly brought the temperature to a comfortable level. Hot water would gush from the tap and we would all use it to bathe and warm up. In the afternoons, clear cool water flowed so readily that we didn't even worry about using the large plastic container for a reserve, almost forgetting that the supply could stop at any time.

We were warm, putting on weight quickly, relaxed and relatively happy. We all spent most afternoons contently napping away.

The only person who didn't partake in the new era of comfort was Julie. She had become a recluse, hiding her body under thick layers of clothing borrowed from others, eyes always averted, lost in their gaze as she stared at the floor or ceiling.

She rarely moved. Most days she slept, or pretended to sleep, tucked into a ball of hay that she had brought down near the water's edge, far away from the others, as distant as she could get from the entry door. She never spoke or interacted with any of us. Once a day Nasha would gently approach Julie with a few gentle words, a small plastic cup of water and some food. Often the food was left untouched by the time the rest of us prepared for bed. Julie was wasting away in front of us while we all grew healthier and happier. I couldn't understand her behaviour, yet kept my concerns quiet, as all of the adults seemed to comprehend some reasoning that was beyond my ability to understand.

It was during one of the late afternoon naps that I first went into the ocean.

Michael and I had been loudly playing a game of kick-the-ball with a nearly perfectly round stone the size of an apple that we saved specifically for this game. Everyone else had been napping for quite a long time and didn't seem to be bothered by the loud noises we were making.

Back and forth we would kick the ball between us, running around the whole barn. Sometimes we would try to steal the stone from the other, while other times we would set up other objects to knock over or divert around.

We had just set up an area against one of the side walls, marking two lines in the dirt as posts in between which we would attempt to kick the stone, while the other person would try to prevent the stone from hitting the wall behind them. Each time we were successful in blocking a shot we would switch places and the other would have an opportunity to attempt a goal.

As our skills quickly improved, the shots on the goal became faster and more forceful in an attempt to sneak the stone past the goal keeper. Michael was in goal. He had been much more successful in getting the ball past me throughout the game and I was determined to prove myself to be as skilled as him.

With a short run at the stone and a great swing of my leg, my foot connected painfully with the stone, launching it towards Michael much faster than any other shot yet. With absolute fear in his eyes Michael instinctively fell to the ground and covered his head with his arms. The stone flew past him, grazing his shoulder slightly, hitting the wall with a thud before ricocheting off the wood, quickly rolling down the sloped ground, right into the water.

The sight paralyzed me.

We had just lost our only perfect ball.

Michael was back on his feet seconds after the wild shot had bounced down the hill. He too looked down the slope towards the water's edge with awe and loss. We each turned and made eye contact, both shocked into immobility. It was the first time that I had ever lost anything.

We stood quietly for a minute or so not knowing what to do before I noticed Michael glancing towards the elders. They were all still soundly resting from what I could see. Even Julie, only a dozen or so steps from where we had been playing seemed peacefully dozing. Before he moved I could tell that Michael was up to something. He looked quickly back towards me, momentarily flashing a look that projected both fear and mischievousness.

Before I could react he was running down the slope past Julie as fast as his legs would take him.

The moment seemed to go on forever.

Fear sparked in every nerve of my body, my chest hurt and my breath locked in my throat. Logically I knew that it had only taken a few seconds before Michael came to an abrupt stop at the water's edge, but all of the fun and laughter that I had been experiencing moments earlier felt like a distant memory.

I stood frozen in terror, still afraid of the great wide open space before me, mortified by the unknown, horrified as I remembered the one and only rule that I had ever known about life in the barn: No one can ever leave.

At this point in my life I was unaware of the details of failed attempts made by others to try to escape through the open wall, but I knew that nobody ever survived. Michael knew this fact as well as I did. I couldn't imagine what was going through his mind or why he would tackle such fear for a simple toy.

As his toes touched the water he looked back at me. I saw nothing but dread in his eyes.

"It's right there," he called to me. "I can almost reach it."

I could hear his words but my mind was racing too quickly to comprehend them. I watched as he splashed his toes back and forth in the water, testing the temperature, testing the rules, testing his own courage. I couldn't react. I knew that a ball was not worth death or punishment. It wasn't worth losing my best friend. At the same time, I could taste a tiny bit of the bravery that Michael was battling with. I wanted to feel it too. I wanted to step up to take his place and protect him from any possible harm. He was older than me, smarter, and new more about the outside world. He was funnier, calm, well behaved, and yet I had always felt that I needed to protect him.

These thoughts all raced through my mind so quickly that it was impossible to interpret them. All I could do was stand there and watch as my best friend was about to take his last few breaths of life.

Michael swished his other foot in the water, moving just inches further towards the ball. My heart lurched and I suddenly regained control of my thoughts and my limbs.

Just as I leapt forward to stop him, Michael jumped.

****

He convinced me to come in.

I don't know how he did it. My heart was still thudding against my chest, my mind still racing.

He had survived.

There were no monsters that rose up from the depths of the ocean, no current to sweep him away. The door did not close on him, crushing him beneath or locking him out of the barn. I don't know what I had expected to happen, but nothing did.

I watched in astonishment for a little while as Michael nervously retrieved the round stone that we had used as a ball, throwing it onto shore within my reach. I had expected him to come right out of the water, but he didn't. He went out further.

The water was up to his shoulders, and when the small waves came they temporarily dunked him under. After only a few moments the worried expression left his face and was replaced by a huge smile. He laughed as he bounced up and down with such ease, sputtering water out of his mouth and nose uncomfortably, but with no effect on his demeanor.

"Come in!" he encouraged with a laugh. "It's cold and salty! I feel so light!"

He laughed as he splashed the water around him, its drops glinting in the rays of the sun like shiny yellow eyes. "Just do it! You'll be okay!"

I couldn't help but shiver in nervousness. I tried to make myself brave, but all I felt was fear. Everything inside me screamed that it was dangerous to go in the water. Everything I had been taught echoed in my head. Leaving the barn equaled death, yet Michael had done it and was still alive.

And he was laughing.

I wanted so much to experience what he was experiencing. More than that though, I wanted Michael to stay as my best friend, to think me as being as fun and as brave as he was. I didn't want to disappoint him. For some reason, this was the overriding emotion in my childish mind, and this alone was what made me jump.

It was the most bizarre feeling. The brisk temperature of the water matched the cold inside me that had been brought on by my fear, taking my breath away and making my skin feel instantly numb. Adrenaline coursed through my veins as I tried to catch my breath, panting and flailing in the unfamiliar sensation of being enveloped in water, fearfully wondering when and how we would be killed.

The water where I was standing was only up to my chest. I could feel the soft sand under my feet and the realization that there was not a bottomless pit below the surface of the water subdued me slightly.

I looked over at Michael. He had cheered and clapped with delight when I jumped in the water and was now laughing as he watched me foolishly thrashing about, shaking both from the ice cold temperature and from my lingering fears, clearly making fun of my panic.

It was the first time that he had ever laughed at me.

My heart dropped. I couldn't let Michael see that I was not as brave as him. Irrationally I felt that this one moment would either lock or destroy our bond, and I couldn't bear to lose his friendship.

I quickly steeled myself. Heart still pounding, I somehow managed to stand upright and still in the water, calmed my breathing and let my hands float to the surface on their own. Michael was still laughing. Embarrassment took over from the fear. I needed to do something now to prove that I was not a coward.

Hesitantly I raised my right hand slightly above the water, then watched as I gently bobbed my palm on the surface. I looked up at Michael again as he continued to laugh. Annoyed by my own embarrassment, I wanted nothing more than for Michael to be laughing with me, not at me. In a burst of frustration I quickly raised my hand above my head and slammed it into the water. The resulting splash exploded towards Michael, dousing his hair and going into his open mouth. I was instantly mortified at my actions and regretted doing it, but Michael's mockery quickly became camaraderie, splashing me back, initiating a battle that made me laugh so hard that my face began to hurt.

Exhausted, we moved to shallower water where we could sit comfortably on the bottom without our heads going under since we hadn't yet figured out how to hold our breath, and sat happily together, Michaels arm over my shoulder. My fears of disappointing or even possibly losing my best friend had abated. I had conquered my fears and successfully sealed the bond between us. I knew we would be friends forever.

Our moment of serenity was abruptly thrown into chaos.

"What are you doing?!" a female voice boomed from the shore. "Get out of the water!"

The panic in the voice was bone chilling. I jumped up from my position so quickly, turning in the process to see the face of the person who was calling, that I fell backwards towards deeper water.

As I stood up in the waist-deep water I could see that it was Nasha who was yelling at us, running at full speed the length of the barn towards us.

"Get out! Get out! You'll be killed!" she screamed. Even from this distance I could see the tears on her cheeks.

Just as quickly, the rest of the group were at their feet and either standing in awe or running just behind Nasha. They must have just woken from their mid-afternoon nap, Nasha being the first to notice our absence.

As Nasha ran, I noticed that Julie, who had been sleeping in her bed on the water's edge when we first jumped in was now sitting cross legged on the beach, her white blonde hair was glowing under the hot sun. She was peacefully watching us, seemingly unaware of the commotion behind her, a perfect image of serenity. For a moment our eyes locked. There was the slightest trace of content in her eyes. Not vindictive or malicious in any way, but somehow just calming. I knew then that she had been watching Michael and I all along.

As Nasha neared the water's edge she continued her panicked demand for us to get out of the water.

"Please come to me! Quickly! It's not safe!"

My trance broke from Julie's eyes the instant that the shot rang out and Nasha fell to the ground.

The popping noise was the loudest thing I had ever heard. In an instant my ears were ringing and all other sounds were drowned out. Nasha had fallen face forward into the sand, sliding a considerable distance until coming to a stop with her head and shoulders underwater. I had no idea what had happened, but I was sure that she was dead.

To my surprise, as quickly as she had fallen, she jumped up and back towards the barn, falling heavily on her bum, her face wet with water and covered in sand, stricken with horror.

POP! Another deafening shot pierced the air and the sand in front of Nasha's feet leapt into the air. In instinctual reaction, Nasha threw her body backwards away from the water, flailing back a full body length, eyes and mouth so wide open in fright that her face was almost unrecognizable.

POP! The third shot rang out, detonating the sand at Nasha's feet yet again. With just as much terror, Nasha's limbs continued to force her retreat.

POP! POP! POP POP! Four more shots spurred the terrified woman back further from the water's edge, each eardrum-bursting bang also forcing the others who had gathered behind her to tumble over one another as they likewise retreated.

Michael and I had fallen together in the water, him lying on across my knees as we cowered our heads, covered our ears and snuck concerned, fearful glances at the events in front of us. With a flick of an eye I quickly stole a concerned peek towards Julie. She had remained relatively unmoved from her serene position on the beach, only turning her head to protect her eyes from the blast of sand that flew through the air.

It took me a moment to realize that the popping had stopped; the ringing in my ears muffled every other noise, somehow amplifying the sound of my own breathing.

Michael and I slowly unfolded ourselves from one another, afraid that any quick movement would bring on another onslaught of attack, worried that this time it would be us who were the targets. Up on the hard packed mud within the barn, far away from the sandy beach and water's edge, the others similarly began to allow their limbs to shift and reposition, their eyes slowly turning towards Nasha, myself and Michael to see if we had survived the melee.

Nasha was the only person who remained unmoved, her gaze locked to the sand at her feet anticipating another eruption of the earth around her, chest heaving in distress and exhaustion. It wasn't until another woman came quickly to her side whispering gently while checking Nasha for injuries that she moved at all, realizing that it was over.

As if suddenly remembering the reason for her initial panic, Nasha's head snapped up in my direction, her eyes staring unbelievably that Michael and I were unharmed.

"What was that!?" I heard her ask despairingly to no one in particular.

"Come. COME! Now!" urged the woman at her side, struggling to lift and drag Nasha back up towards the barn. "Get UP!" she said with one great final tug.

As Nasha staggered backwards using her left hand as a third leg, the woman pulling forcefully on her right, Nasha continued to stare in disbelief and concern towards us.

22

"I don't understand!" I heard her cry out.

Julie had resumed her relaxed position on the corner of the beach; almost completely unchanged since the moment I had first noticed that she had been watching us. Just as before she stared at me, locking her eyes on mine in a glare that was seemingly intent on unnerving me.

"You can get out of the water now," she said with a confidence. It was the first she had spoken in weeks.

I looked at her with confusion. Her composure and certainty displayed in her body language somehow worried me.

"Come on now," she coerced, "It's over for now. Get out of there and dry off."

She was an adult so I felt compelled to obey her, but the events of the past few minutes had anchored me to my place. Looking up to the group who were now watching Michael and I in nervous anticipation, I had hoped to gain some sense of guidance from one of them; some look of safety or reassurance. All I saw was fear and curiosity.

I looked down at Michael. He still sat in the water, body lowered beneath its surface, his hands still covering his ears. Tears streamed down his face from his tightly closed eyes as he suppressed loud sobs. It was the first time I had ever seen him display any sign of weakness; any emotion other than happiness. As fearful and confused as I was, something in me grew in that moment and I knelt down to embrace him gently.

"Don't be scared," I said calmly. "It's over and everyone is okay."

Slowly his eyes opened and met mine; the look of absolute dependency in his grey-blue eyes strengthening my reserve, relaxing my nerves. Michael allowed himself to survey the scene around us, uneasily attempting to interpret the looks from the others up on safe ground.

I pulled his head gently back in my direction to make him look at me again.

"It's okay. I promise," I said, my body confidently betraying the anxiety in my nerves.

As we raised ourselves to stand I could feel the eyes of everyone on us and somehow I knew that the little black domes in the shiny white cylinders that surrounded the barn, whatever they were, were also fixated on our every move.

I took the first step towards the beach while holding Michael's hand. I was as scared as I had been when I took that first step into the water, and now moving to get out, I was so terrified that I had forgotten to breathe. I looked at Michael as he hesitantly staggered slightly behind me, tears still flowing, but no longer sobbing.

The second step somehow solidified my confidence that we were going to be okay. We were still in the water, but I just knew that the danger had abated. With a gentle tug I pulled Michael behind me. Splashing gently onto the sand at the water's edge revived a momentary pulse of concern that the ground was about to erupt into another symphony of explosions, but another step forward reaffirmed my conviction and I kept moving. A few steps further up the slope we had reached dry sand.

Beside me lay the stone ball that had started the whole ordeal. With a false sense of security I scooped it up with my free hand and quickly passed it to Michael.

"Was it your turn or mine," I said with a forced smile.

My heart was still thudding against my chest, my mind was still racing. Again, we had survived.

****

Later that evening as all of the adults except Julie morosely napped in their beds around a small fire I heard Nasha speaking to the group:

"What happened? I don't get why they weren't killed. Everyone else who set foot in that water has been shot instantly."

"I don't know," answered David, the eldest of the group. "Maybe he missed this time."

24

"There's no way!" aggressively replied a young dark-skinned man who called himself Joseph, even though we all knew his real name to be something unpronounceable. "Those shots were intentionally aimed at Nasha! He didn't want her to try to escape with them!"

"Your wrong," said Julie from her distant corner, just loud enough to be noticed.

"What? What do you mean?" questioned Nasha.

"It was a warning, yes," she replied cryptically. "But not a warning for Nasha." Julie turned to look at Michael and I as we quietly passed the stone ball to one another. I pretended not to notice.

"It was a warning to all of us. He wants us to know that he is giving them privileges that we don't have," Julie continued.

"I don't follow," said Joseph skeptically.

"They're his new toys. He wants them to be happy," she said.

"Why would he give them more privileges than anyone else? We've all been his 'New toy' at some point or another and were never treated differently," responded David, seemingly beginning to understand Julie's meaning.

"We've all come here under terrifying circumstances. We were all damaged goods. These boys are pristine, sweet, trusting children." Julie countered, pausing for effect. "He's grooming them."

A silence fell among the group. I didn't dare to ask who this man was that they were speaking of. I couldn't comprehend the idea of some unseen person watching over us, controlling our daily lives. Whatever 'grooming' meant, I could tell that it was bad and it was this moment that I began to fear the future. I looked towards Michael. He still seemed much more shaken than I about the day's events. As much as I idolized him, I suddenly felt that it was up to me to protect him. I was younger, less confident and not as smart as he was, but something in him had been broken today; something that was only strengthened inside of me. My future aside, it was his that I was worried about.

******

25

In the year that followed I became more and more aware that Michael and I were in fact allowed many more privileges than the others. The comment made by Julie stating that we "his new toys," and that he wanted us to be happy echoed through my mind on a regular basis. As Michael and I quickly grew, we were never wanting for clothing that fit us properly or withstood our every-day rough housing. When some article of clothing became too damaged or too small to wear, a parcel of all new outfits would mysteriously arrive behind the entrance door in the middle of a dark night.

The same went for food. Regardless of the appetites of others in the barn, food arrived every other day in the entry room, clearly marked by a sign labeling it as "Michael and Ash only." Even in absolute desperation, none of the other occupants of the barn ever tried to steal a bit of our food, nor would they accept an offering of leftovers.

For the others, food was both a reward and a punishment.

It took me a long time to catch on.

There was rarely ever a time of normality. Either it was a time of famine or a time of gluttony, and each gave rise to the other. Everything that we ever received came to us unexpectedly, arriving mysteriously in the Entry Room during the night. Occasionally one of the elders would be awake to hear a commotion beyond the entry door and rouse the others, excited at the prospect of filling our hungry bellies, though terrified that something bad could be about to happen.

Despite the fact that food for the children came every other morning, for the adults, the food came sparingly. Typically food appeared once every four to six sleeps and would arrive cold, dry and often layered with dirt. It was rarely tasty. A standard delivery consisted of a bag of uncooked rice or beans, two loaves of dried bread and usually one whole, often live chicken, or a slab of browning, uncooked and unrecognizable meat.

Rationing was the rule of survival. The rice or beans could easily be stockpiled, set aside in case of a time when food came less frequently, which happened quite regularly. Bread never seemed to last more than a day or two. Although it was already almost as hard as a rock, the damp sea air quickly took its toll, encouraging rapid mold growth, so the bread was usually eaten within the first day.

Meat was always consumed immediately. On the days when a live chicken would arrive, Joseph would have its neck broken before even exiting the Entry Room. In times when food had not been so scarce in the previous weeks, and the hunger pains were not so bad, arguments often broke out at this. Some argued that we should keep the chicken alive until we were more desperate, to perhaps allow it to lay eggs to give us a continual source of food, or even just to let it starve for a day or so in order to let its bowels clear and make the evisceration less messy. The debate always ended the same, mouths ravenously drooling for the taste of meat.

It was then up to one of the women to quickly pluck and divide the chicken before rigor mortis set in. This task usually fell to the eldest woman in the group, Johnna, as her practiced hands made incredibly fast work of this chore. The feathers seemed to fall off with ease under her strong grip. In a sight that horrified nearly everyone else in the barn, Johnna would lift the carcass to her chest, gripping both legs firmly, one in each hand. With starling speed her left arm would thrust upwards while her right flew downwards, ripping one or sometimes both legs clean off the chicken. Blood would fly several feet into the air, splattering her dark brown skin and staining her curly white hair, as well as anyone else unfortunate to be close by.

The process would be repeated for the other leg, if still attached, as well as each wing. It was a barbaric and disturbing sight to watch, especially at times when the body still kicked and fluttered as its nerves slowly ceased to fire.

The remainder of the segmentation was less brutal and actually somewhat fascinating to watch. Long ago Johnna had created a small cutting blade by smashing one stone against the other, breaking the weaker stone in two pieces. The fragment was sharp enough to draw blood with the slightest touch. With this stone, Johnna was able to slice the bird to pieces with perfection and ease, expertly removing its head and innards, careful to avoid rupturing the bile duct attached to the liver or the glands in the tail.

Within moments various parts of the chicken were skewered and hung over the fire or tossed into a pot to boil into a broth.

Almost every part was used in some manner or another, even the feet.

Even on the coldest days our daily ration of firewood was quickly put to use, favouring food over warmth.

Inevitably, regardless of any careful planning, food would run out.

The elders were often left for days with no food in their stomachs, only able to satiate their hunger by drinking vast quantities of water and sleeping as often as possible. Tensions would erupt over the most pointless of issues and life was generally miserable during these times. Michael and I were always cautious to be on our best behaviour, knowing that the others were envious of our daily food supply.

I came to realize that hunger was not the only source of the negativity during these long stretches of famine. As hunger pains grew and moods fluctuated, each passing day seemed to spawn and intensify feelings of dread and nervousness amongst everyone in the barn. Mornings would begin with a collective sigh of relief as we all surveyed the faces of those around us. At first I thought that we did this to ensure that no one had passed away from starvation during the night.

As the day drew on, tensions would grow, creating endless silences, and awkward glances from one adult to another. Fear would creep in as we all settled to sleep in the evening. The anxiety of the others weighed down on us all and we struggled to allow ourselves to slip into unconsciousness.

Inevitably, one morning we would all wake up to find someone missing.

Most of the time a small bag of rice, beans or other meager rations of food would be found in the Entry Room. Just enough to survive a few more days.

The absent person would return, sometimes more than a week later, always quiet, subdued and often suffering from some kind of injury. Shortly after their reappearance an abundance of food would arrive in the Entry Room and would continue to show up every morning, though each subsequent day with less and less food.

Ultimately, starvation took hold once more, and the cycle was repeated.

****

It was Nasha who taught me structure in my daily life, taught me the importance of following rules, of being kind and helpful, of working hard when there was work to be done, and how to figure things out without asking too many questions. She scorned me when I misbehaved, hugged me and calmed me when I was upset, healed me when I was injured, and did her best to keep me happy. I relished her company. Though she continued to try to maintain an emotional distance, every moment near her was special. Her gentle, soothing voice could lull me to sleep after the worst of nightmares; her warm, tight embraces livened my heart; her dark green eyes encouraged my confidence; the simple sight of her long, shiny black hair, narrow frame and striking face in the morning assured me that we would make it through another day. Without her, my life would have been chaotic and depressing.

It was also Nasha who taught me how to read. Well, reading may be an exaggeration of my abilities. It was Nasha who taught me how to recognize letters and small words.

We would spend full afternoons drawing letters and short words in the sand, stringing together basic sentences over and over until I was able to do it on my own. Michael occasionally took part, but only when there was no one else to entertain him. He found it boring and, as I was so much more skilled at it than he, grew easily frustrated when I got things right and he didn't. This inspired me all the more to excel. I knew that Michael would never be able to read or write properly, so it was up to me to learn all that I could. My duty was to protect him, and to me, knowledge gave me an extra tool to do so.

****

As I aged I began to understand the concept that we were all captives. We were here against our will, unable to choose our own path or live our lives in a manner that we were in control of.

This first struck me in my eighth summer of living in the barn.

Julie had long since ended her self-imposed isolation and re-joined the group, though she was never quite the same. Emotionally she had grown disconnected from life. Nothing seemed to matter to her. The only times she displayed any emotion was when she was angry. Where others would debate, argue or yell, Julie would get uncomfortably close to her opponent, smirk confrontationally and hiss her opinion intimidatingly. Something in her countenance gave her an air of dominance that usually led to the immediate end of the discussion.

She had hardened.

Physically, Julie had become a woman. Due to our age difference, she always seemed to be an adult to me, but in the past few years her body had changed more than anyone else in the barn. Most noticeably her chest had sprouted large round breasts and wide, curvaceous hips that defied her tiny, undernourished frame. I remember seeing her that day on the beach when Michael and I had first gone into the water: She used to have hair so long and blonde that it almost looked unnatural. She had been a vision of serenity and innocence, glowing under the sunlight, a picture of true beauty. Now, with hair growing darker with age, her curvaceous womanly frame, and her newly adopted rigid, mysteriously confident attitude, it was clear that she must have only been a young teen back on the day when I first saw her taken from the barn. One day I finally decided to ask her age. This summer would mark her 18th birthday.

She had been taken many times. More than any other.

Anyone could see that she was the prettiest of all the people in the barn. Although I didn't know at the time what would happen to people who were taken from us, I knew that it was always bad. I couldn't understand why someone would allow another person to be put in harm's way, let alone a beautiful young girl like Julie.

I was always of two minds when Julie was taken. One part of me shared in her fear and anticipation, wanting somehow to comfort her, hoping that this time it would be someone different. The other part of me was relieved in the morning when I would wake up and she would be gone. Her absence meant three things: That, yet again it would not yet be my or Michaels first turn to be stolen in the night. It also meant that only one person was forced to endure the physical and emotional trauma that took so long to get over. The third was the thought of all of the food that would soon be coming our way. Julie always came back with more injuries and trauma than any other. She sometimes would return so bloody, bruised and delirious that it would be weeks before she was well enough to move on her own. As hard as it was to see, the extent of her injuries always correlated to the amount of food that we received. The worse the condition that she was in, the bigger the feast and the tastier the food.

Sometime over the previous summer, Julie's attitude towards being taken had changed drastically.

She used to shiver and hide her head under her rags of clothing in the famine days leading up to another abduction. Horror haunted every bit of her existence, unable to eat or drink, so weak and over exhausted that she could hardly stand. She had come to expect that it would be her each time, and more often than not, she was right.

It was a sense of power.

I could see it in her eyes. Control. The one thing that none of us had. I had never known the concept of having any sort of control over anything or anyone so I had no understanding of how it could be. Up until this point, the barn and its ever watching plastic cylinders were our ruler and dictated our fate.

Her confidence and courage changed overnight. Where she used to cry in fear and rock herself into a paranoid semi-coma as the famines wore on, she now stood tall, calm and reserved. She drank and bathed thoroughly in the cool water from the faucet, even when we all feared that it may run dry. Her hair was smooth, clothes as clean as possible and her posture and poise more womanly than ever.

Julie's first return to the barn after this change in attitude was shocking. With the exception of the blisters around her wrists and ankles, black eyes and red, swollen lower lips, Julie had come back comparatively unscathed from what we were prepared for.

Perhaps most startlingly, she was dressed in new clothes.
As long as I had known Julie she had worn the same knee length blue dress, tattered and frayed along the bottom, and either a thick black sweater or a thin yellow t-shirt, all brown and worn in most places from a long life in the barn.

Standing before me now, in an outfit of tight blue jeans, shiny white shoes and a sleeveless tight fitting red shirt with a neckline that showed the top of her breasts, Julie was stunning. I instantly noticed that her glossy, newly-blond hair had somehow curled luxuriously, her fingernails had been painted a shade of pink that I had never seen before and she smelled sweeter than the few candies that I had tasted in my life.

31

Walking strong, confident and fully alert from the Entry Room on her own, it was clear that this woman before us was no longer the girl that we used to know.

In utter bewilderment, Johnna called out to Julie as she settled back into a relaxed pose in her bed of hay:

"What the hell happened?"

"I figured them out," was her coy reply.

"Who?" questioned Johnna.

"Men. They love to be in control." She paused dramatically. "But you know what they love more?" She looked towards the men, who were staring at her, slack-jawed. "Being controlled."

****

Throughout the following year, Julie continued to be a favourite pick. She was removed from the barn at least once every 15 days. Our reward meals quickly reverted back to being simplistic and sparse, but there was never a lengthy time of starvation.

Occasionally one of the others was still chosen. Almost every time it was a male that was taken. Men didn't seem to be treated as poorly outside of the barn. Almost always a man would come back completely uninjured, yet somehow more emotionally broken than most of the women. The last male that had been chosen, a young, charming, good looking man named Cole who was popular among all of us, came back after his first time of being taken from the barn and cried for a week solid upon his return.

Eventually we all noticed that Julie had begun to put on weight. During her many times away from the barn, she clearly was allowed some luxuries that the others were not afforded. I had learned that her black eyes and puffy red lips were not injuries, but some sort of paint called 'makeup' worn in order to make herself prettier. Her hair grew lighter and lighter. She always smelled like candy and wore new, clean clothes that seemed to appear in the Entry Room every week for her. She even had shiny golden rings hanging from her ears.

It was natural for us all to assume that she had been putting on weight because she was being fed better than the rest of us.

She was constantly ill. It had been weeks since she had last been chosen to leave the barn, others now going in her place regularly. Every morning she would vomit, dragging her body around heavily throughout the days. She was always hungry, but could rarely keep her food down. As her stomach began to grow quickly, her face became gaunt and pale, and I couldn't understand how she could be putting on weight when she hardly ate.

One night, just before the cool evenings turned icy, we all were awoken by ear piercing screams in the darkness. Chaos ensued. I had assumed that someone had woken up to find themselves being abducted. I, as everyone else, fumbled and stumbled in the pitch darkness, running away from the source of the commotion as opposed to toward it, none among us brave enough to help. Having no farther to run, no real place to hide other than pressed up against a wall, shrouded by the night, the group quickly quieted down. In the stillness, the screams continued to chill us all to the bone. My head spun in disorientation, groggy, blindly lost in a wide open room.

"Help me!" came a desperate cry between the screams. I instantly realized that it was Julie. Not one of us moved.

"Please! Someone, my baby…" her voice trailed off into a loud, pained moan.

Baby? My only connection to this word was from my early days in the barn when Nasha would lull me to sleep, calling me a 'sweet baby boy.'

Where would Julie get a small kid from?

A few more moments passed before I heard someone moving to my right, towards Julie. A second later I saw the spark of our fire flint and the silhouette of Nasha flickering in the darkness. In seconds she had a small flame burning. Using some fat drippings from our last meal and a torn piece of cloth, she quickly managed to make a small torch.

In the harsh, dancing light I could make out Julie's shape huddled on the floor near the wall on the other side of the barn. Shock from the sight numbed me. I stared in awe. I had become accustomed to seeing Julie, startling in contrast from the rest

33

of us with her rare beauty, new clothes and cleanliness. Even in the past little while when she was no longer being taken in the middle of the night, Julie had maintained her pristine appearance, poise and air of power. Here in front of us all lay a poor defenseless, weak child.

Julie's legs, thighs and hands were streaked with a thick, black, sticky substance, encasing her fingers as if in a wet glove, contrasting disturbingly with her glowing white skin. She had removed her pants and was sitting naked from the waist down in a pool of reddened mud. From between her legs a crimson stream of blood, glistening almost beautifully in the struggling light.

"Oh god," I heard someone whisper.

Nasha took no time to pause in shock with the rest of us. Her quick hands had a large fire burning close to Julie in mere moments, mostly stoked with hay from our beds and spare clothing. Johnna hurriedly joined in and added our last bits of wood to the fire. Before the logs had even caught flame, Joseph was hanging our only steel pot above the fire using a small the tripod set-up that we used to boil water. Another person was emptying our plastic reserve of water into the pot, while still another was ripping his own shirt into strips, laying the pieces carefully onto a pile beside Nasha. The room was abuzz with commotion, as every single person was frantically preparing in some way to help Julie as if they had previously decided on these duties. Amazingly, even Michael had leapt into the frenzy, collecting the slow brown drips of water from our parched faucet into a small bowl.

I stood alone watching the pandemonium. I didn't understand what was happening. Somehow Julie had become gravely injured in the quiet of the night. Somewhere a child was hiding, people unresponsive to her pleas to save her baby. Hesitantly I took a few steps forwards into the madness, immediately becoming more of a hazard than an aid.

"Move Ash!" yelled one woman, pushing me aside with her hip as she carried wet cloths to Julie's side.

"Get out of here!" called Joseph, as he ran down to the beach with the empty plastic container to fill it with salt water.

At a loss for direction, I stepped out of everyone's way, hiding in the shadows, feeling guiltily useless.

"Help my baby!" came Julie's painful screams yet again. "Please help me!"

Suddenly lurching into clarity, the bewildering fog in my mind lifted and my heart began to race. *Her baby!* Nobody was looking for her baby! They were all so concerned with Julie's injury that they had forgotten to look for the mystery child that she had somehow brought into the barn without us knowing. With that thought, my duty became clear to me: *I must find that baby!*

In an instant I was on my feet at a full run. My first thought was to check the area that Julie had been sleeping moments before her scream broke the silence in the night. Julie and the others were within an arm's length of my searching area as I tore through the blood soaked pile of hay that made up Julies bed.

"What are you doing!?" exclaimed Nasha with bewilderment as she worked frantically between Julie's thighs.

"The baby!" was my blunt reply, scathing with criticism, dismayed that even Nasha could neglect the needs of a child who may also be terribly injured. Too intent on my search, I didn't see her reaction, but by the tone of her confused grunt I could tell that she had dismissed my quest as one unworthy of her concern.

With nothing found in the stack of hay I turned my attention to the ocean. Although the big door was sealed shut, the high tide pulsed gently in the darkness through the cracks and I jumped in without hesitation. The frigid water took my breath away I sunk below its unexpectedly deep surface. Planting my feet firmly on the sandy bottom, standing straight and just tall enough to hold my mouth above the water, I forced myself to gain some semblance of composure. Choking for air between the undulating swells, I felt my way along the wall of the barn, first circling the perimeter before splashing through the open centre area and finally into the shallows. I was certain that I would find the child floating somewhere in the water, face down and breathless.

With both of my feet feeling the depths and my outstretched arms scanning the upper surface, I was dismayed when I emerged on the beach with nothing. Again I jumped in, certain that I had missed an area. With eyes open as wide as possible to take in as much light creeping through the cracks of the walls from the full moon outside and the glow of the fire behind me, I once again searched. Salt stung my eyes and burned my lungs, yet I kept on searching.

Finally, dejectedly unsuccessful, I ended my search of the water and dragged my tired body to the shore.

I was so sure that the child would be there.

The rest of the barn was a wide open space. With my eyes adequately adjusted to the near darkness, I could see that there was nowhere else that a child could be concealed. With failing conviction I dragged myself to the sleeping area. It was unlikely that one of the others had concealed a child under their own hay beds and certainly there were no signs of a child, blood, or any other indication to suspect that Julie's baby were hidden in the hay and cloth, but I searched each bed anyway.

"Somebody control this child!" yelled Cole, the young, good looking man who had last been the victim of abduction only a week before. Yanking my left arm backwards, the ferocity in his grip made me scream out in pain and I fell to the floor in agony. I had searched all but my own and Michaels bed with no luck. There was no conceivable way the child was hidden in the hay or anywhere else in the barn; the rest was vast empty space. There were no concealed corners to hide in, no walls to sneak behind. And then it hit me: The Entry Room.

Spurred on by a sudden rush of energy so strong that I could feel my face reddening, I twisted my hand from the man's tight hold, hopped up from the ground and ran with such speed that I nearly fell over my own bare feet. The child was in the Entry Room. It seemed so obvious! The only way that people came to or left the barn was through the Entry Room! I couldn't believe that I hadn't thought of it before.

In seconds I reached the door that I normally was so fearful of. Without a thought for my own well-being I slipped my small fingers around the frame of the old wooden door as I had seen so many others cautiously do in the past, and pulled.

Nothing. The door didn't move.

I tried again, this time using both hands. Again there was nothing. Maybe the door is very heavy, I thought. Putting my leg up against the wall, pushing as I pulled with my arms, straining every muscle in my body I pulled.

In the background Julie screamed.

In desperation I bashed my fists against the door, kicking my naked foot against the base.

"Open!" I yelled! "Let me in!" Again and again I alternated between pulling and hitting the door, all the while demanding it to magically unlock.

Finally, tired and dejected I fell to the ground, sniveling with angry tears.

Worn out, sure that my failure would result in the mysterious child's death, I turned my eyes back towards Julie. Like fruit flies around discarded food, the rest of my barn mates swarmed her, each one hurriedly occupied with some lifesaving task.

One person alone was unmoving: Julie. Her eyes were locked in my direction, seemingly looking at me without quite seeing me. I could see the look of hopelessness in her eyes and, as her vision met mine, a look of confusion that somehow told me that I had failed her. Moments later her head bobbed forwards and her body relaxed. The commotion around her suddenly came to an abrupt halt. All eyes turned towards Julie, observing as her body lay motionless. Nasha, who had been working hastily to tend to Julie's wounds looked up from her work with panic in her eyes.

"Julie!" she yelled, quickly raising herself to a semi-standing position. "Julie come back to me!" she yelled, louder this time. She grabbed Julie's chin in both hands, holding her own face inches from Julie's open, yet unmoving eyes.

"JULIE!" she yelled again. Nasha's own posture relaxed. "Oh god, Julie," came a defeated sigh.

The barn was quieter than I had ever heard it.

Nobody moved.

Moments later the silence was broken. Behind me a click seemed to boom so unnaturally loudly through the air that it caused me to jump. I surveyed the others. Clearly the noise had not been loud enough for anyone else to hear. Slowly, nervously, I turned my head to the source of the sound. Behind me, in the flickering darkness of the firelight I saw it clearly: Though the difference was subtle, the edge of the door hung just slightly away from the surrounding wooden frame. The door had unlocked.

After a moment of pause and fear I felt my hands pushing myself off the ground, my feet driving me towards the door, half-crawling, half walking the two steps. Drawn on by sheer automatic compulsion, my fingers reached up to the edge of the door and pulled. The door smoothly swung towards me and I fell back to the ground, afraid to impede its movement. Allowing my eyes to adjust further to the near absolute blackness of the entry room, crawling forward to ensure that I was seeing correctly, my heart seemed to drop from my chest. It was empty. The room was empty. There was no child anywhere to be seen.

****

I had retreated to the high platform that hung from the ceiling of the barn, a full 52 rungs above the floor. It was the first time I had ever been off the ground in my life, with the exception of the times that an adult had lifted me to comfort me in times of sickness or play.

The hours after Julie's death had been horrible:

Silence lingered in the air for what seemed like an eternity. In the burgeoning shadows of the morning light, columns of the silhouetted figures surrounding Julie's deceased body stood frozen in morbid stares at the gruesome sight. It was the first death in the barn that was not a direct result of a failed escape attempt. It was also the first death that I had witnessed. The loss of Julie's soul was palpable; somehow the barn, though still occupied, felt entirely empty, small and suffocating. The coolness of the night suddenly seemed amplified as if, at the moment of Julies passing, the temperature had immediately dropped. A collective shiver was shared between all of us.

As if shaking the world back to life, Nasha quickly snapped back to action.

"Johnna!" yelled Nasha, immediately crouching back between Julie's limp legs. "I need you now! We can still save this baby!"

The baby? I thought. *What is she talking about? I've looked everywhere!*

As Johnna raced from the fire pit to Nasha's side, I too bounded into motion, rushing towards Nasha and Julie, determined to figure out where this intangible, elusive child had been hiding.

With an indescribable shot of pain I felt my left arm once again yanked behind me with brutal force as I ran forward. The pull was harsh enough to snap my head forward and throw both feet into the air ahead of me. I fell painfully to the ground, the force knocking the breath from my lungs, cracking the back of my head sharply on the hardened earth.

"No!" screamed Cole. "That's *ENOUGH*!" he yelled, crushing me against the ground under the weight of his hand on my collarbone.

"Whatever the HELL you think you are doing, STOP it!" The fury in his eyes and voice as he screamed at me only inches from my face, startled me in a way that nothing else had ever done before. Never had anyone raised their voice to me in this way. Everyone was always kind, or at least dismissive towards anything I ever did.

"You run around here bumping into people, getting in their way when we are trying to save Julie! You mess up everyone's beds, distract us by diving unsupervised into the ocean, and then you decide to choose the moment of Julie's death to try to escape through the entry door!" he said, radiating with rage. "What the fuck kid! You slowed us down when every second counted! If you would have just sat down and shut up Julie might still be alive now!"

He paused for a moment, staring questioningly into my eyes, possibly waiting for me to react, or maybe trying to think of something more to yell about. I closed my eyes as tight as I could, tears still pouring out the sides. As the man's grip loosened just slightly I was able to catch my first breath and in doing so a wave of sobbing erupted uncontrollably from deep within me.

"Jesus Christ kid..." said Cole, still tense with anger but fading in his violence as he remembered that I was just a child. "What the fuck were you doing?"

Opening my eyes just slightly, allowing myself to peek at him, sensing the threat diminishing, I moaned quietly back, "I was trying to find Julie's kid."

A confused look came over the man's face as he backed slightly away in surprise. "What?"

"Her baby," I answered. When Cole's puzzled expression remained unchanged, I continued : "She was screaming about saving her baby. I couldn't find it. I looked everywhere."

With a look of astounded revelation, he sighed and relaxed his grip on me.

"Oh God. It's inside her belly. Babies come from woman's bellies," he muttered. 'God! All that distraction!"

Releasing his grip entirely, Cole got up and made his way over to the rest of the group. They had been divided between watching the scuffle between Cole and I, and observing the work that Nasha and Johnna were doing on Julie. In the eyes of the few who made eye contact with me I could see disappointment and indignation. Even Michael sat quietly on the ground beside the water faucet looking at me in disapproval.

I was so scared, confused and embarrassed. I couldn't understand why Cole had attacked me so viciously and why nobody came to help. I couldn't grasp the concept that babies come out of woman's bellies. The mental image horrified me. I had been trying so hard to help, yet in the end all I felt was embarrassment, worthless and alone.

Lying on my back in the dirt, my head spun in a mix of emotion and physical trauma; my shoulder throbbing with sharp pains. All I wanted to do was to hide. Having just searched the entire barn for a place that the mystery child could be concealed, I knew full well that there was no place to go.

Resting my sore head back in the dirt, I stared up at the ceiling trying to catch my breath and calm myself. As my eyes continued to focus in the awakening morning light, my eyes fixed on the platform hanging high from the roof. My breath caught in my chest once more as I recognized the distant space to be a potential place of refuge, at the same time instantly fearing the incomprehensible height.

Finally, driven by sheer humiliation I made my way to the first rung of the worn old ladder built into the wall and began hauling myself up. The pain in my left shoulder was debilitating. Crying through the pain I continued to haul myself farther and farther up, whimpering even more as I climbed higher, almost crippled by the fear. I could sense the eyes of some of the other people in the barn below as they watched me clamber clumsily up and I thought I could hear someone calling my name, but fear kept me solely focused on climbing.

Finally making it to the top of rung I threw my body onto the hanging platform, digging my fingers between the narrow boards and holding on with every ounce of strength that I had left. With arms shaky from the strain of the climb, a body weary and cold, and a soul feeling broken and abandoned, I allowed the tears to flow freely, burying my head into the floorboards.

Exhausted through and through, without the energy to sustain my cries, I finally allowed myself to give in to the exhaustion. As I lay there, still shivering with a combination of cold and fear of the astounding height, I slowly opened my eyes and peered through the cracks in the board below me.

Every nerve in my body jumped at the distance below me. My breath locked, my pulse banged through my veins and my already aching head began to spin. Just as my ears began to ring and darkness began to close around my vision I noticed the body of Julie. From my high perch directly above her deflated body I had a perfect vantage point as Johnna sliced her belly wide open in several quick slashes of the cutting stone. The brutal scene sent a great wave of nausea to my stomach, adding exponentially to my already ailing state.

As I mechanically watched, eyes locked in disbelief, the cutting abruptly stopped. With gentle agility, Nasha leaned forward, slipping her hands deep into the gaping, bloody cavity that was Julie's abdomen. My stomach lurched in revulsion, the darkness closing in around my vision just as Nasha leaned back, withdrawing her arms, a tiny hand suddenly emerging, followed by a grotesque wrinkly white head. Somewhere beyond the ringing in my ears, the last thing I remember before passing out was a high-pitched, wailing scream unlike anything I had heard before.

****

I awoke to the sounds of yelling. I had no idea how long I had been passed out for, but the scene below me remained relatively unchanged.

"How could you DO this?!' yelled Nasha and she stood beside Julies butchered body. She spun on her spot, arms outstretched to the sides, head tilted back, her words seemingly directed at no one and everyone.

41

"You didn't have to let her die! You're a *monster*!" she continued, despondent and furious at the same time. "You could have taken her to a hospital! She would have survived!"

The group around her watched in sullen silence.

"What kind of person lets a child get pregnant then sits back and watches her as she dies in childbirth?!" Nasha ranted. "Did that make for good TV for you?! Did it arouse your tiny old dick? Make you feel like a MAN?"

"Nasha, stop!" pleaded David, "Don't piss him off!"

"He let someone die, David!" countered Nasha.

"He's killed others here before and we dealt with it," David said soothingly, slowly getting closer to Nasha who was pacing around aggressively.

"They were trying to escape! It's not the same thing!" roared Nasha, herself stepping toward David as if on the verge of attack. "We all know the rules. Julie obeyed! It's not her fault that she got pregnant!"

"Woah, woah, I'm on your side," replied David, hands up in surrender. "We can't react like this. We have to remain calm and united. Watching us fight would get him off! He wants a reaction out of us!"

"It's not fair!" wailed Nasha. "She did so much to protect us! She survived so much more than any of us—put up with all of his sick games so that we didn't have to!"

David took another cautious step towards Nasha.

"She was just a kid…" said Nasha sadly before falling despairingly into David's arms.

That was when I first understood. Our food, our water, our wood supply, the opening of the big door, the arrival of new people, the abductions: It was all controlled by someone else. Our lives were not our own to live. We belonged to someone. We were not free to make a single decision. Whoever this person was, he was the sole ruler of our existence. He controlled life itself. And now, in shocking clarity, I learned that he controlled death as well.

****

As the morning progressed, I watched from my platform while the mess below was mournfully set back in order. Nobody spoke.

I watched as Johnna gently closed up Julie's body, washing the drying blood and caked mud from her body, rearranging her dirty and torn clothing, attempting to restore her with some semblance of dignity.

Once everything had been tidied and all the blood on the ground covered with straw, everyone seemed to automatically gather around Julie's body. Michael sat quietly on a pile of hay, seemingly unsure of what he could do to help, silently observing the sad scene, apparently in as much dismay as me. Once he realized that the others had come together to surround Julie, he looked up at me, either pondering whether he should take part as well, or perhaps wondering if I was coming down to join in with him. A moment of understanding passed between us, each staying silently in our place, sorrowfully observing.

The group surrounded Julie, heads down, elbow to elbow. Nobody spoke. The silence in the barn fell heavily and eerily. For the first time ever, I noticed a quiet whirring noise. It was coming from directly above my head. Glancing upwards I noticed two of the shiny white plastic columns with the opaque black globes hanging below. The noise was coming from inside them. Sitting up a bit to get a closer look, I could see the tiny eye in each one. The eye in the sphere closest to me was focused back at me. Looking to the other sphere I could see the tiny eye pointing downwards to the group below, slowly rotating to point at each of the faces in the circle.

He was watching.
After a long silence, the group below all moved at once. Four men stepped forward, along with Nasha, while the rest took two steps back in what seemed to be a well-practiced routine. With gentle and smooth synchronicity, each man bent to raise one of Julie's limbs while Nasha lovingly supported her head. In unison they lifted Julie from the floor, the crowd around them parted, and with slow

43

cautious steps, the five pallbearers silently made their way to the Entry Room followed by everyone else in single file.

As the procession entered the small room, a startling realization dawned on me: That's why the door had opened. He knew she was dead. He knew that the body would have to be taken away.

From my vantage point I couldn't see the procession once they were in the room, but I could see Michael intently watching from his bed down below. Straining his neck to watch, I could see the tears fall from his eyes as something emotional seemed to happen. I imagined the group gently placing her body on the floor of the room, each taking a moment to kiss her cheek and caress her soft hair. At this thought, I felt a pang of guilt, as I too should be there to say my goodbyes to someone who had been family to me my whole life.

One by one the group slowly exited the room lead by Nasha. All were silent, all in tears. As the last person exited the room and closed the door behind him, the group stood in one final show of admiration to Julie, chins up, respectfully gazing at the closed door.

In the background, the new child began to scream.

Part 2

Looking down at my hands, surveying the dark, thickening hairs above my knuckles, the worn, cracked skin around my broken and dirty nails, the rough calluses on my palms; they were the hands of a man. In the past few months my voice had deepened rapidly, the furry fuzz on my cheeks had become coarse, though still patchy, and the hair on my crotch had grown like a head of hair.

It was the spring of my 17th year.

Alone I floated in the water of the wide open ocean, far away from the shore, looking back towards the prison in which I had been trapped for my entire life. It was the farthest I had ever been away from the barn. I was astounded by the isolation I felt by being so distant to everything that I had ever known.

The barn itself seemed small from this distance. Perhaps it was my unfamiliarity with seeing such a wide open expanse. It was the amount of land that surprised me the most. It seemed to stretch forever off into the horizon on both sides of the barn, a wide sandy beach lined with lush green, waist-high grasses and bushes blowing in the wind. Far behind the barn, almost a blur in the distance I could see that the land rose high up into great stone mountains that blended into a deep blue-grey with the sky. Other than a distinctly groomed path that travelled unnaturally straight through the grasses from the barn to the horizon beyond the hills and mountains, there was nothing else in sight that was artificial or man-made. The enormity of the world beyond what I knew overwhelmed me more than I could have ever imagined.

I had often spent time swimming and floating in the water. Over the past many years it had become obvious that Michael and myself, as well as our new baby 'sister' Alina, had the freedom to come and go as we pleased. We would often escape the long hot summer days in the barn by leaping into the water, swimming around the walls and landing on the wide open beach to frolic and play. We could spend a whole day outside of the barn, running, playing catch, tag, or kick-the-ball, burying each other in the sand or simply floating in the water all day.

We never wandered far.

We weren't used to open spaces. We had been confined our entire lives. Confinement was comfort. Familiarity was security. We knew the rules and understood how things worked. Life outside the barn was too enormous, intimidating and frightening in its unfamiliarity. On the beach we could see any threat that may come towards us and prepare ourselves. To wander off into the thick bushes beyond was unfathomable. Danger could be hidden anywhere. Somehow, staying within sight of the single black and white eye that hung on either side of the exterior of the barn represented safety to us. Somebody could watch us--save us if trouble ever arose. Our fears were always in our minds, though thus far at least, nothing had ever happened.

As I floated farther and farther out into the salty bay, calmed by the gentle bobbing of the waves, numbed by the icy temperature or the water, I stared back at the barn and thought about how different life had become in the past few years.

After Julie's death, tensions had flared between everyone in the barn, yet everyone fought to repress any open displays of aggression. There had been others killed in the past, those who, before my time had been shot down during an escape attempt, others throughout time here while 'on assignment,' as it became commonly referred to.

Julie's death had been such a blow to our morale though because it had been preventable, intentional and unjustified. Suddenly everyone realized that we were all at risk regardless of how well we behaved or how well someone did while 'on assignment.' To live each day of your life knowing that it may be your last, regardless of your actions or, worse yet, of the actions of others around you, was a frame of mind that kept each and every one of us exhausted with worry.

Silent battles between other barn mates would happen daily. Most of the time they were over the most ridiculous things: an unwelcomed glare, a misspoken word, or even just someone snoring too loudly. Occasionally however, tension would grow too much for one person to bear, resulting in loud, violent screaming matches, ending finally with little resolution of any issues, perhaps only beneficial in that it allowed for a temporary venting of frustrations.

There was almost never a time when moods were light, not even in times of feast, which had been much less frequent than in the past. In fact, everything had become less frequent since Julie's death. The frequency of waking to find that someone had been taken in the night had begun to dwindle in recent years, the barn door was left open or closed for much longer periods of time, and food was scarcer than ever.

I began to feel that, whoever was watching, this figurative 'Mr. Irvine,' he wasn't as interested as he used to be.

****

It was me who chose the name Alina for Julie's baby girl.

After her birth, she had been relatively neglected by the adults. It had become Michael's main pastime to carry the baby everywhere he went and he quickly learned how to feed her and keep her clean. Inexplicably I became jealous of the tiny baby. Although she had no say in it, she had taken away my best friend and I hated her for it.

For many nights I slept alone on my shelf far above the others, alone, brooding in my own discontent and embarrassment for my actions during Julie's death. I would only come down to drink water and eat a bit of food or have a quick bowel movement into the wooden bowl down by the water's edge. Each time Michael would look at me with sorrowful eyes and ask me to come to play with him and the baby. I declined rudely every time, wanting to hurt him for betraying our friendship by fawning over this new child, secretly wishing he would apologize and hug me, making things all better again.

It wasn't until one day many sleeps later that we became close again, all thanks to the child.

"Baby baby baby!!" I erupted as I walked passed Michael and the others on the way to the faucet one afternoon.

"What the hell??" exclaimed an older girl who had been helping Michael tie a cloth around the baby's bum.

"You're so cute baby! Come here baby! Look at me BABY!" I mimicked in their high pitched playful voices that they used while talking to the child. "Every word is BABY! It's so annoying! Just give the kid a real name already!"

"Wow," the girl responded with mocked amazement. "You're so cool aren't you?"

"Can you help me come up with a name Ash?" Michaels tone was calm, almost pleading. I knew it was an intentional attempt to get me to be friends with him again, but I was unwilling to concede that it was me who was being the difficult

50

one. "How 'bout 'STUPID!'" I yelled as I ran back up to my ladder, knowing that I had been too childish, feeling like the loneliest person in the world.

After hours of self-imposed isolation, hating myself for my ridiculous behaviour, I found myself slinking down the ladder in the middle of the night, creeping across the dirt in the darkness and crawling into Michael's bed with him. Hugging him tightly, I could feel him wake up and I whispered, "I thought of a name." He turned to look at me with a slight, sleepy smile.

"Goose!" I laughed, "like your dog!" He rolled over and poked me in the ribs, laughing back as all animosity between us instantly vanished.

Finally hushed by someone in the darkness next to us, I settled to a more comfortable position and whispered once again, "Seriously, how about Alina?"

"That's a good name. Where did you come up with that?" he asked quietly.

"I don't know... it just sounds right," I replied.

With Alina sleeping calmly on an old shirt in the pile of hay next to us, Michael and I fell happily back to sleep.

****

Alina's life started off very rough. She had been extremely tiny when she was born. The talk around the barn was that she had been at least a month premature and, with a frail and malnourished body, she wouldn't survive for long. Nobody else wanted to have anything to do with her, not even Nasha. The general consensus was that it would be better for her to die quickly. Had it not been for Michael's constant care, I am certain that she would have died within the first few days.

Nights quickly grew cold.

Julie was one of the few people in the barn who had been given extra changes clothing, but most had been ripped into rags on the night that she had gone into labour. The one remaining article of clothing was a thick, bright pink cotton sweater. It became Alina's blanket, bed, clothing and even her carrier. On

51

particularly frigid nights, Michael would wrap Alina tightly into her sweater, then stuff the whole package under his own shirt to ensure her warmth.

After her first day, Alina never cried again. In her weakened, fragile state, it seemed that she didn't have the strength to cry, often lying so still and lethargic that checking to see if she was still breathing was a regular task.

She was always sick. On top of pooping and peeing almost constantly, Alina vomited after every meal, regardless of how meager her rations had been. Rashes spread from her bottom and eventually covered most of her body, worsened by her constant scratching with her tiny nails. The area where her belly button should be grew swollen, and red, bulging out painfully each time she coughed or vomited. It was sad to watch as Michael struggled through the endless hours of child care, never having a moment for himself.

****

Winter came early and grew to be one of the worst ones that I had ever experienced.

The first snow had come one morning after a particularly warm and sunny day. The great barn door was wide open and, even in the hours before the storm hit, the gently breeze it permitted into the barn had been refreshing.

Without any sign, the morning sky rapidly grew dark, the chilling breeze forcing clouds to pass overhead at a startling speed and the waves to crash roughly onto the beach. The comfortable temperature dropped in no time at all and we all scrambled to gather what we could to stoke the flickering fire and keep warm.

As the wind picked up in ferocity, the snow began to fall in small, icy specks, blocking the view of the horizon and coating the inside walls of the barn down near the water in a solid white blanket of ice. Within moments the inside of the barn was sunk into near darkness as the dark clouds outside continued to thicken and ice built up between the cracks in the boards of walls.

We were all quick to pile into a huddle as close to the fire as we could safely get, blanketing ourselves under our hay beds instead of on top of them, shivering in icy unison. We all wished that the large door would close, some people occasionally yelling out desperate pleads to the black-domed eyes above that we could not survive this if the door was left open, their voices muffled by the roar of the winds around us.

The wind continued to intensify for a full day and into the following night with no reprieve. We were all too cold to move, to find food, or even get water for Alina. I had long passed the point of thinking that I couldn't take anymore by the time the familiar booms and clicks sounded and the door finally began to close. Freezing and exhausted, Michael wasted no time in leaping from his bedding to tend to Alina. Frantically he fed her some water and washed her bottom before racing back into the comparative warmth of the huddle.

The storm raged for two more days. Winter had arrived, from that point on holding us in its bitter grip under endless storms and bitter temperatures straight through to the spring. In this time the great door never once re-opened, natural sunlight never peaked through the barn walls. We lived in near-darkness for all those months, cold and depressed, quietly loathing every moment of our lives. Towards the darkest, coldest days of winter I began to feel sorry for Alina, sad that she had survived her birth.

****

8. That's how old Alina was. She had grown slowly, still tiny for her age. She had never seemed to be able to put weight onto her tiny frame. It seemed as if Alina was always tired or sick, and her thin blonde hair had lightened as she aged, intensifying her sickly appearance.

Food rations had been very strict in the past two years, as we generally only received our meager delivery of bread, rice and beans once every ten to fifteen days now. There was rarely any meat anymore. If there was it was always a picked over, pre-cooked carcass of some small chicken or rabbit, just enough for a bit of soup for everyone.
Unlike Michael and I, Alina had never been given a special daily meal to spur in her growth, nor did she ever get new clothing, even when her hand-me-down rags donated by other women in the barn became too small or disintegrated entirely. Always clinging to the dirty old pink sweater that she had been wrapped in at birth, chewing a corner with nervous insecurity, she was the quintessential starving, impoverished child. Of course Michael and I divided our rations

amongst the 3 of us equally, but no one else ever once gave her a bit of their insufficient allotments.

Nobody had been taken in a very long time.

There had been snow in the air the last time that we had woken to discover that Cole, the man who berated me on the night of Julie's death, had been chosen again in the night. He had only been out of the barn for three full days and nights, returning unharmed but more withdrawn than before. No extra food came after his return and the water from the faucet remained chillingly cold.

Outside, the dry grasses were starting to green and the days were getting longer. We all knew that another abduction was imminent.

Lying awake for as long as possible each night, we all gradually gave into the inevitable and nervously fell to sleep.

Michael and I had long ago taken to sleeping up on the hanging platform. During the long cold nights of winter the heat from the fire below seemed to get trapped at the roof level, keeping us much warmer than we had been in our beds down below. The layer of straw that we had carried up, handful by handful sufficiently insulated the boards below us, added to the warmth and comfort of our little nest. Just as importantly, our precarious bed had offered something that nobody else had: a semblance of seclusion, a bit of solitude that was unattainable elsewhere in the barn.

We had no idea at the time of how much salvation this sleeping arrangement had brought our way.

We always knew that it would one day be our turn to be 'taken on assignment.' We all knew that Julie had been a young teenager when she was first taken, but the general consensus was that, because we were boys, we mostly likely would be no interest to the powers that be until we were men. Still unsure of what went on when taken, since nobody would ever give us an adequate account of what had happened to them while on assignment, Michael and I didn't understand why we had to be men to be chosen, but were grateful for this fact.

As it turned out, the same rule did not apply to females.

****

Floating so far out in the ocean, all alone looking back towards the barn, my mind raced as I thought about the events of the night before.

I had been violently ill immediately after my meal yesterday. The small portion of food that I had been allotted had fallen to the ground as I ate it down near the beach. I'd been so hungry that I couldn't bear to waste the tiniest bite despite knowing that someone had just washed out the toilet pot in the ocean just moments ago and there was a risk that my food was now dangerously contaminated. Without more than a fleeting moment of concern, I scooped the pile of beans up and swallowed it all in one gulp.

By nighttime the vomiting had become uncontrollable, eventually giving rise to dry heaves so powerful that every muscle in my belly burned in pain. It took every ounce of energy for me to climb up to my bed. I would have stayed down below but I didn't want to be around anybody. I knew that nothing more could come up if I vomited again since I hadn't ingested even a drop of water since the sickness began.

Later in the evening Michael joined me, gently patting my head and telling me that I would be okay. I fell into a woozy sleep shortly after.

I awoke late into the evening to an unusual sound. It was more of a vibration than it was noise, vibrating the boards gently, a deep hum in the darkness. Still too sick to be immediately alerted, I laid unmoving in my place attempting to discern if the noise was something from a dream or if it were in the barn with us. It wasn't until I heard an all-too-familiar 'click' that my eyes shot open. It had been almost imperceptibly quiet, but I knew instantly that the lock on the Entry Door had opened.

Turning my body ever so slowly, I allowed myself to slide close to the edge of the platform to find out what was happening below. In the absolute darkness, a halo of jerky light escaped around the edges of the Entry Door. A second later the door swung quickly open and three long beams of bright white light shot across the barn, illuminating the pile of people who slept around the dying fire. Within moments three dark shadows emerged from the Entry Room, chasing their mysterious beams of light towards the sleeping group before them.

Astonishment had taken over me as my eyes fixed on the scene below, my curiosity battling with my instinctual need to alert the others. The phenomenon of seeing another human being enter the barn made my skin tingle in excitement. Seeing three people was a wonder that my sleepy brain struggled to comprehend.

I couldn't really make out any distinctive characteristics about the men from my platform. In actuality I couldn't even be sure that they were all men. They were all tall and broad shouldered, but, covered head to toe in skin-tight black outfits, their outlines flickering in the bouncing lights in their hands as they quickly slinked across the barn, they all could have been women as far as I could tell.

Silently the invaders made their way to the campfire area where the group was still soundly sleeping. With surprising lack of concern, the three black figures roughly pulled at the sleeping people around them, rolling each person over to survey them, shining their bright beams of light directly in the unconscious faces, often stepping directly on a limb or abdomen in their hurried examination. Iciness flooded my body. It was a search.

They were looking for a specific person.

These people were here to abduct one of us.

None of us had ever witnessed another being taken in the night. It had been a long standing mystery between us all. Often one or all of us would attempt to stay awake throughout the night, mainly out of sheer fear that it would be our turn to be taken, but partially in an attempt to protect the others from an inevitable fate. Nobody ever really talked at length about what they experienced while outside of the barn but I had always assumed that at least some of them had been dishonest about their lack of memory when it came to leaving the barn.

As I sat quietly watching from above, the three strangers continued their unnecessarily aggressive search and I realized that there was no way that a person could be manhandled in that way without waking up. I thought back to the confused, groggy ways in which people were found upon their return to the Entry Room after an 'assignment'. Some of the adults had used the term 'Drugged' to describe the people as they slowly returned to coherent consciousness.

Drugged.

The only way that someone could sleep through all of this chaos was if they had been drugged. In swift recognition, I knew instantly that this must be the case. I had been violently ill all day, unable to hold even a sip of water or a bite of food. If the drug had been somehow introduced into our food or water source, this would explain why all of the others had fallen victim to its effects while I remained conscious.

Daring to risk a simple movement to test my theory, I silently turned my head to face Michael who snored quietly beside me.

"Michael," I whispered, my voice shaking. No response. "Wake up, something's happening!" I chanced to say a little louder.

With a sharp jab of my elbow I struck Michael forcefully in the ribs. When there was still no reaction I knew that my theory must be correct.

Immediately the sinking terror replaced the cold fear in my veins as the reality of the situation struck me: They were here to take someone. What if it was Nasha again? I thought with panic. She had been badly abused the last time that she had been taken.

What if it was ME that they were looking for?

My head swam. I hadn't yet been chosen. I was almost a full grown man, and yet in the past, people who had been younger than I was at this point had been taken. My eyes locked on Michael. With a sickening lurch of the stomach my heart skipped a beat. What if they want Michael this time?

"WAKE UUUUUUUUUUUUUUP!" I screamed, turning to face the group below me. It was involuntary, an impulse from deep within my soul, the sheer volume shocking even to me.

Blinded immediately by the beams of the bright lights in the intruder's hands, I froze in fear. I had given myself away. The predators had been caught in the act and now I would become their prey. Worse yet, they could come after Michael.

Leaping into survival mode, I sat up immediately and yelled again: "GET UUUUUUP! GET UUUUUUUUUP! They're here to take someone!" My voice cracked against the strain of desperation.

Blindly I felt for the ladder behind me, robotically descending faster than I had ever done before. The realization that I was on the move seemed to spur the prospective abductors into panicked motion. Moving quicker than before, the three figures jumped from person to person with practiced agility and efficiency, rolling each sleeping body over while surveying their faces under their bright lights.

As I neared the middle of the tall ladder, all the while yelling to the others to wake up, I heard a deep male voice break through the noise.

"Got it!" he yelled to the other two people, effortlessly hauling a limp body of an unconscious victim over his shoulder. In an instant the other two shadows abandoned their search efforts and joined alongside the other man as they hurriedly made their way towards the Entry Door.

Stunned both by the relief that the chosen victim was neither I nor Michael, and by the feeling that I was already too late to come to the rescue of the poor person who was surely about to suffer unimaginable hardships, I froze in my place on the ladder.

As the three shadows rapidly withdrew with their bounty the lights in the hands cast a dizzying show on the walls of the barn creating a surreal world of moving shapes and contrasting silhouettes. I gasped as I struggled to process what was happening.

Just as the men neared the door a light fell briefly on the face of the small bundle over the leading man's shoulders. I only vaguely remember the feeling of weightlessness as my hands slipped from the rung of the ladder and I fell endlessly through the air.

The tiny, boney body, the light blonde hair, the dirty pink sweater that fell to the floor just as the group reached the Entry Room; it was Alina. They had taken eight year old Alina.

****

The next day I awoke on the floor surrounded by the women of the barn. My head throbbed relentlessly, blurring my vision and muffling the sounds of those around me. I was distantly aware of a sharp pain in my left leg and a pinching feeling in my chest. The sun was up and I could smell a distinct hint of smoke. Opening my eyes for only seconds at a time, fighting against my body's natural will to fall back to sleep, I could make out the foggy shapes of Johnna and Nasha kneeling over me. They seemed to be washing my leg and my chest, yet I could barely feel their touch. My body was both somehow tingling with numbness and extremely sore at the same time, every part of me violently pulsating from the inside in time with the beat of my heart.

Off to the side I could hear someone sobbing and mumbling angrily. I couldn't place the voice.

"What would he want with her?! He'd better not touch her! I'll kill him!" The voice drifted through my hazy mind. I couldn't comprehend anything I heard, but something in me told me that I had been the source of this persons suffering.

Without warning, Johnna pressed down on my chest with suffocating force, the subsequent pain in my ribs setting nerves in my fingers and toes on fire. An ensuing moment of absolute consciousness forced my eyes open as I let out a pained howl and a few choice cuss words. Just as I thought the pain couldn't get any worse, I caught a glint of a glowing red ember burning on the end of a short stick. In a blink of an eye a fiery bolt of pain raced up my leg from where Nasha had been feverishly working, forcing the wind from my chest and curling my body in on itself against Johnna's best efforts to restrain me. A second later everything again returned to blackness.

It was a full day later when I next woke. The fogginess in my mind had abated and the pain in my ribs had been dulled.

Looking cautiously down at my legs I could see that a large gash below the knee on my left leg had a wet cloth neatly folded on it. Beneath the cloth I could feel a warm throbbing, slightly stinging sensation. Vaguely remembering the events of the day before where I had been held down by Johnna, a morbid temptation to look at the wound that I knew was neatly concealed took over me.

Wincing in fear of pain, I was surprised at how painless the removal of the cool wet cloth was; the only painful part being when a few small stings from the cloth pulled themselves free from the dried blood that they concealed.

I should have been more disturbed by the injury that I saw. Something in my mind seemed to still be numb as I looked upon the large black hole in my flesh. About the size of my eye and half as deep, a great chunk of my charred skin glistened under a black crust of dried blood and melted flesh. A great purple bruise, larger than the palm of my hand encircled the scab angrily. I gently touched the surface of the wound. It's hard scab seemed so unnatural that I felt compelled to pic at the hole with my fingernail. A rolling sharpness reverberated up my leg and back down to my toes, yet somehow it seemed tolerable, unreal, as if it were not attached to my body.

"I wouldn't do that if I were you," said a groggy, familiar voice.

Michael laid close beside me on the hard dirt floor, curled into an uncomfortable ball, having clearly spent the night watching over me.

"Do you remember anything?" he asked cautiously, pulling himself up to a weary sitting position.

"No not really…" I said uncertainly. "I remember being sick and going to sleep early."

"Anything after that?" he said, intentionally making deep eye contact as if trying to read my thoughts, most likely trying to determine my level of awareness.

I strained to remember. My head panged with a painful pressure, my ribs pinched as I breathed. I suddenly had the sensation of falling.

"I fell," I said with clarity.

"Do you remember how?" Michael persisted.

I fought through the patchy memories. Rewinding my thoughts I pictured myself climbing down the ladder. I had been racing towards something. Something had scared me and I had let go of the rungs, forgetting that I was only half way to the bottom. Three dark figures flashed in my mind.

"There was someone in here," I said pensively. Michael sat up attentively, apparently shocked by this revelation.

"You saw them?!" he said incredulously.

"I can't remember exactly," I strained. "I just remember someone…. No…three people." I paused to think. "They were carrying light," I said confusedly.

"What does that mean?" pushed Michael.

"From their hand… some kind of light." I could picture them clearer now. Running towards the Exit Door, guided by bright beams of light. One of the people was carrying something.

Suddenly it all came back to me in astonishing clarity.

"Oh my God…" I said quietly to myself, reeling as the reality set in.

Suddenly I became aware again of Michaels stare. Making deep eye contact with him again he finished my thoughts for me: "They took Alina."

****

Relaying my story to the rapt attention of the group my revelation seemed to catch some by surprise, while evidently clarifying what some had long believed in the first place.

"I didn't get any food at all yesterday but I still didn't wake up when the people came in," said Elin, the youngest woman amongst the adults, disputing my theory.

"No, but we all had ample water," countered David before I could respond. "It's the one thing that we all must have throughout the day to survive," he explained. "Sometimes there isn't enough food for everyone. He has to make sure that we all take whatever drug it is that he has been knocking us out with. The only sure thing is by putting it in the water."

The group nodded and grunted in agreement.

"I'd been so sick that I couldn't even keep water down," I trailed. "He must have seen that I was asleep too and assumed that I was drugged like the rest of you."

"I can't believe he would take an eight year old!" cried Michael in renewed despair. Alina had become like a little sister to me. I loved her dearly and

61

protected her however I could. Michael had cared for her like a daughter. The pain he felt was that of a parent who knew his child was in danger. Although I was distraught by the loss of Alina and needed someone to comfort and calm me, I knew that Michael needed me more, but all I could do to offer any sort of support was to hug him.

****

Four restless days later Alina was returned to us.

We had all spent the previous three nights struggling against our body's natural desire to sleep. Despite knowing that it was highly unlikely that another one of us would be taken in the night, we still adopted a regiment of only drinking water in the morning and early afternoon, and establishing shift routine for sleeping. It was a silent protest; a way of letting our captor know that we would no longer follow his rules.

Our demonstration was short lived.

By the beginning of the third day it was clear that we were still at the mercy of Mr. Irvine. Exhausted from both the unnatural routine as well as from the stress of worrying about Alina's fate, resisting sleep had become more and more difficult. I knew that we couldn't sustain this rebellion much longer. Soon we would become so worn out that we would have no choice but to give in and go back to the way that things had always been.

As the morning light began to seep through the wall boards that morning, we all roused ourselves from our semi-coma, begrudgingly moaning and groaning against tired limbs and weary heads. The thick, musty heat of summer had suddenly arrived overnight, filling the barn with an oppressive layer of liquid air that stuck to the skin. I languidly dragged my tired body towards the faucet in need of a cool drink and splash of water to wake me up.

I couldn't believe it when I turned the sharp steel knob of the faucet. No water came at all.

The others all gathered around me, stupefied, staring at the silent tap. We all knew it; Until we proved that we wouldn't defy him again, there would be no more water until evenings.

He had beaten us.

****

It took a while for me to notice that the entry door was hanging slightly open.

I pictured little eight year old Alina's face as she giggled and laughed while jumping in the shallow waters of the ocean with Michael and I, her fragile, thin body with ribs rippling beneath the skin of her chest; looking much younger than her age, Alina was the picture of innocents. A sudden vision of Julie's broken body lying in the cold hay popped into my mind, replacing Julie's head with that of Alina's. All thoughts left me then, subconsciously blocking myself from accepting the horrible probability that Alina may be lying behind that open door, broken, bruised and near death.

I mechanically made my way towards the door, feeling the sensation of each step beneath my naked foot so distinctly that I could almost count the number of tiny pebbles and stray strands of straw as I walked over them. Others may have been talking or moving around me but all I could hear was the sound of my own breathing.

As I neared the door, my arm rose before me like a foreign object and I watched as it grasped the edge of the door tightly and pulled. Quickly the door swung towards me and I jumped back startled, narrowly avoiding a collision.

I stood silent and breathless looking into the shadowy room. Although my eyes adjusted slowly, the image before me was perfectly clear: Lying curiously twisted and still on a small pile of crumpled hay in the back corner, damp areas of skin glistening slightly in the darkness through ripped and torn clothing, was Alina's unmistakably tiny and frail body.
In a blink of an eye my senses flooded back into my body.

"Michael!" I yelled at the top of my lungs as I raced the few steps to Alina's side. Kneeling beside the little girl who I had grown to love so much, my hands struggled to decide if they should hug her or roll her over to face me and attempt to wake her.

63

Softly and gently I found myself caressing her arm, whispering her name quietly despite having just launched myself loudly into the room and screaming for Michael.

"Alina," I said through a cracking, unsteady voice. Slowly I allowed myself to survey her body as she lay unmoving at my knees. Her clothes were wet through and through, her skin clammy and clumped with thick sand. Relieved to discover that it was not a mix of wet and dried blood that clung to her skin, I became conscious of the fact that it was lightly raining outside.

"Alina," I said again, her chest slightly heaving in response as she took a shallow breath. Her head shook side to side ever so slightly and she pulled her hands up to her chest. She was slowly waking and I could sense that she had been in the middle of a bad dream.

"Alina, it's me. You're back," I whispered close to her ear.

Crashing through the silence in panic Michael raced into the room, bouncing off the door frame, nearly landing on top of Alina as he unintentionally pushed me away and fell to her side.

"Oh my God," he cried, pushing his face into her neck and squeezing her in close to him as he lay down beside her. Alina groaned in response, consciousness quickly waking within her.

I threw my right arm over Michael and tucked my other under Alina's head, simultaneously embracing them as I drew my body up against Michael. Together the three of us lay tightly against one another, all three sobbing, overwhelmingly relieved and yet somehow saddened by Alina's return.

My eyes were burning long before I realized that most of the others had huddled in the doorway and were looking down at us with empathy. Making eye contact with Nasha who stood front and centre in the crowd I could see something different on her face; it was a mix of sadness and anger, but more than anything I could sense surrender. Recognizing my comprehension, Nasha spun on her heel and pushed her way through the crowd in front of her. I knew then that things were about to change.

******

64

"No they didn't hurt me," said Alina, head down as she nervously fidgeted with the pink sweater in her lap. She wasn't used to so much attention. We had all gathered awkwardly around her as she warmed herself by the fire, all of us wanting to know what had happened to her, afraid of what we might hear.

"What do you mean '*they*'?" asked Michael, kneeling in front of Alina, looking up at her intensely with tears in his eyes.

"The men," was Alina's vague reply.

"There was more than one?" Michael seemed genuinely shocked by this news.

"There are always different people," interjected Johnna. "Mr. Irvine is the one in charge but the others are different almost every time."

Having overheard some of the stories that Julie had recounted upon her return, this was not news to me anymore, but I distinctly remember how disturbed I had been at this news. To me it meant that there wasn't just one disturbed man out in the real world, but a whole society of them. I could see this revelation flash on Michaels face now; suddenly the world outside became much more frightening to him.

"Five. And one older woman," answered Alina quietly.

"Tell us everything that you can remember," pushed Nasha aggressively. "As much detail as you can think of." Nasha's closed, tight body language and stern, cold face concerned me. The warm, loving person that I normally considered Nasha to be was not present at this moment. Before me stood a confrontational, aggressive, heartless person. The sight confounded me.

"I dunno…" began Alina.

"I was so scared..." she sniffled, tears leaking from the corners of her eyes. "Everything was so different. Things were so shiny they didn't look real. Everything was too perfect like… I dunno.

They had see-through cups to drink out of. Their… their bodies smelled sweet... or I don't know, strong but in a good way. The lady's hair was red like fire and so were her lips, like, almost like not real! The men had smooth faces and shiny hair…

There was light coming through the roof but they could make it come on and off when they wanted… Even in the darkness there were noises all the time…

Everything! Everything was so different! Like a dream… like a bad dream."

A panicked look had come across Alina's face and she stopped to catch her breath. Michael brushed his fingers softly through her hair, and hugged her tightly, calming her gently.

I thought back to the night that I had witnessed Alina being taken. The simple intrusion into our space by unknown people, the sight of their clean, sleek, black clothing, their incredible sticks that threw beams of light out in front of them; those few things were enough to cloud my mind with disbelief. I couldn't imagine waking in a world of unfamiliarity's like Alina had just described.

After a few moments Michael pulled himself slightly away from Alina, still holding her hands in his. "Can you keep going?"

She nodded hesitantly.

"I…. Well, I woke up in small room…on a very soft bed with slippery red cloth on it. My hands were tied against the wall. They were all washing me."

"Washing you?" asked Nasha, seemingly baffled.

"Yah. They all stood around me and they had little white cloths and were cleaning me very slowly…"

"Even the lady?" I interrupted.

"Yah, her too. She kept telling me to smile for the 'camra' and pointed to a little black thing that one of the guys was holding." Several of the other adults in the group nodded slightly in acknowledgement at this foreign word which meant nothing to me.

"It's like the ones that are all over the barn that Mr. Irvine uses to watch us," David explained to me, sensing my confusion. "They take pictures and video.

Kind of like a memory that you can watch later." His explanation confused me even further, but I looked to Alina in encouragement to continue.

"Um, I dunno. I was still out of it. They were all naked and kept touching their… privates. I was scared so I kept closing my eyes."

We all sat in silence waiting for Alina to continue. Her eyes had gone dark and distant. I was afraid to hear more but my curiosity about the outside world left me painfully longing for more.

As the silence grew unbearable, Michael gently caressed Alina's hands. It was a simple, caring, fatherly gesture more heartwarming than anything I had ever experienced. Ever so subtly Alina's body seemed to relax, surrendering herself to the comfort of Michael's support.

"They all got loud and yelled a bit but then they all just stopped….. and then they washed me off some more and…. left me alone in the dark."

"You were gone for days," said Nasha aggressively. "Is that all that you remember?"

Seemingly startled by the reminder that it was not just her and Michael speaking privately, Alina stammered nervously, almost as if she were being chastised for bad behaviour.

"It… it was… was all… they did the same things all the time." Pausing to wipe the tears from her cheeks it was clear that she was holding back an onslaught of sobs. "They did it all the time," she continued with a little more conviction. "If I wasn't in the dark they were in the room with me doing stuff to me like that. Sometimes there were a few different men, but the woman was always the same one. I was attached to the wall the whole time except when they made me pee and stuff into a cold white chair with water in it. They all watched. They even all watched when they fed me. They all took turns feeding me like it was a game. They made me beg for food…like… they made me say 'I want it daddy, give me some please,' or 'Mmm it's so good.' Someone always had a camra."

"They didn't put anything inside you?" asked Nasha harshly.

Confused, Alina hesitated in her response. "Um, just….the food?"

"Nothing in your genitals?" questioned Nasha in the same cold tone.

"Uh I don't ... What do you mean? I..." Alina clearly didn't understand what Nasha was trying to imply.

"Did they touch your genitals?" interrupted Nasha impatiently.

"Uh. Yah," replied Alina, clearly embarrassed. "They cleaned me everywhere all the time."

"Hm," responded Nasha, angrily shaking her head before storming off to the opposite wall away from the group. "PIGS!" She screamed towards the roof. "You're going to HELL ASSHOLE!"

****

No food reward or even warm water came after Alina's return. We had come to expect less and less to be sent to us after someone was brought back, but usually there was something small.
The meager collection of water that did come from the tap in the evenings was not enough to calm the roars of hunger in our bellies, let alone satiate our thirst on these long, hot summer days.

We were being punished not only for plotting against Mr. Irvine, but for Nasha's behaviour. Her outburst had angered our captor. We all knew that it was dangerous to ever say anything negative about our situation as some sort of punishment would be doled out, but this was different. This time there had been a palpable change in mood in the barn: where fear once reigned, anger now took hold. Although few people had ever shown any affection towards Alina, there wasn't one among us who wasn't furious that Mr. Irvine had allowed for such despicable things to happen to a young girl.

The only way to stop the punishment would be to submit to Mr. Irvine's routines and suppress our emotions. As the hunger pains got worse and worse, this became easier and easier.

****

Immediately upon her return, Michael and I decided to make sure that Alina was no longer accessible for the nighttime raids. We both knew that she had to join us at night up in our lofty bed. This one unreachable place of refuge had been our sole protection against our own abduction. Whether the others in the barn knew this or not, it was never discussed, but nobody objected as we forced poor little Alina to climb the impossibly high ladder, screaming and shaking in fear the entire way.

The tiny platform had been small for just Michael and I to sleep on, but now with the added body, it was dangerously tight. With Alina tightly squished between us on her back, tightly holding her pink sweater-turned-security-blanket, Michael and I slept face-to-face, reaching past Alina to hold each other's shirts tightly.

As small as it was, the fear of being unintentionally pushed off in the middle of the night kept us all wrapped tightly together. To us, the fear of falling was less frightening than the fear of being taken by masked men in the night.

****

Food had come sparingly for several weeks before it stopped altogether.

We had stockpiled a small store of beans over the previous months but we had been dipping into it recently, and knew that we couldn't survive for more than a few days on this alone if this forced famine were to continue. Michael and I, being the only two who were allowed to venture outside of the barn besides Alina, took it upon ourselves immediately to find alternative sources of food. We knew it was a risk. We knew that we might anger Mr. Irvine and cause more trouble for us all if he noticed, but we were starving. It was a gamble we had to take.

In the past we had often found small crustaceans along the ocean edge that we brought back to cook over the fire. Most were only bite-sized, but a few of the larger shelled things that we found would feed two or three people. Finding these treats was rare though, and I knew we couldn't rely on this as a daily meal plan if our watcher did not provide food soon.

Fish were everywhere. For most of my life I had sat on that beach watching the fish as they swam along the shore line, sometimes riding the high tide right up to the footings of the barn as they chased tiny prey. Countless times I had tried to devise some kind of method of trapping the fish, often by simply diving into the water in desperation to try to catch one in my bare hands, but was never successful. We had often managed to catch a few small minnows using a hooked chicken bone tied to a long thread, but larger fish would simply strike the bait, snap the thread and take the hook with them. I knew there had to be a way to catch something bigger.

Sitting there on the beach this morning I watched as the tide pulled far away from the shore. In the shallows, darting between exposed pieces of broken corals swam those elusive fish, infuriatingly close but frustratingly unattainable.

The hot summer sun was already beating down heavily on me so I decided to cool down my going for a swim in the cool water. Just as my feet reached the water's edge, movement in the sand off to my right caught my attention. Moving closer to examine, I noticed a few pieces of coral had been pushed onto the very edge of the shore. On the side opposite the ocean, flopping desperately in the sand, twitched a small silvery fish. Evidently it had been swimming in the shallows as the tide receded, becoming trapped by the corals. Excitement immediately overcame me, not because I had found food--this fish was far too small to be eaten-- but because of the way in which it had become trapped. Broken coral was everywhere. I could replicate this kind of trap on a larger scale. I suddenly had a potential way of catching a good sized fish.

The plan was to use larger chunks of coral, stones and branches scavenged from the beach to build a long, low, crescent-shaped wall in the water at low-tide. The idea was that during high-tide the wall would become completely submerged and larger fish would swim past it while chasing some of the smaller sea-life, getting trapped when the tide began to recede. It took Michael and I all day to collect enough building material. Our trap measured an impressive twenty-eight steps in length and was as high as my waist in the middle. By the time we were finished we were exhausted, sunburned and waterlogged, skeptical and disheartened at the thought that the wall would probably not even work.

In eager anticipation, Michael and I were out to check our trap as soon as the sun rose beyond the horizon the following morning. We watched as the tide slowly pulled away almost imperceptibly from the shore, the gentle ebb and flow almost hypnotizing in the early morning haze of drowsiness.

As the tide receded and the top of the wall became visible between the small waves I quickly realized that a substantial section of the barrier had collapsed into the sands and was being pulled back into the sea with the current. Disheartened, I begrudgingly slipped into the water to repair what I could in hopes that the next tide would bring more success. To my amazement, as I entered the water the surface exploded in a great spray of drops. Startled, I fell back in surprise, dunking myself clumsily under the knee deep water. It only took me a second to realize what had happened. A fish! "A FISH!" I heard myself yell.

Michael, who had been gloomily watching from the shore, was immediately on his feet and in the water at the opposite end of our crescent-shaped wall. I could see the fish perfectly clearly and my heart raced as I realized that it was a big one! From where I stood it appeared to be at least the length of my forearm and three times as fat. A fish that size would feed all of us for a whole meal.

Determined to block its escape, I took position right against the edge of the small wall. To my left, the shoreline was about four large steps away, but a natural underwater ledge of sand created by the small waves rose to the surface abruptly at the side of my foot. Judging by the position that Michael stood, it appeared that the same shelf continued to where he stood as well. This meant that our prey had only the narrow gap between our knees through which to escape if it came towards us. Seemingly coming to the same conclusion, Michael and I simultaneously lowered our bodies into the water, effectively damming the sides of the rock wall. The fish, who had not yet found the collapsed section of the wall which was several steps ahead of me, focused its escape attempt on forcing its large body through the small holes between the corals and rocks closer to Michael.

"You've got to block that hole!" yelled Michael, unafraid of causing further panic in the fish. He was at least twenty steps away from me and watched nervously as the fish poked and splashed at the stones close to him. Desperate and full of adrenaline, I was torn between the desire to jump from my place and race the few paces needed to block the hole or to slide slowly across the shallow waters to sneak into position.

Reading my hesitation Michael called out "Slowly, now!"

Doing my best to maintain the physical barrier that I had created with my body, I pulled my body towards the hole in the wall, all the while keeping my eyes locked on the reflective glimmer of the fish as it fought to find an escape.

Finally settling into place, determined to do all that I could to block any potential exit route for the fish, I began taking pieces of the wall from behind me and re-assembling them between me and the fish. Slowly I built a solid blockade from the existing wall right up onto shore. Michael had taken my lead and done the same on his side. Feeling relatively sure that this barrier would hold, the two of us stepped back and watched as the water slowly pulled the rest of the way down the gently sloping beach.

We sat in silence as the fish desperately splashed in the last drops of water and finally resigned its attempts at escape, gasping for water, only getting sand and air. I had expected Michael to get up and grab the fish as soon as the water was low enough. In the end though I knew that he, as I, wanted to watch our invention fulfil its duty. Only when the fish took its last gasp did we get up from our spot to collect it. Triumphantly holding our victim high above our head, Michael and I embraced tightly. This was not just a fish; this was a shift in power; for the first time ever we were no longer completely dependent on the whims of a disturbed stranger for our survival.

****

When we got back into the barn we were greeted with awe and praise. Everyone was shocked to find that we had devised a method of getting food. Over the years people had tried everything to find sources of sustenance. Ideas had ranged from planting seeds found in our food to leaving scraps out in an effort to catch rats. To date, no attempts had been successful.

Following our lead, Johnna immediately grew set on devising a way of attaining fresh water. Knowing that when salt water is boiled too long it leaves the salt behind while the water evaporates, she eventually figured out a method of catching the steam from boiling ocean water, collecting it as fresh water. Though a lot of work, this method provided us with just enough water to last a full day. Through strict rationing, we now had water and food. Everyone shared in our sense of empowerment.

Things were going to change starting today.

It had been many weeks since we had built our trap, yet not a morsel of food had been delivered to the Entry Room in all this time. Our fresh water tap was still running dry. We had never gone so long without something to fill our bellies and quench our thirst. We should have been dead or dying.

But we were thriving.

Michael and I had been incredibly successful with our fishing system. The day after we caught our first fish, we had set about repairing and reinforcing the current trap and soon began to build several more. Some days we found that nothing had been trapped, but other times the stone enclosures would be teeming with bounty. We experimented with baiting traps in different ways to encourage larger fish to explore the shallow waters. We found that our catch was more bountiful when we buried left over fish guts within the crescent walls themselves. On several occasions we were amazed to find sharks the length of my arm, and once a pile of brown stingrays each far larger than my head.

At the suggestion of David, Michael and I had created a drying rack on the hot beach where we hung any excess fish to preserve for later, hungrier times. Alina became quickly adept at carving up and gutting the fish for us using a new version of Johnna's stone blade.

Remarkably, a wide variety of birds quickly discovered our drying rack. The sight of a few birds had been common in the past, but the large flocks that had now made our beach their home was both annoying and a blessing. Scaring the birds away from our drying rack became a constant challenge and at night we had the grueling task of carrying each and every dead fish back into the protection of the barn so that they would not be consumed by the birds in the night. Worse than the amount of work involved was the smell; the smell of dead fish seemed to permeate everything on those hot evenings, suffocating us all under a tangible weight of odour.

Despite all the unpleasantness associated with the birds, the one great benefit was the eggs. Several large white birds had immediately begun building nests upon their arrival on our beach. Within a week Michael, Alina and I were collecting eggs on a daily basis. On top of that, several of the nesting birds fought back when we tried to steal their precious unborn offspring and on several occasions we were able to catch and kill a bird for a meal.

Because the birds tended to nest away from the open beach, I had begun testing the boundaries in terms of how far from the barn I could venture. At first I would stay close to the beach, only going far enough into the surrounding grasses to reach the first nests. In time I found myself traveling slightly further inland to reach an untouched brood of birds until one day I looked up and saw that the barn was out of sight. Unsure as to whether I was permitted to travel this far out or of if I had simply been lucky enough to go unnoticed, I raced back to the safety of the sand, pulse pounding in my ears, breathless not from the exertion, but sheer fear of being sighted and shot down. It was days before I crossed beyond the grasses again, but I was always careful to keep the barn within view.

Michael always stayed at Alina's side. If Michael needed to move any great distance he would simply whistle or call her name and Alina would immediately come to him. It was an unspoken agreement that both preferred, neither could bear the thought that she may be taken again. I did my best to stay close as well, but it was clear that Alina saw Michael as her primary protector.

In my explorations, I continued to seek out other sources of food. Several of the elders would coach me on what to look for, describing in great detail the types of roots, plants and even bugs that may be edible in the area. I had marginal success at best, finding mainly coconuts and large red sea grapes, and a thick grainy root that seemed to grow in abundance in the area. I had managed to catch a few large bugs that others had asked me to search for, but with the profusion of other things to eat, they were rarely eaten and I eventually stopped hunting for them.

Between the three of us, hunting for and preparing food became a full-time job.

Johnna had been able to accumulate a fairly substantial store of sea salt with which we used both as flavouring and as a further preservative. She began to find remarkable ways of cooking delicious meals for us despite the fact that every single meal consisted of fish. I had collected huge piles of branches and driftwood, and there always seemed to be something cooking over the fire.

We had all begun to put on a little weight; even little Alina began looking healthy for the first time in her life as meat began to fill out her sunken cheeks and cover her bony ribs. We began to feel that we had beaten the system, that we had found a way to survive and flourish. We were no longer dependent on Mr. Irving and his sparse, pathetic meals and hazardous water. Our bellies were full and our water was safe. We no longer worried that masked men would be able to sneak into the barn without rousing us all. We were strong, alert and in control.

And then the great door closed.

****

It happened in the middle of one of the hottest days of the summer. As per our usual routine, Michael, Alina and I had been on the beach all day working tirelessly on our stock of fish. Our racks were completely full and I had just come back from the forest with a large cache of long branches to extend our drying surface. Michael and Alina had been enjoying a bit of relaxation, floating and splashing each other in the shallow waters beyond the furthest fish trap, laughing without a concern in the world.

The sun was directly overhead but a cool breeze blew down from the hills providing comfortable salvation for the midday heat. Inside the barn, I knew that the others would be suffering terribly from the stagnant air, still afraid to risk an attempt at joining the privileged three.

I had worked all morning to scavenge for the small, sweet sea grapes that everyone loved and made sure to distribute them equally amongst everyone stuck inside on this hot day. It was all that I could do to brighten their day just a little.

I was just about to climb the newest drying rack to fasten the final cross poles when I first heard the noise.

It was an unfamiliar sound, a click followed by a very subtle whirr. Something mechanical had just been activated. Turning my head to follow the source, I immediately realized that it was coming from the barn, and I knew instinctually that it signaled the coming of something terrible.

Panic rushed through me like an icy breeze. Dropping my load of branches, I spun on the spot, feeling an out-of body sensation as I found myself yelling involuntarily towards Michael:

"THE BARN! GET TO THE BARN!"

Unable to hear the noise from their position, Michael and Alina had been shocked by my sudden outburst and stared at me in utter confusion.

"SOMETHING'S HAPPENING! WE HAVE TO RUN!" My voice cracked as I yelled.

Michael seemed stunned by the intensity of my voice. He seemed to be scanning the grassy areas beyond the beach for the source of my distress while Alina quickly pulled herself over to hide behind him.

"NOW!" I yelled, running several steps towards them to help my voice travel the distance. Behind me a familiar noise now took over from the whir. CRACK! I knew instantly that the great barn door was about to close.

We're still out here! I yelled inside my head. The reality of this realization hit me hard: If we didn't run now, we would be locked outside the barn. Although none of us liked being trapped inside, it at least was a place of familiarity and ironically, safety. Inside the barn we knew the variables to life. We knew the routine, we understood the rules. There were other people to keep us protected and help us survive, people who we relied on for a sense of family support and mutual empathy. If we were to be locked out, we would be vulnerable in every way. Anything could happen to us out here. We would have no support system for survival, no defence against the unknown dangers that may lurk in the night.

For the first time ever I realized that the very barn that had been my lifelong prison was also the only home I had ever known, the only certainty in my life. Like the dirty old sweater that Alina continued to carry around everywhere with her, as awful as it was, the barn was my symbol of security.

Finally grasping the intensity of the situation, yet clearly not understanding what exactly was happening, Michael and Alina bounded from the water, Michael pulling the stumbling girl behind him forcefully as he broke into a run.

"What's happening?" called Michael.

"THE BARN DOOR! I THINK ITS CLOSING!" I shouted back. Michaels face seemed to pale in the bright light as comprehension of the situation hit him hard.

Knowing the two of them were now close behind, I started sprinting toward the barn. I'd never moved so fast in my life! I knew that the door moved slowly but time seemed to be a blur and I had no idea how long it had been since the first whir of movement had broken the serenity of the day.

My body seemed numb. I could tell that my left foot had been cut badly by stepping on some sharp shell or piece of coral, but all I could concentrate on now was making it to the edge of the barn, my pace never faltering.

Before I knew it I had reached the wall of the barn. The creaks and groans of the great door as it descended were deafening from where I stood, but I could see that the door was not yet at the half-way point in its descent. Looking behind me, Alina was having trouble keeping up with Michael as he pulled her faster than her ability to move. Constantly falling and tripping as she went, bleeding profusely from the knees, Alina drastically slowed Michael's progress. I raced back to them and took Alina's free hand, pulling her up firmly to my side, dragging her feet between Michael and I as we rushed towards the barn.

The tide was high, and the open side of the barn extended a good distance into the water. Without hesitation the three of us dove into the shallows together, kicking and splashing vigorously as the door continued to lower.

Alina, never comfortable in the water, flailed helplessly as the water quickly became too deep for her to touch bottom and panic immediately overcame her. Without a moment of delay, Michael had Alina on his back, her arms tightly wrapped around his neck, forcing himself through the water as fast as he could. Swimming slightly ahead of the pair, I reached for Michael's hand. The door was almost closed. Still able to touch bottom with the tip of my toes, I squeezed his hand tightly as I pushed off the bottom, dragging the pair behind me in a storm of splashing.

Approaching the corner, I managed to peer up through the water in my eyes; the door was within an arm's length of the surface of the water. Desperately reaching out for the wall with my free hand, I made contact with the weathered, slimy wood and pulled with all my might. I felt myself cross under the shadow of the door, briefly able to see that everyone inside the barn had gathered along the water's edge and were yelling in worried encouragement.

POP! POP! POP!

My whole body felt like it was on fire.

Beside me, bright red water seemed to leap from the surface.

I felt Michael's hand let go of mine.

My ears burned with a piercing ring blocking out all other sounds.

I saw the door sink beneath the depths of the water as it sealed shut.

Michael and Alina had not made it through the door.

Everything went black.

****

I awoke several days later.

Dehydrated, exhausted and confused, pain coursed through my body with every tiny movement. I resisted all urges to allow consciousness to seep in; all I wanted was to sleep. Visions of giant, bird-beaked sea monsters taunted me. With crazed fervor they chomped at my arm and leg, burned my face with their fiery breath, pulled me under the icy cold surface with enormous finned arms as the water filled my lungs. I fought back violently as the monsters tried to destroy me. There were dozens of them, all much bigger than anything I had ever seen. I knew that I had little chance of defeating them but still I fought with all my might. I had no choice; they had Michael and Alina.

It was the tickling sensation that woke me.

Despite the war that raged in my dreams, the great demons seemed to allow for a time-out each time that I needed a moment to scratch my wounds which, on top of the throbbing pain, felt as though they were being gently tickled from within. In the hazy confusion of my imagination, the annoying sensation seemed oddly definite and tangible, distant and separate from the horrible surrealism of my dreams.

In the midst of the bloody battle, the snapping monsters faded into fractured memories as a foggy crack of light interrupted the violent scene before me, and my eyes pulled themselves open.

Oblivious to my surroundings, eyes caked with cloudy goop, head spinning from fever, all I could think of was scratching the incessant itch in my arm and my leg. As my hand made contact with the patched wound on my arm, a lightning bolt of pain exploded within me. Reactively letting out a guttural roar of agony, I lurched up from my position on the floor, immediately falling back again as the wound in my leg revolted painfully against the movement.

"Quick! He's awake!" a man's voice yelled out as heavy hands force my shoulders back to the ground.

In confused panic I fought back against my unknown captor . Vague memories of being attacked by some sort of monster and a feeling of impending doom and loss flickered through my mind. I screamed in a combination of fear, pain and anger: "Let me go! Let me go!"

Another set of hands held down my arms, while still more restrained my legs.

"Ash! It's us!" came a familiar female voice. "Shh its me, Nasha!"

Nasha? Through foggy eyes I could see a familiar outline of a woman's face; her long, dark hair, her shockingly green eyes… I knew this woman. I felt myself relax slightly as recognition set in.

"Ash, just relax, you're okay," said the same gentle voice.

Nasha. I stopped my resistance and collapsed wearily onto the floor. I was safe.

****

I had been shot twice: once in the upper right thigh and once in the left arm. The pain was unbearable. I felt as if hot cinders were melting into my flesh and every movement shot sparks of fire through my entire body.

In my state of wavering lucidity, it had taken three men to hold me down as Johnna had done her best to stitch me up. Using a rudimentary needle made from a fish bone and short strands of string from my clothing, she had been unsuccessful in slowing the bleeding from the wound in my left arm. The bullet had passed right through my arm and the bleeding had been profuse. She had no choice other

79

than to cauterize the openings with the red hot end of a small log from the fire, immediately causing me to black out in reaction to the searing pain. Once the bleeding stopped, Johnna had cleaned the wound with boiled ocean water and dressed it with a rough bandage.

The leg wound was not as severe, possibly because the water had slowed the bullet. Using her bare fingers, Johnna was able to pull the bullet from my leg and had sewn up the shallow hole with relative ease.

"What happened?" I groaned after Nasha had finished explaining the severity of my injuries to me. My memory was blank. I strained to remember anything at all. In my groggy state, the only clear image that I could form in my mind was that of Nasha's gentle eyes looking comfortingly down on me. I pushed myself to figure out where I was or even who I was but all I could focus on was the pain.

"I don't know why he shot you," sighed Nasha despairingly.

"Who?" I moaned.

"Let him rest Nasha," said another familiar voice. Turning my head slowly towards the voice, allowing my eyes to open slightly, I immediately realized that I knew this woman too. Her dark brown skin, curly jet black hair striped with white, the fine lines around her pink lips; I knew her, but could not place her.

"He needs to know," argued Nasha. "Why not tell him now while he is still a bit delirious? The blow won't sting as much."

"He's too weak, let him rest a bit," countered the darker woman.

"Tell me," I quietly pleaded, eyes closing in exhaustion. A silence fell and I could tell by the shifting of bodies that others had gathered around me and were now uncomfortably preparing for my reaction.

It was a man's voice who suddenly broke through the silence. "It was Mr. Irvine. He shot at you when you were coming back into the barn." The man's voice was cold and matter-of fact. I struggled to picture the face of the man who had shot me, this 'Mr. Irvine,' but the only thing that came to mind was a little black, semi-transparent dome.

"Why?" I mumbled.

"The door was closing. You were trying to get in before it closed," the man responded. "We think he was trying to keep you out."

A jumbled memory grew in my mind. I could feel cold water around me, I could see that it was red with blood as several loud cracks echoed through the air. Above me, the huge wooden door was lowering to the surface of the water.

"Keep me out?" I asked. "Of what?"

"Uh, the barn," responded the man. "We don't think he wanted you guys to get back in."

My mind tumbled over itself as images rushed back in with overwhelming speed. The Barn. I live in a barn. I was outside. Fish. Strange noises. Panic.

Suddenly it all came back to me in jolt of recognition.

Many hands pressed firmly down on me as I fought to get to my feet.

"MICHAEL AND ALINA!" I screamed, my physical pain trumped by that of the emotional distress at the thought of losing Michael and Alina.

"Shhhhh, Ash! STOP! Lay DOWN!" forced Nasha.

Futilely I continued to struggle.

"WHERE ARE THEY? TELL ME THEY'RE OKAY!"

"Stop! Stop. Rest,' soothed the other woman's comforting voice. 'Relax.' Johnna, I remembered. "We don't know what happened."

My body convulsed in response to the stress. Nasha gently coerced me into accepting small drips of water into my mouth. I suddenly became aware of how dehydrated I was and begged for more. Pouring several cupful's into my mouth, Nasha gently caressed my hair and I felt my body allow itself to relax a little.

"Did they get shot too?"

"No," answered Nasha. "At least, we don't think so."

"When the shots rang out they stopped swimming," interrupted David harshly, "But there were only three shots and two of them hit you. The other hit the door."

"The door closed before Michael and Alina could get inside," continued Nasha. "We could hear them through the wall while we were pulling you out of the water. They were yelling at us to let them in, but obviously we couldn't help them. They sounded scared, but not hurt."

"So they're still outside," I said, more of a statement than a question.

Silence lingered awkwardly in the air. Clearly there was something more that nobody wanted to tell me. Both Nasha and Johnna avoided eye contact with me. The small crowd that had gathered around stared at me with sad expressions.

Finally David spoke, first clearing his throat as his voice cracked in an uncharacteristic show of emotion. "They're gone."

My heart felt like it rolled over in my chest as the words left his mouth. I could feel my face pale. My breath caught in my throat.

Gone?

It was my worst fear that one of them should ever leave me, but both of them? The thought echoed incomprehensibly in my mind.

"Wh… Bo…wha..?" I stammered as my mouth tried to ask the questions that my brain was not prepared to hear the answers to.

"We could hear them through the walls at first," David explained. "Michael kept yelling about letting them in. He threw things against the walls and tried to pull at the boards for the rest of the day. We tried from this side too. Alina just cried the whole time."

David paused to take a deep breath, evidently fighting the tears that welled up in his eyes. I tried to brace myself for the blow that I knew was about to hit me but I couldn't even catch my breath.

"By the time night fell they had exhausted themselves and were pretty quiet. After a few hours we were all still awake, we could hear an engine in the distance. As it got closer we knew that it was a car or a truck and it was coming right for us."

My heart was beating so hard that my head began to spin.

"We started to yell at Michael and Alina telling them to hide. They didn't seem to know what was happening--I guess they had never heard a car before.

When they finally saw the car we could hear Alina start to scream and Michael started banging on the walls again, yelling to be let in. The car pulled right up to the side of the barn where they were. I could hear a bunch of men get out and start yelling at them to lay down on the ground and put their hands on their heads but Michael kept pounding on the wall and Alina kept screaming. After a few seconds, or, I dunno, a minute or two, Alina suddenly went silent and I could hear the men fighting with Michael."

David looked me forlornly in the eye. "They were kicking him or something. I could hear him yelling and groaning. Then everything just got quiet. A minute later they were driving away."

****

The winter had been a particularly difficult one. The cold winds had come in early, settled quickly and never let up. Snow and ice once again filled the tiny gaps between the boards of the barn walls, leaving our home shrouded in endless darkness. Alina and Michael had not returned.

We were starved for water. With the door being closed, and the small pool of water that seeped underneath being frozen solid, Johnna was no longer able to collect enough ocean water to convert to safe drinking water with her ingenious little distillery. At first, our only way to get water was to collect the small drops that slowly fell from the rusty old faucet, which had never been turned back on. It would take a full day or night to collect enough water to keep us alive.

As the dehydration took hold, our minds began to falter. Delirious, nonsensical arguments became an everyday occurrence. Great fistfights began to erupt as we began stealing shares of the precious liquid from others who were too lethargic to move quickly enough to get their share. I was shocked at how barbaric people had become. We fought each other without restraint. Male or female, young or old, everyone became fair game. I was equally as guilty as anyone, having drawn blood on Joseph's face, broken Mallie's pinky finger, and been knocked to the ground by a pot-wielding Nasha.

Our only salvation from thirst came from collecting the ice or small piles of snow that had formed on the sides of the walls and melting it in our pot over the fire. It was rarely enough, but the little that we could collect brought us immediate liberation from our dehydration and brought our minds back to some semblance of humanity. It, however, brought on a new problem: Fire.

Fire and food quickly became an issue. Every day we would check the Entry Room to see if Alina and Michael had been brought back to us or if food or wood had been delivered. Even though many of us were awake late into the night, never hearing any commotion from outside, we were always disappointed to see the Entry Room empty each morning.

The collection of firewood that I had accumulated over the summer lasted for a surprisingly long time, though we were incredibly cautious to only burn the bare minimum. Ice was only melted once per day, always while cooking our meager rations of food. Often it would freeze again quickly, so we were quick to drink our fill, and often went to bed thirsty.

By the end of the winter, we had run out of every piece of firewood and resorted to dismantling anything and everything that we could, though there wasn't much in the first place to take apart.

As much as I hated to do it, on one particularly cold day I found myself mournfully ripping apart the boards of my hanging bed. Memories of Michael and Alina and I curled up here flooded back. It had been months since they had been locked out of the barn. I missed them so much. Their absence had left me disheartened and empty inside. I missed Alina's babyish laugh, the feel of her feather-soft hair on my cheek while we slept. I yearned for an embrace from Michael, to look into his strong, reassuring grey-blue eyes, to be comforted by his ever present smile. I couldn't bring myself to think about what may be happening to them right now, or if they were even alive still. These horrible thoughts spent enough time haunting my dreams.

I cried as I pulled at the old boards, one by one removing my only place of sanctuary—the very place that had kept me safe from abduction. By tearing this refuge down I knew that I would be exposing myself to that danger. My hands shook at the thought. It had become a daily struggle for survival and I had to think of the lives of everyone in the barn, not just myself. They had all given up a part of themselves for the greater good of the rest of us. Because of their suffering I had been fortunate to escape the horrors that they had all been subjected to. I couldn't spend my days dwelling on the reality that I was now just as vulnerable as all the others. In a sense, I felt that I owed it to them to be the next one taken.

Having finally removed every board from the hanging platform, the barn seemed somehow larger and more desolate than ever. The two small domed eyes that had hung next to my head every night now seemed impossibly far away. It was strange, but I actually would miss their watchful eyes on me as I slept.

Picking a new spot on the cold hard ground beside everyone else that night I could feel the empathetic eyes of the others on me. Not a word was spoken as we all settled in. As the boards of my old safe haven crackled and quickly burned away beside us, we were all thinking the same thing:

I would be taken next. I knew it and they knew it. And it would be soon.

******

We were literally starving.

Our supply of dried fish had dwindled quickly. Having left the majority outside on the day the door had closed, the great pile that we had amassed was now reduced to a meager stash of scraps and bones. Naively we ate heartily in the first days of autumn, having assumed that the door would open again soon, allowing me to re-stock our store.

It had been four full days since I had tasted food of any kind and two since I had last had a sip of water. The weather had been warmer in the past few weeks and the ocean water once again began to flow freely between the boards of the barn down by the big door, but we didn't have enough wood to keep Johnna's water distillery boiling long enough.

At first the hunger pains had been unrelenting, my belly roaring in anger, begging for sustenance. Thoughts of food consumed my mind so intensely that I was able to distinctly taste anything that I imagined. I would spend hours lost in a fantasy world where I bathed in pools of the sugary, sticky, jiggly worms that I once had as a child; I would wake up from dreams of large chunks of cooked beef and chicken. Even thoughts of beans and rice would set my mouth drooling. As gratifying as these fantasies were, they did nothing to satisfy my appetite, and I wondered if allowing myself to think these thoughts actually compounded my misery.

I was far from being the worst off.

Several people had chosen to give their last scraps of food to other more needy people, apparently thinking that they were better able to tolerate the malnutrition. Looking around the barn, it was painfully evident as to who these people were: Johnna, Aaron, Kevin and Mallie. The effects of starvation worked quickly once they set hold and the sight of these four horrified me. As far as I knew, it had been only a day or two longer than I since they had eaten, but their condition was far beyond that of my own. Hallucinations, confusion, vivid, haunting nightmares and vertigo had been the first signs that these four were in rapidly failing condition. They became so lethargic, virtually unable to move for any reason. Even holding their own heads up to take a drink of water was a strain that they quickly became unwilling to endure.

Johnna in particular became extremely emaciated. It seemed to me at she was melting from the inside. She had become so skinny that the bones of her shoulders and knees seemed like a ball between two sticks hidden beneath her thin clothing. Her head seem unnaturally large for her thin neck, her skin was greying and her mouth hung perpetually open.

I think it was the sunken eyes that frightened me the most. The bony cheeks, sunken temples and dark eye sockets seemed to leave her eyes floating in bottomless caverns, their fixated stare locked on the hope of a quick death.

Seeing Johnna in this advanced state overwhelmed me with strong feelings of appreciation and love for her. Clearly she had been giving her share of food away for much longer than she let on.

Food finally came.

I woke up late in the morning to a distinct rustling noise coming from the Entry Room. It was the first time that there had been any noise from that room in months. My eyes sprung open in recognition. Before I knew it I had flown across the barn and was pounding at the door with every bit of strength that I could muster, desperately yelling out Michael and Alina's names.

They have to be in there!

David and a few of the others had gathered behind me, watching solemnly as I banged on the door in desperation. It was rare that anyone came back to the barn in anything other than horrible condition—everyone knew that—and this thought made me even more desperate to get to Michael and Alina. I needed to hug them, to love them and let them know that everything will be okay now that they are back.

Tears poured down my face as I imagined their battered and abused bodies, their dark, sad eyes, their broken spirits. I retched at the thought of what may have happened to them.

Please let them be okay.

After what seemed like an eternity I slid down the door, exhausted yet electrified from within at the thought that soon I would be holding the two people that I loved most, hoping above everything that they weren't in really bad shape. Around me, everyone had now silently gathered, sitting together in a morose semi-circle, some watching me with sympathy, others staring warily down at their hands.

All sound from within the Entry Room had long since stopped. The hum of an engine had long since vanished over the horizon outside of the barn. Whoever had dropped Michael and Alina off were now far away.

There was no shuffling inside, no voices, no noise at all.

The door should be open by now.

He's making me suffer.

I felt myself drifting off into a weary sleep. Images of earlier, happy days on the beach with Alina and Michael floated through my mind. They had been so happy. The three of us had been happy. We were not alone in this horrible old barn, but we were different from everyone else: We were a family. My heart burned to hold them again.

Behind me, a distinct and familiar noise brought me back from my happy daydreams. I recognized it instantly. The lock had clicked. The door had finally opened!

With a renewed surge of energy, I quickly pulled my weak body to my feet, swinging the door towards me in one continuous movement. Stumbling inwards, the darkness of the room temporarily blinded me as my eyes strained to adjust.

"Michael! Alina!" I called into the blackness.

No response.

"Guys, you're okay, you're back," I said quieter.

Still nothing.

They're drugged, I thought, feeling stupid. Of course. Everyone is drugged when they come back.

Dropping to my knees, I began to feel my way along the floor into the room, reaching out with my free hand for the feel of one of their bodies. My eyes quickly adapted to the change in light as I searched. I was sure that I had crisscrossed the entire room.

There was no Michael.

There was no Alina.

My heard dropped at the realization. I was frozen in disbelief.

They aren't here.

It was a blow that I had not been prepared for. I felt more forlorn than ever.

Floating back to reality, I forced myself to think: Scanning the shadowed room, I knew that the door would not have been unlocked for no reason. The only times that this door every opened was when someone was being abducted or brought back, or when food was being delivered. Looking around me a second time, I still couldn't see anything.

All of a sudden I became aware of a faint but sharp smell.

There is something here.

Moving slowly around, it was the stench that led me to the strange items hidden in the back corner of the room. There, on a single wooden plank, hidden against the darkest corner of the dirty floor were several small piles of brown goop. My stomach recognized it before my brain caught up: MEAT. In an instant, my animalistic instinct suddenly took over I fell to the floor, forcing one of the piles of cooked, salted entrails down my throat without a moment of thought.

Choking and gagging on the rough, sinewy meat, shaking with a mix of pleasure and desperation, I didn't taste a thing as the food went down. My pulse raced. My only thought was to eat. I felt instantly alive.

Suddenly, strong hands gripped my shoulders and I was pulled up from the floor, thrown back from the food and held down with vicious force.

"You selfish prick!" yelled Nasha. "We're all starving!"

I was floored by the ferocity in her voice. I had heard Nasha angry before, but never anything like this. I felt as if I had just been hit in the stomach.

I understood immediately what I had done wrong: I had succumbed to my own selfish needs without thinking of the others first. It was so uncharacteristic of me, so heartless, and I found myself in disbelief at my own actions.

In a mix of embarrassment and fear, I half crawled, half ran from the Entry Room, pushing through the others who stood angrily in my way, having witnessed my treacherous behaviour.

Out of habit, I ran for the ladder to my loft, shocked when I got there to remember that I had removed all of the rungs for firewood during the winter.

With nowhere to go to escape my own shame, I crumbled into a ball right there on the dirt floor and let myself cry. I could feel everyone's eyes on me, angry at me for my actions, disappointed by my selfishness. I could tell that they all hated me now. Especially Nasha, the only person who I really cared for in this group. I had let her down the most and would never earn her trust again.

More so, I cried for Michael and Alina. I had been so sure that they were in the room. I had gotten my hopes up, had allowed myself to believe that they had come back, had allowed myself to feel a bit of happiness again. I missed them now more than ever.

****

"There's a note," I heard Nasha announce to the group as she carried the small plank of food from the Entry Room. Her voice shook uncharacteristically and I could tell by her flitting glances as she look at everyone around her that she was nervous about something.

The members of the group who could still walk had circled around her, all anxious to have a bit of food to appease their hunger pains and fatigue. In the background, weak moaning haunted the air as the four who were close to death caught the small scent of the food.

Hesitantly Nasha put the small platter on the ground beside her, shaking slightly at the urge to take a quick bite. From my distant position at the base of the old ladder I could see the sharp bones in her cheeks and the greyness of her skin. I never imagined that Nasha could ever look as frail and tired as she did now. She was almost unrecognizable.

Turning to face the group, Nasha nervously cleared her throat as she held the white note in front of her.

"I," she stuttered, sadness dragging at the corners of her mouth. "I found this note. It… it was beside a platter that has some food on it," she said, ensuring that she spoke loud enough for those who were too ill to have witnessed what she had brought out of the room with her.

People shuffled their bodies impatiently, some clearly out of curiosity for what the note said, some out of anticipation of having their share of the food.

"It's not good," continued Nasha weakly. Pausing to strengthen herself, she bravely pushed on.

"My Children,

I have been generous and kind enough to take you all under my wing. I have fed you, given you a place to live and have kept you safe from this dangerous world. You should have been praising my charitable ways, and yet you have betrayed me.

I am your provider. I control what resources are available to you. After all that I have given you, you attempt to supersede my power by finding your own food and water sources. This is very disrespectful.

There must be consequences. You will pay for your insolence.

There are 14 of you left. You are all hungry. I have graciously brought food but you will notice that there are only 13 portions. As punishment for your misbehaviour, one of you will not eat. There will be no sharing allowed. If you attempt this, further punishment will ensue.

Decide amongst yourself who will suffer.

I will be watching you all closely.

Your divine leader,

Mr. Irvine."

Silence hung in the air like a dark cloud when Nasha had finished reading the note. She lowered her head in shame as if she were somehow more than just the messenger of the letter. Nobody seemed to know what to say.

My conscience had overcome me while Nasha read and my mind spun into another world as I tried to process what was going on. It was because of me that this was all happening. It was me who had broken all of the rules: I had allowed Alina and Michael into the safety of my platform in the ceiling. I had abused the freedom of being allowed to leave the barn. I had been the one who came up with a way of catching the fish. I had built the racks to preserve it. I had gathered firewood to keep us warm at night. It was because of me that Alina and Michael had been locked out.

And then there was the fact that I had eaten a full portion of food; I was not as sick or malnourished as the others so it should have been me to go without food. Everyone else needed it more than I did.

Someone was going to starve to death and it would be entirely my fault.

The overwhelming anxiety was unlike any emotion that I had ever felt. My stomach tightened and my hands began to sweat as I fought the urge to vomit. I held my breath as the food came into my mouth. I couldn't bear the thought of the added hatred I would face if I wasted such a precious and vital meal. My eyes watered as I held the food there, the acid in my stomach burning at my cheeks and gums. Finally, I swallowed it again.

****

"How the hell do we decide this?" shouted David, unfairly directing his rage at Nasha. "None of us can go another week or more without food! He's forcing us to KILL someone!"

"How can he say that we betrayed him?" yelled the normally timid brunette named Kristy. "That door was open all summer. None of us heard or saw ONE of those camera's move the whole time. He wasn't watching! We would have all died if the kids weren't able to get us food!"

"What the fuck does he mean he's been generous to us?! He's starved and tortured everyone for fun!" screamed another voice from behind Nasha.

"I can't go another day without food!" interjected Elin meekly. "I can barely walk now…"

"Stop it everyone!" said Joseph with force, stepping protectively in front of Nasha. "This isn't Nasha's fault so stop fucking taking it out on her! We're all starving so let's just do this. We know we have to."

"WHAT DO WE DO?" barked David, flailing his arms in crazed frustration. "Draw straws? Or hey, how bout we go by age? I've lived the longest so I should be the first to die right?"

The sarcasm in David's voice stunned me. Being the oldest person in the group, I had always seen him as our leader. He had always been so rational, so in control. Everyone looked to him for support and guidance. To see him so angry underscored the extent to which malnourishment could affect our emotions. He had snapped.

"You're being an ass David!" answered Joseph, tension flaring in his voice. "Sit down and shut up for a minute so we can discuss this!"

At this, David exploded into motion, pouncing on Joseph with startling speed. Joseph, not expecting an attack from someone who was normally so reserved, didn't see him coming until it was too late. His head crashed hard against the solid dirt floor as David fell on him with the full force of body, punching Joseph in the face with quick, ferocious bursts.

"CALL ME AN ASS? YAH, TRY IT NOW!" David raged as he threw punch after punch. The two rolled across the floor as Joseph fought to gain some leverage. To my surprise, instead of stepping in to stop the fighting, the crowd around the two men began yelling encouragements to their choice for victor.

"Hit him in nose!" yelled Elin.

"Break his neck!" yelled Kristy, kicking David in the leg as the two rolled past.

"Knee him in the balls!" shouted someone else.

The sight horrified me. I was watching a pack of animals. Before I could stop myself I was up and running into the melee. My heart was pounding as I threw myself through the audience around the two men. It wasn't anger that drove me forward, it was fear. Fear that our group was self-destructing. Our unity was the only thing that we were in control of. To lose that would be the end of everything.

With a sudden burst of strength I reached for Josephs shoulders as he rolled on top of David. Wrapping my arms quickly around his neck, I yanked backwards, ripping the two men apart so forcefully that Joseph rolled into the on looking crowd and knocked over two bystanders.

"ENOUGH!" I startled myself by the power in my voice. "Enough!" The crowd around me froze in surprise, their wide eyed faces emphasizing their shock at the

93

fact that I had intervened in such a commanding way. Neither Joseph nor David got up from their positions on the floor, both exhausted and confused.

Taking a moment to centre myself, struggling to maintain my authoritative façade, I moved back to the centre of the group.

"This is exactly what he wants!" I said powerfully, turning as I spoke to address everyone. "He's watching and LAUGHING right now! Laughing at ALL of us!

We can't fight among ourselves! We are all on the same side for fuck sakes!" I had never sworn before and I saw several people blink uncomfortably at this. I suddenly felt awkward and childish but I pushed myself to stay strong.

"Look," I continued as calmly as I could, "Fighting won't get us anywhere. It'll only wear us down quicker. Let's just work together on this."

"Easy for you to say," accused David, still lying on the ground rubbing his bleeding hands together. "You've got food in your belly!"

The bitterness in David's voice stung, and for an instant I wanted to run and hide like a child. I knew that I couldn't think of myself though. At this moment, someone had to stand up and save our group and I seemed to be the only person who was thinking even remotely clearly.

"Hey, look, I'm sorry okay?" I said back as calmly as I could, "I didn't think, I just reacted. I didn't know there wasn't enough for everyone or that this was some sort of messed up game. I can't change the past.

Maybe it's a good thing. I mean, honestly, I am still the 'kid' around here. You guys would have made me take my share no matter what. That's the plain truth of it so get over it. My head is already feeling less cloudy while you guys are all going nuts from starvation, so yah, maybe it is easy for me to think logically about this."

I noticed a few heads nod slightly in defeated agreement.

"So how do we do this?" asked Nasha quietly, her eyes fixed on a bare spot on the ground ahead of her.

"Yah who choses who starves to death?" said David angrily as he pulled himself up from the ground and stepped towards me threateningly. "You, kid? You're gunna do that? Cuz I'm not!"

"A second ago you were willing to snap Joe's neck and now you're not willing to come to a democratic and fair decision?" The tone in my voice was more sarcastic than I had intended.

"You little PRICK!" Yelled David, inches from my face. "I should snap YOUR neck! You've been a mooch on us your whole life! If we had let you die when you first got here like we all wanted, we would'a had a LOT more food for the rest of us!"

"DAVID!" shouted Nasha, racing to put her body between us. "How dare you say that? He's been a great kid!"

"Sit down bitch!" commanded David harshly. "You've said lots of times that we should have let the kids die, so don't act all innocent!"

A stab of pain shot through my chest. All in one moment I felt surprise and that David was behaving so uncharacteristically, love that Nasha had stood up for me, and hurt to know that she had once wanted me dead.

Nasha's hand flew up from her side and smacked David roughly across his cheek, stunning him momentarily.

"We were starving! I couldn't stand to see the kids suffer!" cried Nasha. "Even you're not that much of an asshole!"

In an instant, David's fist had crunched into Nasha's face knocking her mercilessly to the ground, David falling on top of her in a barrage of flying fists before any of us could react. "It's your fault! All of it!" he screamed.

I immediately launched myself on top of David, punching him viciously in the head as I fell on him. Shifting my own weight to pull him from Nasha, his target quickly changed to me. For an old starving man, the force in his blows was surprising and I struggled to defend myself.

Suddenly David was off of me and rolling on the ground again with Joseph, who had apparently come to my rescue. Elin threw herself into the battle now, leaping onto Joseph, scratching at his face and stomping on his body. A second later, Kristy was dragging Elin backwards across the dirt by her hair, both girls kicking and screaming like wild animals as the two men continued to roll.

And then it all just stopped.

I didn't know why at first. I had still been lying on my back in the dirt, catching my breath and trying to comprehend the wild scene around me.

It was Joseph and David who had stopped moving first. Frozen in mid-tumble, Joseph on top of David with his right fist held high about to send down another agonizingly ferocious punch. A second later I saw Elin and Kristy freeze in the exact same manner, all eyes fixed in the same direction.

Confused, I pulled myself up to a seated position and followed their stare.

Johnna.

She had dragged her frail body across the floor towards the fight and had collapsed just steps away from David and Joseph.

The entire group fell silent and still.

"Me," she moaned, her voice rough with dryness.

We all watched in shocked bewilderment.

"It has to be me," she groaned painfully, her tired head falling to the dirt having used her last bit of energy.

We all knew what she meant. Starvation had already driven her close to death. Johnna was volunteering to die.

The gesture floored us all. The idea of having to choose someone to die was one that none of us would have been able to make. We would have continued fighting to the death or until Mr. Irvine issued some kind of unimaginable punishment. By volunteering, Johnna had saved us from destroying ourselves, from living in fear of what Mr. Irvine could do, and most importantly, the guilt of having to end someone's life.

****

We made sure that Johnna's last days were as comfortable as possible. She was given the largest pile of straw to sleep on, the thickest of clothing to keep her warm, and someone held her hand at every moment.

It was terrible to watch her die and to be unable to do anything about it. The worst part was the fact that she didn't have to die. All she needed was food and the only reason that she couldn't get any was because some sick asshole took pleasure in watching her suffer. We were all teeming with anger at Mr. Irvine for doing this, but we were all too afraid to speak of it in case he should be listening. We couldn't bare the idea of any further punishment.

It took Johnna thirteen more days to pass away. We had all hoped that this was some kind of test for us—that Mr. Irvine would be content that he had proven his point that we should all be on our best behaviour—and that he would send in life saving supplies to restore poor Johnna back to full health. When food did come just two days after she had volunteered, an attached note left little doubt as to his true intentions.

It simply read: "Watching closely."

In a heartless move to further Johnna's suffering, the food that came was bounteous and filled the barn with alluring, appetizing scents that set our mouths watering. Even in an unconscious haze, Johnna's body recognized the presents of sustenance, immediately convulsing and reaching out in primal desperation.

We all ate heartily, sitting as far away from Johnna as possible with our backs turned to her to numb the guilt, wordlessly devouring as much as our pained bellies could handle. Many of us ate so much that our stomachs revolted at such a sudden introduction of food, vomiting it up in great heaves, yet we kept eating as our bodies screamed for nourishment.

There was so much food: a mound of cooked seafood, a large chunk of raw beef smothered in a salty brown sauce, four fully cooked chickens, hundreds of tiny cubes of cheese, a mountain of creamy deserts, boxes of cold milk, and bags of rice and beans. There was enough food to feed us a dozen times over.

It wasn't until I couldn't swallow another bite that I realized that most of the food had something in common: Much of it would spoil by tomorrow. I knew immediately that soon we would be rationing leftovers, starving again. This was yet another part of Mr. Irvine's cruel game.

I looked at the others as they continued to ravenously force more and more food into their already full mouths and I decided to keep my revelation to myself. I couldn't bear to take away from their one moment of happiness.

In the background Johnna moaned in agony. She would not be the last to be sacrificed. This game was going to continue.

****

We had all gathered around Johnna. Aaron, Kevin and Mallie, who had also been secretly giving away their shares of food until she had volunteered, were recovering quickly from their advanced state of starvation and had pulled themselves up to join in our circle as well. To do anything else seemed rude, ungrateful. All we could do was to be there with her and watch as she slowly faded.

Johnna was almost unrecognizable, only her long curly white hair bearing any resemblance to her former identity. Her skin alternated between being ice cold or as hot as a fire to the touch . Every few minutes she would break out into a rib breaking shaking cough that made us all wince in sympathy. In the rare moments that she was completely at rest, one would think her already dead were it not for the almost unnoticeable rise and fall of her bony chest as she struggled for each breath. Nasha said she would die of pneumonia before her body gave out from starvation, but being as skinny and frail as she was, it would be a close race for one of the two to take her.

We had been sitting quietly with Johnna for much of the morning. The silence around me was unnerving. I could hear people breathing; the occasional sniffle sounded deafening; the movement of an arm to wipe away a tear seemingly echoing through the depths of the old barn.

I looked around at everyone as they stood in the quiet circle.

"Someone should say something," I whispered to the group. Every single person avoided eye contact with me. "She needs to hear that we are here with her...how much we appreciate her."

People shuffled insecurely but no one said a word. I looked to Nasha. She had always been someone who knew just the right thing to say.

"Nasha?" I hinted. A tear dropped down her cheek as I looked at her, yet she said nothing.

I understood the silence: Johnna was dying because we were being punished for misbehaving. Her frail body was a cautionary example of what could happen to any one of us if we did something that would upset our captor. We were all too afraid to speak in case it should be seen as rebellious behaviour.

Ultimately, it was me who finally began to speak. I couldn't let this great woman die for us without any sort of recognition for her sacrifice.

"Johnna," I said quietly, crawling close to her on the cold floor. "It's Ash... We're all here. We're all right here with you.

I don't know if you can hear me but we wanted to tell you that we all love you. We will never be able to thank you enough for what you did for us."

I reached for Johnna's hand and held it tightly. It was startlingly cold and felt like a pile of chicken bones. I took a moment to fight back tears that were threatening to burst from my eyes.

"For everything. You took care of us....You cooked our food, comforted us when we were sick or injured... You saved Alina's life... You made life here tolerable and sometimes even happy. You were a mother to all of us, a friend. You loved us all and we all love you."

I sensed the slightest squeeze of a finger as I held her cold hand. Her chest slowly rose as she took a slightly deeper breath than normal, releasing it slowly through cracked, dried lips. Her eyes flickered slightly below thin eyelids and I could see a faint pulse beating in the large vein in her throat.

"You can go now Johnna," I whispered, choking back tears. "We'll be okay now," I said as confidently as I could, knowing that this was not the truth.

Johnna took in another deep breath and this time I distinctly felt her hand gently squeeze mine. She exhaled heavily with a slight hiss and for a moment I thought she had whispered my name.

"We love you Johnna," I said quietly.

Around me, one by one, the others echoed my sentiment.

When the barn fell silent again, I laid down in the hay bed against Johnna, holding her hand as I moved. Nasha mirrored my position on Johnna's other side, draping her left arm gently across Johnna's thin belly. Around us, others followed suit and found a place on the floor close by to settle down into.
"Don't be afraid anymore," I said quietly into her ear. "We'll all stay with you."

It was mid-afternoon before Nasha realized that Johnna had stopped breathing. In silent tribute we each kissed her forehead one by one.

Without a word, David gently scooped Johnna's tiny body into his arms. A few of us stepped forward to help him, but he waved us away with a simple shake of his head. Somehow Johnna appeared relaxed and content.

In single file we followed David as he slowly crossed the barn holding Johnna tenderly. As he reached the Entry Room door, we all heard the familiar 'Click' as the lock unlatched. It was not a surprise to any of us. We all knew that Mr. Irvine would be watching.

We stood outside the room as David single-handedly placed Johnna's body tenderly on the cold bare floor. Softly he caressed her cheek and did his best to arrange her hair. Under his breath David mumbled a few quiet words that I couldn't quite make out, then kissed her cheek once before standing up, and exiting the room.

He swung the large door shut silently, heaving a great sigh as it locked, then turned to face us. Tears streaked down his face but he stood tall and strong.

"She was my twin sister," he said emptily. We all froze in surprise. In all the years that they had been trapped here, nobody had any idea that they had even been related.

"He killed my sister."

****

Five days after Johnna had passed away we awoke to the sound of running water. It had been weeks since our tap had flowed and we had left it open so we would know as soon as it was turned back on again.

Before my brain had even processed what the source of the noise was, Joseph was on his feet and running towards the tap with the large plastic water container in hand. He reached the faucet with both hands out stretched, scooping a small amount into his palm and splashing the water into his parched mouth while simultaneously placing the container under the running tap. I could see him shaking from where I sat, so thirsty that it must have been difficult for him to hold the jug instead of drinking for himself.

And then it stopped.

With a look of confusion on his face, Joseph turned the rusty handle of the tap to the left and right with his free hand but nothing happened. The water was off. He held the jug up to his eye level. Even from where I sat I could see that there was only enough liquid in to cover the bottom of the container.

There were thirteen of us left. It had been almost three days since we had last had anything to drink. As the others began to stand up and stalk towards Joseph I sensed that they were all following the same carnal need that was driving me up as well: Get water before it's all gone.

I didn't know what had come over me. There were no other thoughts in my head. All I could feel was a mixture of panic and desperation.

The battle that ensued was savage.

Everyone seemed to pounce at the same time. Joseph hadn't noticed the impending attack until a moment before we were all upon him, clawing like animals to pry the precious liquid from his strong grasp.

Ferociously we pulled at each other's hair, scratched at eyes, and stepped on the faces of the fallen. Women, men, young and old cursed at each other coldheartedly, their grunts and screams filled the air.

A fist hit my face hard and I could immediately taste blood. The force of the blow disoriented me yet I continued to pull myself through the tangled limbs of the crazed mob.

Water. That's all I cared about.

I seemed to be the last person to stop fighting; the group around me just stopped in their places falling silent as I threw a violent fist at Elin, hitting her cheek horrendously hard. I flailed a moment longer before noticing that the battle had stopped.

Then I saw it.

Off to the side of the pile of bodies, the water jug had been tossed from the group and now lay on its side, cracked down the middle, empty.

There was a mournful pall in the air as the mound of people painfully pulled apart from one another. We had acted like barbarians, attacking people we loved without hesitation for something so basic, and in the end we had destroyed they very thing we sought.

As the group parted, I was appalled at the injuries that I saw. There was blood everywhere. Not a single person seemed to have escaped without a major gash on their face or arms. Nasha cradled her ribs with both hands as she limped painfully towards a soft bed. Elin's face had already swollen up where I had hit her and she was missing a front tooth.

My scalp stung tremendously. Rubbing my hand through my hair, I could feel that there were several patches of missing hair, all oozing with blood. Someone had kicked me in the back and I could feel the stiffness already setting in.

The last few people were slowly dragging themselves up from the pile. I could see Kristy's eyes watering as she used her hands to push herself back away from the scene. She had been near the bottom of the pile and seemed to be struggling to move her legs. She had always been so meek, so timid; she was the definition of a Wallflower, and yet she had been one of the first to fly into attack mode at first sight of water. She was the truest example of desperation. Seeing her like this brought me back to my senses and I stepped forward to help her up.

"Shh, it's okay," I said softly. "It's over. Where are you hurt?"

Kristy continued to use her hands to shuffle herself backwards. Tears were streaming down her face as she stared blankly ahead of her. It was like she didn't even notice my presence.

"Kristy," I said. "Look at me." I gently grabbed her chin and turned her head towards me. "The fight is over. Let me help you. Where are you hurt?"

Her eyes blinked as her brain registered that I was talking to her. She stopped pushing herself backwards. "It's not me..." she said weakly, freeing her chin from my hold and looking ahead of her again, breaking into sobs. "I killed him..."

I turned to follow her eye back towards where the fight had been. Alone on the ground, perfectly still, Joseph laid with his arm outstretched towards the fallen jug, his head twisted inhumanly over his shoulder. His open eyes seemed to be staring accusingly at Kristy, his mouth gaping in a silent scream of disbelief. Joseph was dead.

****

It wasn't until we had carried Joseph's body off in our now all-to-familiar funeral procession that we found the food in the Entry Room.

Perhaps the most shameful moment of my life was that moment that the door swung open as we silently carried Joseph toward his final exit from the barn: It was the sweet smell that hung in the air that first caught my attention and froze me in my tracks as the others who had also been tending his body continued forward. We had been carrying Joseph feet-first, one person on each limb, me on his left leg, as his lifeless body dangled between us. My sudden halt had caught Elin off guard as she lost grip on his left arm and Joseph's body fell hard to the ground. All eyes turned to me in indignation. Just as I was about to say something, Elin's head suddenly snapped around to face the opening of the Entry Room.

"Do you smell that?" she said. The others all turned their head in towards the door, lifting their noses as they caught the sweet scent in the air. Nasha and David, who had been supporting Josephs other two limbs slowly bent to softly lower the rest of the body lightly to the floor.

Straightening herself Nasha let out a quiet sigh. "Food."

With mixed restraint, some rushing forward, some trailing cautiously behind, the group coldly abandoned Joseph where he lie and followed their noses to the food.

The smell in the room filled my lungs and set my heart racing faster with each breath.

It was a feast unlike anything we had seen in ages: Cakes lathered in icing; cookies decorated with crunchy smiley faces; cooked spicy chicken that made my mouth water and burn at the same time without even tasting it yet; a dripping chunk of beef with mashed potatoes all covered in gravy; a table full of different varieties drinks in shiny glass and plastic bottles. It all sat on tables draped with immaculately white cloth, beautiful live flowers filling the small gaps between the elegant gold and silver platters. I had never seen something so beautiful. Attached was a simple card that read, "Bon Appetite!"

We all rushed the table holding the beverages first, our bodies literally dying to have liquid. There was a lot of shoving and pulling, but with such a bountiful amount of options, we were able to keep calm enough to avoid the scene that had occurred earlier around the faucet.

My hand closed around a dark brown bottle. I chugged its contents in one go, tasting nothing but its icy coldness as it chilled its way down my belly. A second later I could taste a bitter, almost tangy flavour that was not entirely pleasing. After letting out a huge belch, I reached through the group to grab another.

"Woah there big guy!" laughed David. "Take it easy on that stuff! That's beer!"

I had heard people talking of beer before. Alcohol. The stuff that makes you silly and stupid and lose control, then leaves you sick and tired the next day. The only thing that I knew of similar to alcohol was the mystery chemical in the tap water that drugged us to sleep each night before someone was taken. The thought that I had just downed an entire bottle on my own frightened me. I didn't want Mr. Irvine to take me in the night.

I reached for another bottle that was clearly marked 'Water,' gulping it down greedily before joining the others in front of the great mound of food, and proceeded to indiscriminately eat as much as I could.

When I could eat no more, I sat down lazily beside one of the empty food tables. It was only then that I realized that not one of us had heard sounds of engines in the distance or noises in the Entry Room throughout the morning. This could only mean one thing: The food had been there since nighttime. They must have come while we were sleeping.

Joseph's death, the fight; it had all been pointless.

******

"It's not your fault you know."

Elin had been sitting quietly by herself in the corner of the room while the others crowded around the food. I had noticed her once I started to feel full and now that the room was beginning to clear out, I decided to join her.

She had a large bottle of juice in her hand and drank hastily. I noticed that her hands were shaking badly. I still had a large wedge of beef in my hand, so I offered it to her, knowing that she hadn't eaten a thing, but she refused.

"Yeah it is,' she said, taking another large sip from her juice. I slid my back down the wall and sat beside her.

"We all did..... Mr. Irvine did," I said, struggling to say the right words. Elin shook her head slowly, her eyes fixed on the opposite wall.

"Look, have some food," I said, pushing the chunk of beef into her free hand. "You're starving. You aren't thinking correctly."

"No. You don't get it..." she replied dully.

"Yah I do," I said empathetically. "We were all starving and extremely dehydrated. We were going nuts. We all snapped when we saw that there wasn't enough water for everyone. We all did. We all trampled Joseph."

A sarcastic smile crossed Elin's lips. She continued to stare at the wall across from us, shaking her head from side to side.

"Look," I said supportively. "If the roles were reversed, Joe would have done the same thing and would have been just as guilty as the rest of us. You were desperate. We were desperate. He just got in the way."

Elin took another great swig from the bottle.

Still shaking her head slowly, she turned to look me square in the eyes. It was a look so intense that I actually jolted my head back in surprise.

"I did it on purpose."

Unsure of what she meant, or what to say next, I stammered awkwardly. "You... uh, no I don't think... Uh, I, we all did it. It wasn't on purpose."

"I got to him first," she said pointedly. "When everyone else jumped, I pushed him down and stomped on his neck."

Bewildered, I just stared, wide mouthed, unable to respond. I pictured the scene in my mind but I could not imagine what it would feel like to intentionally and heartlessly murder a friend. I too had been driven mad by thirst, but even in my worst state I knew that my soul had limits to what it could do.

Elin turned her head to face frontwards again.

"If I couldn't have it, nobody else would." She took a large bite of the meat in her hand.

I became aware that several others now stood around us, all apparently as mystified by Elin's recount as me. I looked up at Kristy who stood at my side. She had believed that she killed Joseph in the scuffle. It had torn her apart on the inside.

"How… how COULD you?" she hissed incredulously, fresh tears pouring from her eyes.

"Please bitch," retorted Elin cruelly. "We're all gunna die here eventually. One less mouth to feed means more time for me to be in this awesome world."

"What the hell Elin!?" choked Nasha incredulously, stepping in front of Kristy protectively. "How could you do that!?"

Elin shrugged dismissively, holding her empty bottle towards Nasha. "Nothing matters anymore. Make yourself useful and get me more wine."

****

Nobody noticed the bags of rice and beans until all the food was gone. They had been under the table, concealed by the cloth that draped down to the floor. Had it not been for Nasha's insistence that we clean up every fallen scrap to avoid a mouse infestation, we never would have found them.

Nobody commented other than to say how great it was that we now had enough food to last a long time. The famine was over. Everyone seemed pleased by that.

I don't know why, but my instincts were telling me that something bad was about to happen.

****

Several days later I sat alone, quietly watching the group go about their day. With ample food in their bellies, moods had once again lifted, and people hummed and laughed as they went about their normal routines. It was astonishing to me that they seemed to have forgotten the horrible state we were all in just a few days ago. Even Elin, someone who had heartlessly murdered one of our own had been accepted back into the group as if nothing had ever happened at all. Every time I heard her giggle with one of the other women I saw the image of Joseph in my mind, mouth open, eyes staring blankly, dead on the ground because of her, and I shuddered. It felt as if the others had just forgotten him. Forgotten Johnna.

107

Forgotten that Michael and Alina were out there somewhere being tortured and beaten and who knows what else. Almost all of them had been abused at the hands of our captor. Worse still, they all knew that it would happen again eventually. It angered me to watch as everyone got along so well, acting as if we had a privileged life. They were naïve to think that things were going to continue so prosperously, and heartless for forgetting the sacrifices that had been made to keep us all alive.

They were living in a mindset where yesterday was forgotten and tomorrow was not worth thinking about.

As I watched them stuff their mouths with food, fill their cups with cool beverages, their bellies grow and their skin regain a healthy glow, I wanted to knock the food from their hands, to smack the smiles off of their faces. I wanted to yell at them to respect the memories of the people we had lost, to remember that bad times would be coming again soon! I wanted them to remember that we should be living in constant fear and that life was not good! In the past few months things had been worse than ever!

But I didn't say a thing.

I understood why they were all behaving this way: it was too scary to think of the reality of our situation. To live blissfully unmindful of anything other than this exact moment was their only means of keeping their sanity.

As I continue to watch them carry on, I found my mouth drooling for a bite of that food, thirsting for a glass of that juice, longing for someone to hug me and make me smile too. It was like they were a bunch of happy zombies and I found that I wanted to live in the moment, to forget like they had, but I knew that this was impossible.

Maybe I could block my mind from thinking about the weeks of starvation; maybe I could put aside my sadness over the loss of Johnna and Joseph; maybe I could even forget for just a moment that we were all prisoners here in this horrible old barn and that one day, I too would be taken from here and subjected to horrible tortures, but I could never forget that Michael and Alina were out there somewhere, hopefully still alive, and were likely suffering through unimaginable cruelty.

Hearty food had come again. It was the third time in three days. Just as before, several tables were laden with platters of cooked meat, trays of exotic fruits, and steaming bowls of colourful vegetables. There was an entire section of beverages, both alcoholic and not, hot and cold. On a separate table lay a spread of deserts decorated with mounds of icing, glazed coatings, and even real flowers.

Nobody touched any of it.

On the opposite side of the Entry Room from the food stood a large table around which everyone was swarming like flies to leftovers. Being the last to come into the room, I couldn't immediately tell what all the commotion was about. It wasn't until several of the women sprinted out of the room, cheering in delight with arms full of strange things that I was able to get close enough to realize what was happening. My mouth literally dropped when I saw it: before me stood a long table piled to the roof with soaps, perfumes, makeup, toothpaste, brushes and best of all, new clothing for everyone. We had never been given 'stuff' before. In the past our most prized possessions had been the cheap plastic bottles, bowls, cups or cutlery that occasionally came with our food. The only time I had ever seen new clothing had been during the short time that Julie had been Mr. Irvine's favourite and would often return wearing something fashionable and clean.

There was no note.

When the crowd finally dispersed from around the table of clothing, I silently moved in to take a closer look at what was left. The table had been picked almost clean. All that was left was a crisp white shirt, some white socks that were far too small for me, a very short skirt made out of some kind of plastic, and a few bottles of soap. A quick vision of what I would look if I dressed in this outfit flashed through my mind and I laughed for the first time in weeks, feeling instantly guilty as soon as I did it, knowing that good times always foreshadowed the bad.

Still, the sweet, fresh scent of the new clothing and soaps pulled at my senses and I couldn't help but allow myself to give in to the excitement of wearing real clothes and being clean.

The atmosphere in the barn was electric. Despite the cold air, most people had gathered around the water faucet and were already stripped naked, having discarded their old rags as if they were useless trash. I was amazed by the mounds of white, glistening bubbles as people lathered each other aggressively with the fancy soaps. I have never seen bubbles before. At first I had expected them to be cold like snow, but as I joined the group in bathing, I was amazed to find them light and fluffy, warm even, and to discover that they do not taste good.

All around me people laughed as they scrubbed each other, making each other's hair stand in tall spikes or had bubble ball fights with one another. Again I felt myself tingling with happiness and had to concentrate to control my rising excitement.

The most startling change was to see the men clean shaven. One of the many things found on the table of presents was a shaving kit complete with a sharp razor, scissors, shaving cream and a strongly scented after shave balm. I had never seen any of the men with anything less than a short scruff on their faces. All we had to trim our hair with was a sharp stone similar to the cutting stone that Johnna used to butcher meat, and because of that, most men had full beards and long hair.

I found the men to be entirely unrecognizable. In a way it was a little scary to be seeing them this way; it felt as if there were strangers amongst us.

The change in David was astounding. With his greying beard gone and his thick brown hair cropped short to his scalp he went from looking like an old man to looking like someone half his age. Looking around the group I noticed that this was the same for everyone else around me. It was clear to me then that the others here in the barn with me were all much younger than I had always thought.

I didn't like it when the women put the makeup on their faces. It seemed ridiculous to me that someone would think that putting paint on their faces made them more attractive. To me their black-rimmed eyes, blue or pink eyelids, red cheeks and glossy red lips looked like they had just been badly beaten. The make-up took away from their natural beauty and hid all the character in their skin, and yet the women all complimented each other profusely with words like 'hot' and 'wild' or comments like 'You are a natural beauty!' I didn't get it.

Getting dressed into the new clothes was the most fun part. The guys tried on every piece of men's clothing, putting each thing on to test for fit before quickly removing everything and passing to the next man. Eventually we all settled on a few items for each guy to keep as their own, as well as a few that would be shared amongst us all.

The women were ridiculous to watch in comparison. Arguments immediately broke out over clothing that one woman or another had claimed as her own without even trying it on, promptly by that same person laughing or complaining about how that item made her butt look big or her boobs look saggy. A moment later that same outfit would be tossed to another woman with a comment like 'Your fat ass would look great in this!' Then they would all laugh again like best friends.

Once all the woman had chosen an outfit, they almost simultaneously broke into what they called a 'Catwalk' and would parade back and forth across the barn with their hands on their hips towards the ogling men, posing awkwardly and spinning as they turned back. It was fun to watch their enthusiasm but almost embarrassing to see them behaving so unnaturally.

That night we feasted on the food that we had neglected earlier and spent the evening dancing to a symphony of clapping hands and poorly harmonized, slightly intoxicated voices, as our old clothing burned away in the fire pit in the centre of the group.

'You're prettier than I have ever seen you," I heard Aaron say lightly to Kristy as they swung past me in a tight embrace.

That's when it hit me: He had given us all this food to fatten us up, all these clothes to make us as attractive as we could be. This was not a reward. It was a culling.

****

"Stop! Stop!" I yelled at the top of my lungs, running into the centre of the dancing group. Immediately the clapping and singing came to a stop, although a few people who were too drunk to notice my sudden intrusion continued awkwardly dancing in the sudden silence for a few more seconds.

"What the heck are you doing, Ash?" groaned a woozy Nasha, holding onto David for support.

"You've got to stop!" I cried to her. "All of this!"

"What are you bitching about?" called Kevin. "We're having a good time for once in our lives. Let us be happy for one god damned minute."

"No! Don't you see? Don't you get it?" I pleaded, spinning to address the whole group who were now all glaring at me with distain. "All of this! This is not a reward for something! We haven't done anything!"

"It's the beginning of spring. We survived another winter," countered David dismissively. "That's reason enough to celebrate."

"Or maybe he is enjoying his time with Michael and Alina!" interjected Elin with cruel sarcasm.

The harshness in her words enraged me and I flew across the space between us. Before I knew it I could feel my right fist crash into Elin's jaw and we fell to the ground together, my body landing hard on hers.

"You're a monster!" I screamed as I pinned her down by her shoulders.

A second later I was being pulled backwards.

"Get off of her!" yelled David as he forced me to the ground. Nasha and Kristy jumped in to restrain me as I fought to attack Elin again.

"How could you say something like that? They're innocent kids!" I screamed.

Elin, having shaken her head to straighten her thoughts, pulled herself up to a sitting position. Rubbing her sore jaw she looked toward me with an empowered, taunting smirk.

"They were, you mean."

With that, I struggled even harder, almost managing to shake off Nasha's grip.

"You BITCH! You are an animal!"

"Calm down!" said Nasha punitively, twisting her body to force my chest back to the ground with her knee. "SIT – DOWN."

Stunned by the power in her push, my mind reeled to process what was happening. Looking around me with their painted faces and newly cut hair, the group had all gathered and was staring at me as if I were a stranger.

"Listen to me!" I pleaded. "Why do you think he gave us all of this stuff? Why this year? We've survived a lot of horrible winters and never got this kind of stuff!"

David's eyes rolled as I spoke and I heard several dismissive groans from the others.

"You have to listen to me!" I continued as I sat myself back up. "Look at each other! We're clean, we smell nice, we have fancy new clothes. We're not boney and emaciated anymore. We look better than we ever have! Why do you think that is? Because he likes us? Because he wants us to be happy? No! He's never done that! Every time we get something there is a consequence! We get food one night and the next morning someone's taken."

"Yah but we've been getting food for a while now and we're all still here," David argued, rubbing his hand with frustration through his newly shorn hair.

"But think of how bad we looked! We were skin and bones! Sickly! Our clothes were full of holes! We stank!" I countered. "He clearly enjoyed watching us suffer, but think of how long it's been since he took Michael and Alina! MONTHS! He's got to be bored by now."

I watched everyone's faces as the idea took hold in their minds. I could see the fear creep in to their eyes. Even the paint on the girls' faces couldn't hide the nervous blush that overcame their cheeks.

"What if he's right?" asked Kristy to Aaron. "It kind of makes sense."

"Nah I don't think he is," replied Aaron dismissively. "If he was gunna take one of us, he would've only brought food and presents for that person and left the rest of us to suffer like when he used to always take Julie."

"That's exactly it! Why give us all new clothes and food unless he is planning on taking us all? Or at least the most desirable picks!"

"He is getting old," offered Nasha, "He took me when I was fifteen and he seemed old then. I'm almost forty now. He's going to have to get rid of us all one day soon."

Silence fell over the group and several people shuffled uncomfortably as they processed their emotions.

Subtly, Aaron messed up his hair.

****

It was obvious that everyone was surprised that we were all still here as the sun came up. There seemed to be both a collective sigh of relief and an intensified sense of fear as people slowly rose to begin their day.

The change in the group the following morning was astounding. Gone was the jovial, relaxed atmosphere of the previous night. The women had all washed the makeup off of their faces and now looked tired and stressed.

Everyone, including myself had gone to extreme lengths to soil their hair and new clothing with various mixtures of dirt and food from last night's feast. Several people who had used milk based products to ruin their clothing now gave off a sour, pungent scent that made my throat water in disgust. In an effort to be on the same level of filth, many others now rubbed themselves down with any leftover milk products that they could find.

Elin allowed herself to pee just a little bit with her clothes on.

Nobody wanted to be seen as 'attractive.'

****

Not one of us ate or drank a thing all day in fear that some of the food or drinks could be laced with drugs to knock us out. A few of the others had difficulty with this as they suffered through painful hangovers that seemed to last all day.

We were a miserable group.

Night fell and not one of us had uttered a word all day. My stomach rumbled painfully. I had become accustomed to having a full belly again and was finding it incredibly difficult to get used to the feeling of hunger that used to feel normal to me. Despite the stench of the people around me, I could still smell the sweet scents of the cooked meat and sugary cakes that now sat in random heaps amongst us. My mouth watered hungrily.

I thought about our situation. I knew that I was not wrong about another impending abduction. I could just feel it. It was the only scenario that made sense. If he wanted just one of us he would have done what he always did in the past and simply taken that person in the night. He was going to take us soon too. I had never quite been sure of what happened to people who he took--even at this age people guarded me from hearing the gory specifics of being taken--but I knew that he preferred to take people who had a healthy appearance. He would take us before we allowed ourselves to become withered and sickly again. On top of all that, for whatever reasons, I was the only person who had never been taken before. I knew that Mr. Irvine would be eager to get a chance to finally take me. The thought made my skin erupt in goose bumps, but I knew it was inevitable. I thought of Alina and Michael. I hoped they were still alive. I missed them so much. Maybe this would be the only way for me to ever see them again.

"Screw it!" I said, pulling myself up from the ground and reaching into one of the piles of food. Finding a large muffin, I stuffed it voraciously into my mouth.

"No! Ash stop!" cried Nasha as she jumped up and tried to knock the muffin from my hand.

"It doesn't matter anymore," I mumbled as I chewed. "I might as well keep myself strong."

"You can't!" she argued. "We have to make ourselves look less appealing! You were the one who pointed that out!"

"It's too late," I countered. "He's watching. He's seeing what we are doing." I reached for a large banana and ripped the peel off of it before shoving half of it in my mouth.

"So what? Who knows when he will act?" cried Nasha desperately. "It could be weeks or months!"

Struggling to speak as I chewed, I replied "He won't wait long enough to let us starve ourselves again. He wants us to look good!"

"He may not take you though. Don't risk it!"

"Don't kid yourself!" I said too aggressively back to her. Catching myself, I turned to look at her. Her green eyes that had once been a symbol of strength to me now glistened with tears of fear.

"Sorry," I sighed. "It's just... I know that he's gunna take me this time. My platform in the roof is gone and that's all that kept me safe until now. I don't have anywhere else to hide. And to be honest, I shouldn't keep hiding. Everyone else has sacrificed themselves for the benefit of the rest of us. It's my turn now."

"No, you're wrong," said Nasha. "We've done our best to sacrifice ourselves because we didn't want you to have to go through those horrible things. Yah, in some ways I am sure some of these people have resented you for going through this unscathed, but at the same time we all want to see you get out of this without ever having to go through what we went through. You don't owe us anything!"

"Speak for yourself bitch, not for me," interrupted Elin. "I'm gunna do whatever it takes to never go through that again. I'm all for the kid taking one for the team this time."

"Look, I'm an adult now," I went on, ignoring Elin entirely. "I'm smart, tall, strong... I can handle it. I don't wanna see you guys suffer anymore."

"You don't understand what he does to you...." said Nasha through flowing tears.

"I've seen how you all come back. I remember how bad Julie was that one time," I replied. "I'll get through it."

Just shook her head slowly. "No... That's just the physical part. There's... so much more."

Nasha's face had gone white and she hugged herself tightly suddenly get lost in horrific memories. I leaned in to give her a comforting hug and I could feel her shaking. She squeezed me back tightly, sobbing on my shoulder. I could feel my own emotions washing over me.

I hated seeing Nasha in such a weak emotional state. I felt for the horrors that she and the others had gone through. I missed Michael so much and wanted to see him more than anything. I could hear Alina's laughter in my mind and wondered if I would ever hear it again. Worst of all, I knew that everything that I had ever known was about to change.

I was so afraid.

I took a large bite of the banana still in my hand and turned to face the camera closest to me.

"I'm ready. Come take me now."

****

I stood boldly in front of the entry door doing my best to conceal my shaking hands and knees.

Within moments of announcing that I was ready to me taken away into the unknown outside world, the quiet click of the lock on the door unlatching broke through the silence of the barn.

Everyone stood behind me as I faced the door, nobody speaking or moving. The tension in the group was palpable; this would be the first time that's someone willingly chose to be taken through the Entry Door.

As the door hung loosely ajar, I could sense that Mr. Irvine, our divine controller, was excitedly watching, waiting for me to step forward into the dark room yet I stood my ground.

Several minutes passed and yet nobody including myself moved. My stomach trembled in fear and I struggled to maintain a normal breathing rate, but a pulse of defiance coursed through every piece of my body. I may have volunteered to be taken. I would not fight this but I was not going to leave this barn without making a point.

117

A camera above me whirred in its casement and I watched as the eye spun to face the Entry Door. In the stillness the lock clicked several times. It was a sign to remind me that the door was unlocked and that Mr. Irvine was ready for me to enter the room.

Again I turned to address the camera closest to me.

"I know the door is open: I heard it unlock the first time." I paused for a moment of dramatic defiance. It was a spontaneous act of rebellion. I don't even know where it came from, but it played out as if I were watching it from the eyes of an observer and wasn't actually doing it myself.

"I told you that I am ready for you to come and get me. I didn't say that I was going to escort myself into hell. I won't fight back, but if you want me you will have to send your people to come and get me."

Behind me I could hear several people gasp in shock as they understood what I was saying: I was challenging our keeper. By being the only person in the barn who he had never taken, I was offering up the very prize that he wanted most, but by insisting that his soldiers—soldiers that only I had ever seen-- were to show themselves in broad daylight, I was proving to everyone that Mr. Irvine was not the great and powerful being that he wanted us to believe him to be, but that he was a mere mortal who was dependent on the actions of others to maintain his control. Although my fate was still ultimately in his hands, for this one short moment I had demonstrated that Mr. Irvine was not the only one who could take control of another.

It occurred to me that Mr. Irvine could simply just wait until nightfall-- or several more days for that matter-- to have his people swoop in while I slept, taking me silently and effortlessly like he did with all others in the past, but something in me knew that I had stirred some nerve of excitement in this man who I had never met. I knew that he had already pictured having me in front of him in real life instead of through a camera. I knew that he was a man who got what he wanted and would now be unwilling to wait for this to happen.

I held my position in silence for what seemed like an eternity. Fatigue began to take over my muscles which now began to shake because of that as well as from fear, but I did my best to hold my head high and give no sign of my fear or pain. Behind me others held their positions as well, silently supporting my tiny act of defiance.

Just as the need to change positions became desperate, a low rumble became audible in the distance and I knew that Mr. Irvine's men were approaching.

****

My heart beat so roughly against my chest that I could see my shirt fluttering slightly because of it.

As I listened to the sounds of the armed men nearing the building outside, a hundred different scenarios raced through my head: Part of me wanted to run and hide, part of me felt like I was about to pass out. I thought of storming the Entry Room just as the men entered, somehow attacking them and allowing the others to escape. I wondered how quickly I could barricade the door. The thought even crossed my mind that I should kill myself as the men entered as an ultimate act of rebellion.

In the end I held my ground and forced myself to lock out any thoughts about what could potentially happen to me after I walk through the door in front of me. The only thing I allowed myself to focus on was the hope that I would soon be with Michael and Alina again.

The men arrived at the side of the barn in mere minutes and made no effort to keep their voices low as one person dictated to another the method by which they were going to bring me in.

"Jackson, you get the door," yelled one deep voiced guy. "We'll go in, guns up. If there's any problem, shoot to kill anyone who gets in the way but try to take the boy unharmed."

Shoot to kill. I could feel the blood drain from my face as it occurred too late to me that by offering myself up for sacrifice to save the others, I had inadvertently put them all in more danger than they would have been had I just followed the normal processes. I was relieved when I noticed that everyone around me took a few silent steps backwards, some even lowering themselves to a seated position on the ground, obviously afraid of coming across as any sort of threat to the armed men.

Overhead, a camera whirred around in its casing, its gears noisy in the tense silence, settling its eye directly on me while another camera spun to face the door. Behind the slightly open door I could hear the men locking the exterior exit behind them.

"Ready!" the deep voiced man barked.
I sucked in a quick, sharp breath and realized that my head was dizzy because I hadn't been breathing.

This is really happening.

The next few moments flashed before me with startling speed:

The Entry Door flew open so quickly that it slammed against the inside of the barn with a thud that made everyone jump in surprise. Four people dressed head-to-toe in rigid black suits burst into the barn all at once, faces protected behind shiny black domed helmets with clear visors, their tall, muscular physiques seemingly super-human. In their hands each man held long, bulky, white objects that I knew to be guns, though I had never seen anything like them before. My mind flashed back to the night when I watched as Alina had been chosen: the men from that night looked like children compared to these massive soldiers.

With startling synchronicity, the first two of the armed men rushed ahead of the others, falling to one knee on each side of the door, guns raised towards the group of stunned onlookers, a mirror image of each other. Between the two kneeling men, a third heavily armed man quickly made his way around the surrounding crowd smashing the butt of the weapon into the faces of anyone who looked at anything but the ground.

"Eyes DOWN!" he yelled at the rare few who dared stand firm. "Any trouble and you're dead!"
After completing his circle around the onlookers, having beaten everyone into a painful compliance with the exception of me, he quickly made his way back to the Entry Door and stood between the two kneeling men facing me, gun pointed directly at my head.

The fourth man stood still in the doorway, his face locked straight ahead, and though I couldn't see his eyes due to the reflection on his visor, I felt his gaze locked on me. There was a moment of complete stillness as we stared at each other. The four armed men in front of me somehow lost any semblance of being human, blending together into some sort of rigid steel weapon of battle.

Nobody moved, not a person made a sound.

With striking calmness the lead soldier suddenly adjusted his hold on his weapon, seemingly detaching himself from the mass of glossy black steel around him, and quickly made his way across the barn towards me. His confidence and poise united with his sheer size to project an altogether intimidating persona. I felt my head spinning again and reminded myself to breath.

"You will come with me," the man commanded in an overwhelmingly powerful voice. "Any resistance will result in your immediate death."

A blast of cold ran through my veins. I felt like I was deep underwater, in danger of being too far under to make it to the surface for another breath.

An image of Michael popped into my mind. He was maybe only four or five years old, chasing our ball into the ocean for the first time, defying all known rules, knowing that others had been killed when they went into the water. He was terrified, but that ball had been one of our most prized possessions, one of the few joys in our lives. He knew that we had been given special treatment over the others here in the barn and was willing to risk everything to keep that one little item. He was only a child, but that act of bravery had always stuck clearly in my memory. To me it defined exactly who Michael was at the core of his being. I had always admired him for that, secretly wishing that I would one day be even half as courageous as he was. I needed to see him again.

Looking at the frightening behemoth in front of me, I imagined myself as Michael about to take that very first leap into the ocean, and I took a deep, refreshing breath. I suddenly felt a warmth course through my body as my heart began to beat powerfully in my chest, infusing my muscles with a rush of energy, filling my head with a sense of power unlike anything I had ever felt. I was immediately empowered and unafraid.

Holding my chin high, feeling more self-assured than ever, I looked straight back at the soldier before me.

"I will go with you without resistance," I said, "but if you and your men hurt any one of these people as we leave, you will have to kill me. Mr. Irvine has always given me special treatment and I am the only one that he has never managed to take from here, so I know enough to understand that I am a prize to him. He will want me unharmed. If I am injured or killed, you can bet your life that he will have you severely punished."

The soldier stood in silence for a moment after my speech and for just a moment I was certain that he was about to shoot me for my defiance.

Through the quiet I became aware of a faint voice coming from somewhere inside the helmet of the man before me. I could just make out the words: 'He's right. Touch him and your ass is mine.'

With that, the soldier in front of me spun on his heel and said "Follow me."

Part 3

The moment that the Entry Room door clicked shut behind me, the rear wall of the Entry Room slid open with a breezy hiss. Two of the armed men led the way into another room that was as dark inside as a moonless night. The third guard lightly prodded me in the back with his gun.

"Move."

I walked slowly out of the Entry Room, barely able to see the two men in front of me, my heartbeat thudding in my ears.

Behind me the other two men followed closely behind and the great sliding wall of the room hissed firmly closed behind them.

For a moment there was absolute darkness. I had expected that the armed men would take me out of the barn and onto the beach outside where their transportation machine would be waiting. All I could see were four red glowing dots that hovered motionless where the four men around me had just been standing, and I guessed that these must be some sort of tiny red flames inside of the men's suits.

A thick, bitter vapor seemed to be hanging in the air, burning my throat and eyes, immediately causing me to cough violently. Somewhere nearby a deep, steady rumbling echoed in the enclosure around me, making every bone in my body vibrate.

"Locked and ready," said one of the men.

As if the darkest night suddenly changed to the brightest day, the room instantly flooded with bright white light, temporarily blinding me and making my already watering eyes feel like they had exploded into my head. I fell to the ground and covered my eyes with both arms, my head now pounding in pain.

"Get into the truck," ordered one of the men. At first I thought he was speaking to me but I could hear the other men grunt in acknowledgement and move towards the rumbling machine, closing themselves inside with three heavy thuds.

"Open your eyes," said the remaining man. This was definitely an order directed at me and yet I didn't move a muscle.

"Open. Your. Eyes," he growled in a voice so threatening that I lost all concern for the pain in my head.

My eyes stung and my head pounded as I forced my eyes open. I felt myself inhale nervously as I allowed myself to take in my surroundings. We were in a crisp white room. Light seemed to exude from every inch of each of the four glossy walls, causing them to blend seamlessly into one another, masking any sense of depth perception. Even the floor and the ceiling glowed with the same glossy white light. I felt as if I were floating in a bright white cloud somewhere far up in the sky.

In stark contrast, the soldier stood before me clad in his glossy black armor looking even less human as reflections of light bounced off of him like he was suddenly covered in stars. Floating in this white room, he somehow seemed twice as large as he had moments ago.

Behind the soldier, also seeming to hover in space, was an enormous box sitting on perfectly round legs, its glossy black surface similar to the material in the man's uniform. I could tell right away that this was the source of the low rumbling and the noxious fumes as a steady stream of thick black smoke spewed from the rear end of the machine.

Truck, I thought. I had heard stories of these machines in the past but never imagined them to look like this.

Through the semi-transparent black panels on the upper part of the machine, I could see the other three men enclosed inside.

"Get up," demanded the man in his loud, powerful voice. Obediently I stood. He took a single step towards me, seeming to cross the great expanse between us, suddenly only a breaths travel from my face.

Nervously I tripped backwards, my tailbone thudding hard against the unforgiving floor. I knew right away that this was an intimidation technique. I forced the images of Michael and Alina into my mind. I saw them beaten, bruised and scared. I had to stay strong for them.

Slowly I drew myself up from the floor, taking time to straighten my shirt and purposely trying to come across as annoyed. Equally as slowly I turned to face the soldier. He was grinning with malicious pleasure but instead of cowering in fear, I felt my resolve strengthen. Locking my eyes with his, I stepped leisurely forward, my feet on either side of his, our chests and noses almost touching.

"Let's get going," I said firmly. The tiniest glimmer of satisfaction fluttered in my belly as the soldiers smirk turned to an angry scowl.

****

Anxiety shook me to the core the moment that the heavy steel door of the truck clicked closed beside me. Never before had I been in an enclosed space like this. The vast openness of the barn had even seemed small and claustrophobic to me after those long summer days where I had been allowed out onto the beach. I now felt as if the whole world had shrunken around me; as if the doors of the truck would never again be opened, trapping me in this small space until my lungs collapsed from lack of air.

The unfamiliar sensation of vibration as the truck grumbled around me, the hundreds of bright lights flashing all over the front section of the vehicle, the feeling of the tight strap fastened across my chest holding me tightly against the cold, smooth and unnaturally soft black seat, even the sweet smell of the interior of the vehicle—something between a soapy scent and that of cooked meat—it was all so new to me that I could feel my brain struggling to keep up and stay clear.

"Take this," said the soldier seated next to me. In his open metal palm sat a single yellow orb the size of a pea. I struggled to focus my thoughts enough to speak.

"Take it where?" I said with exasperation.

"Eat it," commanded the man.

"If that's one of your drugs, you can't get me to take it. I've seen what those things do to people."

"Suit yourself, I just didn't want to be cleaning up your barf later," he replied mockingly. "Just wait till we get moving."

Moments later the room around us went completely dark. The sudden transition to absolute blackness was nearly as shocking to my system as the moment when the bright white lights had come on. I concentrated my attention on the bright green, red and white lights at the front part of the truck to give myself some sense of the space around me and keep my mind as focused as possible.

"C1 Holding for departure," said the man at the front left side of the vehicle.

"Roger that, C1," responded a voice that sounded as if it came from within the walls of the truck. "Opening outer hatch."

With that, another wall of the room around us slid open with a muted hiss and light poured in from outside, this time nowhere near as blinding as the unnatural light had been in the glossy white room. Through the transparent wall in the front of the truck I could see the familiar beach and distant forest that surrounded the barn and I suddenly had an intense urge to run.

The truck lurched forward with a roar.

The sensation of moving in a vehicle was all together overwhelming for me. My stomach churned as I felt my own weight pressed heavily into the soft seat by an unseen weight. The feeling of moving without actually walking with my own two feet was surreal to me. Knowing that I no longer had the power to choose when to start or stop moving left me feeling more out of control of my own body than I ever had.

The truck exited through the large door with a wobble as its wheels transitioned from the smooth floor to the soft, uneven sand of the beach and bounced over the small ripples and dunes. My stomach twisted and fluttered with every motion and I suddenly understood the saying of 'having butterflies in your stomach.'

As the vehicle crossed through the tall bushes that lined the beach I turned back to look behind me and I realized that this was the farthest I had ever been from the barn. It already seemed impossibly distant and small. As we crossed over a large mound, the barn slid behind the landscape and I suddenly felt a gut wrenching sense of loss. Everything that I had every known in this life was there behind me. It was my home. My prison. My world. And now, despite knowing better, I felt as if it all ceased to exist.

Everything from this point on was like a whole new planet.

****

129

We passed through the area of low brush surrounding the beach with surprising speed. The low mounds and hills that had already wreaked havoc on my stomach and equilibrium grew steadily into large hills and windy trails that left me even more woozy and nauseous than I thought possible. I felt as if my head were underwater, floating and bobbing on with the waves and the current, and although I desperately wanted to watch everything that we passed, I soon had to close my eyes and lower my head to keep from being sick.

"Re-thinking that pill now aren't ya?" snickered the soldier beside me.

He laughed again when I didn't respond.
"They all think they can handle the first time they get in a car eh Jack?" he said to the man behind the wheel that appeared to control the direction of travel. 'Jack' laughed along pitilessly.

"What're you drivin' like Miss. Daisy for anyway?" grunted the soldier beside me. "Why don't we show this kid a real roller coaster ride?"

"You got it boss," responded Jack with a malicious chuckle.

At that, the truck roared and I felt the weight of my body press even heavier into the seat behind me . I fought to keep from swaying too much as we raced around curves and flew over the tops of hills but the nausea rose to my throat and my head began to spin. After only a few sharp turns I knew I couldn't take much more.

"I'm gunna be sick," I groaned.

"Told ya kid," laughed the man next to me. "Should'a taken the pill."

I felt something light land on my lap and allowed myself to open my eyes just long enough to see what it was. It was a single square sheet of paper.

"It's a barf bag," said the man, seeing my confusion. "Unless you want to spend the rest of the day covered in your own barf you'll wanna puke in that."

Seconds later the entire contents of my stomach emptied violently into the thin bag.

****

A groggy haze clouded my thoughts. I was awake, but not yet fully conscious.

Everything felt wrong: The soft padding beneath me; A tight strap across my waist; A constant hum.

 My stomach churned in discontent as my mind raced to remember what was happening to me.

"Hey, I think he's awake.'

I shook my head quickly to help myself wake up and focus, but my brain felt like it was full of rocks and my eyes burned to close again.

It all came back to me in a startling rush and I lurched in my seat, instantly alert.

I was no longer in the large truck, but the same four soldiers who had removed me from the barn were sitting all around me. We seemed to be in a long narrow room lined on each side with rows of soft white chairs, each with their own little circle of clear wall to look outside. I was immediately aware of the fact that the air in this space was thick and dry, feeling somehow oversaturated with the exhaled air of others. The low ceiling added to a sense of being trapped and about to suffocate. Feeling as if I were on the brink of panic, I closed my eyes again and told myself that I had no need to panic as long as the men around me were sitting calmly.

"Well look at Sleeping Beauty," laughed the man on my right, clearly speaking about me. "Knocked ya out pretty hard huh?"

"What did you do to me?" I said, feeling more weary and nauseous than I had ever felt in my life.

"Just a shot of something to keep you out. It's a long trip and I don't like babysitting."

"You drugged me?" I groaned.

"Yeah man, and I got a good 6 hours of sleep because of it," the soldier said with a boastful smirk.

"6 hours? How long is that?" I asked, confused.

"Oh right, 'time' is probably something you've never worried about. Uh, let say it's a little more than half the night," he responded, clearly amused.

The concept of traveling for most of the night confounded me. I had never imagined that the world could be this large.

Looking through small round clear spots in the walls I could see that it was still nighttime, but off on the horizon, the faintest glow of orange was emerging in the distance.

"How much longer?" I asked.

"We're almost there," answered the soldier who had been driving the truck, with a grunt of exhaustion in his voice.

"See that city over there?" said the man next to me, pointing his finger towards the faint line of the sun rising on the horizon. "That's where we're headed. Another two hours or so."

I squinted my eyes, scanning the darkness for any sign of a building.

"I don't see it," I said.

"Are you blind, kid?" the soldier said with disbelief. "All those lights? On the horizon. Right there."
"All I can see is where the sun is about to come up," I said, even more confused.

"Wow, you barn kids are so fucking stupid, " he laughed. "Dude, those are lights. Like from buildings and cars and shit. The sun won't be coming up for another hour."

"But it covers the entire horizon…" I said in amazement.

"What did you expect? A bunch of old barns?" snickered the man.

Yah, kind of, I thought to myself, bewildered by the enormity of what I was seeing. I couldn't even begin to imagine the number of people that must live in a city of that size. It was more people than I had ever imagined to live in the entire world.

The entire horizon, I thought again to myself, suddenly feeling like a single grain of sand thrown by a great wave onto an endless beach.

****

I had blacked out. I don't know when it had happened, but I distinctly remember the moment of extreme panic when I realized that we were in a machine—an airplane—high up in the sky where only clouds and birds were supposed to fly. I had thought that we were in some large vehicle cruising slowly over the top of a hill in the darkness.

The airplane had begun to bounce violently, tossing my stomach into my mouth repeatedly as I alternately felt weightless and then extremely heavy in my seat.

"What's happening?!" I screamed to the men around me, all who had braced their hands tightly on the seat in front of them.

"Turbulence," said the man named Jack, trying to look tough despite clearly suffering almost as much as I was.

"What the hell does that mean?!" I cried out, sure that we were falling to the earth like some giant stone.

"Calm down!" yelled the man directly next to me. "Think of it as bumping into clouds. They're bumpy but soft."

We're in the clouds, I remember thinking.

****

The truck continued to travel along a long windy road for what seemed like an eternity.

I had woken up in the same seat that I had been in when we left the barn, but I could tell that this truck was different.

Instead of a shiny black material, the seats were brown and fuzzy and smelled like an ocean breeze.

"What happened?" I moaned.

"Dude you gotta man up!" taunted Jack cruelly. "I've seen five year old girls who can handle more than you!" In my groggy state, Jack's statement hit me hard, knowing that he probably wasn't kidding about putting such young girls through this.

All around, fields stretched far off into the darkness, lined unnaturally with straight lines of trees and long piles of stone that were almost perfectly rectangular as they divided one type of crop from the next. In time we began to pass the occasional building, and every so often my heart jumped out of my chest when I saw one that resembled the barn that only hours ago had been the boundary of my entire world.

As we neared the city, the halo of light that I had seen earlier gradually morphed into millions of individual pinpricks of light, some moving in great snake-like lines of red or white, while others remained motionlessly illuminating every last object in a golden glow. Artificial lighting was everywhere, and I soon lost track of whether it was daytime or if it were still night.

I watched for a long time as the city seemed to grow before my eyes. Individual buildings of the city began to come in to view and I was in awe as each one seemed to be more enormous than the last, creating a solid wall of stone not unlike that of the distant mountains that surrounded the barn, blending into the yellow-grey clouds high above. I remembered how scared I had been the first time that I had climbed my ladder in the barn: my pulse had quickened, my breath locked in my chest, my blood banged through my veins and my head began to spin. That had only been 52 rungs above the ground. The idea that people could be in those buildings standing amongst the clouds dumbfounded me.

I felt as if I had had the wind knocked out of me the first time that I spotted the first person on the outskirts of the city. It was a tall blonde woman dressed only in what looked like black underwear, her hair pulled back tightly, and she seemed to be running from something. For a brief moment I almost gave into an intense urge to call out to her for help but I was stopped by the fear that all people on the outside world were crazy, strange, awful people like Mr. Irvine and his four soldiers. Confirming my suspicions, the woman stopped moving forward yet continued the motions of running in the place where she stopped and began talking to herself as if she were with someone else. Crazy for sure.

Little by little, all sorts of vehicles began buzzing around us, disappearing around a maze of rows, endless corners, hills and holes in the ground. Some vehicles only held one person, while others carried dozens inside their steel bellies.

Still moving further into the depths of the great city, an unfathomable number of people began to come together on either side of the rows of vehicles. Most of the people were dressed similarly: Black pants, black jacket with a bright white shirt underneath, shiny shoes. The hoard of people soon grew so thick that each person was shoulder-to-shoulder and chest-to-back with the people around them, walking in a rhythmical stop and go wave of organized pandemonium. Most people were carrying black or brown bags in one hand, while the other hand held a small object to their head. Many people were talking, but it didn't seem that any were talking to each other.

I couldn't think of one good reason why all of these people would be awake at such an early hour. Everybody out here must be crazy.

I knew before we stopped that we were about to arrive at our destination. Directly ahead, an enormous tower loomed high over all of the other buildings, piercing the clouds like a giant needle. It was a place that I distinctly remembered from some of the stories that Michael told early on after his arrival at the barn: The tall needle that he once went to the top of where he could see through the floors and where people below him turned into ants. The ensuing mental image had lingered for many years in my nightmares, and although I knew now as a young adult that Michael had meant to say that people looked as small as ants because of the distance, the very sight of this building still brought on the same tremor of fear as it had when I was dreaming as a child.

As we passed the giant needle I could feel my anxiety growing. I looked through the front of the truck along the pathway up ahead, knowing full well what I was looking for. Sure enough, glistening like a reflected sunrise on the surface of the ocean, another tall building loomed high above, paneled all in gold, contrasting itself from the otherwise grey, man-made valley around me.

The Golden Tower.

I knew from Michaels story that this was Mr. Irvine's home, the place that Michael was taken before coming to the barn, the place with a hot pool in the clouds and fish bigger than a child that swam in the walls. It was another powerful ingredient in my years of nightmares and I felt my body shiver nervously. Within those golden walls, every person that I had ever known had been tortured, abused, treated indignantly and had their spirits shattered. Worse yet, Alina and Michael had been brought here so many months ago, and though my heart longed desperately to see them, I was mortified by the thought of what they may have had to endure over all this time.

More frighteningly, I was terrified that they may not have survived.

"Coming up on entrance two," said the driver. "Copy that. Support not required."

The sudden interruption of my thoughts surprised me and I had to shake my head to bring myself back to the moment at hand. The men around me shuffled in their seats, pulling dark shields over their head and adjusting the grips on their weapons.

The truck had slowed down substantially and was now turning onto a much less congested artery between the gold building and another mammoth stone structure. A moment later the vehicle was turning again, this time descending down a steep but short hill, straight for a large white wall.

"Entrance two, prepare for arrival of cargo," said the driver. A moment later, the white wall before us began to raise into the wall above, revealing a large underground cavern hidden beneath the mountain of towers.

I quietly held my breath as we slowly rolled into the belly of the cave. Despite the enormity of the room, I suddenly felt as if I were deep underwater.

"Any fucking around and I'll taze you, kid," warned the man next to me, his voice echoing hollowly behind his clear face shield. "Stay calm and you'll make it through this alive. This part of it at least."

I was surprised at how far down the tunnel went. After four complete spirals downwards, my head began to spin and, despite the fear of not knowing what would be happening to me once I got out of the truck, I found myself relieved to feel the vehicle come to a stop. I finally allowed myself to slowly release my breath.

Out of nowhere, a half dozen soldiers appeared and surrounded the vehicle, all mirroring each other's pose: one leg far in front of the other, right eye against their raised weapon which was pointed directly at me.

"For Christ's sake!" yelled the driver as he exited the vehicle. "What part of 'support not required' don't you get?

"Back off Jack," snapped a tall man as he lowered his weapon and stepped aggressively towards Jack. "You have no rank once you pull in here."

"Fuck that," barked Jack, standing his ground assertively. "My duties are to get the kid from the barn to Irvine's office. We're not in the office yet. Till then I am still in charge."

"Don't push me Jack!" yelled the tall man, nearly pressing his chest up against Jacks. "I don't care who the hell you think you are or what your duties are, but I am in command here and you will do as I say. You don't like it, you're out. Simple as that. Now get the kid out, hand him over then fuck off. "

I watched as Jack attempted to stand his ground, clearly fuming from rage but unable to come up with a good counter argument. A moment later his shoulders dropped ever so slightly and he spun on his heels to face the truck once more.

"Get him out! We're done here."

The door beside me swung open.

"Out," barked one of the soldiers.

For a brief moment I hesitated, suddenly very afraid to exit from the relative safety of the truck that I had originally felt to be suffocatingly small. Now with all the unfamiliarity of the enormous world around me, my body begged me to stay put in the familiar space, certain that I wouldn't be able to handle all of the stimulus and constant change.

"Now!" yelled the man, raising his weapon in warning.

I practically fell from the vehicle in scared response, hanging myself from the belt across my chest.

"Idiot!" cursed the man, leaning past me to detach the belt.

I fell heavily to the ground, smashing my left cheek and shoulder into the cold stone floor.

"Oh for God's sakes!" groaned the same man.

I struggled to pull myself up from the ground, my vision blurring as the pain in my cheek throbbed. Fear coursed through my body, blatantly circumventing any attempt to feign some sort of composure. I could feel my hands shaking as the world lightly bobbed like a gentle wave on the ocean. My ears rang loudly in my head. Looking around at the armed group in front of me, my brain began to over stimulate again: all the lights, the constant noise, the strange textures of every surface, the semi-circle of strangely clad, unfamiliar men who all held me at gunpoint.

"Here 'e goes," I heard a voice groan as the word went dark before my eyes.

****

I had fainted. I knew it before I even dared to open my eyes. There was too much happening around me. My brain couldn't keep up. Even now with my eyes closed, my brain raced to process all of the noises and sensations.

I could hear the men around me grumbling about how much of a mess I was. Apparently I had peed myself when I fainted, but it wasn't until it was mentioned that I could feel the cool dampness in my crotch.

"I'm not changing him," said one man who seemed to be supporting the right side of my body. Another man was on the left side, the two men apparently dragging me forward.

"I don't envy Sarah," joked the man on the left with a slight snort.

"Yah this kid's worse than his little bitch was!" mumbled the other man.

My bitch? Does he mean Alina?

I kept my eyes shut and my body limp as the men dragged me, doing my best to tune out any other background noises in an effort to keep calm enough to carry off the act of still being unconscious.

My shoulders started to burn under the strain of supporting my body weight and I fought desperately to keep myself from instinctually changing my body position. Just when I thought I couldn't take it anymore, the men came to a stop. I felt the man on the right slightly adjust his grip on me as we stood still and the slight change brought welcome relief to my tired muscles. A moment later a quiet bell rang and we stepped forward a few more paces before spinning around and coming to a stop once more.

"46," said the man on my left side.

To my surprise a new voice responded.

"Penthouse Level, sir?"

"Yes, of course the Penthouse Level," replied the soldier impatiently.

"Passcode?"

"Alpha 4113820."

"Thank you sir," replied the third man timidly.

A second later there was a slight hiss in front of us and I could feel the air stop moving. The room seemed to have closed in around us . I immediately felt suffocated again and fought to keep from panicking. Suddenly the whole room seemed to lurch upwards and my stomach seemed to launch itself into my throat before depositing its meagre contents all over my chest and the floor at my feet. In response the two men at my side abruptly released their hold on me, my limp body falling directly into the vomit.

"Jesus!" said both men simultaneously.

"You'd better not have gotten any on me kid!" grunted one of them.

"Sarah's gunna hate us!" laughed the other.

I had opened my eyes the moment that they dropped me. We were in a tiny steel room. One other man dressed in a red and black outfit stood rigidly facing a wall of yellow circles with numbers, dutifully ignoring the events around him. The room felt as if it were floating in water. I looked up to see a green number on one wall as it changed from 44 to 45 to PH1.

"Up! Quickly!" Commanded one of the soldiers.

'NOW!" yelled the other man with frightening aggression when I didn't move. I stood quickly, turning in the same direction that they faced without having being told.

The room stopped floating with another stomach churning lurch and I staggered slightly to prevent myself from falling.

"No speaking, no trouble," commanded the man on my right.

Just then a quiet bell rang as it had only moments before. With a quiet hiss, the wall before us split down the middle and slid silently away.

Before me stood a short, thin woman with dark black hair, squinty eyes and a tightly wrapped dress covered in red and white flowers. A shiny golden plate above her left breast read 'Sarah.'

"Hello Asha. Welcome to Irvine Industries."

****

I staggered as I followed Sarah through a long, narrow room, pressing myself up against the solid wall on my left for stability, doing my best to steer my eyes away from the transparent wall to my right. My legs felt like they were about to give out underneath me. My vision felt as if it were closing in on me. The world outside was unimaginably far below us.

Sensing my anxiety, Sarah stopped walking and turned to face me, obviously cautious to maintain an air of formality as the soldiers behind me watched.

"Don't look through the windows. What you're feeling is called Vertigo." Her dark brown eyes locked on mine in the same protective gaze that Nasha often shared with me when I was in need of comfort, her voice soft, but cold.

"It will pass quickly if you keep calm and breathe normally. In time you will get used to it." Sarah's voice cracked slightly as she said the last part.

It may have been my panicked state, but something in me sensed a hit of sympathy in her demeanor.

I focused my eyes on the floor in front of me as I followed her onwards, carefully regulating each breath to a count of three. My head felt immediately clearer, my nerves less on edge.

I reminded myself that I had to be strong; Michael and Alina could be somewhere in the building.

Sarah led me around a corner and in to a large, bright room with no windows. I felt the tension in my shoulders relax just a little bit, relieved by the fact that there was no longer any risk of plunging off the edge of the building to the hard ground below.

"You may wait outside," Sarah said firmly to the soldiers.

"Our orders are to guard the boy," responded one man in an inhuman, disconnected grunt.

"And you will do that by standing guard in the hallway while I examine the boy," snapped Sarah with a hiss of authority that contrasted her tiny stature.

The two stood facing each other for several seconds in a silent stare down. Sarah looked impossibly meek and vulnerable next to the tall, muscular and heavily armed soldier but she held her ground.

"That will be all," she said with absolute finality, stepping forward to rest her hand on the open door next to the soldier, clearly intending to close it on him.

The soldier remained motionless for a second or two longer and I caught him blinking self-consciously, clearly annoyed to be bossed around by someone half his size. Then, with a quick shake of his head and a huff of irritation, he spun on his heel and led the other soldier from the room.

Sarah closed the door quietly behind them and clicked a button, locking it firmly.

"Are you hurt at all?" she said to me, grasping my shoulders with both hands, squeezing gently and inching her way down my left arm.

Surprised by the sudden physical contact I stepped back defensively.

"Yes? No?" Sarah asked, undeterred from her examination of me.

"Uh, no," I stuttered self-consciously as she repeated the action down my right arm, continuing down my torso, and then down each leg. I had never been touched like this before. I could feel myself blushing in embarrassment.

"Your face," she said, carefully touching my left cheek with two fingers. "Does it hurt when I do this?"

Despite the nearly intolerable pain I prevented myself from wincing. I shook my head no.

"Well it's not broken, but I can tell that it must hurt like a bitch."

She gently rubbed a wet, strong smelling cloth across my cheek, cleaning away a surprisingly large amount of blood, instantly numbing the majority of the pain.

"Hold this against it," she said, passing me a blue bag that was as cold as snow that stung my skin as it touched it.

"You've soiled yourself," she said matter-of-factly, quickly unbuttoning and removing my pants. Having never owned a pair of underwear, I was now naked from the waist down, legs streaked from my own filth, humiliated.

Without a moment's hesitation, Sarah immediately began wiping my genitals, bum and legs with an assortment of damp cloths.

"This happens to almost everyone," she said plainly.

Tossing the dirty cloths into a shiny white bin with a self-closing lid, I saw Sarah turn to me, but in my embarrassment I couldn't bring myself to make eye contact with her.

"Hey," she said gently, stepping closer. "Ash. I'm not here to hurt you. My job is to make you as comfortable as possible. You've been through a lot. This surely is overwhelming for you."

I allowed myself to briefly look at her before locking my eyes on a stark part of the white wall. I felt the burn of the ice on my throbbing cheek, the cool breeze on my exposed and slightly damp crotch, the gentle but constant hum of all of the unfamiliar machines around me. Nothing was as it should be. I was suddenly so overwhelmed, so exhausted that I couldn't fight it any longer and I could feel tears welling up in my eyes.

"Hey, hey, hey," comforted Sarah, lowering the bag of ice from my cheek and gently grasping me on either side of my face, turning my head to face her. "Breathe. You're okay."

Our eyes met and Sarah forced me to hold her gaze. The effect was steadying, calming. Her eyes somehow blocked out everything else in the world and it became just the two of us, alone in a quiet, safe space, sharing a moment with one another.

I breathed in a deep and heavy breath, letting it out in a steady, slow stream. I felt my heart rate slow and my body relax a little.

"See? Better, right?" asked Sarah with a smile, still holding me by my cheeks.

I exhaled heavily again and nodded subtly. Sarah took a slight step back and moved her hands to hold me gently by the shoulders, her eyes still locked in a comforting stare with mine.

"You're exhausted. You've been traveling for a whole day with no food or water and I assume very little rest," she said, "God, I can't imagine what you're feeling like. All of this unfamiliarity! I can't believe that you're, what, eighteen? And you've never once been out of the barn?!"

All of a sudden Sarah stopped talking, released her hold on my face and turned quickly to fumble with some strange items on the table behind her. A moment later she turned to face me again, a small rod with a light shining out of it which she held close to each of my eyes.

"I'm the head nurse here," she began, sounding much more formal than before. "I take care of sick or injured people in the company. I don't see anything of concern with you but I will want to get a full scan and a range of tests done on you." She turned then to put down her tool and to pick up a flat wooden spoon.

"Stick your tongue out please." she asked, and I obeyed as she pressed down heavily on my tongue.

"Now, you've never been vaccinated or exposed to some of the everyday bacteria and viruses that we face here in the outside world, so I am going to give you a few shots. I need you to swallow these so you don't get sick," she said quickly, handing me several multi-coloured spheres.

Seeing my confusion, she went on. "They aren't going to put you to sleep, if that's your concern. They will protect you against illness. Side effects will be limited to difficulty sleeping and perhaps diarrhea for a few hours."

Methodically she placed a small paper cup filled with water in my other hand. "Take them now please."

Confused by the sudden change in demeanor, I hesitated for a moment before swallowing the pills, but did so as directed, placing the empty cup back in Sarah's hand, hoping silently that she would offer more water.

"Good," she said. "Sit, please,"

She motioned to a seat in the corner and I obediently followed orders, shocked by the coolness of the chair against my naked bum and genitals.

"Hold this tightly but don't move your arm," Sarah commanded flatly, placing a squishy ball in my hand and wrapping a stretchy band around my upper arm. I watched calmly as she inserted a small glass tube onto the end of a long, thin needle. It wasn't until she pressed the tip to the flesh of my inner elbow and pierced the skin that I jumped slightly, my mind going a little bit foggy as I watched my own blood fill the small chamber.

Sarah grabbed my upper arm firmly and reminded me to sit still. I couldn't imagine why she would intentionally make me bleed.

When she had two vials filled, Sarah put them down and grabbed another tray of tools, including many more needles.

"You will feel a couple of pricks, like mosquito bites, but it is important that you do not move . These prevent you from getting many diseases." Subsequently, Sarah began sticking the needles into my shoulder one by one. What she described as feeling like mosquito bites felt more like bee stings. I fought to keep myself from moving, yet Sarah still had to use her free hand to hold me steady.

As she withdrew the fourth needle, she mumbled a quiet but emotionless 'Very good.'

After several other painless tests with almost no words shared between us, Sarah sat down onto a black stool in front of a glowing rectangle in the wall and began hitting her fingers on a pad on the table.

"Do you have any other health related issues or concerns?" she asked coolly, her eyes locked on the machine in front of her.

I struggled to get words to come out.

"Where are Michael and Alina?"

Sarah shook her head slightly, avoiding eye contact.

"I honestly don't know."

"Are they okay?"

"I haven't seen them since they first arrived."

We sat silently again for a few moments while Sarah mindfully tapped on the machine.

"What… what is going to happen to me?" I asked finally, my words shaking as I spoke.

Sarah stopped tapping on the pad in front of her. Her shoulders slumped almost imperceptibly. She stared blankly at the machine in front of her for a few seconds before spinning on her stool to face me, straightening her posture purposefully, making stern eye contact with me.

"The results of your test will be back within forty-eight hours. Should there be any concerns, I will contact you."

The callousness in her words stung me. I didn't know this woman and I had no reason to distinguish her from any of the other strange and evil people that I had thus far encountered in the outside world. I had no reason to trust her. But for some reason, in those first few moments with her, I had instantly come to rely on her support. Something had happened in the past few minutes, but I knew that the woman who had just held me by my cheeks and calmed me down was still there in front of me. I just couldn't understand why she had become so cold all of a sudden.
I choked back a sob as I stared into her dark eyes.

"No…. I mean, what are they going to do to me?"

At that, Sarah's head drooped low and she took a noticeably nervous breath. As her head came up again, Sarah's eyes locked on mine once again. Before she spoke, her eyes flickered up to and to the right, the back to me, slightly wider than before. She repeated this odd flick of the eye once again before speaking. Following her gaze I looked up to the ceiling, almost falling over as I saw the familiar crisp white cylinder with the black eye watching us from above. Mr. Irvine was watching me even now.

Sarah passed me a thin, crinkly sheet to wrap around my waist.

"Now you will go with the soldiers," Sarah said, clearing her throat. "They will take you to be bathed, fed, groomed and dressed.

You are dismissed."

I stood between the two soldiers as we walked single file to another room at the other end of the long hallway. Windows seemed to be everywhere, but I remembered to control my breathing and did my best to focus on the crinkling sound of the paper around my waist as I walked, blocking out any other outside stimulus.

We came to a stop outside a plain white door marked with a sign that read 'Wardrobe'.

One of the soldiers pulled a small white rectangle from his pocket and held it against a black box next to the door. Immediately the box beeped and a green light appeared. I could hear a faint click from the door as it unlocked itself. The soldier then pressed down on the handle and threw the door open, gesturing with his hand for me to go inside. Silently I obeyed.

I couldn't believe what I was seeing: The large room before me was filled to its limits with clothing, ranging in style from simple white outfits to bizarre, multi-limbed, human-like monstrosities made of clear plastics and rigid fibers. The amazing array of colours and textures was unlike anything I had ever seen before. Every wall in the large room was covered floor to ceiling in crystal clear mirrors that reflected into each other over and over again, creating the illusion that the room of clothing stretched off to the horizons in all directions .

I never knew that there could be so many varieties of each colour. Having only ever owned a few outfits in my life, it seemed incredible to me that there would be any need to have so many un-used clothes at one time, and the thought that most of these outfits were completely impractical for everyday life confounded me. To me, clothing was a necessity for survival: A light, airy outfit for the hot summers, a heavy, thick sweater and pants to keep me from freezing during the winters. I could see no reason that anyone ever want to wear these cumbersome, heavy outfits.

The door thudded closed behind me.

I didn't have to turn to know that the soldier had remained in the hallway—I could see my reflection in the mirrored wall ahead of me. For the first time since sitting on the beach outside the barn, I was completely alone.

I didn't dare to move a muscle.

Cool air blew through the room like a natural summer breeze blowing in off of the ocean; silence filled the room like a welcoming hug. I didn't realize until now the extent to which my senses had been so overloaded from all of the stimulus in this new world. Had I been brave enough to close my eyes for a second I could have convinced myself that I was standing at the water's edge back inside the barn. I wanted to be back there so badly that even just the brief memory calmed my pounding nerves just slightly.

I scanned the room slowly. Despite the stillness, my instincts still tingled with the reminder that I was under constant surveillance, and I knew that I wouldn't be left alone for long.

There was no sign of the familiar black eyes that had watched me all my life.

I searched again, listening attentively this time for the distinctive whirr of the eyes as they moved.

Nothing.

Could this be the first time in my life that I am not under constant surveillance?

I was surprised at the revelation that I was somehow comfortable being under observation, that it was all I had known--as if, despite all of the horrors, hardships and pain that I had witnessed in my life, there was some sick comfort in knowing that someone was watching from above.

I felt goose bumps raise the hair on my arms and the back of my neck as I felt eerily alone.

"Well you must be Ash!" declared an oddly high pitched, jovial voice.

I was so shocked but the sudden intrusion in the silence that I staggered to keep myself from falling backwards into a wall of ornate fabrics.

I steadied myself against the material beside me, holding my body rigid and still, instinctually attempting to hide simply by being motionless.

Nobody had entered the room. I hadn't heard or seen anyone moving. For a moment I thought that the voice had come from some disembodied source in a similar way that I had heard while in the truck on the way here, but something in the echo told me that there was in fact a person somewhere in this room.

I quickly scanned the rows and rows of outfits again.

"Oh my!" said the strange voice again. " I didn't mean to scare you!"

I was dumbfounded to see movement only a few steps from where I was standing. Out of nowhere the figure of a lavishly dressed, heavily painted, androgynous person, neither distinguishable as a male or female, seemed to bloom from the flowery camouflage of colourful tapestries behind it.

With dramatic flair, the person before me stepped into the open isle between the rows of clothing, spinning on their right toe in a full pirouette which made their odd outfit explode outward in a burst of whirling, flower-like patterns. The dress settled and the person struck a well-practiced pose: the left leg jutting unnaturally outwards between a slit in the fabric, hands rested daintily on the hips, chin high, teeth bared in a wide, almost creepy smile.

I noticed instantly an overpowering scent of flowers.

"I'm Florian," said the figure before me, thrusting a surprisingly muscular, hairy hand palm down in my direction.
Frozen where I stood, I looked cautiously up and down the bizarre person in front of me. All superficial signs—the vibrant dress, the glittery makeup, brightly painted red fingernails, the effeminate mannerism--told me that this person before me was female. On closer inspection, undeniable signs of masculinity—the broad shoulders, the shadowy chin and cheeks, the hard lump of an Adams Apple—all betrayed the illusion and affirmed to me that this oddity in front of me was in fact a man.

As if sensing my realization, Florian squeezed my hand nearly tighter than I could tolerate and gave me a subtle, knowing wink.

A second later, he was back in character, swishing his wrists and speaking in an impossibly high pitched tone for a man.

"Florian, of course means 'Flower,'" he said with a squeaky giggle as if I should already know this, once again spinning to make his dress fly out in a rippling spiral that, I had to admit, looked surprisingly similar to a giant blossoming flower. "You can call me Flo if you want."

Stunned, I didn't move from my awkward position against the wall. It was only when Florian stopped spinning and gave me a look of mock disappointment that I realized I still had my hand outstretched as if waiting for my hand to be shaken again.

"Oh come on now honey, I'm not that hideous am I?" she—he said with a playful pout. I slowly lowered my arm, but held my stance.

"Come, come now baby, let momma look at you!" Florian said reaching out with both hands, pulling me up to a standing position.

Momma? I thought. *You're a dude! And probably not any older than me!*

Self-consciously rigid, I stood in the position that Florian placed me in: legs slightly spread apart, hands on hips, chin up. I felt ridiculous as he looked at every inch of me, circling like a bird searching for prey. As he passed behind me I suddenly remembered that I was wearing a paper skirt that was open at the back, and I quickly reached to pull the two pieced tightly over my cheeks.

"Oh that's no fair," giggled Florian, smacking my hands playfully as he continued his inspection.

After completing his circuit he stepped in front of me and crossed his arms, his posture and body language immediately switching from effeminate and aloof to stern and commanding. His eyes locked onto mine: it was an intense stare that made me bristle with nervousness, yet I forced myself to hold a defiant gaze. I knew that this was a war of wills and that I could not risk losing if I wanted to maintain any semblance of control over my time in this room.

It went on for far longer than I thought, and I could feel my eyes start to burn with strain, yet Florian seemed to be steadfast in his determination. I felt myself wavering, struggling to stand perfectly still, concentrating as hard as I could to keep my eyes focused on his. Anger began welling up inside me as I realized that I was about to lose this battle.

And then he stuck his tongue out.

I was so thrown off by this odd action that my eyes involuntarily blinked, and at that moment I knew that I had lost.

Florian's head flew back he let out an ear piercingly high laugh .

"So serious!" he chuckled, tapping me on the elbow playfully. "I'm just messing with you! Lighten uuuuuuup!"

I stared at him in disbelief. I didn't understand what was going on or what to think.

Florian's smile faded after a moment of silence and I could see his mood became sympathetic and serious.

"At least say something," he said, pausing for my response. "Okayyyyyyyyyyyyy. Um, okay, your name. Let's start with your name."

My name. Easy enough, I thought.

"Ash," I said.

"Ah! A breakthrough!" Florian laughed. "Okay so I knew that already, but it's a nice courtesy to introduce yourself when in the company of a lady like me!

A pleasure to finally meet you. Of course, I already know everything about you!

Welcome to my humble office. As you can probably tell, my job is to make you dapper and sexy!"

Seeing my confusion, Florian continued his explanation, his voice chirping up and down like a songbird.

"You barn kids are, um, shall we say….lacking a bit of polish. I'm here to teach you etiquette, hygene, posture, and of course to make you HANDSOME for your meeting with Mr. Irvine."

"What do you mean you know everything about me?" I mumbled.

Seeming caught off guard, Florian's cheeks seemed to somehow redden even more under all of the paint on his face.

"Oh, well, I know because," he stumbled, his eyes flickering to the wall of mirrors to our right as he tried to explain himself. "I've read some of your medical report, so I know everything that has been documented about you."

"I just met with the doctor right before coming to this room," I said skeptically.

"Oh dear boy," Florian laughed artificially, his tone sounding uneasy, "I forget how out of touch with reality you are! Here in the real world, information can be passed from one place to another in less time than a blink of the eye!"

His answer didn't surprise me at all. Nothing in this crazy place seemed unimaginable.

"The real world," I repeated quietly, my eyes once again circling the absurd costumes all around the room.

A darkness came over Florian's face, his presence abruptly changing from jovial to sullen. He stood before me for a moment, his left palm flat against his cheek, his right hand over is heart. His eyes were once again focused on mine, yet I could tell that he wasn't looking at me, but through me, lost in thought.

Suddenly, with a flick of his wrist and a toothy smile brighter than the sun, his demeanor once again changed like crack of lightning and he was behind me, pushing me forcefully towards a mirrored wall in a corner.

"Don't react," Florian whispered in my ear from behind as he shoved me along. His voice was deep, masculine and aggressive. The change threw my mind into a tailspin as I struggled to understand what was happening.

"They can see everything we do but they can't hear us," he continued hurriedly. "Just keep acting stunned and defiant."

"I don't think that will be a problem," I replied with all seriousness.

He pushed me right into the corner, my face nearly touching the mirrors on both sides. To my left side, a row of rainbow coloured materials was stacked to the ceiling.

"There aren't any cameras pointed into this corner," Florian whispered again in a startlingly masculine tone.

I looked at him in the reflection in front of me. His gaze was burning with a seriousness and fearful determination that both scared and intrigued me.

"We can't stay in this corner for long or they will get suspicious but just listen to me for a minute. They can't hear us in here. I know the guy who runs the surveillance and he's disabled the sound system in this room, blaming a tech issue. There are cameras behind the mirrors on the two large walls. It's imperative that, when we step back out into view that you act as though you are still skeptical of me. Defensive even."

"It's pretty accurate, actually," I replied with hostility.

"Look," Florian continued earnestly. "There's a group of us here who are trying to help you. We're all prisoners here like you were in the barn. You're our only hope. I can't explain right now—I don't know how much time we have."

My head spun in disbelief. Moments ago I had felt entirely alone--a simple kid trying to stay alive and sane in a surreal world full of crazy people. I didn't have a plan or a goal, no idea as to what was going to happen to me out here. Until this moment I didn't realize how hopeless I had really felt. To have a friend out here, a group of secret allies to watch out for me was like a breath of air after diving just a little too deep in the ocean.

And yet I couldn't bring myself to believe anything that any of these insane people said.

"Take off your shirt," Florian suddenly commanded.

"What?!"

"Just do it!" Florian demanded. "We have to make it look like there is a reason that I pushed you against the wall!"

I held my ground, not quite comprehending his intent.

153

"Look," he continued with nervous impatience, his voice deep and serious. "The world out here is a shitty place. People do shitty things to others--especially here. Someone like me being locked alone in a room with a guy like you... well people would expect me to try something."

Memories flashed through my mind of all the others from the barn who returned beaten, broken, and, to my best guess, horribly abused sexually. A shiver went down my spine as I realized not only that Florian's idea seemed logical, but also that I would soon be isolated from these secret allies that Florian spoke of, if they even existed, and would be forced to face those other people who would actually try something with me.

I had no friends out here. I had no understanding of how things worked in this insane city. I didn't even have any idea how to get out of this tower if I were to somehow make an escape. All I had was the frantic whisperings of some looney that I just met who thought he was a woman.

I had no choice.

"Okay here," I said, ripping my dirty shirt in several places before passing it to Florian. "To make it look like I struggled."

"Good idea!" said Florian quickly.

Catching a glimpse of myself in the mirror I remembered that I was still wearing the paper skirt. It looked ridiculously flimsy, and I realized it was very unlikely that it would have stayed on in the event of a struggle.

Without a second thought I gripped the crinkly waist strap with both hands and ripped the skirt from around my waist, crinkling it into a loose ball before covering my crotch insecurely. Florian jumped back slightly in surprise.

"Might as well make it believable," I explained shyly.

"Oh, well, okay then," he smirked.

I don't know what came over me, but I suddenly felt very vulnerable. Seeing my naked reflection, I became aware of how disturbingly thin my arms were—how boney my knees were—how frail I looked compared to everyone else here. I was tired, weak, hungry and feeling disoriented in this foreign environment where I had to assume that everyone was my enemy. I pictured myself being attacked and abused by faceless strangers. A weak kid like me would have no chance defending myself.

Images of Michael and Alina floated into my head and I realized that they too would stand no chance defending themselves against these people; that they were almost definitely being abused beyond imagination, tortured to the limits of their young bodies. I had come here willingly in a naïve attempt to rescue them. Now, standing here naked in front of this mirror, the reality that I was powerless to do anything left me feeling like I was being slowly buried in the sand.

I was suddenly brought out of my thoughts by Florian's hand smacking me lightly on my cheek.

"Ash," he said loudly, "Hey, Ash!"

A combination of fear, panic and anger suddenly erupted inside of me and before I could stop myself, my right arm launched out in front of me, fist clenched, and cracked brutally into Florian's sparkly cheek.

He staggered backwards in a mixture of pain and surprise, and I instantly regretted what I had done, not sorry for hurting him, but afraid of what my punishment would be.

"Holy Ffffffffuck!" he sputtered, steadying himself against the wall as he rubbed his cheek . "To make it look like you fought back, right?

Man you got a good right hook there bud!"

I moved toward him aggressively. "Why didn't you help Michael and Alina?!"

Stepping back quickly with both palms up in submission Florian responded gently: "Woah, woah! Ash calm down. I tried. We tried. We're still trying."

I stepped toward him again, my fist clenched tightly, prepared to strike again.

"What does that mean? Where are they? What's happened to them?" I roared, tears welling in my eyes.

Florian had backed into the centre of the room and tripped backwards over the hem of his absurdly large dress. His left hand propped his upper body off of the floor as he reached up towards me with his right, protecting himself from another blow. In his eyes I could see genuine fear.

"Not everyone is on our side, Ash!" he said, almost pleading. "When they passed through here I told them both that there are people who are secretly trying to help them! The problem is that the people who are assigned to handle Michael and Alina aren't on our side. We can't get to them. It's different with you. We know who all of your handlers are going to be. They are with us."

"What do you mean 'handlers'?" I asked.

"There's a department of people who organize the schedules of people like you who come through here: what you eat, when you eat, how you look, any …. 'appointments' that you have. They control your every move while you're here."

"Appointments…" I muttered. "Sexual stuff, you mean."

Florian flinched before nodding regretfully. "Mostly."

"Are they both still alive?" I asked, lowering my fist slightly, nervous to hear the response.

"Yes," he responded with certainty. "Let me up and let me do my work and we will talk as I go. I don't have much time left with you today."

I nodded in cautious agreement. Florian pushed himself off the floor and made a grand display of dusting himself off and adjusting his rock solid hairdo, reminding me that now that we were back in view of the cameras, the act was back on.

Thrusting his chin high in the air, both hands placed on his hips in a very feminine stance he approached me slowly but assertively.

"I'm going to act like I'm angry at you and treating you like a troublesome kid, but remember, they can't hear us," he said in his deep voice. "Just stand there, listen and do what I say."

Once again he circled me slowly, looking me up and down like a bird about to swoop in on its prey.

"For the record," he said assertively, his hands prodding me to stand up straighter, "just so you don't feel completely uncomfortable, this, " he stopped, gesturing to his outfit, "is just an act. I actually like girls. I wouldn't dress and act like this if I didn't have to."

I shook my head in disbelief. "What?!"

"Yeah... I've been here all my life," he began. "I didn't have the luxury of being in a distant barn to isolate me from the things that happen in this effed up place. Sorry, I don't mean to call the barn 'luxurious,' but I just mean.... the people here have been using me for their own entertainment since before I can remember." His voice cracked with a hint of shame. "Some of the things they did to me could have killed me. Sometimes I wish it had.

When I was about ten, some guy was brought in to fulfil Mr. Irvine's sick needs after I had failed to fulfil him. He was extremely feminine—long blonde hair like a girl, walked with a swish—even had rags stuffed in his shirt to look like he had boobs. The ugliest girl you'd ever seen too! It wasn't just the look though. It was an attitude: So over the top flamboyant and bitchy that it was almost disturbing. Most people couldn't stand to be around him."
Florian ran his fingers through my tussled hair, feigning effort to get it to look presentable as he continued.

"Mr. Irvine wouldn't let this guy near him even though the guy seemed to be genuinely interested in letting him have his way with him. The strange thing was that Mr. Irvine seemed amused by this fem guy and they ended up talking and joking with each other. A week or so later, this guy was Mr. Irvine's personal assistant."

Florian let out a heavy sigh.

"That's when I gave up everything about who I truly am: Over a few months I started acting more and more feminine, dressing in outrageous woman's clothes and talking in that annoying high pitched voice making sure I was as talkative and irritating as possible. I hated it, but eventually Mr. Irvine lost interest in me.

For a while he sent me out to other clients, but even they lost interest quickly.

I was 15 the last time anything like that happened.

Because I was so flamboyant, I was set up as an assistant to the wardrobe consultant at the time. She vanished a year ago, so now I am in charge here and people generally leave me alone."

"I—that's awful," I whispered, feeling genuine sympathy for Florian.

"Hey, don't worry about me. I'm not looking for pity," Florian replied sharply, waving his hands around as if he were furious with me. "I just need you to understand who I am so you trust me."

I thought about what he said for a moment. If even half of what he said was true, Florian had lived through a nightmare. He would have felt so terrified at every moment of his life; so alone.   Florian would have every reason in the world to take part in this secret mission to rally troops against Mr. Irvine and his people.

I looked into his light green eyes searching for any sign of deceit. All I could see as he stared back were the sad eyes of a man pleading for help.

"What is it that you're trying to do?" I asked coolly, concealing any indication as to whether I believed his story or not.

He looked at me with conviction.

"Kill Mr. Irvine," he responded bitterly.

****

My stomach rumbled with hunger .

A young woman with skin as black as night and short hair as white as a cloud had interrupted our conversation and taken me wordlessly into an adjacent room where she set me down in a tub of hot water and scrubbed every inch of my body with unabashed meticulousness.

Florian had told me that her name was Chiku as she ushered me from the room, explaining that she was just going to take me to be washed properly and that she would bring me back to him to be dressed. Just as the door closed behind me, he poked me in my rib to get my attention. As I turned to look at him he shook his head ever so slightly: This woman was not on our side.

The bubbles in the tub smelled like sweet fruits, yet a quick sampling proved that they were clearly not edible. My mouth drooled in reaction to the bitter taste so I scooped a palm full of hot water as it fell from the faucet.

Seeing my actions, Chiku handed me a small bottle of cool water from behind her. Distrustful of her motives, knowing that the sleeping drug was often given to us through our water source in the barn, I shook my head 'no' and pushed the bottle away. Surprising to me, Chiku shrugged her shoulders before picking up the bottle and taking a small sip. Again, she offered the bottle, having figured out my concern and proven it unwarranted.

Other than the small bit of water that Florian had given me, I hadn't eaten or drank anything since yesterday. My stomach rumbled again as the smell of pineapple tempted my hunger, the bitterness of the soap in my mouth begging to be rinsed away. At this moment I needed that water more than anything else.

Gently, I took the clear bottle from Chiku's hand. I watched her eyes as they followed the bottle to my lips. Her face was unreadable and emotionless. I sniffed the opening for any sign of contamination without really knowing what to smell for: everything was different here, even the water. I was used to the musty, brackish water that flowed from the faucet in the barn.

Finally giving in to my body's demands, I closed my eyes and took a sip.

The feeling of cool, clean, tasteless water on my tongue was unbelievably refreshing and I was barely able to stop for a breath of air as I poured the rest of the water down my throat. The physical gratification sparked a wave of euphoric panic inside me as my body seemed desperate for more.

Chiku, seemingly having foreseen my reaction, took another bottle from behind her, twisted the lid off with a snap and sipped it lightly before replacing the drained bottle in my hand with the full one.

I drank it voraciously.

"Thank you," I said lightly as she took the second empty bottle from me and began scrubbing my arm briskly.

For the remainder of my bath, neither Chiku or myself said a word. As she scrubbed I noticed that both of her dark wrists were calloused and rough like the soles of my feet after a long summer of walking on the shelly beach.

Following the skin up her arms, a pattern of pink scars led like ladders to her shoulders. Dark black, uneven rings circled her neck, some scarred permanently beneath her flesh, others raised and raw, clearly fresh. I looked up to her eyes, which remained downcast and averted from mine, but despite her coal-black skin I could see dark bruising and puffiness around both eyes.

This girl had been beaten and tortured very recently.

As if reading my thoughts, Chiku's hands began to shake as they lathered my skin. I wanted to whisper some words of comfort, but I had no concept of what she had been through, or what I could say that would even remotely soothe her.

I thought back to the moment when Florian poke me and shook his head as Chiku took me from the finishing department. I realized then that Florian hadn't been warning me that this poor girl was against us, he was asking me to be gentle with her.

******

After bathing me and cleaning my teeth, Chiku escorted me back to Florian's room. I was completely naked as we walked the few steps from one room to another, passing a small group of men dressed in ornate gold, silver or red jackets and matching pants. Not one of the four men showed any hesitation in stopping to touch my body in various places, mumbling in some unknown language, sizing me up as if they were picking out a fresh piece of fruit before moving on as if it had been the most normal thing in the world. Chiku stood off to the side, cowering in the shelter of a fake tree until the men passed.

Shaken, I walked into the room to find Florian waiting with a scowl on his painted face, looking convincingly annoyed.

"Finally!" he said rudely to Chiku as she skittered back down the hall behind us.

"Well that's better," he said with an explosion of flair, apparently forgetting to drop his fake accent. "My, my, you do clean up well! Let me look at you!" As he did before, Florian walked in a circle around me, looking at every inch of my body.

"What happens now?" I asked quietly, afraid of the answer.

"We get you dressed and ready for dinner," he replied perkily, his voice chirping an octave sharper than normal.

"Okay," I said impatiently, having expected more information. "And then what?"

"Thennnnnnnnnnn…," Florian replied playfully, tapping his finger on the tip of my nose. "You. Go. To. Dinner."

"Enough Florian."

My heart felt like it leapt into my mouth. I had no idea that the door behind me hadn't closed, or that someone was standing there. I stood frozen in my position, watching my reflection in the mirror ahead of me. Whoever was at the door was hidden from my view by my own body.

"Get him dressed now," commanded the mysterious voice . "Dinner is in five minutes."

The door slid shut with a hiss.

Florian hurriedly pushed me into the centre of the room.

"We don't have any time," he said in a muffled panic. "He will want you in the dining room before dinner's served so you need to move quickly."

"That's Mr. Irvine," I stated blandly.

"Yes," Florian said, pausing momentarily to acknowledge the significance of this first meeting.

"What's going to happen?" I asked for the second time, hoping for an honest response.

"Hopefully just an introduction," Florian said without conviction, sliding a crisp white shirt over my shoulders. "It's going to be a formal dinner. Be polite, don't talk much, follow what he does. Just, PLEASE don't pick the food up with your hands. I haven't had enough time to show you proper manners!"

"How do you people eat without using your hands?!" I asked, thoroughly confused. In the barn, we had no other means of picking up food other than our bare hands.

"Utensils! Fork—knife—Spoon!" he said with exasperation. "Just watch what Mr. Irvine does and copy him."

For the next few minutes Florian raced around the room in an attempt to find a suitable pair of matching pants and shoes for me to wear to dinner. Flustered by the strict time constraints, he eventually decided on a pair of plain white pants and similarly plain white leather shoes, all of which felt just a bit too tight.

The door slid open at the end of the room just as Florian secured a white belt around my waist despite the tight fitting pants.

"Oh god," he whispered, stepping back to have a dissatisfied look at me. "It'll have to do."

He ran his hands hopelessly through my messy, damp hair before smearing a thick white paste through it to flatten it down.

"Be polite, be humble, don't cause problems. Do what you're told."

In his voice I could hear compassion and the promise that he would continue to be on my side, but in my heart I worried that Florian's words were just empty promises of hope that he could never deliver on.

****

162

The crunchy white shirt and pants that I was wearing scratched at my skin like a burlap sack and the tight shoes tripped me up with every step as I walked behind an armed guard. Dizzying windows looking out onto the vast city far below were everywhere and I focused on the uncomfortable clothing to keep my brain from succumbing to vertigo.

Emotions rolled like waves over me as I headed towards the man I hated despite having never met him: Fear made my hands shake, nervousness dried my throat, anger clenched my jaw, sadness left my gut sick as I thought about what condition Michael and Alina could be in.

I was about to meet the person who stole my life away from me; the person who used me and everyone I had ever known as toys for his amusement, who made us starve and suffer for almost every moment of our lives. The person who tortured, abused, and even killed people that I loved. He had been watching me every moment of my life. He knew everything about me yet I knew nothing about him.

And yet, for some reason, the overwhelming feeling that washed over me was a sense of power.

The soldier leading me came to an abrupt stop in front of one of the many plain white doors in a long corridor, spinning mechanically in his spot to face me, his weapon held firmly across his chest prepared for conflict.

I stopped in my tracks in front of the man. Behind a clear protective shield, the face of an old, battle weary man stared back at me with menace. I stared back defiantly as he swiped his white card over the black mechanism that opened the door. My heart jumped at the sound of the swishing door but I fought every natural impulse to show any outwardly signs of fear.

I turned as casually as possible towards the open door, reminding myself to breathe as I stepped over the threshold, every sense in my body suddenly alive and burning with activity.

The room before me was astoundingly beautiful. Enormous, heavily draped windows stretched from the floor to the elaborately carved, barreled ceiling hanging high above, painted with brightly coloured images of remarkably realistic clouds and dozens of fat children and young kids with wings.

Every solid surface glistened with gold embellishments in the shape of more winged children in various poses, as well as leaves, spirals and other geometric shapes that reflected the beaming sunlight onto the blood red walls and curtains like a burst of stars. The highly polished white stone floor was like a mirror as I stepped onto it, reflecting my upside down image amongst the clouds of children that floated in the ceiling above me.

Golden urns of flowers encircled the room, all varying in colour, type and size, filling the large room with their sweet scent, somehow seeming surreal and natural at the same time.

In the centre of the grand room, hanging like an upside down, multi-tiered tree decorated in clear glittery jewels, a light fixture illuminated the room from branches adorned with a hundred flickering candles.

Beneath the grand chandelier sat a thick rectangular table with golden legs that resembled the paw of one of the many unknown animals that I had gnawed on many times in the barn. A heavy red cloth covered the surface of the table, spiraled with thick golden patterns that were impossibly elaborate.

Two matching chairs sat facing one another at either end of the table.

I was alone in the room.

Dark clouds had completely enveloped the world outside, making this room feel more like it was simply situated at ground level during a particularly foggy day, quickly diminishing my fear of actually being up so high.

I held my spot for only a moment before stepping further into the room to examine its incredible details more closely, shaking from a nervous eagerness to finally meet and confront Mr. Irvine.

My hard-soled shoes clicked on the stone floor as I made my way around the room looking at all of the incredible aspects of the room. I was drawn in particular to the faces of all the children painted into the ceiling and sculpted into the walls. Each one was unique, some just babies, some teenagers, so startlingly realistic that they almost seemed like live children, and I half-expected some of them to turn to look at me as I came close to them. So many of them seemed familiar to me, like the faces of old friends long since forgotten. I followed the images around the room and noticed that they seemed, clearer, newer somehow as I moved, as if they hadn't all been created at the same time.

It wasn't until I neared the fourth wall that I saw it: A life sized painting half way up the wall of a small, smiling boy, just a toddler still, with distinctive blue-grey eyes and brown hair and a smile that lit up the room. I flashed back instantly to one of my first memories, the vision suddenly clearer than it ever had been: a strange young boy with light brown hair, wearing a bright white shirt and clean shorts, waking up happily on the floor of the entry room in the barn, his blue-grey eyes meeting mine with a huge smile before he embraced me and we ran off to play together.

Michael.

I couldn't believe it. I leaned in to look closer. The smile, his eyes, his posture even; it was undeniably him.

Flabbergasted, I looked to the faces of others painted on the wall. Moving to the right along the faces, none rang familiar, but each one was so unique and detailed that I couldn't help but feel that these faces too were those of real children.

My feelings were confirmed as I moved along the wall. Tucked in a corner, almost hidden by the shadow of a heavy red curtain was the image of a tiny, frail little girl with thin blonde hair and sad eyes: Alina.

Quickly I set about searching the faces of others that I had passed thus far on the wall. At first I didn't recognize anyone. Michael, Alina and I were the only kids that lived in the barn. The rest were much older than us. It was a picture of Julie that I found next. At first I thought it was a second image of Alina. I had almost forgotten that Julie was Alina's mother. I was astounded at the similarities: The same striking facial features, the sad eyes, the strikingly blonde hair, the boney body. She was much younger than my first memories of her, but it was definitely Julie.

I then started imagining what each person that I knew from the barn must have looked like when they were children or teenagers. Johnna, Elin, David, Mallie, Nasha.

They were all there.

My mind reeled as I spun to look at the dozens of faces scattered all around the room and the realization set in: this was a shrine to every kid that Mr. Irvine have ever kidnapped.

"I see you are admiring my art," said a familiar voice as the mechanical door whooshed open.

Mr. Irvine.

I was astounded at the sight of the man in front of me.

Over the years I had developed my own mental image of Mr. Irvine. He was the man who ruled and controlled every moment of my life; the man who watched me late at night as I slept; the man who provided me with food or starved me close to death; the man who tortured the only people I had ever known.

He was a god in my mind: an all-powerful, all knowing deity. I had always pictured him as standing twice my height and doubling my width with impossibly large muscles. I saw him as having long, thick black hair that flew in the wind and a well-manicured, short beard that sparkled with specks of red.

I didn't expect to see an elderly, frail, hunch backed man who couldn't walk without the support of a cane.

Of course it made sense: Some of the people in the barn had been there for decades, taken by Mr. Irvine in their teens or early twenties. Several had become grey haired and lined with wrinkles themselves. He would have been older than them for sure.

I watched as Mr. Irvine shuffled his feet slowly across the large room towards the table in the centre. He was dressed immaculately. His black pants lined with grey stripes matched his jacket perfectly, tailored to compliment his thin body in a way that gave him the appearance of a slightly stronger stature as he walked. A shiny silver tie, subtly adorned with tiny reflective jewels, coordinated with a glittering silver chain that hung loosely from his left pant pocket. Thick glasses rested over the bridge of his nose, their shiny reflective rims complimenting the silver accessories.

Above everything, his shoes stood out the most. Predominantly black with wide white sections over the toes, the shoes were so shiny that they reflected the room around us almost like mirrors. To me, someone who had rarely owned shoes, let alone shoes that were even remotely clean, this was the grandest sign of true opulence.

Mr. Irvine completed his trek across the room and stood for a moment, both hands rested firmly on one of the chairs to catch his breath.

"I have waited a long time for this," he said eventually, his voice wheezing with strain.

"Come, let me see you," he said, first coughing to clear his throat when I didn't respond.

I didn't move.

"Come," he said gently, waving me over with one hand as the other held his body steady. "Don't be afraid. I have a feeling that you have the wrong opinion of me."

I wasn't feeling anything—no emotions at all. I had come into the room feeling afraid but confrontational, expecting to have to square off against a worthy competitor, not some weak, defenseless old man.

Everything that was happening seemed like a dream; that I was simply an observer with no influence or actual participation in the scene.

I was numb.

Somehow I found myself floating towards Mr. Irvine.

I stood calmly in front of him looking blankly into his black eyes. I had expected to see the eyes of the devil himself, but was shaken by the softness and sincerity that shone back at me.

A faint smile curled the left side of his mouth, barely visible beneath a heavy white mustache as he reached up to caress the side of my face.

His hand was ice cold, electrifying the nerves in my injured cheek like a splash of water in the winter, but as his fingers traced its way around my face in a motion of delicate affection, my face warmed with embarrassment.

"You've turned into such a good looking young man," he said softly, "And so kind as well. I am very proud of you."
He rested his hand lightly on my shoulder.

"You have always been my favourite you know." His voice was soothing now—somehow comforting and respectful, like the words of someone caring for a small child who had just suffered an injury.

I now realized that I was exhausted physically, emotionally strained to the limits of fear and uncertainty. My stomach had given up its roaring for sustenance and my head was dizzy with malnourishment. I felt myself lapping up his gentility, my entire being just wishing to disengage from the feeling of being constantly on guard just for a moment.

"Where are my manners?" Mr. Irvine said lightly. "Please, sit. You must be completely exhausted."

He pulled the chair out and gestured for me to take a seat. I hesitatingly obliged, relieved to be sitting once again.

"Let's get some food and drink into you and have a little chat. I'm delighted to finally get to spend some time with you. I bet you have a million questions," he said warmly, winking slyly at the last part.

Mr. Irvine moved slowly around the other side of the table and lowered himself painfully into the chair across from me. As if a pre-planned signal, two men came quickly into the room from opposite ends, both sharply dressed in suits that mimicked that of Mr. Irvine's, though clearly lower quality. One man carried a shiny circular tray supporting two heavily etched glasses and matching bottle filled with a translucent brown liquid. The other man carried a slightly larger tray holding two small loaves of steaming bread.

In absolute mirrored unison, the men placed one of each item in front of Mr. Irvine, then repeating their synchronistic routine in front of me before swiftly exiting the room from their respective doors.

My mouth began to visibly drool as the sweet scent of the warm bread hit my nose. It took every bit of restraint to keep myself from shoving the entire loaf directly into my mouth, but all I could think was that this food might be poisoned.

Seeing my desperation, Mr. Irvine leaned forward in his chair with a laugh.

"My dear boy, you can't live your life thinking that every item of food might be laced with drugs. I'm here to have a nice dinner with you. The last thing I want is for you to pass out in the middle of it!"

When I still didn't move he leaned forward again, sliding his plate of bread towards me.

"You pick which one you want and I will eat the other. Same with the drink if you would feel more comfortable," he said with a dismissive laugh.

Sensing that he was being genuine in his display that there was nothing to worry about, I tore off a piece of the bread on my plate and wolfed it down, barely chewing at all. My body seemed to suddenly operate on its own free will as it shoveled the bread into my mouth, my mind simply locked on the fact that there was food in front of me.

I found myself not only devouring my own helping of bread, but moving onto Mr. Irvine's share without the slightest hesitation.

It was only as I looked up from my plate while taking the last bite that I saw Mr. Irvine's disappointed eyes on me as he swirled his drink pensively in his left hand.

I wiped the soft crumbs off of my chin and sat up from my hunched position, suddenly aware of the spectacle that I must have been.

Self-consciously I reached for the glass of brown liquid, desperate to clear my dry throat. The drink smelled foul—like milk that had soured or fruit that had gone bad, and its odour burned my nostrils. I locked eyes with Mr. Irvine. His expression had not changed, yet, with a simple upward movement with the hand that held his glass, he encouraged me to down my drink without a word.

I hesitatingly obliged.

The taste was as foul as the smell, if not worse, but it was the burning sensation as it went down that made me almost lose my lunch right there on the table.

As the tingling subsided, the watery feeling in my throat quickly passed as well.

169

I looked down at the two empty plates in front of me.

"I'm sorry," I mumbled.

"It is I who should apologize," responded Mr. Irvine gravely.

Confused at this response I looked to his eyes once again.

"My men who picked you up were told to treat you well," he began to explain. "They are supposed to give you food and drink on the way here. They're supposed to keep you comfortable and make sure you get enough rest as well. I suppose they didn't do that?"

"They offered me some drugs but I said 'no'. "

"Motion sickness pills," Mr. Irvine stated. "Even I take them. I am impressed that you were able to tolerate your first trip in a vehicle without being sick."

"Well, I wouldn't say that…." I replied quietly.

"Ah, I see," said Mr. Irvine considerately. "It's hard to find good help these days. You will learn that people here in the outside world live by their own rules. I do my best to maintain order in my business but people will do whatever they want."

I nodded my head just enough to acknowledge that I had heard him.

The two servants quickly rushed into the room in perfect unison as they had done before, picking up the empty plates with a swift flick of their wrists, replacing them with larger plates full of thickly sliced beef, mounds of fluffy potatoes and glistening vegetables, all coated generously in a thick brown sauce. The aroma took my breath away.

The servant men disappeared as quickly as they had come. I was dying to bite into the thick slab of meat on my plate, but forced myself to wait until Mr. Irvine picked up his utensils and took his first bite before I allowed myself to start eating.

I remembered what Florian had said about copying the way that Mr. Irvine ate. I had never used a proper utensil before and found it frustratingly purposeless— more of a hindrance than helpful—but I struggled to make the fork and knife mimic what Mr. Irvine was doing with his own, finally getting a small piece of meat into my mouth around the time that Mr. Irvine had taken his third or fourth bite. It was the best thing I had ever tasted.

I looked up at Mr. Irvine briefly as I chewed the flavourful steak. He was looking back at me with a look of empathetic humour and I couldn't help but crack a faint smile, knowing that I must look ridiculous.

"Use your hands if you want," he laughed with a wink. "I won't tell anyone!"

I practically inhaled my food from that point, wiping every little speck off the shiny plate with my fingers—even the gravy. Mr. Irvine hadn't even finished half of his food by the time I started licking the food from my fingers.

"There's a napkin there, if you want it," said Mr. Irvine with a smile. I looked at the crisp, white, perfect little fold of material beside my plate and couldn't imagine soiling anything so nice. Seeing my hesitation, Mr. Irvine picked up his own napkin, which had been resting on his lap, and wiped his mouth with it. I followed in turn, changing the colour of the napkin to a streaked yellowy-brown in the process.

I sat in silence as Mr. Irvine took a few more bites of his food, before neatly crossing his fork and knife and covering his plate with his napkin.

"Old men like me don't have the same appetite as young bucks like you," he joked.

The servants once again swooped in to clear away our plates, this time leaving a tiny dish of thick white cake topped off with a single strawberry before swiftly leaving us alone once again. I could have eaten the cake in two bites, but I held myself back, using a new fork to slowly scrape away tiny pieces in an effort to make it last longer.

It wasn't until we had both completely cleaned our plates that Mr. Irvine spoke again.

"I hope you liked the food."

I nodded in acknowledgement. "I did. Yes, thank you," I muttered, sipping on the bitter beverage once more with just as much distaste as before.

"Would you prefer water?"

"Yes please," I responded. A moment later one of the servants had come and gone, replacing my brown drink with a tall glass of crystal clear water which I sparingly savored.

"So," Mr. Irvine began gently, leaning back in his chair and turning his palms towards the ceiling. "Now that we have finished our nice meal and are both relaxed, where would you like to begin?"

I didn't hesitate in my response: "Where are Michael and Alina?"

"How gallant of you!" Mr. Irvine said through a delighted smile. "I expected you to ask about this place—about me and who I am or what we do here. Surely your mind must be racing! All of this new stimulus, all these unfamiliar people and objects!"

"I'm only interested in Michael and Alina," I said coolly.

"Well now!" he said with amusement on his face. "I am impressed with your dedication to your friends."

He paused to take a sip of his dark drink. I held my stare, awaiting his response.

"I will have to inquire as to specifics," he said calmly, "but I promise you that they are dealing well with the outside world."

My heart leapt at the small glimmer of reassurance that the two were well, let alone alive, though in my mind I could not yet judge what was true or not.

"What does that mean exactly?"

"There's so much to explain, my young man," Mr. Irvine said with a grand smile. "Much of the story will be too much for you to understand. The world outside of the Barn is much larger, much more complex that you could possibly fathom at the moment."

I leaned back in my chair and crossed my arms calmly.

"Try me."

The large smile remained fixed on Mr. Irvine's face, but something ever so slight flickered in his eyes. I couldn't tell if it was a hint of annoyance, if he were happy that I asked, or if he was simply just thinking of where to begin.

"Well…," he started, clearing his throat with a cough. "I am impressed with your eagerness. Let me begin with this: I am not a bad man. I know why you may have that impression of me: Time after time you have seen your friends—people you have known your entire life—come back to life in the barn in bad shape. They have been beaten, abused, neglected and in some cases, maimed for life. Some, to my great sadness, have even died.

Again and again, these people who you love have been brought from the barn into this outside world—to me—and nearly every time they return in poor shape.

From your perspective I must look like the Devil himself. I can understand that. But you don't know the truth." At this, Mr. Irvine turned in his chair and leaned forward to lock his eyes with mine.

"I am here to help," he said softly.

I stared back unflinching.

"Ash," he continued, leaning back in his chair reflectively. "Asha. Do you remember being called that?"

I nodded slightly. It had been my childhood name. I hadn't heard it used since I was a toddler.

"I always liked that name. In Hindi it means 'Hope'. Did you know that?"

"No," I mumbled.

"It's usually a girl's name, but I always thought it suited you. I've always had high hopes for you.

I like 'Ash' though. It sounds tough, manly!" he laughed, grunting as he said the word 'manly.'

The smile on his face faded when I still remained unmoved. He repositioned himself in his chair, wincing slightly in discomfort in the process.

"I knew your mother," he said emptily.

I felt as if I had been punched in the gut. In all my years in the barn, I had never wondered about my real parents. The idea that every child had parents that were anything more than biological donors had never occurred to me. I knew from Michael's stories that he had had parents. I had heard others talking of the families that they desperately missed--I had even witnessed Alina's grotesque birth--But all I had ever known was the group of people in the barn with me. They were my family. They were my parents. Nobody ever led me to believe otherwise, leading me intentionally away from questions of the normal outside world as much as possible.

The concept that someone had once cared for me as their own child floored me.

"She was a sweet, intelligent girl," Mr. Irvine explained. Content glimmered in his eyes as he realized that he had peaked my interest. "You have her brown hair and eyes."

He leaned forward as he spoke, whispering softly enough that I had to lean in to hear him.

"She was from a very powerful, very well-known family. When bad times befell them, I was the only person left who could help her. She brought you to me when she could no longer care for you. She had no choice." He paused for dramatic effect. "Her and I were friends. Nobody here knows that."

He leaned confidently back in his chair.

I pondered his words for a moment before finally speaking.

"What happened to her and her family?"

"They disappeared."

"Dead?" I pushed.

"Possibly," he said with a hint of sadness. "I would be inclined to believe so."

174

My heart felt heavy at hearing this. Only moments ago I felt the first pangs of love in my chest for someone I had never known, and already the possibility of ever finding out if that love could actually exist was smashed to bits.

"What do you mean she brought me to you because she had no choice?" I mumbled, looking down at my fidgeting fingers.

"Her family—your family—had been under a great amount of public scrutiny because of some political dealings that went awry. They were forced to flee in the middle of the night." He leaned forward again to lock eyes with me and spoke softly.

"She knew that she would not be able to protect you from the people that were chasing them. She asked me to hide you from them and keep you safe."

I shook my head with confusion. "So you locked me in a desolate barn for my whole life?"

"It was the only place that I knew people could never find you," he said earnestly. "That's why I had cameras everywhere—for your own security. To be prepared if the barn was ever discovered."

"And the others? Why were they in the barn?"

"They all have their own stories," he explained. "And unfortunately, I can't share their secrets with you. Some don't even know themselves why they are there. The common thread though is that not a single one of those people in the barn would be alive today had I not been able to take them in and keep them hidden."

"So you're saying...." I struggled to process this new line of thought. "You're saying that you saved me. Saved everyone in the barn."

"I've never thought of myself as a savior. What kind of person would I be if I stood back without offering to help?" he replied humbly.

"Then why would you steal people from the barn in the middle of the night, torture and abuse them, then send them back clinging to life?" I snapped angrily.

"Ah," he sighed, his head drooping forlornly. "That is something that haunts my dreams every night.

What I try to do is rehabilitate. When my associates and I perceive that the threat to an individual in the outside world has diminished or has ended entirely, we begin a re-integration program. The individual is removed from the barn, brought to us here to be cleaned, fed and schooled on the workings of a normal everyday life.

For some, particularly those who don't remember life outside of the Barn, that education is a lengthy process and can be completely overwhelming. Even for those who had a life before being put into hiding, it is a process that can be too much to handle.

Once it has been determined that a person is fit to re-enter society, they are placed in half-way houses—homes where they are free to interact with the general public, but still have a stable place to call home.

Unfortunately, there are often complications.

People get mixed up in the wrong crowds, often in an attempt to locate people from their old lives. I try to intervene, but do my best to encourage them to make their own path in life.

Sometimes people just have bad luck." He let out a great sigh. "I step in only when it is clear that their rehabilitation attempt has failed."

"So you bring them back to the Barn until you think they are ready to try again." I said.

"Precisely."

"But what about people like Julie? People that you took every week or two and only kept for a few days at a time?" I challenged.

"Again, everyone has their own story and I can't go into specifics," he replied formally. "But Julie passed away years ago. Strictly between you and I," he lowered his voice slightly and winked at me. "Julie got into the wrong crowd: a group of 'Women of the night.' Prostitutes. She enjoyed the power that she had over men when she had them alone. She was very popular and made a lot of money."

"What use is money if she was being sent back to the barn all the time?"

"Sent? She requested it. She felt safe there. It was her way of rejuvenating herself," explained Mr. Irvine. "As for the money, I don't know what she did with any of it. That secret died with her."

"Why take people in the middle of the night if this is a project to benefit them?"

"Fear," he replied quickly. "After being in a secluded barn, coming to the outside world is a scary thing. Collecting a person in the middle of the night keeps everyone calm."

My head was spinning. It was all too much to comprehend. Mr. Irvine had an answer for everything and it all made sense. Everything about him—his body language, his eye contact, his tone of voice—came across as genuine and sincere. He said it himself: I had always thought of him as the Devil; a horrible man who held us captive and used us all for his own pleasure. This man before me sat in stark contrast to any image I had ever imagined him to be.

I found myself doubting my old opinions about him. I could understand now why the others from the barn had come back so terrified of the outside world; why they blamed Mr. Irvine for all of their suffering. I couldn't specifically remember a time when someone had outwardly said that it had been Mr. Irvine himself who had hurt them. Sure, some hated him, but if what Mr. Irvine had said about some people not even knowing who or what circumstances had brought them to his care, I could understand their skewed perception of him.

"You let us starve. You sent us a *letter* telling us that one person had to be chosen to starve to death. " I said in a final plea for clarification.

Mr. Irvine's head once again drooped sadly.

"There are times, yes, that I did not provide the necessities of life for you." He crossed his arms over his chest as body language tightened, evidently ridden with guilt. I detected a faint crack in his voice as he continued: "I admit that there are times when I intentionally withheld food or water. It was punishment. There were a lot of things that went on while you were asleep in the barn, or while people were here at the tower with me. Things that would compromise my ability to keep everyone safe and hidden. Those who were the culprits knew exactly why everyone was being reprimanded. I never intended for anyone to die."

He leaned forward, picking up my glass of water and drank the last drop.

"Over the years there has been many times where the connection to the barn was lost: power outages, storms. Times where my company was under close scrutiny from others and I had to remain distant to protect our secret.

And then there was my health: I am an old man. I have been in the hospital for weeks at a time for years now and have no protégé, no 'second in command' with the authority to monitor the well-being of the people in the Barn.

Only once has this been a problem: The weeks leading up to Johnna's death. The day after she had volunteered and I sent the feast, I underwent emergency surgery to clear a blocked artery. I had intended to send a message permitting Johnna to begin eating again. By the time I got out of the hospital it was too late for her. I walked into my office just as you were all huddled around her, kissing her forehead one by one. I felt horrible. I will carry that guilt with me until I die."

Mr. Irvine paused for a moment to pull a scarlet handkerchief from his breast pocket and wipe an invisible tear from behind his thick rimmed glasses.

"I always tried to make up for my shortcomings by providing grand feasts," he said, almost pleading for forgiveness. "I did everything that I could to keep you all safe. You have to believe that."

I felt myself nod just slightly despite myself, still not sure how much I could believe.

Silence lingered for an uncomfortably long amount of time. Mr. Irvine sat quietly in his chair, staring thoughtfully at the handkerchief in his hand, occasionally wiping beneath his silver-rimmed glasses. All indications presented the image of a broken, defeated man who was being haunted by his failures in life.

I felt a twitch of sympathy for him. If even a portion of what he spoke of were true, I owed this man my life.

"I believe it is time for bed," Mr. Irvine said finally with a sigh.

I suddenly realized how absolutely exhausted I was. It had been almost a full day and night since I had a natural, undisturbed sleep, but it was the mental and emotional exhaustion that now drifted over me like a thick cloud.

Mr. Irvine tucked his handkerchief into his breast pocket and straightened his coat, then reached for his cane as he struggled to lift himself from his chair. I stood quickly and waited obediently as Mr. Irvine rocked forward a second time to propel his old body upward. He managed to get himself halfway to a standing position before falling heavily back to his chair with a groan.

"These old knees aren't what they used to be," he said breathless and embarrassed.

I held my position, surprised to see the effects of aging to this extent.

He tried again, this time rocking his weight forward even harder. Mr. Irvine popped up from his seated position with surprising speed and I could tell immediately that he had too much velocity. I saw his left foot trip over his right and his cane fall from his grip before he even realized what was happening. In an instant I found myself in front of him, arms outstretched to catch him as he tipped forward towards the hard ground. He fell hard into me, his chin slamming forcefully into my chest and his right arm wrapping over my shoulder as I threw my arms under his.
A second later it was over and we were left in a stunned, awkward embrace.

Mr. Irvine slowly pulled his feet forward and raised himself to a steady position, still holding me tightly for stability. He raised his dark eyes level with mine, his nose so close to mine that I could smell the sweet mixture of cake and alcohol on his breath.

With his free hand he reach up and held the back of my neck tenderly.

"Thank you," he said breathlessly.

Feeling suddenly very uneasy, I took a small step back, putting a few inches of distance between us, still supporting the majority of Mr. Irvine's weight.

One of the servants silently swooped into the room, quickly picking up the fallen cane and placing it back into Mr. Irvine's hand before rushing back out the same door he came through.

Mr. Irvine steadied himself, keeping his left arm tightly around my waist in more of an embrace than a means of support.

"You're a good boy," he said lightly, squeezing me tightly as he spoke.

I didn't know how to react. I felt so uncomfortable being this close with a complete stranger. Physical contact with another was something that hadn't had much experience with. The only people who ever really embraced me had been Nasha, Michael and Alina.

While I found something distressing about being so close to this old man that I had previously thought of as an enemy—and was still uncertain of-- somewhere inside I felt a tiny tingle of comfort in the tightness of his grasp.
I wasn't sure if I should peel myself away or stay close in case Mr. Irvine had another fall, but soon had no choice as Mr. Irvine took a step towards the door, guiding me beside him.

We walked in silence together towards the door. As it whooshed open, I caught one last look at the image of Michael as a toddler painted on the wall. His wide smile shone up at me brightly but this time I noticed something in his eyes—a sadness, a pleading—as if he had just witnessed something scary but was putting on a brave face.

I felt like I was abandoning him as the white door hissed shut behind us.

****

We had wound our way through a maze of hallways, up an elevator, and past several people who pressed their backs against the walls and lowered their eyes.

I couldn't tell whether it were out of respect or fear.

Just before entering the bedroom, Florian rounded the corner in front of us, lowering his head and backing away just as all the others had done. As Mr. Irvine and I passed, he briefly raised his eyes to mine. In them I saw a mixture of sadness and support.

The bedroom was not at all as I had expected.

As in the dining room, huge windows stretched across the length of the left wall from the floor to the ceiling, draped with thick, textured red and gold curtains that matched the luxurious blankets on the massive bed to the right of the door.

The wall directly across from the door held a giant, blurry painting of a small child on a bright red background, the details of the face entirely indistinct save for piercing green eyes that stared back at me with innocence, and seemed to follow me as I moved around the room.

Below the painting, stretching the full length of the wall, a fire raged inside a narrow recess, radiating heat throughout the entire room, its silent flames casting flickering shadows that seemed to fill the room with movement. Despite the heat, my skin crawled with goose bumps and I shivered with a chill of nervousness.

A huge glass tank covered the entire wall to the right of the bed, teaming with bright fish, corals and sea creatures, many similar to some of the fish that I had caught and eaten back at the barn. My memory flashed back to the day when Michael first spoke of being brought to the barn. He had said that Mr. Irvine had a 'wall of fish'. I could never quite picture what he meant by this, but I understood now that this is the wall he was speaking of. He had been in this room.

I wasn't surprised to see that cameras hung from all four corners of the ceiling.

"Welcome to my sanctuary," Mr. Irvine said with a grand swoop of his arm, encouraging me to enter further.

I took a few steps into the room, stopping to lean against one of two large padded chairs that faced the fireplace.

Mr. Irvine approached me surprisingly quickly compared to the way he had been shuffling in the dining room, stopping at my side to drape one arm over my shoulders while he patted my belly with the other. I felt myself twitch involuntarily at his touch.

"Now that you have some food in you, you must be exhausted," he said softly.

I nodded slightly.

"Yes?"

"Yes," I said obediently.

"Good, good," he said, moving his hand from my shoulder slowly down my back.

"We should get you washed up then," he said, still speaking gently. "Come with me please."

I felt his hand slide down my arm and into mine, interlocking our fingers gently before guiding me into a side room that I had not spotted before. I noticed again that he was walking much more sure-footedly than he had been before.

The next room was nearly half the size of the bedroom. The floors and the walls were made from large glossy white tiles that were nearly as reflective as the large mirror that spanned the length of the room. Dim lighting grew brighter automatically as we entered.

A camera whirred above, turning to watch us from above.

"Let's get you out of this starchy outfit," Mr. Irvine said, unbuttoning my shirt, slipping it off of me in a slow, careful motion.

Next he knelt down slowly but with ease to slip the heavy shoes and socks from my feet.

From his kneeling position, he gently reached up to unzip and remove my pants. He pulled them down unusually gently, as if he didn't want the 'starchy' material to scratch me as it slid down my skin.

I felt myself tense up as he exposed me. Having grown up in a barn with no privacy, nudity around others had always been a normal part of my life, but until today no one had ever helped me undress.

I had been shy and uncomfortable as both Dr. Sarah and Florian had examined or dressed me, but something about this situation felt different; Mr. Irvine's touch was somehow more personal, more intimate than the others had been. It felt indecent, but at the same time somehow instinctually stimulating despite my conscious discomfort. My face warmed with embarrassment as my skin seemed to grow ice cold with nervousness.

I stood naked in front of him as he remained kneeling in front of me, looking me up and down confidently.

"You are a good looking young man," he said, stone faced as he stood up effortlessly, stepping back to get a full length view of me.

He pulled a small white object from his pocket and held it in front of him as I stood motionless.

"Turn around," He said, somewhat directly.

I obliged.

"Beautiful," he said under his breath.

He put the object back into his pocket, stepping close to me and resting his hand on my lower back.

"Let's get you into the shower," he said with a smile and a gentle push, guiding me into a large glass enclosure.

Although the walls were transparent, the small space made me feel too closed in and I felt my anxiety growing. The tension must have shown on my face, as Mr. Irvine stepped in with me and caressed my back.

"You're not accustomed to all these walls," he said with a tone of consideration, his face so close to mine that I could feel his breath on my bare shoulder.

"You'll enjoy this though. It will help you relax."

Mr. Irvine leaned forward, his chest pressing on my back, as he reached to turn an ornate, golden knob on the wall.
I jumped in surprise as ice cold water shot from a silver plate in the ceiling like a midsummer rain storm, instantly soaking my whole body and all of Mr. Irvine's left arm as he backed out of the stall. A moment later the water turned warm, then hot.

It felt amazing.

I had really enjoyed the bath that Chiku had given me—it had been soothing to my sore, dirty skin—but the sensation of a million tiny drops hitting my flesh in a gentle massage, streaming down my neck, over my chest and back, tickling my legs and feet was unlike anything I had ever felt, and despite the heat, goose bumps of pleasure spread across my body.

I stood under the steady rain flow enjoying the comforting warmth for a while, my eyes closed, my mouth occasionally sputtering water that filled my mouth as I breathed calmly. I found myself transported back to the barn.

It had been extremely rare to have hot water pour from our little rusted pipe—a luxury that was mainly reserved for cleaning our tattered clothing or our rudimentary cutting tools and serving plates. Occasionally the adults would collect some warm water in a basin and bathe themselves with an old rag, but by the time it was my turn the water had been luke-warm at best, soiled from the filth of the others who had come before me. During the summers I would bathe in the cool ocean using coarse sand to scrub the layers of filth from my skin. It had been the only way to get clean.

"Wave your hand under the silver spigot and soap will come out," echoed Mr. Irvine's voice from outside the stall, bringing my mind back to reality.

I did as he suggested, getting a palm full of a thick, green gooey liquid that smelled musty but appealing. I stepped away from the direct flow of the water as I lathered a bubbly white foam over my whole body, my hands sliding over my skin in a way that I found oddly entertaining.

I massaged the suds through my hair, surprised to not feel fine grains of sand that I had always been so used to.
"The other spigot has shampoo in it for your hair," Mr. Irvine said with a laugh.

Surprised by the concept of using two different types of soap, I decided to try it and was pleasantly amazed that my hair still grew softer, my fingers sliding through it effortlessly as the crunchy paste that had been holding my hair so firmly in place washed away completely.

"That's perfect," mumbled Mr. Irvine.

I looked over at him, confused by his statement. He was leaning back against the countertop casually, his eyes locked on the white device that he held in his hand.

In the mirror behind him I could see a reflection of the other side of the object that he was holding. In the window of the small machine I saw a miniature version of myself standing naked in the steaming shower, staring confusedly back.

A camera.

****

I dried myself off with the softest towel that I had ever felt before sliding into a pair of bright white underwear that Mr. Irvine handed to me. He led me over to the sink and used his fingers to style my hair in a way that he thought suited my face, then showed me how to brush my teeth properly—something that I had never done before.

When he was satisfied with my efforts he took my hand and led me back in to the bedroom.

"I'm absolutely exhausted," he said with an exaggerated yawn. "I can't imagine how you must feel."

"A little tired I guess," I responded blandly even though I felt tired enough to fall asleep standing up.

He walked to the side of the great bed, turning down the sheets and indicating for me to get in.

"Make yourself comfortable," he said soothingly.

The bed was unlike anything I had ever experienced. I had been so accustomed to sleeping on a rigid wooden platform or a cold, sometimes damp dirt floor with little more than a pile of dusty old straw to soften the base. I had never found that set up to be comfortable, but it's familiarity had always inspired immediate sleep. As I slipped my nearly naked body beneath the heavy comforter and silky smooth, warm sheets, I felt as if I were crawling into a warm pool of air that wrapped itself around me like a hug. The pillow below my head, something that I was entirely unaccustomed to, felt instantly relieving and I wondered how I had gone my whole life without one.

Mr. Irvine tucked the sheets in around me loosely.

"It feels nice doesn't it?" he hummed, sitting on the edge of the bed, looking down on me with a smile.

"So soft," I replied with a slight nod of my head. "Where are the others?"

"The others?" he asked, confused.

"Everyone else," I clarified. "When do they come in to sleep?"

He smiled in comprehension.

"Ah, all of the employees. Of course." He stood up from the bed with ease and removed his striped black jacket and folded it gingerly on one of the chairs near the fire.

"You are accustomed to sleeping in the same room with everyone. Things are a bit different here than they are in the barn," he said with a wink. "This is a very large building. There are many rooms to sleep in, so we often only have a few people in each bedroom."

"Just us in here?" I asked, sounding like a small, nervous child.

"Just us, yes," he replied, unbuttoning and removing his shirt, revealing yet another sleeveless white shirt beneath, lined heavily around the openings with a mat of thick white chest hair.

He untied and slid off his shoes and pulled off his dark pants and socks with ease, his eyes locked in my direction, though I intentionally averted my gaze to other things around the room.

"I don't look bad for an old man, do I?" he asked softly, drawing my eyes back towards him for a quick moment. I looked him up and down quickly. He stood straight-backed and broad shouldered in stark contrast to the hunched over way he had stood when we first met.

"You seemed older when I first saw you," I pointed out.

He laughed lightly. "I always feel much better after a hearty meal."

186

He walked around to the other side of the bed, drawing the covers back meticulously, then crawled in quietly beside me. Although the bed was huge, he slid right over beside me, pressing his chest lightly against my side, draping his arm across my chest in a way that reminded me of how I used to sleep with Alina and Michael.

"I know this is all very new to you, and your mind must be racing," he whispered lightly. "but I will be right here beside you. Try to relax."

I nodded my head lightly, my eyes wide open as the lights dimmed slowly.

I could feel myself shaking despite the warmth in the room. I had spent countless nights unashamedly curled up tightly with others from the barn trying to retain body heat, or simply holding each other for emotional support. The sensation of Mr. Irvine's bristly, dry arm across my chest brought me neither warmth or emotional support. Instead, I felt restrained, trapped.

Light from the fireplace flickered around the room.

I felt Mr. Irvine's hand slide slowly from my shoulder towards the centre of my chest. My pulse thudded in my throat.

The hairs of his chin were scratchy against my shoulder. His sour breath stung my nostrils. I tried to breathe through my mouth but even then I could almost taste the bitterness as he exhaled.

His body was loose and relaxed against my tense muscles.

After a few minutes I felt his hand slide slowly down towards my navel.

I focused my eyes on an empty spot on the ceiling and tried to control my breathing. My heart was beating so strongly in my chest that I could barely stay still.

A moment later I felt Mr. Irvine's hand reach the band of my underwear.

My eyes flicked to another empty spot on the wall and I felt my fists involuntarily clench shut.

We laid in unmoving silence for several more minutes before I felt his hand move once again.

As his finger slipped beneath my underwear I suddenly found myself jumping up from the bed and running to the side of the fireplace, shaking with disgust and fear.

"I'm sorry Ash!" pleaded Mr. Irvine. "I didn't mean to make you feel uncomfortable. I must have moved in my sleep."

I knew that he was lying. I felt that he knew what he was doing, and that it was completely intentional. I wanted to run, to hide somewhere, but I didn't know where to go.

"Look at me, Ash," Mr. Irvine said quietly, siting up in the bed. "I'm sorry. Excuse an old man. I am the only one out here who cares about you."

I stood silently beside the fire, still shivering despite the warmth. My nerves were completely shot. My head was spinning. I was exhausted. I felt so alone and lost.

"Come back to bed," Mr. Irvine said gently. "I'll stay here with you, but I'll put a pillow between us so I don't bother you in my sleep."

Staring into the flame of the fire I was suddenly brought back to the first day that Michael and I had been allowed to venture out into the ocean while others were kept back by gun fire. Julie had explained to the group that Michael and I were allowed special privileges because of the fact that we were sweet, pristine, trusting children that Mr. Irvine was grooming. I had never understood this conversation but now it all seemed to make so much sense to me now.

"Ash?"

Feeling the soft carpet between my toes I heard myself mumble "I'll just sleep here."

Mr. Irvine let out a light sigh. "Suit yourself."

I laid down on the soft floor, turning my back to Mr. Irvine and stared into the flickering flames of the fire. Behind me I could hear Mr. Irvine slide out of bed. He was walking slowly towards me. In my mind I heard myself screaming 'Leave me alone!' But nothing came out of my mouth. My already quickly beating heart began to beat even quicker as he drew closer and I was more afraid of what was about to happen than I had been of anything all day.

And then I felt a sheet drape lightly over me, heard a pillow being placed gently beside my head, and hear Mr. Irvine's footsteps as he walked back to the bed and crawled in.

"Goodnight Ash," he whispered.

I thought I would never fall asleep, but there was something familiar and comforting about slaying in front of a fire, even though this modern fireplace was vastly different than the smoky fire pit that I was used to.

Within seconds my eyes began to feel overpoweringly heavy and before I knew it, my mind was lost in dreams of sleeping on an uncomfortable wooden platform, tightly hugging Alina and Michael.

****

I woke up shivering from the cold.

Not a single flame flickered in the fireplace in front of me. The room was almost completely dark except for a small clock on a table beside the bed whose green numbers shone "2:34." I felt as if I would be able to see my own breath had there been sufficient lighting.

I laid a still as I could, willing myself to forget the cold and fall back to sleep as I listened to the rhythmic pulse of Mr. Irvine's breathing. The room seemed to just keep getting colder.

Finally I couldn't take it anymore.

I found myself silently tip-toeing up to the bed and sliding silently under the heavy blankets, the need for warmth far surpassing my discomfort of being in bed with this strange man. As I crawled in Mr. Irvine didn't move a muscle, continuing to inhale and exhale with a slight whistle. I listened for any deviation in his breathing, but he seemed to be in a very deep sleep.

189

Subtly I slid my pillow between us, my only barrier of protection against any of Mr. Irvine's ill intentions, but it gave me a modest bit of comfort.

Gradually I felt myself stop shaking beneath the heavy blankets as exhaustion took over. My mind started to drift back off into another world.

I fell asleep with the image of Michael's face painted on the wall of the dining room, staring back at me with tears in his eyes.

****

I had been deep within a sad dream of walking down the beach back at the barn with Michael by my side, my arm over his shoulder. Dark clouds and heavy, cold winds threatened rain, and waves crashed with startling force at our feet. I was trying to talk to Michael but no matter how loudly I yelled, my voice was drowned out by all of the noise from the storm.

My eyes flew open. I was alone in the bed.

Through cracks in the thick curtains I could see that the sky was just beginning to turn from the grey of dawn to the blue of early morning.

I didn't have to look around the room to know that I was the only one in the room; an eerie quiet hung in air so thickly that even the sound of my own breathing seemed erroneously loud.

I laid perfectly still. I knew that the cameras would be watching me, but I didn't want to give any signs of movement just yet.

My heart was already racing with anxiety about what the day would hold and I needed time to process the events of the previous day and arrange my thoughts. Already I felt overwhelmed by all of the unfamiliarity around me.

I closed my eyes tightly, trying to take myself back to the barn, back to my uncomfortable little bed of straw and mud, hoping to trick my mind into thinking I was laying there surrounded by all the others as if it were just another typical morning. I imagined Nasha sitting up by a smouldering fire warming leftover scraps of food for breakfast while the waves lapped up against the sides of the barn and crashed on the beach. I could almost smell Michaels musty hair near my nose and feel the familiar press of Alina's knee in my stomach.

I never thought I would think of that life as luxurious, but all I craved was familiarity, and to me this morning, familiarity would be the greatest form of opulence.

My eyes wouldn't stay shut. They kept popping open, involuntarily forcing me from my comforting memories of the barn back in to the cold, grand, empty room, forcing sharp blades of anxiety back into my veins and lungs.

I could see that the sky outside was now fully bright. It was nerve wracking to be left alone for so long.

When I couldn't take laying down anymore, I slowly slid myself from the bed and raced across the cold stone floor to the washroom.

Closing the door behind me, I quickly relieved myself before climbing under the hot shower which calmed me marginally.

Steam filled the room like a thick spring fog and I felt a small comfort to be hidden from the eyes of the cameras which were surely trying their best to get a clear view of me.

When I couldn't tolerate the scalding water on my skin anymore, I finally turned the knob off and turned to reach for my white towel to dry myself off.

I nearly fell over in shock when I rubbed the water away from my eyes to see two young teenagers, a boy and a girl nearly identical in every way, standing shoulder to shoulder just inches from the shower stall.

The two were an eerie sight in the fog, and it wasn't just because I hadn't expected to see them: Both kids somehow appeared inhuman—thin and short, bodies more appropriate for a child of eight or ten years old, yet faces that showed the early signs of adolescence: smooth, powder-white skin with dark freckles and light acne, a shadow of darkening hair above the boys lip. Both children had yellow-blonde hair; the girl's flowing down to her waist in thick spirals, while the boy's

191

was closely shaven to his scalp. Their matching eyes, a deep blue that seemed to glow from their sockets, were a shade that I have never seen before.

Most shockingly, both children had an identical scar as wide as my pinky finger that ran from the corner of their left ear to the bottom of their nose.

The young girl held my towel towards me, her face blank and emotionless.

"We are your handlers," the boy said, his voice cracking with puberty.

"My name is Emmaline and this is Kyal," said the girl flatly the very second that the boy finished speaking. "You may call me Emma."

"Please dry yourself off and put these clothes on," Kyal croaked not even a split second after Emmaline spoke, holding up a pile of black clothing.

"We are available for assistance should you require it," shot Emma as quick on the draw as before.

I stood dumbfounded before them, frozen in place as they stared back, waiting for me to follow their directions. The monotonous yet rapid-fire way in which they spoke seemed disconnected and inhuman. These creepy children were certainly not representative if the image I had in mind when Florian had told me that I would have 'handlers' to watch over me.

"Begin now please," directed Emma plainly.

Hesitantly I took the towel from her outstretched hand and followed their directions as they observed.

"We trust that Florian has explained our participation in this operation?" asked Emma.

I nodded with uncertainty. "I think so."

"To clarify," Kyal began, "We are members of the same group who are trying to take Mr. Irvine from power."

"Shh!" I hushed apprehensively, "the cameras!"

"Mr. Irvine has a strong dislike for any sounds related to bowel movements," explained Emma. "As such, microphones are not installed in private bathrooms in the building, and are generally the best place to speak openly. This is why we waited for you to come in here before approaching you."

"The rule does not apply to public restrooms in the building," clarified Kyal quickly. "Avoid speaking as much as possible if there is more than one stall in a restroom."

"To continue," Emma went on, "Kyal and I are here to schedule and guide you through your day. To maintain stealth, your schedule will not be any different from any others who come here for the first time."

"This means that you will be subjected to many unpleasant things," picked up Kyal. "We cannot avoid this without arising suspicion."

"We will, however," said Emma, "ensure that you are placed with people who are less likely to do you harm wherever possible."

"We ask that you comply without conflict to any situation that is asked of you. Attempt to be personable and confidant in everything you do and it is more likely that you will get through this with little physical harm." I couldn't help but look at the scars on the two kids faces as Kyal said the words 'physical harm,' and was certain that they both noticed.

"Do you understand?"

I pulled on the pants that Kyal had handed to me and stood to look the two strangers in the eyes.

"I don't know what the hell is going on!" I said with all honesty.

"What information have we not effectively communicated?" questioned Emma, her head tilting slightly to the left in confusion as she spoke.

"Uh!" I grunted, throwing my hands up in the air and rolling my eyes in exasperation. "Tsk! Where do you want me to start?"

Both simply stood staring at me waiting for an answer.

"Oh my God." I huffed. "What's going on here? Where are Michael and Alina? What the hell am I supposed to do to bring down Mr. Irvine? NONE OF THIS MAKES SENSE!"

"Ah," said Kyal as if these were questions that he had not considered.

"To go into a detailed explanation of what happens here at Irvine Industries would take far more time and mental capacity than you have available at the moment," he stated.

"Michael and Alina are on separate floors in the building," continued Emma, "It is impossible for us to re-unite you at this time."

"In terms of," began Kyal before I interrupted.

"Wait!" I said holding my hands up in front of the boy to make him stop talking as I stepped close to Emma.

"They're here?"

"Michael and Alina? Yes," affirmed Emma factually.

"Mr. Irvine said that they were in the outside world and that he would have to inquire as to their exact whereabouts!" I was nearly shouting.

Emma calmly looked at me. "Clearly he was being untruthful."

Frustration boiled up in me.

"How do I know what the truth is?!" I yelled. "Why should I trust you freaks!?"

Kyal flinched at the word 'freaks'.

"What other choice do you have?"

******

194

I ate a simple breakfast of boiled eggs and soft, sweet white bread in a small, dimly lit room while the two twins observed in silence. An armed guard held post almost inhumanly motionless.

When I had eaten my fill, Emma and Kyal led me robotically through a maze of hallways, elevators and corridors. It was moderately unsettling how the two of them navigated the many corners, doorways and even steps upward while stepping at exactly the same pace with their shoulders pressed tightly against one another. It seemed somehow mechanical—certainly not natural.

The armed guard followed only a step or two behind me at all times.

Eventually we ended up at a large, bland white room across the hall from the room where Florian worked.
The four of us entered wordlessly. The main door to the hallway remained open.

In the centre of the room there appeared to be a raised walkway in the shape of a 'T' that was lit from underneath somehow. At one end stood a wall of portable mirrors that seemed to reflect every angle of the room. Behind the mirrors, several wardrobes full of clothing surrounded the outer walls.

Off to the left, a large white board covered the surface of one wall. I noticed that it was covered mainly in slang words and their proper counterpart such as 'Ain't vs. Isn't' and 'Gunna vs. Going to.' In front of the board stood one large desk with a smaller desk facing it.

On the right side of the room, a fully set dining table with one lone chair, complete with a variety of food and even burning candles sat empty.

Still appearing as if they were attached at the shoulder, Emma and Kyal stood rigidly against the wall behind the dining table. The guard held position in front of the open doorway.

"HellooooOOOOoo!" chirped the familiar high-pitched voice of Florian as he fluttered his way past the guard and into the room.

I couldn't help but be taken aback by his outfit. I didn't think it could get any more shocking than yesterday's crazy get-up but today's dress was unbelievable: Florian's legs were squeezed into skin tight, green leggings, each leg sprouting one large leaf out the side. Pink petals as long as my arm sprouted from a dark green band around Florian's waist, circling him completely in a thick bouquet. In the front the petals spread apart across his chest to reveal a thick mat of black hair carpeting very convincing, voluptuous breasts that Florian had somehow created from pushing together his own flesh. A large, beautifully coloured hat in the shape of a butterfly sat slightly off centre on his newly platinum, tightly curled hair. He walked effortlessly on a pair of transparent glass shoes that made him seem half a foot taller. As always, the makeup on his face looked like a rainbow had thrown up on him.

The effect was mesmerizing in the most undesirable way.

Despite the huge, toothy smile that stretched across his face, I felt sorry for him. I couldn't imagine how odd he must feel prancing around all day pretending to be a character that was so opposite from his natural self-identity.

I was surprised at how detached and impersonal Florian treated me as he spent the entire day training me to hold proper posture as I walked, to speak and write using more refined words and expressions, and, most difficult and frustrating of all, how to sit at a formal dining table and eat properly. I couldn't believe that there was such a variety of utensils and orders in which they must be used. It all seemed ridiculous to me to require anything more than a spoon for liquids and a knife on the rare occasion that a piece of meat was too tough to rip apart with my teeth.

It was late in the afternoon before Florian finally dismissed me, having become frustrated with my complete lack of progress.

I was just about to complain that my stomach was sore from eating so much food during the training, but then I noticed the twins standing silently in the exact same place along the wall that they has chosen when we had first entered. They looked tired and weak and I caught Kyal looking hungrily at the leftover food on the table. It had been at least nine hours since the two had met with me in the washroom this morning and they had not had a bit of food or a drink of water since at least then. Just steps behind me I heard a low grumble coming from the guard in the doorway and caught him subtly rubbing his belly. He too had not eaten all day.

Whether these people were looking out for my best interest or not, I knew how horrible it felt to be without food for long periods and I wouldn't wish that feeling on anyone.

In a moment of compassion I swooped back over to the dining table and scooped up 3 large loaves of oily, cheesy bread, passing them to Emma and Kyal before moving towards the guard with the third loaf.

The guard looked at me in confusion. It was a mixture of humour and annoyance. I heard his stomach rumble again.

"Take it," I said, pushing the loaf against his chest.

He looked at the loaf. I could see the hunger in his eyes.

"We can't take this," a crackly voice from behind me said.

"It is forbidden," continued Emma's.

The guard looked up at my eyes. I thought I could see appreciation glimmering back at me.

"Step back," he commanded forcefully, adjusting his grip on his weapon.

****

Silently the four of us made our way through another maze of hallways to an unmarked white door. The soldier tapped his small white card against the black box outside the room and the door slid open with a noisy hiss.

Behind the door, a tiny room, it's walls close enough for me to touch from the doorway and not much longer in the other, held nothing more than a thin, narrow white pad to sleep on that blended seamlessly into the floor, and a matching blanket.

There were no windows.

Somehow the walls, ceiling and floor seemed to disappear into one another, illuminated from within in a way that made the room seem both enormous and suffocatingly small at the same time.

"In," commanded the soldier with a nudge to my back.

197

I felt instantly claustrophobic.

My knees locked as he nudged me again.

"What is this?" I sputtered.

"This is where you will sleep tonight," stated Emma.

"What?!" I gasped. Just the thought of having to sit in that room to wait for someone for a few minutes made my lungs feel like a great weight was pressing down on them. The idea of spending a whole night in there alone made me instantly start to panic.

"I thought Mr. Irvine had me sleeping in that big room with him!" I said, surprising myself by how disappointed I sounded. In truth, I couldn't stomach the thought of another minute in that room alone with Mr. Irvine. Who knows what he would try this time? On the other hand, that tiny white room would feel like the walls were closing in around me.

"Mr. Irvine has noted your inability to rest last night," said Kyal matter-of-factly.

"He has determined that you would perhaps sleep better in a calm, private enclosure," Emma continued.

"That's bullshit!" I yelled as the guard forced me into the tiny space, my heart thumping fearfully against my chest.
"He knows I've never been in a room as small as this! He knows that being alone scares the shit out of me!"

"If you would prefer to spend another evening alone with Mr. Irvine," said Kyal.

"Mr. Irvine will permit that," finished Emma.

Their tone was as robotic and formal as ever, but something about the manner in which they moved was clearly an indication that it would be best for me to sleep in this room tonight.

I hesitated for a moment, weighing my options.

The idea of being locked in this small room scared me, but the thought of laying with Mr. Irvine again made me feel sick to my stomach.

I didn't need to speak my decision out loud for it to be known.

"Should you need to relieve yourself," said Emma, stepping slightly into the room with me, "Push this button."
As she demonstrated, the thin mattress on the floor raised up flat against the wall to reveal a small steel toilet and matching sink hidden in a space beneath.

I was mortified. There would be no leaving this room for any reason until the morning.

Before I had time to process anything, Emma had stepped backwards out of the room and the door slid shut.

****

I had no idea how long I had been in the room for—it could have been just minutes or it could have been all night.
I felt like I was floating in the clouds, high up out of sight of the golden tower. The air in the room was stagnant and at a temperature that seemed to match my internal warmth exactly.

The self-illuminated walls, floors and ceiling blended into one another so perfectly that I had no depth perception. I couldn't tell if the ceiling was just out of arm's reach or if it were as high as the sun.

It was deafeningly silent.

My breathing echoed in my ears like the eerie sound of an unseen stranger whispering right next to me, and several times I held my breath just to make sure it was only mine that I was hearing. I could hear my heart thumping in my chest as if it were a sound coming from another room. It seemed to echo off of the walls as it beat. I swore I could even hear my muscles tensing and my eyelids opening and closing.

After a while I had become so aggravated by the sounds of my clothing crinkling as I breathed that I stripped myself naked and tried to stay as motionless as possible on the mattress below me.

Being trapped in that tiny room felt as if the whole world had evaporated into a fog of mist; as if there were nothing left on this planet but me and my memories.

As I floated in that empty space I tried desperately to calm myself by closing my eyes and thinking about life back home in the barn.

At first I tried to trick myself into thinking that I was floating out in the ocean on a calm day, enjoying the sun, taking a peaceful moment away from the monotony of life with the others. I imagined that the echoes of my breathing were the sounds of rolling waves gently sweeping over the sands on the shore and I could almost hear the seagulls off in the distance.

The moment of calm passed quickly. The sound of the seagulls in the distance somehow changed to the sounds of screaming and I was instantly brought back to the night when Julie gave birth violently to Alina—her voice bone chilling as she begged for help.

My eyes flew immediately open and I sat up to catch my breath. The room was now pitch dark. I couldn't even see my own hands in front of my face. It had gone from feeling like I was trapped alone in a cloud of fog to feeling like I had been buried alive and I struggled to keep myself calm.

In the darkness I backed myself into a corner to give myself some sense of my physical surroundings—some way to ground myself back in the physical realm of reality.

I longed for someone to turn to for comfort. I had never imagined that I would feel this alone.

I don't know how long I sat propped up in that corner, holding back tears and trying to wrap myself in imaginary hugs from the people that I missed.

At some point I must have drifted off because the sound of a quiet voice jarred me from my uncomfortable position.

"Ash, it's time to wake up." I jumped as if the words had been screamed in my ears.

The lights in the small room were on and the door was wide open. On the other side of the door Emma and Kyal stood shoulder to shoulder gazing in at me with blank expressions. The same soldier stood immediately behind them.

It was if they hadn't moved from their spots from the moment the door had locked me inside.

My muscles and bones ached with stiffness and exhaustion as I stood up from my corner before my brain had even woken enough to process what was happening.

****

The next two days and nights were a direct repeat of the previous one. Florian tirelessly schooled me on manners, posture, grammar and articulation mainly, all of which I quickly began to adopt as habit. I still had problems using cutlery and eating in the refined way that Florian pressed upon me, but much of that was simple rebellion; it seemed ridiculous to me to eat so slowly while the food quickly grew cold.

Although I watched carefully, there was no subtle hint of camaraderie or conspiracy between myself and Florian or Emma and Kyal at all.

The silence and isolation of the tiny room still brought on a state of near panic, but a restful sleep finally came to me on the third night simply due to complete exhaustion.

The following morning I woke moments before the lights came on and door slid open. It was just enough time to stand and shake soreness from my muscles.

Kyal, Emma and the soldier were not the slightest bit fazed to see me standing there waiting for them, proceeding in their morning routine as usual.

I was surprised when we rounded a familiar corner and turned the opposite way than we had in the two previous mornings.

"Where are you taking me?"

"Medical," was the simple response from the twins as they walked on, shoulder to shoulder in front of me.

"Why?"

"The nurse requested it," answered Kyal, matter-of-factly.

We rounded another corner and I found myself standing in front of the door to the medical room. Without a word, the soldier took out his white key-card and swiped it in front of the black box beside the him causing the door to slide open.

My three escorts stepped back to allow me to pass through the room, which I did without hesitation. I turned briefly as the door slid shut, just in time to catch a glimpse of Emma's left eye as she winked secretively at me.

Nurse Sarah stood quietly facing me in the centre of the room, her vivid yellow dress peaking from behind an open lab coat in shocking juxtaposition to the stark white, windowless walls around her. A sympathetic smile curled her lips ever so slightly. Despite the fact that I had no idea why I was here, I immediately felt more relaxed and safe.

"Are you okay?" she asked softly.

"Yes," I whispered back, nodding slightly.

"Have they hurt you?"

"No."

"Good."

A moment of awkward silence lingered between us before Sarah spoke again.

"I'm sorry, I'm just very nervous," she said, stepping closer to me.

"You?" I asked in surprise, lowering my voice as much as possible to keep my comments from the ears of the camera. "What do you have to be nervous about?"

"There's just a lot going on," Sarah said dismissively. "Oh gosh! I should tell you that the cameras have been disabled!"

I almost jumped in amazement. The strain of being unable to speak freely since those few brief moments with Florian had worn me down and made me feel like I would explode if I had to keep censoring every comment or movement before I made it. Even though I didn't know if I trusted Sarah or not, I felt like I could literally feel a weight off of my back.

"What?! How?!"

Sarah winked. "*Technical difficulties*. Our contact in the control room had arranged to do scheduled maintenance on the video server in this part of the building today, so Emma and I took the opportunity to coincidentally book a follow up appointment for you at the same time."

"So... he can't hear us or see us?"

"Nope, nada!" She smiled. "We only have a half hour to talk, and I do actually have to do some tests to prove that I had you in here for a reason, so we have to be quick."

I felt my ears grow red with anticipation. After so many hours of isolation my mind had grown full with a blur of unanswered questions, theories, and escape plans. I just needed to sit down and have everything explained once and for all.

"Come," Sarah said, guiding me towards a paper covered bed in the corner. "Let me hook you up to some things while I try to explain stuff to you."

I looked up at the camera in the corner as I walked across the room. It stayed fixed on its position towards the door. Sarah was telling the truth about that, at least.

I laid on the bed and felt the paper sliding and crunching beneath me.

Sarah slid her finger tips gently down my cheek bone. With everything going on I had forgotten that I had fallen out of the vehicle and injured my cheek when I got here.

"How is your face?"

"Uh, fine, I guess," I said, wincing as she pressed unnecessarily heavily on my eye socket, causing pain to shoot up over the top of my head.

"Sorry," she said apologetically. "I just wanted to double check that there was no break. Have you had any side effects from the inoculations? The shots, that is?"

"No."

"Good. Remove your shirt please," she asked, reaching for a coil of wires. I did as she asked and she began suctioning several little cups all over my chest and arms.

"This is just to check your heart," Sarah explained. "Nothing to worry about. Like I said, I just have to show that I did tests on you."

Sarah fiddled with the machine attached to the cables for a moment before turning back to face me.

"Okay then," she sighed. "I don't even know where to start."

"How about with what the hell is going on here?" I asked with exasperation, thinking that this would be the obvious first place to start.

"Well that's a loaded question," Sarah sighed. "There's a lot more going on here than even I comprehend."

"Give me the basics," I said.

"Well," she started. "Hmm. Okay. Irvine Industries is a multi-national company with offices all around the globe. The company deals in everything from Industrial Manufacturing in China to Coal mining in Chile, to Bio-engineering in England—all countries in other parts of the world very far away from here.

Mr. Irvine is also a leading political powerhouse. Not just in Canada, but all around the world. He acts as a special advisor to the Prime Minister—the leader—of Canada, he is a leader in the World Economic Forum and has close personal relationships with the President of the United States, the Russian Prime Minister, and several big name celebrities—all people who hold serious influence in this world. In short, directly or indirectly, Mr. Irvine has more influence than pretty much anyone else on this side of the planet other than the World Leaders themselves."

"So your little group of rebels don't like him because he has too much power," I said perhaps a little too coarsely.

The expression on Sarah's face turned from light hearted and eager to inform, to cold and cross.

"That's not it at all. He's kept us all prisoners here. Against our will!" She stood up and walked across the room in frustration, her arms crossed and her body tense.

"You don't know what he does to people like us."

"He says that he is protecting us all, keeping us from people out there who want us dead," I argued, sitting up on the bed despite the suction cups and wires on my chest. I could feel the hostility between us growing quickly.

"What!?" Sarah exclaimed in utter disbelief. "That's ridiculous! Nobody wants me dead!"

"He says that some people don't know why they were brought to them. That they don't even realize how much danger they were in."

"That's absolute bullshit! I had a happy family life. I was grabbed off the street when I was 16 by three men in a black van, beaten, repeatedly raped, knocked unconscious, then brought here."

"Who brought you here?"

"I don't know, those three guys in the black van I assume."

"Maybe he saved you from them."

Sarah's jaw dropped in disbelief.

"He says he protects people here then slowly tries to rehabilitate them and re-introduce them into normal lives once they are prepared and safe to try."

"I can't believe you would even think for a minute that any of that makes sense!" Sarah said, struggling to maintain composure. "Have you not seen how badly abused people are when they are sent back to the barn?"

"Yes I have," I said, proudly feeling as if I were winning the argument. "Those were people who got involved in the wrong crowds when they went back into the real world."

"Oh my God…" she said, looking me directly in the eye and shaking her head.

"It makes sense," I stated with certainty.

She continued to stare. Her whole body seemed to be exuding a feeling of betrayal, her posture deflating with exasperation.

"If you believe that then we're done here."

Surprised by her sudden willingness to just give up her argument, I suddenly lost a bit of my conviction, worrying that maybe I was severing a potentially imperative relationship before I truly knew all the facts.

I stared at her while she stood there scowling. I couldn't read her. She seemed to believe what she was saying, but did she know the real story, or was she just trying to use me as some sort of pawn? Mr. Irvine had answered all of my questions calmly and rationally and explained himself well. He hadn't been aggressive or confrontational like Sarah was being right now. Maybe that was the reason I let her continue; Even though Mr. Irvine's explanation of things made more sense to me, I couldn't see why Sarah would be so passionate and personally hurt by my distrust for any reason other than that she honestly believed what she was saying.

"Fine, tell me what your side of the story is."

She hesitated before answering, clearly weighing out whether it was worth continuing this conversation any longer or abandoning it, and me, completely.

"Human trafficking," she finally said coarsely.

"What? What the hell is that?"

"He buys, sells and trades people."

"People can't own other people!" I snickered. "We're not objects."

"No, you're wrong. People can and they do," she countered aggressively. "They shouldn't, but they do."

"What do you do with someone you own? Stand them up in a corner and hang decorations from them?"

"Don't be ridiculous. If someone owns you, they will make you do whatever they want you to do. Slavery, mainly in the sex trade is the big thing. They do horrible things to their sex slaves.

Sometimes they just need people to work for them without pay. Everything from housekeepers to sweat shop workers where people—even children—are sometimes worked to the death.

Sometimes they keep you to themselves. Sometimes they rent you out to other people.

You lose all control over your life. You lose every one and every *thing* you ever had: Your family, your dignity... your hope."

"If that's true, why don't these 'slaves' just run away? Or better yet, unite and fight back?"

"Because the owners have too much power," Sarah replied, pointing to the camera in the ceiling. "There's no way to escape! Someone is always watching!"

"Then why hasn't anyone stepped in to stop this? Why didn't you and your little group of rebels step up to rescue these people before this? Why now?"

"Don't you get it? We're all slaves! Every one of us! Me, Florian, Emmaline and Kyal, even all of the soldiers! Everyone! He owns us all!"

I thought about this for a moment, letting the magnitude of this possible explanation settle in.

"Why would soldiers—people who are trained for battle—people who carry deadly weapons and are free to come and go as they please—why would they not turn their guns on Mr. Irvine and save themselves and everyone else?"

Suddenly lowering her voice from her near state or hysteria to an odd, dejected tone, she replied, "Because they believe him.

He's probably told them all a similar story as he did with you—convinced them all that he was some sort of hero. Someone to fight for instead of against. I know that some of them have been training under his command their whole life."

"No," I said firmly, not yet sure of what I believe. "That doesn't make sense either. People talk. If that were true they all would have figured it out by now and fought back."

"Some people are pretty easy to convince," she replied with subtle jab of mockery.

"Yeah well, like Mr. Irvine said, there's a lot of people here who don't know the real reason that they're here. Maybe your little group has the wrong idea."

Sarah stared blankly at me, shaking her head.

"You know deep down inside that you get a bad feeling when you're around him."

"I get a bad feeling about everything!" I argued.

Sarah shook her head again. I could see that she was frustrated and out of arguments. She stared at me through her dark squinty eyes. I could tell that she truly believed what she had told me. I wanted to believe her. I wanted to be on her side; if what she said was true, a lot of people were suffering at the hands of a powerful and ruthless master—people who, somehow, would rely on me for their freedom.

I just couldn't swallow the idea though. The concept that one person would not only hold that much power, but would use that power to enslave, humiliate and torture countless others was mind boggling to me. No human being could be that cruel—so heartless. Mr. Irvine's explanation that he was a good man attempting to protect and rehabilitate people who didn't even know that they needed his care was the only option that my heart would let me believe. Sure, being alone with Mr. Irvine made me feel uncomfortable, but I understood that everyone has their own issues and preferences. His interest in me was awkward and unpleasant to face, yes, but it wasn't threatening.

"I'm sorry," I said genuinely. "I can see why you believe what you do; a small group of people who don't understand why they're here and have had some bad experiences. Of course you'd get together and try to fight back. It's understandable. But what Mr. Irvine says makes more sense: He's protecting us, not enslaving us. He's our only hope."

"My *GOD!*" Sarah exploded. "You can't be that naive ! That gullible! *ONE* conversation with him and you're his biggest advocate!"

"I have faith in people. They are inherently good. Sure, people may not understand what he is doing and may hate him for it, but what you are suggesting would just make him a monster!"

"People are *NOT* inherently good!" She said, almost yelling. "You've literally lived in a *BOX* for your whole life! You have no idea how horrible some people can be! I'm the nurse here! I've seen it all first-hand!

Here!" she said, fumbling in a bag that sat on her desk for a small white object that she fiddled with before passing to me with a shaky hand. "I didn't want to have to show this to you, but I don't have any choice."

I took the object from her cautiously. The nervousness in Sarah's movements suddenly made my skin bristle with hesitation, uncertain if I wanted to see what she was about to show me.

I nearly dropped the machine as I saw the picture on its screen: a young boy in a dark, smoke-filled room, his arms and legs tied to the bed in the four corners, his naked body covered in bruises and lacerations, his mouth open in agony as several naked but masked men and women laid with him or surrounded the bed.

Michael.

I felt a rush of vomit welling up in my throat. The insides of my ears started to burn and ring simultaneously. I felt light headed, enraged, horrified, scared, sad. Tears immediately slid from my eyes.

"Who..." I choked.

"Slide your finger to the left on the screen," whispered Sarah warily.

Everything inside of me begged me not to do as she said, too afraid to see what else there could be, but I watched my own hand as it touched the screen on its own and swiped its finger from right to left.

The image on the next screen was of the same scene but from a different angle, and taken from farther away.

Several steps away from the bed, three fully dressed men stood in various positions holding a variety of machines and lights directed towards the bed where Michael was restrained. Off to the side of the three men, a fourth sat in a tall, bright red chair, observing the scene with a smile.

Mr. Irvine.

"What do you think of your hero now?" Sarah asked with empathy.

I sat silently for a moment while I forced my mind to process what I just saw.

"What do you need me to do?"

****

It was the first time that I had been in a room with so many people since being in the barn.

Sarah, Florian, Chiku, Emma, Kyal, and the guard who I now knew to be named Solomon all sat in a circle around me as I lay on the bed. Nobody said a word as the final stitch was sewn into my cheek.

The pain was excruciating. I didn't expect that the needle would hurt this much.

It had all gone to plan:

Kyal had knocked on the door only moments after Sarah had shown me the pictures of Michael.

"We must go!" he called before the door had opened fully.

"Now!" said Emma with more urgency.

Mr. Irvine had unexpectedly requested my presence at morning brunch and it had set everyone to scrambling to have me cleaned, dressed and prepared for the meeting.

"Wait!" cried Sarah just as the twins began to usher me from the room. "This is the perfect opportunity!"

"Now?" Emma said in disbelief, seeming to comprehend what Sarah was implying.

"Yes, now!" Sarah replied, spinning around to grab a syringe from the table behind her.

"We don't have time to brief him," responded Kyal flatly.

"He'll have to wing it," said Sarah, jabbing the needle deep into my arm before I even realized what she was doing.

"Oh shit," I heard Solomon mumble.

"Sorry Ash, no time to explain!" Sarah quickly. "Don't be scared, you'll be fine, I promise."

I raced through the twisting halls with Emma and Kyal leading the way while Solomon, who I still believed to be an enemy, prodding me forward hurriedly with his weapon.

"It's now!" called Emma as we rushed into Florian's area.

"What!?" He exclaimed with horror, seeming to understand what she was speaking of. "Today?"

"Yes! *Now!*" replied Kyal impatiently. "Get Chiku in here!" he ordered the guard.

"What's happening?" I cried, suddenly feeling like a scared little child.

Florian approached me hurriedly, tossing a shirt in my arms while subtly reminding me with his eyes that there were cameras watching.

"Mr. Irvine has requested his second meeting with you," he said formally with his voice trilling in panic. "We were not informed of this in advance, so if you please, do your best to expedite this process and make this easier on us all."

A few seconds later, the guard re-entered, dragging a terrified Chiku forcefully by the arm.

"Now!" called Florian to Chiku, who instantly flew into action, cleaning my skin with scented sponges and cloths as Florian helped me get my new white suit on.

I could feel my cheeks flush as the duo raced around me without speaking. I didn't understand what was going on and just wanted someone to explain.

I felt a drop of sweat fall from my underarm and slide down the side of my chest towards my waist.

Florian spun me on the spot to tuck a belt through the loops in my pants and it took the room a moment extra to stop rotating around me.

"What do I have to do?" I asked, my voice shaking.

"Just go to lunch," replied Florian sternly. "We'll be there to make sure everything goes well."

"We need him in there right now," said the soldier from the door.

Without a moment to step back and review my look, Florian pushed me towards the door and the whole group of us left the room at a jogging pace.

My body felt suddenly hot, burning from the inside as we ran through the halls, though I could feel a cold sweat on my back and forehead. My head began to feel cloudy. It was all too much. Things were happening too quickly.

Suddenly we were in the dining room with all the paintings of the small children. Florian and Chiku were fluttering around me, getting my appearance just right, while Emma and Kyal were quickly re-arranging the setting on the table in front of me.

In the madness, Chiku dabbed the sweat that had dripped into my eyes, momentarily giving me the faintest hint of a gentle smile as she did so.

"Out!" commanded a familiar voice from the doorway.

Around me the group scattered like an army of ants disturbed by a sudden rain fall.

Jack, the soldier from the car ride entered the room in full battle gear. Mr. Irvine followed a step behind.

An ear-piercing ring filled the room and my head began to pound.

My five helpers filed quickly from the room, followed by the soldier Jack as Mr. Irvine approached me.

"Nice to see you again, Ash," said Mr. Irvine with a grand smile. "Please accept my apologies at the hurried nature of this meeting. I suddenly found myself with a change in schedule."

I stood still as he spoke, supporting my weight on the back of the chair in front of me.

The ringing in my ears intensified.

Mr. Irvine gave me a look of concern. "Are you okay, son?"

I heard the familiar hiss of the door sliding shut behind Jack.

Everything went dark.

******

"That really must have hurt!" a deep voice groaned from the foot of the bed.

"It looks bad but it's mostly blood," said another voice.

I felt a hand pressing heavily on my forehead as searing hot blades seemed to be tearing my face apart.

Suddenly completely alert, I leapt up from where I had been laying, instinctually trying to escape from whoever was torturing me.

I was astonished to feel myself being forced to the ground even before I had an opportunity to assess my surroundings.

"No you don't!" barked a man's voice.

My face was pressed hard to the ground, my arms pulled tightly behind me while a heavy weight pressed down on my legs.

All I could see was floor and an empty white wall.

"Let him up Solomon!" said a familiar voice. Sarah.

As the man pulled me up from the floor, immediately recognised that I was back in the medical room. It was a disorienting feeling to not remember how I got here.

I steadied myself on my feet and shook off the soldier's grip with as much strength as I could muster.

"He's okay, Ash," Florian said in his masculine voice.

I was surprised to see the group of people that surrounding me. At the same time, I felt rescued and ambushed.

"What happened?" I demanded, looking directly at Sarah.

"Everything went to plan," Sarah assured me. "Get back on the table and let me finish stitching you up?"

"What do you mean? Stitch what up?"

"Your cheek, you need stitches."

I raised my hand up to my cheek. It was sticky with blood and pain shot through my head like a shot from a gun.

"Lucky that it's the same cheek you already injured," commented Florian.

The group parted as I made my way back to the table to lay down.

"It couldn't have gone better," said Emma with a stone face that betrayed her delight.

"You went a bit overboard by cutting your face up but it helped," remarked Kyal as blandly as his sister.

The needle stung like a bee as it pierced the flesh of my cheek over and over. Sarah apologized profusely with each stitch, saying that she would have given me some sort of localized numbing agent but it would cause a bad reaction with whatever she had given me to make me pass out.

"I'm afraid that you will always have a scar from this," Sarah sighed when she was done cleaning the wound. "You cut it right down to the bone."

I groaned as I sat up on the table, my head still pounding from the combination of drugs and injury.

"So can someone explain now please?" I moaned.

"We needed time to talk," said Florian.

"We are almost never in the same room together," interrupted Emma. "This was a good excuse."

I shook my head uncomprehendingly. "What do you mean?"

"Since we were so rushed to have you ready, we were all in close proximity to you," explained Kyal. "Having you pass out right when we were leaving the dining room gave us the perfect opportunity to have an excuse to meet."

"Emma, Kyal, Florian and Chiku were needed to carry you out of the dining room, while I 'stood guard'," interjected Solomon, using air quotes at standing guard.

"We didn't expect you to get hurt," said Florian with concern.

"We thought you would just pass out in your chair," explained Sarah. "We didn't think you'd pass out while standing up."

"Your face smashed your dinner plate in two!" smiled the guard. "We're lucky your knife didn't stab you through eye!"

Nobody else smiled at his comment.

"You should have seen Irvine's face!" he joked again, looking around for a reaction from the others, focusing regretfully on his shoes when he didn't get one.

"Moving on," said Emma sternly. "Let's focus on our plan."

"Emma's right," Kyal concurred. "We don't have much time."

****

I laid awake in my isolation room for what seemed like hours. The pain in my face has eased, but was far from dissipated. My head was still foggy from the drugs that Sarah had given me, and I felt numb in a way that I had never experienced before.

I couldn't stop my mind from racing.

"We need you to act as if you don't know anything."

That was the phrase that kept repeating itself over and over in my mind.

It had been Kyal who had said that. His robotic tone was so empty of emotion that it seemed that he would have no difficulties suppressing his fears and lying about all of this if he were in my position.

"Mr. Irvine basically had you convinced that he was a good person. You need to show him that you believe him."

"How do you expect me to do that?!" I replied loudly, turning to look at Sarah, "After the picture that you showed me?! There's no way that I'll be able to fake being nice to him!"

"We need you to do more than that," said Emma calmly. "We need you to submit to whatever he asks of you."

The magnitude of what she said struck me like a punch to the gut.

"What?" I stammered. "You mean, you…. I am supposed to…"

"It's not as bad as that with him," interjected Sarah, placing her hand on my shoulder to calm me. "He's a very old man. He may have a sick mind, but his body doesn't function the way it used to."

"Just do what you did the other night with him," said Florian attempting to keep his voice positive. "Squirm away or something."

I thought about this for a moment. My mouth watered with disgust at the idea of having that man touch me again.

"Why me?" I said quietly.

"You're a prize to him," explained Sarah. "He's watched you for your whole life and has never been able to get close to you. He's tried many times, but either someone has volunteered themselves in your place, or he has simply been unable to get to you."

"Mr. Irvine is always protected by at least one guard—two, most of the time. There's someone in the room with him when he eats, when he sleeps, even when he uses the restroom. He's never alone," said the soldier. "I've been doing this for ten years now. You're the only person he's ever demanded to be left alone with. It's something he's been saying since you were a kid. We were even taught that in basic training."

"We were all told that," said Emmaline.

"It's one of the cardinal rules of our job," continued Kyal.

"What about Michael and Alina?" I questioned. "Why not them? They were kept away from him for almost as long as I was."

Sarah looked at Florian with sorrowful eyes, searching for approval to divulge a secret. Florian simply stared back at her.

After a moment she turned to speak.

"To Mr. Irvine, Alina is nothing more than garbage. Every person in that barn has been hand-picked for one reason or another by him. Alina's mother, Julie, got pregnant by someone who Mr. Irvine viewed as lower class than his standard. She kept her pregnancy hidden until it was too late for him to do anything about it. Julie was here a lot and was respected by pretty much everyone. To directly kill her or make her abort the baby would have caused an uproar with the staff and he knew it.

When it was discovered that the umbilical cord was wrapped around the baby, Mr. Irvine sent Julie back to the barn, certain that the child would die before or during birth. When she survived and Julie died, Mr. Irvine was furious! He refused to provide any care for the baby. He wanted her to die.

He even took his anger out on Nasha and Johnna—the two who were directly responsible for removing Alina from Julie's belly after she had died. He brought both of them here and had them beaten to within an inch of their lives.

When they were sent back to the barn, they and everyone else were too afraid to care for Alina. She was weak and frail to begin with and was on death's door with nobody paying attention to her but Michael.

It was Michael who saved Alina."

"Mr. Irvine was enraged at Michael for saving her," said Florian. "Until Alina started to get better, Michael had been as much of a Golden Boy as you had been."

Sarah drooped her head. "He never got over it."

"You're saying that he's been planning on torturing Michael and Alina all that time?" I asked, shaken once again by the thought of the pictures that Sarah had shown me.

Florian, Sarah and the soldier all nodded slightly.

"Where are they?" I asked miserably.

"We don't know for sure about Michael," replied Sarah.

"How did you get those images of him then?"

"They were sent to me from our ally in Surveillance. He found them on a server when doing upgrades. We think Michael is still in the building somewhere, but we only have access to the top ten levels."

"And Alina?" I asked, dreading the answer.

The room fell silent.

"Tell me!" I demanded.

"Alina has been sent back to the barn," answered the soldier solemnly.

"What? When?"

"The day they picked you up. They dropped her off right after they had secured you in the car."

I sighed a breath of relief. "At least she's not here being tortured by these psychos anymore."

Silence.

I looked around the room. Everyone's face was either downturned or had their eyes locked on some unseen place in the distance. I could sense their apprehension immediately.

"What's wrong with Alina?"

Everyone shifted uncomfortably in their seats.

"Someone tell me," I begged, terrified to hear the response.

Sarah cleared her throat. Just as she was about to speak, Kyal jumped in to save her from being the bearer of the news.

"She's in very bad shape," he began. "She's been put through everything imaginable. She's been repeatedly sent out to some of the worst clients. "

"She's almost unrecognisable," interjected Emma callously. "Bruised and swollen. Broken bones. Nearly catatonic from fear."

My heart dropped. My head felt light. I could feel the skin under my eyes tingle with warmth and the contents of my stomach rise up towards my throat.

"She'd been in intensive care for weeks before they sent her back to the barn," mumbled Solomon.

My head snapped up towards Sarah. I suddenly felt like I was going to explode with rage. "You lied to me! You told me you didn't know where she was!"

Sarah nearly fell over in her chair as if I had hit her squarely in the face.

"I didn't know, Ash!" she cried with real tears already coating her face. "I swear!"

"She was in another building!" defended Florian, leaning forward into the space between Sarah and I. His voice was shockingly masculine and intimidating. "We've only just uncovered the details today."

"Sit back, please," Solomon warned, looking very much like an enemy again. I realized that I was shaking with rage.

I felt a gentle hand rest on my shoulder. Chiku.

I turned to look at her.

"Calm," she said in a meek, childlike whisper. "Okay. We help."

Once again the room fell silent. Everyone stood slack-jawed, shocked that Chiku had spoken.

"Did..." started Florian, looking to the others around the room somewhat comically. "Did you guys just hear that? Chiku, you can speak?"

Chiku kept her eyes on me and patted my shoulder. "We help."

I felt my rage subside—her simple words and gentle touch somehow affirming to me that this small group of people were definitely worthy of my trust.

Sarah straightened herself back out on her chair again, running her fingers self-consciously through her thick black hair.

"Alina's wounds were all superficial, according to our source," she said formally.

"So she'll recover quickly?" I asked, hopeful.

"The bruises and bones will heal, yes," Sarah replied, her voice dropping to a more morose tone. "Her emotional scars will take longer."

"Sticks and stones may break your bones…" trailed off Solomon obtusely.

"There's something else," Sarah said nervously, looking to Florian for emotional strength.

I felt my body grow tense and rigid in fearful trepidation.

All eyes turned to me, awaiting to see my reaction.

"Alina is pregnant."

******

"I'm not the ringleader in all of this."

Sarah looked at me with concern as I paced around the room trying to work the rest of the medication out of my system. I was still feeling lightheaded and my fingers tingled as if I had fallen asleep on my arms.

I had completely lost my mind when she had told me about Alina's pregnancy. I immediately remembered poor Julie staring at me, her eyes glazing over while trying to give birth and I knew that little Alina could suffer the same fate. I screamed at the group for not doing more to protect Alina, blaming them all for everything. My fists had flung out in a violent tantrum at anyone and everyone, connecting squarely with Emma's right ear, Sarah's belly, and the hard shell of Solomon's armour before he was able to pull me to the ground and have Sarah sedate me again.

"I'm just the one who has the most access to you right now," said Sarah.

"Who is, then?" I asked angrily, looking around the room for someone to vent my frustrations on.

Sarah crossed her arms aggressively. "The ringleader? Who do you think?"

I threw my arms up in frustration. "I don't know! I just met you people! I can't figure any of you crazy people out!"

"Emma and Kyal."

My face must have registered pure surprise because Sarah's mouth cracked the tiniest of smiles.

"The twins?!" Emma and Kyal looked back at me calmly, their faces registering no emotion.

"Well first off, they're not twins," said Sarah. "They're two years apart, Emma is the eldest. And they're not even related."

I stared, dumbfounded.

"They're genetic experiments. Both kids were genetically engineered— manufactured in a sense--to suit Mr. Irvine's ideal of physical perfection. Unfortunately for Mr. Irvine, they are exceedingly intelligent. By the time Emma was six, they had both figured out what Mr. Irvine had intended to use them for. To deter his attention, they took sharp knives to each other's faces, giving themselves those hideous scars. They did the same to their genitals. Mr. Irvine stayed away from them after that. He thinks they're emotionless monsters with one good brain between the two of them."

"It sounds like that's a pretty accurate judgement," I said without thinking.

Somehow without movement, Emma's face subtly changed. She looked saddened. Hurt.

"On the contrary," Florian stepped in. "They've been observing and researching every detail of this building and this company since day one. They know more about this place than anyone. Maybe even more than Mr. Irvine."

"Why? What can two kids do?"

Solomon suddenly spoke up. "Without them none of us would know anything. We wouldn't have any way of communicating or even knowing that there are others on our side. Nobody suspects a pair of stone-faced zombie-children who look like they don't give a shit about anything in this world to be sneaking around all day and night gathering valuable intel. No offense kids," he said, turning to them briefly.

Sarah gestured for me to sit down so she could take my blood pressure.

"They've single-handedly organized a rebellion which, hopefully, will save us all."

"Except Michael and Alina," I argued.

"We can still save them," said Emma, her voice annoyingly emotionless. "They've suffered a lot, yes, but with the right care they can learn to deal with what's happened to them and live a full life."

"That's why we have to act now," continued Kyal. "We have to get this plan going before he can hurt them, or anyone anymore."

"So what's the plan then?" I asked.

Sarah looked at me cautiously.

"As we've said, we need you because the guards stay away from Mr. Irvine when he has you in the same room as him. You need to convince Mr. Irvine that you believe everything that he has told you—that you're on his side. We need him to trust you."

I realized I was already shaking at the idea. "I hate that man! I can't possibly even look him in the eye! How am I supposed to convince him that I believe him?"

"Just be distant like you were before. Show that you're uncomfortable. Pull away just like you normally would. The main thing is to ask questions. Ask anything and everything. Ask him to show you around the building. It will show him that you are at least interested in what he does. Avoid bringing up Michael, Alina or any of us. Keep it about him and he'll feed right into it."

"So that's it?" I said harshly. "You just want me to be nice to him? Why didn't you tell me this last time? Why did you have to drug me and drag me back in here?"

"No," replied Emma bluntly. "The second phase of the plan is to gain access to the main office."

"It is the only room that Emma and I have not ever been able to get into," continued Kyal. "Nobody has been in that room other than Mr. Irvine and his personal bodyguards."

Emma took a half step forward. "That room contains every access code in the building. Nobody will be able to get in or out of the building without those codes."

"Woah woah!" I said. "You want me to get into a room that nobody else has ever had access too? How the hell do I do that?"

"No," said Kyal simply. "We need you to slip this into his food."

I looked at Kyal's outstretched hand. At first his upturned palm appeared to be empty. I leaned in closer and saw a flat, pea-sized section of transparent plastic glimmering under the overhead lighting.

"What is that?"

"It's a drug that Mr. Irvine is highly allergic to. It will stop his heart almost instantly," he replied.

I choked in disbelief. "What? You want me to kill Mr. Irvine now?"

"It's our only option," said Emma.

"I can't take someone's life!" I cried.

"You're going to have to," said Florian. "He's taken the lives of so many people-- several of those who you've loved. He's destroyed the lives of so many others. We have to stop him!"

Sarah leaned forward. "Think of Michael and Alina. Think of all the others who are going through what they are going through right now."

I stared at an empty spot on the floor. "I don't know if I can do this."

"You must," said Chiku's soft voice.

The room was silent for a while as the others let me process the information. A dozen thoughts and questions raced through my mind at once but I couldn't slow them long enough to ask out loud. I forced myself to see the image of Michael tied to that bed, his mouth open in a frozen scream. My skin grew cold and the bile built back up in my throat. I thought of Alina. So young. I couldn't let her suffer the same grotesque fate as her mother.

"What do I do with that?" I said looking at Kyal.

"It will be stuck onto your fingernail on your pinky finger," he replied.

"You must get Mr. Irvine to swallow it," said Emma.

"Dip your finger in his drink or peel it off and mix it in his food when he's not looking."

"Why me? Why can't the cook slip it into his food?" I asked shakily.

"He's not on our side. The food is under guard from the moment it's prepared until the moment it is served."

"When do I have to do this?"

Emma looked at me with her typical stone-faced gaze.

"Tomorrow. Breakfast."

My breath felt as if it were knocked from me. I needed time to prepare myself. Tomorrow seemed too soon.

"Ash," said Florian gently. "We know this is hard but it has to be done."

"It'll be easy," commented Solomon. "No weapons, no fighting. He won't see it coming."

I shook my head slowly. I couldn't believe this was happening.

"Listen to me Ash," Florian continued, pulling my chin softly to face him. "Listen. This is important: Take your time with it. Don't rush. He will be watching you like a hawk. If you don't get an ideal opportunity, don't risk it. If it doesn't happen tomorrow, so be it. There will be several opportunities, as long as you can convince him that you still believe his story so that he lets down his guard."

I thought for a moment.

"What happens once I do it?"

"You open the door to let us in," answered Emma.

"We'll take it from there," said Kyal.

****

I had finally fallen asleep. Dreams of little nine year old Alina, her belly ripped open, dripping with blood as she walked towards me coddling a tiny baby—its screams blending horrifyingly with those of Michaels, who was somewhere in the background—haunted me all night and I woke in a near state of panic several times.

I hadn't eaten at all the day prior and I woke up the final time with hunger pains so overwhelming that I couldn't lie still any longer. I didn't understand how, back in the barn, I could go for days without food and not have pains like this.

I laid there awake for a very long time before the light finally came on and the door slid open. The familiar faces of Emma and Kyal stood before me. Nobody said a word. They simply turned and I followed them without delay. An unfamiliar soldier followed behind, his heavy boots clicking on the stone floors, thankfully masking the sound of my beating heart.

In complete silence, Emma, Kyal and the soldier stood back and watched as Florian and Chiku performed their morning duties on me, bathing and styling me to Mr. Irvine's liking.

I longed for someone to say something—just one or two small words of support. Something to give me strength. Even just a subtle, gentle squeeze of my arm. I waited for that as Chiku scrubbed my skin with a coarse cloth. I hoped for it as Florian buttoned up my shirt. All I felt was their shaking hands.

When the two had completed my styling, Chiku snuck a tiny white tube from her pocket and unscrewed the lid. With a quick sleight-of-hand motion that was almost imperceptible, she pulled out the nearly invisible slip inside and applied it to the nail on my pinky finger smoothly. It vanished entirely.

I was armed.

Standing before the mirror I looked myself over. I had been dressed in slim fitting, perfectly tailored black pants and matching shirt with rolled up sleeves. My black shoes were so heavily polished that I could see my own reflection. My thick brown hair, normally messy and matted, was smooth and slicked evenly off to one side of my head. The compound that Chiku had plastered so heavily over my injured cheek nearly concealed the wound completely.

I looked every bit the part of a young, tough, confident man.

I stepped closer.

I stared deeply into my own dark brown eyes. Despite the fancy outer shell, a terrified young kid peered back.

Mr. Irvine would see through me right away.

******

The air hung heavy and humid in the dining room as I waited for Mr. Irvine to arrive. A cool breeze whistled forcefully through a vent in the ceiling, yet I could feel sweat soaking into the armpits of my shirt. I wished that my clothing were looser.

227

The sun was fully up in the East, and though its direct rays were blocked by other impossibly tall towers all around, the room was filled with light that seemed to make the paintings of children on the wall seem all the more real.

Slightly to the South, a great lake stretched off into the horizon. I found myself sniffing the air for the familiar scent of salt water but all I could smell was a mixture of manufactured air and strong perfume from the many flowers in the room.

I forced myself to look down towards the ground outside. People were everywhere. I couldn't believe that there were that many humans in the world, let alone in one city. It was unfathomable to me as to how they could go about their daily lives in a world of such chaos.

Did they know what was going on in this big golden tower? Did they have any idea that people were being enslaved and tortured, rented and sold for the entertainment of wealthy, powerful people?

I wanted to bang on the window and yell down to them, but I knew I was too far away for them to hear me. I doubted that anyone would care anyway.

My vision began to blur in and out as I looked down at the world below and I felt myself swaying, so I decided to move to one of the two chairs at the dining room table, lowering myself down into its soft padding as quietly as possible.

From somewhere behind the walls I could hear the deep mumble of voices. It sounded eerily like the children on the walls were whispering about me.

I looked at the image of Alina in the corner. Despite all the light in the room, she was still darkened by shadow. Her face looked sad and afraid, but the look on her face was not fear for herself; she looked as if she were afraid for me.

As sweat dripped further down my arm, I focused my eyes on my fidgeting hands and tried to focus my mind. I had to convince Mr. Irvine that I didn't know anything other than what he himself had told me; that I didn't know how he tortured and sold people; that I didn't know what he had done to Michael and Alina; that a secret group hadn't recruited me to kill him.

I tried to think of questions that I would ask him that would make him believe that I was interested in what he did here. Questions that would make him trust me. Ways I could talk to him that would make him believe that I was okay with, and even invited his attention.

Nothing came to mind.

My left leg was bouncing up and down uncontrollably with nervousness and I felt myself taking short, ineffective breaths. I suddenly became aware of a sour taste in my throat.

I forced myself to breathe normally. If I was going to do this, I had to toughen myself up.

After an agonizingly long wait, the mumbling voices within the walls moved towards the door way, and with a whoosh, the door slid open.

A shiver went up my spine as Mr. Irvine walked confidently in.

"My boy!" he called out, his arms up as if ready to give me a hug despite being on the opposite side of the room. "How are you feeling?"

I leaned forward slightly in a move to stand, a rule of proper manners that Florian had drilled into my head, but I felt myself leaning back again involuntarily. I gritted my teeth and made another attempt but my legs just wouldn't co-operate. I looked down to see them both shaking wildly.

Mr. Irvine looked at me with concern as he crossed the room. I noticed that he was not carrying his cane.

"Don't get up!" he said. "We don't want a repeat of last time!"

I gripped both of my knees in an attempt to conceal the shaking.

"Ash? Are you alright?" he said with genuine concern.

I caught myself clenching my jaw and fists and tried to relax them.

"Still a little off," I forced myself to say, not entirely untruthfully.

"You gave me quite a scare there!"

I nodded wordlessly as Mr. Irvine walked behind my chair, placing both of his hand on my shoulders. I cringed on the inside in reaction to his touch, trying my hardest to not show any external sign of disgust.

"Let's hope it's out of your system," he said, his mouth inches from my right ear, his tone wavering somewhere between caring and threatening.

He left my side with a gentle squeeze of my shoulders and lowered himself easily into his chair. As he did, two servants, different ones than the last time I had a meal with Mr. Irvine, came into the room, serving us simultaneously with a generous plate of fried eggs, thick slices of ham and bacon, toast, steaming tea, and ice cold orange juice. Mr. Irvine didn't seem to notice them at all as they flitted about, his eyes meticulously examining me.

The two servants disappeared back out of the room quickly. "You look petrified."

I searched my thoughts rapidly to find an appropriate response. "I am."

He looked at me curiously. I felt like he had already discovered my deceit.

"What can I do to help you relax?"

I shook my head quickly. *SPEAK*! I yelled to myself in my head.

With a cough to loosen my throat I replied : "No, nothing. I'm sorry. Everything is all so overwhelming still." I felt a little of the fear fall away as I realized that I could be honest to an extent as to why I was behaving so oddly.

He laughed. "Well of course! I would be concerned if you weren't!"

I reached for a piece of bread on my plate, more for something to fidget with than to eat—I had absolutely no appetite—but dropped it back onto my plate after remembering my manners.

"Oh gosh, I'm sorry! The aroma of this wonderful food must be difficult for you to resist! By all means, dig in!"

When I still didn't move, Mr. Irvine looked at me with a big smile and rolled his eyes.

"You still think I might have had your food drugged?"

The thought hadn't even crossed my mind, but I didn't want him to know exactly how nervous I was.

"Do you want to switch my plate with yours?" he asked.

I shook my head. "No sir, just waiting for you to begin."

"Ah, of course. By all means, don't wait for me."

"Thank you," I replied, not sure if I could even eat.

"Have they been treating you well?"

"Yes sir, just fine thank you." I picked up my fork and knife, laying the crisp white napkin gently across my lap in the process. I nervously pulled my chair in closer to the table and reminded myself to sit up straight.

Just as I went to cut into a steaming sausage on my plate, I caught a glimpse of Mr. Irvine staring at me with a smirk on his face. Awkwardly I lowered my cutlery, feeling suddenly insecure about every single motion I made.

"Are you going to eat as well?" I asked, more of a ultimatum to him that I didn't want to be stared at than a question for which I cared about the answer.

He looked up and laughed. "Oh yes, yes. Don't mind me! I just find your new manners to be adorable!"

I squirmed a little on the inside at the world 'adorable', but I did my best to not let it register on my face.

I waited until Mr. Irvine took his first bite of food before I followed suit. The meat was oily and sweet, very tender and very juicy as I slowly chewed it. On any other day, I wouldn't have been able to hold myself back from devouring every last morsel, but this time I couldn't seem to get my throat to swallow.

I subtly rubbed the coating on my pinky finger with my thumb as I chewed the same piece over and over, staring blankly at my plate in front of me.

"Is there something wrong with your food?" he said after several minutes, his eyes curiously upon me.

I realized that I had eaten less than half of a small sausage.

"No" I said with food still in my mouth, shaking my head. "I'm just..." I choked on the bite in my mouth and felt it slide half-way down my throat as I inhaled. Instantly tears filled my eyes and I began to cough uncontrollably.

"Water, take a sip of water," Mr. Irvine said with genuine worry.

Between coughs I reached for the glass in front of me, knocking it over in the process. Water went all over the table, into my lap, and splashed onto the floor beside me.

"Here, here," Mr. Irvine said, leaning over to pass me his drink. Graciously I threw the liquid down my throat, sputtering in to the glass as I gulped it down.

Finally the muscles in my throat relaxed and I wiped the tears from my eyes.

"Thank you," I said quietly.

"Better?" he asked, dabbing at the water on the table with his napkin.

I nodded. "Yes."

A moment later, the two servers swooped back in through the door pushing a large cart full of new table linens, cutlery and food, and in the time it took me to dab the drops of water from my pants, the table was fully re-set and all new, dry food was steaming on our plates.

"Let's try this again," laughed Mr. Irvine, picking up his utensils eagerly.

I followed suit, cutting once again into the hot sausages. As I chewed the first bite carefully, I realized that I was rubbing my thumb on my fingernail once again.

The coating had dissolved.

I somehow felt instantly more at ease—my stress somehow melted away just as the coating had done. I was no longer about to murder someone.

I took a deep breath and ate heartily.

"So what do you think of this place now that you are becoming more comfortable here?" Mr. Irvine said, wiping the last remnants of food from his lips.

I purposely prolonged the process of chewing my last bite of food as I thought of how to answer. Part of me wanted to tell the truth—that I wasn't getting any more comfortable here; that I was just as scared and nervous as I had been on the first day—but I remembered what the group had told me about trying to win Mr. Irvine's trust.

"It's still a bit overwhelming, to be honest," I mumbled, catching a bit too much negativity in my tone before correcting myself: "But it's incredible"

"Oh I can understand how you would feel overwhelmed. There's so much that is new to you! So many new stimuli! Your brain must be working overtime just trying to process everything that you see and hear!"

I forced a weak smile. "And all the new faces, all the action, all the scheduling. I've never had a schedule before."

"I've never thought of that!" he said with a laugh. "What an alien concept that is to me! Every moment of my life is scheduled!"

"Did you just call me an alien?" I said, forcing my best attempt at a joke.

Mr. Irvine locked eyes on me with curiosity and let out a small chuckle. "So you do have a personality."

I looked down self-consciously at my hands in my lap. "When I'm not scared for my life."

Mr. Irvine let out a heavy sigh and the atmosphere in the room once again felt heavy and dark. I could sense Mr. Irvine was staring at me but I kept my eyes down. I was angry at myself for changing the mood of the conversation. I was supposed to be winning Mr. Irvine over, and here I was going backwards.

"I bring news on Alina and Michael," Mr. Irvine suddenly said brightly.

My heart instantly sank and anger raged through my veins. I could feel my ears growing red and the hair on my arms stand up. I knew that he was about to give me some bullshit story and I fought every urge to jump up and attack him, screaming '*I know what you did to them!*'

I forced myself to push through it. I knew that I didn't have a choice. I wouldn't have a chance if the guards outside the door were to bust in to stop me, and I knew that the rebel plan would fall apart without me.

It killed me a bit inside as I slowly forced myself to look up into Mr. Irvine's eyes and feign a look of interest and hope. It took every bit of focus to suppress the need to grit my teeth and flex my furious fists.

"Oh yah?"

Mr. Irvine's smile seemed to stretch ear to ear. He looked absolutely delighted, as if he was genuinely about to give me the best news I had ever heard.

My lungs strained to breath calmly.

"My sources tell me that Alina has been taken in by a lovely host family outside of Montreal. They say that she is fitting in well with three other girls her own age in the neighborhood and has transitioned successfully into normal life outside of the barn."

A sourness welled up in my chest. I wanted to spit at him. To hit him square between his silver-rimmed glasses.

Out of nowhere a quiet voice spoke. "That's great to hear." It was my own voice.

Mr. Irvine's head tilted to the left for a moment as I spoke. His smile faded slightly.

"Michael, however," he went on, suddenly serious. "Michael has had a difficult time. Being older, he was released into a half-way house for young adults and has had issues understanding the concept of getting a job and earning money to pay for every-day living. Obviously that's something that you both would have trouble understanding, having never experienced that necessity."

I nodded, not quite understanding the concept.

He continued. "The good news is that he has had a lot of support and guidance and in the last month, he has been more successful. Despite the struggles, he is very happy, although he has been asking for information on you as well."

Through all of the anger inside of me, I suddenly felt a tiny twinge of sadness. Even though I knew Mr. Irvine was making the story up, I wondered if Michael had actually asked anyone about me. I knew that he must be terrified, but I knew as well that he would have been more worried about what was happening with me and Alina than he was about his own situation. I wished that I could be with him to let him know that I was okay and that I was coming to save him.

I watched as the clouds floated peacefully above the buildings outside. It was the same sky that I often looked up at from the beach back at the barn; the sun was the same sun; the clouds were the same clouds. How was it possible that the world that it hovered above could vary so much?

A small black bird suddenly darted past my sightline as it angrily chased a much larger one around the building, pecking at the larger birds tail feathers as the pair swooped and rolled through the air. I wondered what the larger bird had done to deserve such an attack--wondered why it didn't turn to fight the smaller one. Above all, I was amazed by the smaller bird's courage.

I suddenly became aware that Mr. Irvine was still speaking.

"And I want you to remember that, Ash. I won't abandon them. I will make sure they have all of the resources necessary to ensure their continued success in society."

I felt myself nod automatically. My pulse was still raging, but my mind was locked on the image of the little bird chasing the larger one. I knew that I had to focus.

"Thank you for that," I said formally, steeling my nerves and hardening my resolve. "What is next on the schedule for me."

Mr. Irvine seemed pleased for the change in subject.

"Ah, an eager lad. I can appreciate that." He wiped the corners of his mouth and turned in his chair to face me. "I have plans for you my boy. Big plans."

****

I was rushed out of the dining room the moment that Mr. Irvine stood to dismiss me with an uncomfortably long hug.

"What the hell happened?" whispered the soldier as he prodded me to walk quicker through the winding halls.

"Sorry!" I said in an angry whisper. "I spilled my water and the stupid tab disintegrated!"

"Fuck!" he cursed.

Emma and Kyal trotted ahead of me without saying a word, but I could tell that they had heard what I had said.

Soon we rounded a familiar corner and were rushing back into Florian's room. It was filled to the brim with even more lavish and outlandish outfits than I had seen earlier in the day. A sweet, fruity smell hung heavily in the humid air, nearly strong enough to make my eyes water.

"Back so soon?" he chirped with delight in his girlish voice.

Emma brushed past him, reaching for a rack of black suits against the wall. "We must immediately prepare him for the auction."

Florian's face changed suddenly from a look of happiness to one of absolute distress.

"What's going on?" I asked, my voice shaking slightly.

Kyal plunked himself dejectedly in a chair against the wall in an uncharacteristic display of emotion. "We must get you ready for the auction," he echoed.

I stood silently, dumbfounded and confused as Florian stripped me naked while the others watched disinterestedly. I looked up to the cameras that were hanging from the ceiling and could see them move slightly as they monitored the room. I understood why nobody was speaking but I was desperate to know what was happening.

Looking to the eyes of Emma, Kyal, Florian and Solomon, it was as if they were complete strangers to me. I couldn't see even the tiniest hint of acknowledgment that we even knew one another. I was suddenly so angry at myself for failing in my mission, so afraid that I had ruined everything.

I felt entirely alone.

Chiku raced into the room as soon as Florian had finished undressing me. She and Solomon whisked me out of the room and through the hall with such urgency that I didn't have time to be insecure about the fact that I was completely naked as I passed curious onlookers.

As the door slid shut behind us, Solomon remained on guard out in the hallway. It was just Chiku and I.

The air in the small room was thick and oppressive and I immediately felt the need to sit down, but there wasn't anywhere to sit.

In the corner, steam poured like a heavy morning fog between the cracks in a glass bi-fold door. I could tell right away that this was the source of the heat in the room. To the left of me, the bath tub that had been filled with frothy bubbles the previous time that I was here was now filled to the brim with clear water and large chunks of ice. Next to the tub, a towel was laid out on the floor, and beside it, a bottle of bright green liquid, a strange, black glove, and a sharp, 'L'-shaped blade.

"Shh," I heard Chiku say, indicating with her hands for me to relax. I turned my gaze away from the sharp blade laying on the towel to look at her. I noticed immediately that her hands were shaking, and despite her coffee black skin, it seemed as if she were pale. For some reason, Chiku was even more terrified than me.

I felt a flutter in my stomach as Chiku indicated for me to wait for a moment as she adjusted some knobs on the wall. The few times that she made eye contact with me, I could see that her eyes were cold and distant. Her movements were stiff and rigid as she pushed me into the dark steam-filled room.

I stood there in the darkness for several minutes, my lungs burning with heat, my body perspiring so profusely that I could feel streams of sweat flowing continually down toward the floor. I had never felt so hot before.

My head quickly began to spin with dizziness. I tried to focus my mind by reviewing the events of the day or by trying to guess what would happen next, but my mind would only concentrate on how hot and uncomfortable I felt.
Soon the heat became unbearable and I let myself squat, then finally sit on the hot wet floor.

I didn't understand what was happening. Was Chiku punishing me? How long would she force me to boil in this heat? What had I done so wrongly? I wasn't a trained soldier—they couldn't have possibly expected me to succeed in my mission on the first try. Or maybe Mr. Irvine had figured it all out and was responsible for what I was being put through.

Just when I thought my lungs were about to give out from the heat, a crack of light appeared in the doorway. Chiku's dark face peered in cautiously, her white hair illuminated by the light behind her like some sort of halo.
Upon seeing my level of weakness, she abruptly threw the door wide open and dragged me by one arm from the room, rolling me roughly onto my stomach on the out-spread towel.

Fog from the steam-room seemed to be lodged in my mind. Every muscle felt weak. My limbs didn't want to co-operate. An overwhelming heaviness filled my entire body.

The rim of a cup pressed against my mouth and I felt my lips instinctually draw the liquid in. It was hot as it touched my tongue, but it wasn't until I swallowed the first few drops that the incredible bitterness registered, burning my sinuses and lungs like fire, awakening the pulse in my heart in a jolting ache that seared its way through my veins.

My body made an attempt to push itself up from the floor to escape this torture, but my arms failed to move me more than a few inches before giving up. A moment later I realized that Chiku was sitting on my back, holding me down with her own body weight.

238

"It okay," I heard her whisper as she pushed the cup to my mouth forcefully. "It bad, but it help."

There was a comforting hum to her voice that reminded me of being lulled to sleep as a sick child and I felt myself relax just a little, despite choking down another taste of the bitter liquid.

Once I had drained the entire contents of the mug, Chiku slowly slid off of me and began rubbing my skin briskly with a course cloth. The sensation was at the same time painful and soothing as thick frothy bubbles began to build up around me, smelling of flowers and sugary treats.

Soon my muscles began to relax and my mind began to let in brief memories of warm ocean waves and gentle breezes.

I felt my body roll over. I was now on my back as Chiku rubbed and lathered and rubbed and lathered. The tension slipped away completely, and for the first time since being in the barn, I was entirely at peace.

A gentle, warm splash of water flowed slowly over me as Chiku's free hand slowly caressed away the froth from my skin. My eyelids flopped open on their own just enough to see the layers of old skin, rolled in tiny black logs, wash off of my chest; the freshly revealed skin glowing pink, feeling clean and rejuvenated.

Out of nowhere I felt a sudden and stinging pain as Chiku's hand slapped down fully on my belly. I lurched up in surprise, letting out a loud yelp in doing so.

I was abruptly and entirely conscious and alert. Chiku stood before me like a scared mouse, entirely convinced that I would lash out at her in defense, and I knew instantly that she had only hit me to wake me from my haze.

She led me back into the steam room despite my objections. The steam stung at my newly raw flesh and a renewed flow of sweat immediately began dripping down the small of my back. After only a few moments, Chiku opened the door and pulled me out once again.

This time she guided me into the bath tub. Chunks of ice parted as I hesitantly slid my body below the surface, my skin feeling as if it were engulfed in flames, my breath sharp like knives being driven into my lungs as the water surrounded my neck. Chiku slowly drained a small bucket of icy water over my head, my ears feeling as if they froze on contact, the sensation on my skin suddenly changing from burning to freezing. My heart began to flutter like a trapped bird, and just when I felt that I couldn't take it any longer, Chiku gently helped me out of the tub and back onto the warm floor.

I immediately felt entirely exhausted. My brain did not want to think, my body did not want to move.

Chiku hummed a quiet, gentle tune as she moved around the room dimming the lights and lighting vanilla scented candles.

I was vaguely aware of her gentle touch as she lathered my face with foam. I didn't even realize that she was using the sharp blade to scrape away the subtle blonde fuzz and patchy coarse hairs from my chin.

The next thing I knew, I was opening my eyes under a stark white ceiling. A familiar, cool breeze blew across my skin, and a subtle scent of roses tickled my nose.

"Oh finally he's awake!" said an effeminate voice.

Florian. "Let's get this going!"

****

I was still in a fog of sleep when I sat up to look at the room around me. As usual, every rack hung heavily under the weight of every style and colour of clothing that could be imagined, though it seemed that this were an entirely different selection of items from the last time that I had been in this room.

I had no idea how long I had been asleep for.

Despite having no windows, a fresh summer breeze blew steady enough through the room to ruffle the frills and edges of the lightest fabrics, making some of the clothing seem as if they had a life and character of their own.

240

Towards the centre of the room, Florian towered above a rack of clothing on impossibly high white shoes that added a full foot or more to his height. He was wearing a tight fitting, curve enhancing, canary yellow dress with ruffles at the shoulders and a neckline that plunged clear past his odd cleavage to his hairy navel at the front and down to a dark tuff of fur just above the small of his back. On his head perched a beehive of platinum white hair at least eight inches high, with lavish, wide curls trailing down to his waist. As he spun to face me, I was both disturbed and astonished by the makeup that plastered his face. Despite his masculine features, he had somehow managed to make his lips full and glossy, his eyes dramatic with long lashes and thick liner, and his nose smooth and graceful. Long, hot pink nails with glossy white tips hung from his fingers like jewels. Had I not known otherwise, I would have never guessed that he were male.

I stood and stretched my tired muscles in an attempt to wake myself up quicker.

In the reflection of the mirrors behind Florian, I could see Emma and Kyal standing shoulder to shoulder behind me, their bright blue eyes glowing against the background of the white wall and the drab, cream coloured clothing that they wore. From this distance, the matching scars on their faces seemed to give them an eerie, sad looking, lop-sided smile that stretched all the way up to one ear.

The pair regarded me blankly, as if not registering my presence at all.

Beside them stood a short, thin soldier clad in the standard white armour, his weapon held at the ready. I did not recognize him.

"I trust you had a wonderfully refreshing nap after your spa treatment with Chiku," said Florian in his sing-song voice as he approached me and clasped both hands on my cheeks. "My you look baby-faced without those tiny sprouts of facial hair!"

I looked deep into Florian's eyes, hoping for some subtle hint that acknowledged our collusion, but saw nothing. Florian was entirely in character.

Once again I felt very abandoned.

"Tonight is a big night for you!" he said through an enormous, excited smile. "It's Auction Night!"

Florian pinched my cheeks gently before twirling away towards a dark rack of men's clothing. He thumbed through it quickly, pushing rejected items away as if he already had an idea of what he was looking for. Settling finally on the desired item, he twirled again in my direction and held up a dark grey suit to my chest.

"Ah perfect! Let's hope it fits!"

I had been wearing only a towel, but was surprised at how comfortable and soft that the new outfit felt against my skin.

Florian helped me to button up the stark white dress shirt with a high collar and adjusted the shoulders on my jacket before stepping back to take a look.

"My, my, what a stunner you are," he said with genuine astonishment.

I stood awkwardly as his eyes surveyed me, uncertain of what to do.

Catching himself lingering too long, he laughed and stepped aside, stumbling slightly on his high shoes.

"Look at yourself!"

I almost didn't believe my own reflection.

At some point while I was asleep, someone had cut my hair shockingly short on the sides, blending somehow seamlessly in to long hair on the top which was slicked back loosely, and somehow highlighted in muted, undefinable streaks of lighter shades of my normally dark brown hair.

Somehow, my skin seemed more golden in tone, my eyes darker and more striking than before.

The suit jacket surprised me the most: It was slim fitting and very complimentary to my broad shoulders, but that wasn't what made it interesting. The smooth, dark grey suit featured strategically placed padding stitched to the outside of the material around my arms, chest and abdomen, just a shade or so darker than the rest of the material, textured like the sinewy strands of muscle beneath the flesh of a newly skinned animal. The affect made me look as if my own muscles were just below the surface, straining against the material to escape, giving me an air of robustness that seemed to naturally suit me. At the same time, the patches somehow looked fashionable, practical and clean-cut. Paired with a simple, thin black tie, dark pants, and sleek, dark shoes, my reflection was more attractive than any man I had seen before.

"What do you think?" Florian said with a smile.

I hesitated as I struggled to believe that the reflection in front of me was in fact my own.

"When did you do this to my hair?"

"You were completely out, no drugs or anything!" Florian laughed. "Honestly! You must have been exhausted! We had no choice but to prop you up and get to work.

Tell me you like it."

I stood up straight, cocked my head to the side and tucked my hands into the pockets of my pants. I looked good.

I nodded. "Yes. I do."

"Oh good, I'm glad to see that you are taking pride in your appearance now."

My eyes caught sight of Emma and Kyal in the background once again. Their stone-still presence and unflinching expression bringing me back to reality.

"What is this 'Auction' you guys talked about."

Florian's cheerful demeanor deflated like a flower begging for water.

He stood still, fidgeting with the clothes hangers in his hands, his eyes focused away from mine intentionally.

Behind me, I heard the soldiers suit rattle slightly as he changed positions and I could see in the mirror that he had adjusted grip on his weapon just slightly.

"It will be a nice evening for everyone," said Florian with a sigh. "People are anxious to meet you."

"People? You mean clients?"

Florian's body language deflated just a little more, but it was enough to confirm my suspicions.

This was it. Tonight I would be auctioned off to the highest bidder.

My insides went cold and felt as if they were shaking. I had to remind myself to breathe.

Not another word was said as Florian finished his final touches to my outfit and dismissed me into the care of Emma, Kyal and the soldier.

It wasn't until the door hissed shut that I heard Florian call out to me "I did your nails while you were asleep as well."

I looked down at the nails on both hands. All were cleanly clipped, sanded and shiny with a clear gloss. Each one looked exactly the same except for the nail on the pinky finger of my right hand. It had been groomed just like the others, yet the glossy polish was slightly different, slightly slimy, and it felt thicker than the others. Florian had applied another film of poison.

****

The room was almost as large as the barn.

It was a vast, open space with small round tables, each with either one or two red velvet chairs at their side, dispersed far away from one another throughout the room. At one end, a massive wall reached up into the darkness above, a huge stage spanning the length of its base. Thick red velvet curtains draped on each side, both concealing a small door from the audience. Down the centre of the huge room, extending out from the stage, a narrow walkway crossed the length of the room about five feet above the existing floor.

Light illuminated the runway while the rest of the space was shrouded in darkness and the fog from dozens of cigarettes. The smell reminded me of cooking rotting food over a campfire.

244

Every seat in the place was full.

I stood on stage at the end of a line of about 30 others—men, woman, children--all immaculately dressed and fidgeting nervously.

A few steps in front of the line, a middle aged man dressed in a dazzling golden suit and matching shoes stood beaming towards the crowd. Lighting from above sparkled off of his bald, glossy head and the metal frames of his thick, golden eye glasses.

"Welcome ladies and gentlemen," His voice boomed unnaturally through the theatre, amplified by some unseen machine. He strode across the stage with practiced, authoritative movements and a serious look on his face that silenced any mumbles from the audience. The excited twinkle in his eyes was visible even from where I stood.

"We are delighted that you are all able to join us this fine evening," he said monotonously. "Please, make yourself comfortable. Servers will be around throughout the night to top up your beverages so drink up. We hope to get through this quickly. Remember, we are offering our best candidates this evening, so get your check books out. Competition will be stiff, if you know what I mean."

In a motion incongruous to his attire, the host grabbed his crotch obscenely at the last part of his speech and the audience clapped and laughed politely.

"Without further ado, let's get on with the show."

A faint round of applause trickled through the darkness.

Seeming to know the routine, the first man at the front of the line nervously adjusted his outfit and took a small step forward and moved to the centre of the stage. He must have been only a few years older than me, his light blonde hair still thick and full, his shortly cropped facial hair not yet completely covering his entire jaw. As he took his position in front of the catwalk, I could see that he was missing several fingers on both of this hands and he walked with a slight limp. A scar glimmered across the back of his head as the spotlights shone down on him.

The audience clapped obediently.

"For those of you who have not yet met Matthew," bellowed the host, swinging his arm to indicate the man in the centre of the stage. "He is one of our most prized candidates."

A bright light flickered and suddenly the walls at either end of the building lit up with a full length image of 'Matthew' standing entirely naked against a white backdrop. The massive image moved entirely life-like--a pre-recorded video of Matthew. I felt a fluttering in my gut as I looked up at the moving picture of him; his muscles so large, his body so toned and attractive. He was physically perfect and intimidating.

Almost every inch of his flesh was covered in a scar or wound of some sort: Multiple interlaced slashes across his back, healed in raised, hardened lines; white, ugly patches that looked like melted plastic; blackened, dimpled areas of tightened skin that resembled large pock-marks of someone who had dealt with bad acne as an adolescent. It was horrific to see and sickening to imagine what he had been through to acquire those scars.

The audience was deathly silent with the exception of a few gasps; some of disgust and others of intrigue.

Beside Matthew's image on the wall, the word "Bidder" lit up in bright green, followed by a golden dollar sign . A moment later, the number 78 lit up beneath the word 'bidder', and the number 1 000 illuminated beneath the dollar sign.

As if on cue, Matthew began walking strongly down the runway in front of him as the announcer spoke again:
"Matthew, as you can see, is one of our finest representatives. He has the looks of a cover-model, the assets of a god, and the obedience of a family dog."

The numbers beside Matthew's image changed. 102, 1 500.

Matthew continued to walk powerfully across the room.

26, 2 000.

"Matthew will do it all, ladies and gentlemen. Aggressive, passive, submissive. You name it. He has been with us for twenty years and has all the experience that you dream of."

The numbers began to change quickly.

11, 2 500.

78, 3 000.

94, 4 500.

Matthew reached the end of the runway and began removing his jacket and shirt.

"Matthew has been tested, treated, and certified healthy by all accounts. Your mind can be at ease as you do with him as you please."

The numbers continued to change rapidly. My mind struggled to understand what was happening. Why was Matthew participating so willingly? Why was he trying to get attention? With a body like that, why hadn't he managed to escape?

"Let it also be known," continued the announcer, his voice growing more dramatic by the sentence. "Our subject is an accomplished chef, a skilled handyman and a detailed domestic servant."

To my left I heard one of the small children begin to whimper.

In one quick motion, Matthew removed his shoes, then slid off his pants, pushing his clothing off the edge of the stage with his foot and into the arms of a waiting servant. In a motion that mimicked his image on the walls, he spun slowly in place, revealing all of his naked body to the audience.

"Last chance," called the announcer. "Don't miss out on our prime offering."

I looked up to the numbers again. They were changing quicker than I could follow.

A hum of activity rumbled through the audience.

"Bidding will end in 5.... 4.... 3.... 2...." The announcer paused for effect. "Bidding is now closed."

11, 14 550.

"Congratulations to bidder number 11."

Matthew gave a simple wave to the audience and hurried back across the catwalk. I felt my eyes locked on him, still trying to figure out why he was so compliant. He passed so closely in front of me on his way to the left stage door that I could smell the sweet cologne on his skin. For a brief second his eyes met mine. They were the emptiest eyes I had ever seen.

"On to lot number 2," blared the announcer.

Once again the room rumbled with commotion. At the end of the line, a young girl, no older than eight or ten swayed timidly. In her hands she held a small wicker basket carrying several yellow flowers that matched her poufy, knee-length dress, white stockings and large hair bow. She stared out into the audience with sheer terror.

From the darkness behind us, a thin person dressed head to toe in a tight fitting spandex unitard that completely concealed his face darted out like a shadow and shoved the girl forcefully out onto the catwalk before slinking back behind the red curtains. Tears began to pour from the girls eyes as she struggled to keep from falling.

The woman two people down the line from me began shaking uncontrollably as she watched the young girl move towards the centre of the stage. As the girls naked image appeared on the walls, I thought for sure that the woman would lunge out in an attempt to save the child, but she stood her ground, lowered her eyes to her feet and sobbed openly.

I felt cold all over as I looked up at the girls image. Already the numbers changed by the second.

52, 12 000.

21, 12 500.

36, 13 000.

I heard the announcer use words such as 'innocent,' 'sweet,' 'untouched,' and phrases like "an unpicked flower," and "a rare treat."

It seemed as if I were floating away. Visions of waves lapping against the wooden boards of the barn chased by a warm summer breeze of salty ocean air filled my head. I thought about the comfort of my old loft bed, cuddled tightly against Alina and Michael, so far away from danger and worry. I could smell Johnna cooking a small meal over a fire and hear Nasha's musical laughter. I floated high above, watching the group smile and tell each other happy stories as they watched the sun set through the open barn door.

I was a lifetime away.

I fell to my knees as the man in the unitard scurried back behind the stage like a scared rat after shoving me painfully between the shoulder blades.

I was suddenly back in this horrible reality.

Only the announcer and I were left on stage. I must have been completely lost in my memories while the others had all been auctioned off.

The room was dead silent as I slowly stood.

"Our final lot for the evening," blared the announcers voice from above. "Number 36451. Ash."

I looked to the host as I heard him call my name. My blood was running cold again and my stomach seemed to roll over within itself. I could feel that my eyes were open wider than what was natural, but I couldn't do anything to relax them.

The announcer stretched his arm out towards me, his palm up, his fingers curling then reopening quickly, beckoning me to come towards him. My mind screamed at me to rebel and stand my ground but my feet seemed to be obeying on their own accord and I found myself walking right up to the man's side.

The room was so still and silent that the sound of my own breathing seemed to be coming from somewhere else.

"Ash is a particularly special treat for us all tonight!" bellowed the man, his voice displaying more excitement than earlier. "If you can believe it, Ash has been with us since he was a toddler and this is his first time taking part in the Auction!"

The walls at the end of the ends of the barn lit up with my naked image. For a moment the picture was frozen and I struggled to remember when it had been taken. Then the image began to move. I saw myself standing in a steaming hot shower, nervously lathering myself with foaming soap, turning just enough to give the viewer a clear image of every inch of my body. I knew right then that it was the footage that Mr. Irvine had taken of me on the night that I had slept in his room.

My skin felt as if it were crawling with bugs as I watched the short clip repeat itself over and over, seeing it now for the first time being almost more humiliating than when it had actually happened.

The crowd came alive with excited mumbling and movement.

"That's right, ladies and gentlemen," the announcer called out loudly to maintain the audience's attention. "This is the Ash. The one that you have all been anxiously waiting for!"

The numbers appeared.

19, 1 000.
"For those of you who have been following us all these years, you will already be aware that Ash is our most prized asset. He is young and virile with all the innocence and eagerness of adolescence and virginity. He is completely unspoiled, pristine and ready to be moulded."

06, 3 000.

22, 4 500.

The man placed his hand firmly on my back and pushed me forward toward the runway. The world seemed to spin as lights hanging from the ceiling moved robotically to focus more intently on me, their heat causing my forehead to begin dripping profusely with sweat.

Cigarette smoke circled all around me and as I walked, the bright lights seemed to thicken the haze, making it feel as if I were walking through a cloud. Voices mumbled all around me like unseen monsters:

"Bid on him! I want him sweetie!"

"Take it off! Take it off!"

"Do you know what I would do with that?"

"Oh I would LOVE to break him!"

"I hope he's a crier!"

I couldn't control my shivering. My hands were trembling so much that I tucked them under my damp armpits as I walked.

I stumbled over my own feet as I reached the end of the runway, nearly falling into the crowd. I tried to make out the faces of people closest to the catwalk, but they were all carefully concealed by the darkness.

I looked up at the moving image of myself as the announcer continued to speak to the audience, my ears seeming to go deaf to his words and the other murmurs in the crowd.

54, 5 000.

85, 8 500.

126, 13 000.

45, 15 500.

I felt as if I had stood there for hours as the crowd ogled me and the announcer drummed on.

My thoughts once again turned to Michael and Alina : Had they been put through this too? Had Michael been brave like the first man, Matthew, or weak and terrified like me? Had Alina wept like the little girl in yellow? Which one of these sicko's bought them?

Finally I heard the announcer bellow triumphantly: "Bidding is now closed! Wow what a record!"

The audience began to clap wildly. Some people even whistled loudly with excitement.

My eyes raised up to the numbers beside my image on the wall.

132, 66 500.

****

I was delirious with fear as a hand pushed me from behind, quickly guiding me through one of the doors at the rear of the stage.

Behind the door, a dimly lit elevator stood open. There were no other exits from the room. I stepped in wordlessly, my mind still locked on stage, shaking as I watched the numbers beside my image as they skyrocketed, the jeering words from the crowd circling in my head like voices from a nightmare.

I was surprised when the rear doors of the elevator opened. I didn't even notice that we had begun to move.

The concrete corridor ahead was dark, long and very narrow. The air smelled musty and damp like sweat after a hard day in the hot sun, but was cold and stale as if it had been trapped for a long time.

At the far end, dull light gave just enough illumination to travel through the passageway without difficulty, but it wasn't until we were half way along that I realized that there were many doors on either side, each one with a number engraved on a silver plaque. The sound of someone crying slipped under the cracks of door number 21 as I passed.

Close to the end of the hallway a hand gripped me from behind, pulling me to a stop in front of door number 28. A cold chill ran down my spine as my brain struggled to prevent itself from thinking about what may be waiting for me behind the door.

The hand released its grip on my jacket.

I kept my eyes locked on the dull light at the end of the corridor. It was only a few strides away. There didn't seem to be anyone up ahead and any noises I heard were coming from behind me.

My already rapidly beating heart pushed blood even quicker through my body, infusing every vessel with adrenaline. I felt instantly energized.

I didn't know what was out there, but I was certain that it would be better than what was waiting behind door number 28.

The person behind me seemed to be busy fidgeting with the lock on the door.

I could do it. I could run.

I clenched my fists tightly, readying myself, emboldening my own feet to move.

The lock on the door clicked.

Now! Run now!

"Ash."

I instantly felt my body deflate: I knew that voice.

"Ash, you have to go in."

Emma.

I slowly pivoted to face her.

In the hurriedness and darkness of our departure from the stage, I hadn't even glanced at the person who egged me into the elevator and down the long tunnel. My mind had been too overwhelmed and terrified to focus on anything other than my basic movements. I had barely registered the thought that someone was even behind me.

I was shocked once again to see Kyal standing dutifully behind Emma, his chest almost pressed against her back in the narrow space. His face was unusually emotional: his eyes were red and bloodshot, the corners of his mouth slightly downturned. I noticed that he did not interject in that usual rapid-fire way that he and Emma were known for.

I felt a powerful sense of hopelessness and relief at the same time: I knew the pair were about to send me into a situation where I could be forced to face unimaginable horrors, but a tiny part of me held out hope that they would be able to help me somehow.

I expected her to give me instruction or an explanation of what lay ahead for me; some sort of breakdown of rules or expectations, or advice to make it easier on myself. My full attention was on her for this. My head and heart were desperate for guidance. I was out of courage, out of strategy, out of energy. I needed some kind of hope.

Emma blinked several times suddenly, as if coming back from a dark place in her own mind, shocked to see me standing in front of her now.

She stared at me for a moment before speaking again, her eyes boring deep into mine in a soulful, warm way that I didn't think she was capable of.

A tear glistened on the rim of her lower eye lid. Kyal remained behind her, silently staring downward.

Her hand touched my elbow softly. "I'm....I'm sorry, Ash."

With a gentle push of her other hand, the black steel door beside her swung open.

I couldn't see anything other than an empty black hole with no indication of its size or contents. A rancid, spoiled-milk smell poured out of the opening.

"Please. There is no point in delaying any longer," Emma said softly, indicating with her hand for me to enter.

I looked to the two of them for a moment longer, hoping to hear them say something helpful—anything at all in fact—but when nothing came forth, I gently nodded my head and stepped into the dark space.

****

The room was completely dark.

I stood completely still for a few minutes waiting for my eyes to adjust, but when there was no change I felt my way further into the room until I found a hard bench to sit down on. It was cold and slightly damp, my hands sticking to a thin layer of slime that coated its surface.

The air was absolutely stagnant and the sour-milk smell was now layered strongly with that of mildew or mould.
I could hear my own breath echo against the stone walls so clearly that I could tell that the room was not very large.

I felt nothing. No fear, no nervousness.

It was as if my mind and body had given up. I fought the urge to lay flat on the bench and just close my eyes. Maybe I would fall asleep and my mind would have time to rejuvenate itself. Maybe I would wake up and feel like I had even the tiniest bit of control over my situation. Better yet, maybe this was all just a bad dream. Maybe I would wake up and be back in the barn on my cozy nest by the fire and none of this would have ever happened.

But no, I knew it wasn't a dream. Even in the darkness, everything felt far too real.

As time wore on, I began to grow very uncomfortable. My back was hurting and I started to feel weary from the absolute darkness. I needed an anchor in this black, undefinable space, something physical and recognizable to keep me from feeling as if I were falling into some endless hole--somewhere to rest my exhausted body.

I slid my hands along the bench below me. As my fingers traced along the slick, greasy surface, I began to feel as if I were seeing through my fingertips. The bench seemed to be made of wood, bound tightly in a plastic covering. A small bump here, a seam there, a grain of sand grinding incongruously across the slimy material.

As I reached further, the opposite edges were still out of reach and it became clear that this was not a bench that I was sitting on. My fingers followed the side as it turned ninety degrees. I leaned back, resting on my left elbow and continued to slide my hand into the darkness. It wasn't until my body was completely stretched and my knuckles bumped against the rough brick of the wall that I moved my hand in towards the centre of the surface to feel the soft, damp pillow.

This was a bed.

I'm not sure if I felt relief for having a place to lay down or fear for not knowing how long I was expected to sleep in this horrible place, but I pulled my feet up onto the bed and found the pillow with my head.

The sensation of the damp, squishy fabric felt odd on my newly cropped hair; somehow similar to the feeling of laying my head onto a chunk of raw pork fat, but its coolness was surprisingly comfortable. It was the smell that bothered me most: the putrid, bitter scent of a damp rag that hadn't been cleaned properly, left out on a hot day. I forced myself to ignore the odour and laying perfectly still on my back, staring blankly into the darkness as the moisture from the surface of the bed seeped through my clothing and onto my already clammy skin.

Exhaustion overcame me quicker than expected and I realized that I felt the tiniest bit grateful that I had been forced to sleep in the tiny room back in Mr. Irvine's tower that had deprived me of any outside stimulation. A few days ago, being locked in this silent, pitch black room would have made me curl up in a ball of panic. I was now thankful for the isolation.

Somehow I drifted into a dreamless sleep.

****

I don't know how long I slept for. It could have been hours, it could have been minutes, or maybe I had only blanked out for a few seconds, but I awoke feeling instantly alert. As my eyes popped open, I saw nothing but absolute darkness. My breath caught in my lungs as my hands flew up to my eyes to feel if something was covering them—my heart almost stopping when I felt the burning sensation of my fingers touching my open eyeballs. I was certain that I had somehow been blinded in the night. It wasn't until I noticed the odd crinkle of the wet plastic on the bed below me and felt the moisture in my clothing that my mind clicked back into motion and I was brought back to reality and remembered where I was.

Hell.

I sat up on the hard bed and hugged my knees as I forced my heart to control its beating. Gone was the calm, disconnected mindset of before I fell asleep. I felt like ice pellets were thundering through my system as last night's events on stage flooded my mind with renewed disgust and horror.

Also gone was any doubt at all about Mr. Irvine's true motive for holding me and everyone I had ever known captive.

I had almost believed him.

His openness and sincerity when he spoke of having no other choice but to step in to save all those people seemed so genuine. It made sense. I wanted to believe it.

The story that Sarah, Florian and the others told had seemed unbelievable. It was unthinkable that anyone could do that to other human beings. Everything in me had doubted their version of events and wanted to believe that they were just disgruntled rogues who wanted a scapegoat for their actions.

But thinking of that line-up of scared, fidgeting people up there on stage— handsome Matthew, covered in scars, eyes as dead as night; the tiny girl in the yellow dress with the matching bow; the woman, who I have taken to assume was the girl's mother, whimpering hopelessly as she watched the child being auctioned off in front of a room full of sicko's—I knew now without a doubt that anything and everything could happen out here in this strange outside world.

Sitting up on the hard platform, I shook my head in an attempt to clear my thoughts and cool my nerves. I realized that my hands were shaking. I alternated between clenching my fists and shaking my arms wildly but the trembling wouldn't stop .

I felt my way to the edge of the bed and lowered my feet to the ground. My clothing made a slight sucking noise as I lifted my damp body from the sticky plastic covering, my hands outstretched scanning my surroundings for obstructions. It was good to stand. My muscles were sore from the hard platform and strained from the emotional stress.

I suddenly felt a burning in my bladder that I had been unaware of earlier. It quickly grew unbearably intense and I realized that I hadn't relieved myself since the previous morning.

I had to go now.

"Hello?" I yelled, hoping someone on the outside would hear me. My voiced boomed in my ears as the room echoed my call eerily. "Is anyone out there?"

I listened intently for a response.

Nothing.

I remembered hearing the muffled sound of someone crying from behind the heavy steel door of room number 21 as Emma and Kyal has ushered me down the dark corridor. Maybe someone would hear me if I got closer to the door.
I felt my way along the cold stone wall, my fingers every so often bumping into small steel hooks and loops that protruded from the mortar.

On the third wall I felt the smooth, cold surface of the steel door and immediately began calling out.

"Hello! I have to take a leak! Hello? Anybody!"

Silence.

I banged heavily against the steel, the echo in the room sounding like thunder from a violent storm.

"Hello!?"

Nobody was coming. I think I knew that before I had even began calling out.

The pain in my groin was growing stronger by the minute. Like a child, I literally held my penis to avoid urinating all over myself. In the barn, we never had the luxury of toilets, but always had a designated spot in the farthest corner of the barn in which to relieve ourselves, far away from where we slept, ate and hung out. Here, in this small, dark room, where the walls were nearly within reach of each other, there was no place far enough away to distance myself from the smell of mess.

In final desperation, I unzipped my pants and urinated onto the steel door.

Finding my way back to the wooden bed, I crawled once again onto its sticky, plastic surface and rest my back and head against the wall behind me.

Ice continued to scrape its way through my veins. I struggled to fight against my own mind to prevent it from picturing various scenarios as to what might be about to happen to me; images of myself chained to a bed, surrounded by old naked people wearing mask just like I had seen in the image that Sarah had shown me of Michael; visions of myself being beaten and forced into servitude just as Chiku had been—ladders and cross hatches of scars climbing from bleeding wrists to a band of oozing rings around my throat; the reflection of myself in the mirror as I carved a crooked, disfiguring smile up my cheek to my left ear, just as Kyal and Emma had done. Every time a new image popped into my mind I shook my head violently to escape the thought, though moments later a new, more gruesome one followed.

I tried to think of other, happier things from life in the barn: The large stone that Michael and I used to play with as kids, laughing and screaming with joy—my mind flashed once again to the image of him screaming on that bed.

The memory of little Alina in her pink sweater, smiling up at me as I we cuddled beside a warm spring fire—flash to the memory of her mother, Julie, screaming herself to death as baby Alina got stuck in her birth canal.

Moments of successful fishing ventures, stacking row upon row of fish upon our drying racks under the hot sun, finally providing adequate nutrients to our starving group—skip to the moment the door of the barn closed, trapping me inside, and Michael and Alina out.

I tried to think of a way to get the upper hand: When the door finally opens, maybe I could dash out and out run whoever was out there.

Maybe I could hide behind the door as it opened, jumping on the person that came in and force him to let me go.

Maybe I could just talk calmly with the person and convince them that I was a good person and didn't deserve all of this.

I knew of course that none of it would work.

There was no escaping.

I didn't even know who I would be trying to escape from. It could be a lone man. It could be an old woman. It could be a solider, or a team of soldiers. It didn't matter anyway. I was weak, tired and disoriented. Whoever came through that door would be more ready for me than I was for them and I knew it.

As scenario after scenario and worry after worry raced through my mind, I realized that I was exhausted with tension. Saliva was building up in the back of my throat, my stomach felt sour and empty, my face felt damp with sweat.

I started to feel myself growing impatient with waiting for something to happen. It must have been hours since I woke up.

Sitting here in absolute darkness and silence knowing that something horrible would eventually be happening to me became maddening. My fears began to blend with a sudden infusion of anger and I wanted to throw something. I got up from the bed and felt my way once again along the cold wet walls and began pounding on the door with both of my fists.

"Let me out! I dare you! Come get me! I can handle you!"

I punched and yelled until the flesh on my hands throbbed, my lungs burned, and the smell of urine finally turned my already tortured stomach, dry heaving small mouthfuls of rancid saliva into a the pool of piss.

But still no one came.

Exhausted in every way, I found my way back to the bed, laid my head down and cried.

I just wanted it over with.

****

I heard the jingle of keys only a second or two before I heard one slide into the keyhole of the thick metal door.

I had been laying in a semi-unconscious state staring blankly at the unseen ceiling, too tired to think, somewhere far off in the depths of my mind, straining my eyes to see if I could see any stars.

The noise brought me back to reality immediately, once again throwing my heart and my nerves into a turbulent storm.

I sat upright on the bed as if a lightning bolt had hit me, staring in to the darkness towards where I knew the door to be, wanting to hide, afraid to move, fully aware that there was nowhere to hide.

The heavy lock turned with a thud.

A thin line of light crept around the frame of the door, glowing like a daytime eclipse of the sun.

Suddenly the door exploded open with a bang as it slammed into the stone walls, the outside light stinging my unaccustomed eyes as if the sun itself had landed in my brain, giving me an instant headache.

Four hands were immediately upon me, forcing me down onto the bed, ripping my suit jacket, shoes and socks off me before I could resist. Suddenly one person was stretching my arms above me against the cold wall, binding my wrists tightly together and into a steel eyelet in the brick using some sort of plastic tie in a prayer-like hold. The other person did the same to my feet, hooking them to a steel chain that rattled loudly as it was pulled from under the bed.

I fought back as they restrained me, but their hands were too quick, too practiced, and before I knew it, they were retreating from the room as quickly as they came. Through squinting eyes I caught a glimpse of Emma's long golden hair as she left through the door.

A feeling of utter betrayal washed over me. I couldn't believe that she would have taken any part in this without trying to help--some sign of camaraderie at least. Even just an acknowledgement that she knew me would have brought me a small measure of strength.

Frustrated and scared, I twisted my body and tugged at the plastic ties that held me, hoping one would snap or come free somehow, but the muscles in my arms and legs were stretched so tightly that each movement came with searing pain.

A man's voice mumbled something inaudible to the others in the corridor and I froze in fear. It was about to begin.

With a blinding flash, the ceiling suddenly lit up, once again slamming my eyes and the back of my head with pain.

I could hear his footsteps as he entered—the slow click-clack of expensive, hard soled shoes on the concrete floor.

The steel door thudded shut. I heard the key turn in the lock.

I strained to open my eyes but the light was just too much. I could feel his presence as he stood silently by the entrance.

Watching me.

I forced my left eye to open just a crack. The light was becoming less painful with every second, and in the quick glimpse that I had, I was able to see the wall to my left. Its cement bricks were dark with dirt and various stains three quarters of the way up, but white and clean above that. Every few feet, little round eyelets or holes alternated around the room at varying heights with rusty brown chains sticking out a link or two from the occasional hole. A strange system of pulleys and ropes hung from the ceiling, just high enough to be out of the way. I recognised it instantly as being just like the room in the picture where Michael had been tortured. My eye squeezed tightly shut in horror as I willed myself to push Michael's image from my mind.

The click-clack of his shoes echoed once again as he crossed the short distance to the bed side. His sharp cologne stung my nostrils.

Again he stood deathly still. I could tell that he was only inches from the side of the bed. I couldn't bring myself to open my eyes. I wanted to be in some faraway place. To open them would to accept that this was really happening.

A gloved hand touched my chin, holding it gently even though I tried to pull away. It was smooth and warm, but I could tell there was strength in the wide fingers.

Against my will I felt my eyes slowly open.

A gold belt buckle was the first thing I saw. Embossed into its ornate swirls and lines was the face of a crying child looking straight at me, the wide wings of an angel stretching out from each side of the head to the edge of the clasp.

Looking up, my eye stung all the more as the light bore down from above. The man before me was silhouetted, his bright white suit glowing like a cloud on a sunny day. I could see that his well-kept, white hair sat in a tidy wave across his head, glowing like a tarnished halo. A thin line above the bridge of his nose hinted that he was wearing glasses.

I didn't figure it out until he spoke.

"Good to see you again, Ash."

Mr. Irvine.

I felt as if I had had the wind knocked out of me. Mr. Irvine. He was the last person I had expected to see here. I guess I had just assumed that by putting me up for auction, that he was done with me.

I struggled to understand what he was doing here.
.
I opened my eyes fully.

He was staring down at me through his silver rimmed glasses, looking just as proper and professional as ever, but something was different; something in his eyes. Gone was the soft, sincere gaze that I had been so surprised to see in him when we first met. He looked tense--angry even, despite a subtle grin. I felt almost as if I were a child being scolded for something that I had done wrong.

But there was something more. Something darker. As he stared down at me, looking my stretched body up and down carefully, I recognized that look. Hunger.

"You're surprised to see me." His voice was dark and heavy. Challenging somehow. The stench of booze and stale smoke flowed over me like a fog.

I ran through a few quick responses in my head. I wanted to yell at him--to tell him off, to spit in his face for what he has put all of those innocent people through. I knew that he had the upper hand though. I would gain nothing from berating him other than the satisfaction of getting it off of my chest. Deep inside I still hoped that there would be some way to get out of this—to get back up to the safety and solitude of the quiet room that I had been sleeping in; to convince Mr. Irvine to let me go back to life in the barn.

I decided to reply as politely as I could.

"You could say that," I said, attempting to sound relieved, but coming across as annoyed.

He let out a little huff of amusement. "You had hoped to be rid of me by now."

I went on the defensive. "No, no, not at all! I… I didn't…. understand why you let me in that situation. When you said that you had big plans for me, I thought that you mean with you. In the company. Not this."

He backed away with a laugh of disbelief.

"Cut the shit, kid!" he yelled, slamming his fist against the stone wall. Anger raged across his face causing a vein in his forehead to bulge forward. I turned my head in fear as spit from his mouth flew in my direction.

"YOU'RE FULL OF IT! You're a *horrible* actor! I could see the way you were clenching your fists and averting your eyes when I saw you last! Hell, I could almost feel lasers burning into my skull every time you did make eye contact with me! You were shaking like a leaf on a windy day and don't try to tell me it was nervousness! You were furious!"

"No!" I choked out, horrified to be called out. "No you're wrong! I was exhausted and overwhelmed!"

"Bullshit!" he yelled furiously, his face only inches from mine. I held my eyes, nose and mouth shut as if I were diving under water.

"I've watched you for your entire life! I know your body language! I know your genuine smile! I know every fucking thing about you!"

He took a deep breath and seemed to calm himself a little. I could see him contemplating his next thoughts.

"Who got to you?" he asked finally.

I felt the hairs on the back of my neck rise. How did he know?

"Wh… What?" I stuttered.

He turned towards me. His face was cold and blank.

"Let's not play games."

I stared back with what I hoped was a look of confusion.

"I could tell the moment you walked in for breakfast. You looked like a cross between an angry bull staring into a matadors red cape and a terrified fawn about be hit by a Mack truck!"

"I don't know what you want me to say," I pleaded softly, his words about me being a terrible actor screaming in my mind.

He leaned back against the wall casually, though I could see an air of hostility in his motions. His eyes were locked on mine. I could feel them boring into my brain, reading my thoughts, knowing the truth without me needing to say it. I could feel him manipulating words in my head, threatening me from within.

I shook my head slightly and shrugged my shoulders slightly despite the restraints.

I could tell immediately that he wasn't falling for it.

"Chiku," he grunted, a look of bitter comprehension spreading over his face. "I saw her whispering to you." My heart dropped and I found myself flinching at the mention of her name.

He tilted his head slightly, as if my simple movement had spoken volumes. "And someone else."

I felt sick to my stomach.

Pushing himself off the wall, he came toward me slowly, glaring down at me bitterly. "Florian."

"No!" I coughed out. "No you're wrong!"

265

He smiled confrontationally.

"It's not them, leave them alone!"

"So you're admitting that someone did get to you." I felt myself flush with stupidity as his smile grew impossibly wider.

"No, that's not what I said!" I squirmed uncomfortably. "They're all... none of them...none of them told me anything!

Mr. Irvine slowly shook his head, his eyes still reading me like a blurry word written in the sand.

"Shit!" he yelled suddenly, turning to pace the room in fury once again. He turned back to me with rage in his eyes. "What is this? A coup or something? A little army of boy scouts trying to bring down a god?"

He snickered with irritation, stepping aggressively towards me again. "What do they think they're going to do, start a little support group? Call the police?!

They'll all pay, you know," he grunted vehemently, his eyes cold and dark. "All of them. I own them! I control everyone! "

He backed away and paced a few steps angrily. Just as in Mr. Irvine's bedroom, I noticed that there was no sign of a limp, no sign of the helpless, frail old man that I first encountered. If anything, he seemed younger and stronger than ever.

"Why are you doing this?" I asked softly, hoping that by getting him to explain, he would feel the tiniest sense of compassion and go easier on me. "Why now? Why bother putting me in that auction if this was your goal all along?"

He turned to face me with a look of enjoyment flashing behind his menacing eyes. "First rule of business in my opinion, my dear boy is to create interest in your product. You drive the price up, you create demand." He began loosening his tie. "Of course, the second rule is to test out your product to make sure it is up to par."

I understood it now: It had all been a ruse—a smoke screen to make me feel sorry for him, to believe his sob stories of having no choice but to take in so many innocent people who had nowhere else to go. It was a ploy. A Game. Get me to trust him and believe him and feel safe with him, then swoop in and break me into a million pieces—a shattered, empty void of a soul to be used and moulded for his own purposes. It gave him a sense of power and control that I could never fully understand or would never want to experience.

He had already started to pull off his white suit jacket, folding it neatly in half before dropping it uncaringly onto the dirty floor.

I didn't see it coming.

All of a sudden my face was stinging and my head felt thick and heavy. My ears began to ring loudly. I looked out at the blurry room and felt a mixture of tears and blood flowing down my face.

My eyes were still twisted in murky confusion as his fist hit my face for a second time.

"You'll see, you little fucker!" I heard Mr. Irvine yell. "I'll show you why you should never cross me!"

A second later I felt the buttons on my shirt pop and fly across the room as he tugged forcefully at it with both hands, ripping it wide open, exposing my chest and stomach.

With a forceful yank, Mr. Irvine undid the clasp on my belt, pulling it clear of the loops in one swift motion.

I heard the first lashing before I felt it, my belly suddenly feeling as if hot embers were searing through the skin from one side to the other. The snap of the leather against my flesh seemed to echo over and over in the room as he hit me harder and harder, my lungs too stunned by the pain to inhale enough to let out a scream.

Suddenly he was yanking at my pants. The momentary break from the whipping provided precious seconds of relief as I caught my breath and was able to let out a much needed roar of agony.

He seemed to have trouble pulling my pants and underwear down towards my feet, swearing as he tugged, the material warming my skin like a rope burn as it slid down.

My head spun as it tried to process the pain. I felt him hit me again, this time his belt grazing the sensitive skin around my penis as it cracked down.

In my haze I sensed Mr. Irvine step back . I could hear him pulling at his own clothing. I knew what was about to happen.

In my head I was screaming, cursing like I had never cursed before; my arms and legs were flailing violently, fighting against my restraints, slowly loosening them, but in reality I knew I was barely moving. My head and face was throbbing, my eyes were already swelling shut, my mouth hung open, begging for a breath, my skin felt like it were on fire, my body was stretched just a bit too far to allow me to move at all.

I could do nothing to help myself.

"You're mine you little shit!" he grunted almost under his breath as he pulled off his own pants.

With surprising force, Mr. Irvine gripped me by the hips and rolled me over onto my stomach. The raw, bleeding wounds seemed to stick to the plastic sheet on the bed, tearing them open further. I felt as if the muscles in my arms were ripping right off the bones as the restraints around my wrists now pulled them backwards, painfully arching my back and shoulders.

Sweat dripped down into my eyes and into the bleeding cuts on my cheekbones, rolling off of my chin in pink drops, absorbing into the brown pillow under my face. I was both cold and hot at the same time, shivering from within.
I felt empty, dark.

Mr. Irvine's weight pushed heavily onto the back of my legs, driving my boney knees into the wooden surface of the bed with a new shock of pain. The bare skin of his smooth legs and rear felt surprisingly cold against my own, sticking uncomfortably as he adjusted his position.

Acid burned up into my mouth, my face felt flushed and tingly. I heard myself start to whimper.

He leaned forward, pressing a hand firmly onto the small of my back. I felt his mouth beside my ear.

"Let's see if you're as good as Michael was."

He shifted his weight again, moving his body further up my legs, pushing my upper body down further into the hard bed, straining my arms to their limit.

Suddenly I felt a sharp pain in my right hand and I could feel blood flowing down between my palms. For a second I thought my flesh had ripped open under the pull of my weight against the straps. I let out a yelp of pain.

Mr. Irvine laughed and smacked me violently on the back with his open hand. I shuddered in reaction, tugging hard against the plastic bindings involuntarily.

Then I felt it.

There was something squished between my hands. It was small, but its sharp edge dug into the flesh of my middle finger, cutting through the skin and muscle with ease.

I flashed back to the moment when the door to this dark room flew open and two people ran in to tie me down. I hadn't realized until they raced out of the room that one of them had been Emma. I had felt sickened and let down that she hadn't done anything to help me. In my heart I had known that she couldn't have even if she wanted to, but from that moment I doubted her loyalty to me. I now understood: showing any sign of acknowledgement to me would have focused attention on her as she slipped a tiny knife between my palms as she bound me. I hadn't noticed it before because it was so thin and short that it fit perfectly--the pain in my wrists, arms, and now the wounds from the belt blocking out any other sensations.

Adrenaline rushed through me. As Mr. Irvine positioned himself, I focused all of my attention on the knife. It was my only hope. With all the strength I could muster, I began rubbing my hands together. Because of the weight pulling down, there was very little movement, but I could feel the small blade slicing upward, cutting towards the tip of my finger.

Mr. Irvine pressed himself hard against me, the course hair of his groin scratching my smooth skin as he prepared to get in to a position that suited his desires.

The knife slid slowly up. I could feel the handle pressed tightly between the index and middle fingers of my hands now.

Mr. Irvine was trying to use his legs to force mine apart. The shackles around my ankles cut deeply into my skin. I flexed my legs as tightly as possible.

Another great slap echoed off the walls as he smacked me with his open hand again. I threw my head back, yelling out in pain.

"Scream all you want, kid!" he laughed, yanking my head back by the hair. "It just makes it better for me!"

With my head in this position, I could clearly see the blade. It was just a hairs breadth from the plastic tie that looped through the ones around my wrists and up into a ring in the wall.

My muscles were shaking and burning from trying to resist him. My whole body was covered in sweat now. As he pushed down harder on me, he grunted with satisfaction.

My eyes were locked on the blade. It rubbed gently against the plastic loop, but wasn't cutting through it.

He pulled my hair back further. My hair felt as if it would come out in one big chunk.

His smoky, boozy breath burned my nostrils.

"I think Alina fought harder than both of you."

For a split second I pictured frail, sweet, timid Alina in my position, her naked little girl body held down under the weight of this heavy, disgusting old man as he forced his way inside of her. I hadn't allowed myself to picture this before-- somewhere in my mind, I knew that it must have happened, but until now it hadn't been a reality to me.

Rage coursed through me, pushing the adrenaline to the tips of every nerve in my body. I suddenly found myself bucking my hips and twisting like a trapped wild animal. Mr. Irvine lost his grip on my hair and was thrown from my back, falling hard onto the foot of the bed. With his weight off of me, the tiniest bit of slack was released and I was able to press up on the blade, forcing it against the plastic tie that looped through the metal ring in the wall.

It popped apart with a snap.

I felt my chest fall to the bed, my face scraping against the coarse wall as I went down.

Without a thought, I was already in the process of rolling over onto my back, pulling my knees to my chest and lunging towards Mr. Irvine.

It had all happened in a matter of a second or two and he hadn't had time to realize what was going on. His eyes seemed to pop out from behind his glasses as I leapt onto him, his left hand on his penis, the other only half way up to his face to defend himself.

I had meant to jab the knife into his throat but my arms felt too light and weak to co-operate. With my hands still bound at the wrists, it felt as if I were diving into water as my fingertips smashed into his abdomen. I could feel the blade pierce the soft area above his navel as my shoulder crashed into his cheek. I shoved my hands forcefully inward as we both rolled off the bed and onto the cold, slimy floor.

Mr. Irvine's head cracked grotesquely onto the concrete as I landed on him, but he shoved me hard and quickly rolled out from under me.

My arms were tingling as blood flowed back into them. The butt of the knife hung from the tips of my fingers and I fumbled to keep hold of it. Only the top part of the blade had blood on it, and I knew that I hadn't injured Mr. Irvine enough to disable him.

He was already scurrying to his feet, using the edge of the bed to pull himself up. One hand covered the wound on his stomach, blood trickling between his fingers, past the fold of skin under his belly and into the white hair of his crotch. I could see that he was in severe pain and seemed shaken and disoriented.

I knew that I only had a few seconds to free myself.

With a twist I pulled myself into a sitting position--the metal restraints around my ankle looked as if they were ripping my flesh right off the bone as I moved. Blood oozed around the cuffs like a freshly killed animal. Another wound which I didn't have time to dwell on, but knew I would suffer from later. I tucked the knife, blade up, between my two big toes.

Out of the corner of my eye I could see Mr. Irvine reaching for his belt—the one with the huge golden buckle.

I swung my wrists down hard towards the blade. I felt a sting in my ankle as my hands hit my feet. The blade had missed the plastic tie completely, slipping right between the tight coil. A bit further off to the side and I could have slit my own wrist. I pulled my arms upward, freeing the blade and swung again, this time slower and more precise. The blade hit the plastic dead on and the tie snapped off immediately.

I was mortified to see that it wasn't a coil, but several individual ties.

Mr. Irvine swung his belt powerfully. Fire ripped across my left arm as the leather hit my skin. The buckle smashed like a rock into the bones of my right elbow. A shockwave of agony sent shivers through my body.

All of a sudden he was kicking me. It was so rapid-fire that I couldn't protect myself. His foot smashed into my leg, then my arm several times, then my shoulder. The force of it knocked me over and he kicked me in the back, right between the shoulder blades.

I heard him yelling but my ears were ringing too much to make out his words.

As he swung his foot to kick me again, this time in the back of the legs, I twisted my body and pulled the knife from between my toes.

In a flash I found myself rolling towards him. I saw him stagger backwards to brace himself for another kick.
Everything suddenly felt as if it were moving in slow motion.

I lurched my upper body towards him, scraping my left side along the rough floor, throwing my arms towards his feet. His back hit the wall behind him as he hopped to dodge my strike. I swung again, the knife tightly between my fingers. He raised his left foot as the blade came near but couldn't get his right foot up quick enough. The blade sliced easily through the area of tendons behind his ankle, sending him crumbing to the floor.

His torso landed squarely on my legs, his head at my feet, entangling our bodies in an awkward pile as he howled loudly. Blood from our wounds mixed in a pinkish slime as we struggled, kicking and pulling at one another, partly trying to attack, partly trying to get away from each other.

He kicked with his uninjured leg and threw his knees into my stomach while I elbowed his groin and bit his thighs.
I looked for a vulnerable spot to stab him with the knife again: somewhere where the short blade would do more than just superficial damage. I made contact with his skin a few times, causing nothing more severe than a simple flesh wound. As we rolled and twisted, his body was sliding further away from mine, his toes now down by my waist.

I couldn't believe that this old man had more stamina than I did. I had always been thin and weak—years of malnourishment and low activity had taken its toll on my body—and I was now exhausted and sore from all of my wounds. The adrenaline in me was pushing me forward, but my body was starting to give in.

I could tell that Mr. Irvine was suffering too—his breath was pained and wheezy, his face contorted in a mix of pain and anger—but even in his old age, his muscles were more developed than mine and his fighting skills were more practiced and efficient.

Soon he would be free from my hold and once again grab the upper hand.

I knew I had to strike now.

Just as I was about to drive the blade into the back of his knee, the only debilitating spot within my reach now, his foot crashed into my arms and the knife went flying across the room, rattling into a corner.

Without a moment's hesitation, I pulled back on his leg and rolled my body up and over his waist until our faces were just inches apart. His hands were immediately around my throat, squeezing so hard that I could feel his long nails digging into the flesh. Somehow he rolled me onto my back and used his body weight to push down harder.
I pushed up against his chest with my bound hands but couldn't get the leverage. I began twisting and wriggling my body like trapped fish, but the chain around my ankles was pulled tight and he had straddled my hips in a way that kept me pinned to my spot.

My face began to burn and my brain started to hurt as the blood trapped in my head had nowhere to go. I gasped for air but couldn't get anything past the spot where he held my throat shut and my lungs began to feel as if they would explode.

He pressed down harder still, grunting and yelling with fury, and I started to feel light headed. My struggles dwindled down to nothing more than a feeble flailing.

At some point, Mr. Irvine's glasses had fallen off. His eyes somehow looked colder without them. Meaner. He smiled as I weakly reached up towards them with my clasped hands. I wanted to so badly to rip them from his head.

With a slight stretch of his neck he was able to keep my fingers just below his nose. My nails scored bright red lines into his cheeks and the space above his lips, but I didn't even have enough strength to draw blood.

His maniacal smile grew.

I started to see dark spots and nothing felt real. Every part of me felt cold and weak. My arms began to feel limp. I was fading quickly.

I looked up at my hands, willing them to find the strength to reach that inch or two more.

Darkness was creeping in. My eyes flickered shut for a second. I felt my hands drop slightly. The tips of my fingers grazed his lips. They were soft and wet with saliva. My eyes popped open, for a moment thinking that I had touched his eyeball.

That's when I saw it—the shiny surface on the nail of my pinky finger. It was dangling half off like a flake of sunburned flesh, but it was still intact.

With my last bit of energy I shoved my pinky between his lips.

He bit down hard but still I pushed. He gagged suddenly and I forced my hand in further still, all four of my fingers now between his jaws, feeling the silky softness of the back of his throat.

His hands flew up to mine, easily wresting them away but I could see that the damage was already setting in.

Saliva oozed from his lips and fell on my face as he toppled backwards. His mouth hung open wide, sucking in short wheezy breaths in between violent retches.

I pushed myself away from him, sliding myself across the floor to lean my back against the bed, my mouth sucking in air like a fish out of water, my eyes locked on Mr. Irvine.

He had dragged himself towards the wall and tried unsuccessfully to stand up. He fell to a seated position, his back against the wall, facing me. I felt as if I were floating somewhere up near the ceiling, staring down at the scene as if it were happening in another world.

His eyes seemed to bulge from his face, somehow pleading with me, begging for help, while at the same time staring me down with sheer viciousness.

His naked body began to shake.

He seemed to be reaching for his heart but his hands got stuck in the air just inches from the grey hair on his chest.
I could hear his throat gurgling as if he had just inhaled a mouthful of water, but the saliva had stopped flowing from his mouth.

His eyes rolled back in his head slowly, almost as if he was fighting the muscles that pulled his vision from me.

Every muscle in his body was visibly contracting. His fingers and toes curled under freakishly. It was like if he was being crushed from the inside.

With a great spasm, his head lurched backwards, thudding so brutally on the concrete wall behind him that I flinched in shock.

I felt almost bad for him. Part of me wanted to lean in and hold him still--to smack him and bring him back to consciousness and somehow stop the drug from taking effect; no human should suffer this way—but mostly I felt satisfaction. As horrific as it was to watch him dying in front of me, I thought of all of the disgusting things that he had done to so many people—what he had done to them himself, what he had let others do to them; Souls broken, bodies tortured, lives ruined and even ended because of him. Michael, Alina, Julie. Almost every person I had ever met. If anyone deserved to die such a hideous death, it was Mr. Irvine.

Slowly he slid sideways down the wall, resting his shoulder and head softly onto the hard floor. His breathing became short and intermittent. His skin seemed to be turning a deeper shade of grey.

I had been watching him for several minutes. My heart was still pounding in my ears but my breathing was beginning to regulate. I didn't move a muscle. I just stared.

Eventually his body stopped twitching and his wheezing faded away. It wasn't until I saw a small pool of urine growing beside his leg that I felt myself blinking and coming out of my stupor.

Mr. Irvine was dead.

It took me a while to believe it. I kept my eyes locked on him for any signs of movement—a twitch of a finger; a rise and fall of his chest; a flicker of an eye.

Nothing.

A chill rushed down my back like a cool breeze. This would change everything.

I was suddenly spurred into motion and I dragged myself over to the knife that laid in the corner. Again I placed the blade between my toes and hacked at the two remaining ties that held my wrists together. One by one they popped off, leaving alternating purple, red and white rings in their place.

My wrists ached with stiffness and I rotated them to get the blood flowing again. My fingers tingled and burned as they regained feeling.

My underwear and pants were twisted around the steel chain and shackles around my ankles. I fumbled to untangle them as I pulled them back to my hips and zipped them up.

An arm's length away, Mr. Irvine's clothing sat in a messy pile. I pulled them towards me and quickly located a ring of keys in one of his pant pockets. Every key was shiny and new except for two. Both were thick, old and tarnished, but one clearly match the colour of the restraints around my ankles. I tried it first and the lock popped open with ease.

Blood oozed from where the steel had bitten into the flesh--ages of oil, grease and god knows what else that was on the shackles mixing into a purple-brown goo that dripped down onto my feet. It felt like fire as the air hit the newly exposed sores.

My whole body ached. My muscles fought against every movement. The whip marks in my skin tore open a bit further with every motion. My ribs seemed to be stabbing me from the inside with each breath. But I knew I had to keep moving.

I pulled myself up to stand beside the bed. For a second I had to steady myself against the wooden mattress as my head spun and my vision blurred but it quickly passed.

All but two buttons were missing from my shirt, so I did them up and tucked the bottom into my pants as tightly as I could. The belt that I had been wearing was now covered in my blood so I grabbed Mr. Irvine's and quickly threaded it through the loops in my loose pants. My suit jacket, socks and shoes were in a pile on the floor at the head of the bed and I slipped them on quickly.

I checked myself over, straightening my collar and tucking adjusting the belt. I knew that I had to look as normal as possible if I got out of here—I couldn't risk drawing any additional attention to myself. Once I was confident that everything was on properly and that I looked as presentable as I could, I took a deep breath and stared at the door. It was the only way in or out of this room and I would have to go through it at some point. I knew the second dark key on Mr. Irvine's ring would fit the oddly shaped lock in the door. The only thing stopping me was fear. I didn't have any idea what to expect once that door opened. My best hope was that Emma, Kyal and Solomon were standing on the other side waiting to see if Emma's risk with planting the knife between my hands had worked out, but I had no way to know if this would be the case. They may have left the hallway by now, ushered away by guards or off to fulfil other duties. There might be soldiers waiting in the hall, armed and waiting for me to emerge after hearing all the commotion that I had cause. There might not be anyone out there at all, leaving me lost in an endless maze of corridors, rooms and elevators where I would inevitably be caught and held to pay for what I had done.

Goosebumps crawled down my arms as I stood staring at the steel door, the key jingling against the others like a bell in my hand.

I was a little kid again, standing on the edge of the forbidden ocean while Michael splashed happily, laughing as I watched him. I wanted to jump in so badly but fear

277

had frozen me to the core. I thought of Michael's face. I could hear him calling to me. Just do it! You'll be okay!

I had no choice.

I could almost feel the ice cold water of the ocean hitting me as I stepped forward. The key fit easily into the hole. Slowly I turned it, trying to keep the metal-on-metal sound of the lock turning in its chamber to a minimum.

With a thud the lock disengaged and the door swung towards me just a hair. I took a deep breath, then pulled it towards me just enough to see through the crack to the other side.

My fear immediately became reality: directly in front of the door, an armed soldier stood with his back to me. He had already begun turning, having apparently heard the lock open. Our eyes met just for an instant. I realized that it was not Solomon.

He too recognized that I was not Mr. Irvine.

I slammed my body against the door but it was too late. He too had rammed into the door and despite my efforts, it flew open, throwing me to the ground.

The soldier stepped in with his gun pointed directly at me. His eyes only left me for a moment as he surveyed the room.

"Sir?!" He called out to Mr. Irvine's dead body. "Sir can you hear me?"

He stepped forward again trying to get a better look at the body, which was slightly concealed on the other side of the bed. The tip of his weapon was only inches from my face. When no response came his head snapped back to face mine. His teeth were clenched tightly shut and his face was bright red. Tears of pure rage glistened on the whites of his eyes.

"You'll pay in hell for this!" he growled, adjusting his grip on his weapon.

This was it. I had no defence, no energy or means to fight back. I held my right hand up towards him, hoping that somehow it would keep the bullets from inflicting too much damage. The old bullet wounds in my upper right thigh and left arm stung painfully as if warning my body what to expect.

"No....please no..." I begged.

Out of nowhere a thin, white arm shot under his from behind, driving a long thin blade up and into his unprotected jaw.

He fell immediately, flopping to the ground like a piece of discarded clothing.

Above him stood Emma, the sleeve of her airy white shirt wet with dark red blood.

Kyal had launched into the room not even a step behind her and was already rummaging through the pockets in Mr. Irvine's jacket.

My eyes felt as if they were about to pop out of my head with surprise, my brain not yet having enough time to register what just happened.

"Get up!" Emma was reaching out a hand to me. "Now! Move!"

"Got it!" called Kyal, flashing a white key card before running to my side and pushing me towards the door.

"Come on Ash," he said assertively, "you can process all of this later!"

As I stepped over the dead soldier, Emma bent down quickly and in one quick motion yanked the steel shank from the man's chin.

****

There wasn't anyone else in the long corridor.

We ran in single file, Kyal in front, me in the middle, my hard shoes clicking with each step while Emma and Kyal somehow managed to run in absolute silence. I had no idea what was happening or where we were going but I was too shaken to speak, my mind still locked on the image of Mr. Irvine swallowing his last breath.

I couldn't believe that I had killed somebody.

I felt dirty. Empty. It was as if, by taking someone else's life I had lost a part of myself.

279

My clothing burned at my wounds as I ran. Tears poured down my cheeks. I didn't know myself whether they were tears from the pain or tears of emotion. It was all too much. I felt as if I were going to break down at any moment, both physically and mentally. I just wanted to be back in the barn again, climbing the 52 rungs to my private little platform where I could cry myself to sleep, far away from the rest of the world.

A hand touched me lightly on the shoulder as we neared the end of the corridor.

"You did really well Ash," came a whisper from behind me. They were just a few short words, but there was a gentleness in her tone that I wasn't expecting . It somehow took away a bit of the guilt that I was feeling.

I didn't even notice at first, but a clear glass door completely enclosed the tunnel that we were in. I would have walked right into it if Kyal hadn't been in front of me. Emma tapped her white access card against a small black panel on the wall and the door disappeared into the bricks.

Kyal knelt down at the corner, peering out into the hallway in either direction so rapidly that it seemed impossible that he had been able to get a good look at anything at all.

"Two friendlies to the left," he said militaristically. "One hostile to the right, armed."

Emma turned to me and straightened my clothing and flattened my hair. She clicked her tongue negatively at the blood that was seeping through my white dress shirt.

"Nothing we can do about that," she said, pulling the lapels of my jacket together. "Try to keep this closed and walk normally."

I nodded slightly, unsure how I was supposed to walk calmly when I knew that, at any second, nearly everyone in the building could be after me.

Kyal stood up beside me, his face concerned and supportive. "You'll be fine. The hard part is over."

I swallowed hard and nodded my head with a bit more conviction.

Emma and Kyal looked at one another for a moment as if reading each other's minds.

"Go," they both said in unison.

Emma stepped into the hallway first. I was mortified to see that she turned to the right, directly towards the armed soldier and not to the left away from possible conflict. Her posture was straight and tight, moving with the familiar robotic motions that I had come to recognise both her and Kyal for. She seemed calm and distant, as if nothing unusual was happening at all.

Kyal nudged me gently in the back, unintentionally hitting me right in the middle of one of the worst lesions, causing me to jump forward into the hallway awkwardly. I thought for sure that my reaction would garner the attention of the soldier for sure. He simply turned and glanced at me as if I were just another distraction from his thoughts before turning and looking back in the other direction. I reminded myself that to him I was just another nameless prisoner being escorted through the halls; an everyday mundane event. I pulled my jacket together, ensuring that the single button was firmly in its hole, and marched on obediently between my two handlers.

Part way down the hallway we turned left into a stairwell. It was brightly lit and I noticed immediately that a camera hung from the ceiling above the landing. Two guards stood at the base of the stairs, both staring blankly ahead like statues. Emma didn't hesitate for a moment as she passed between the two men. Out of the corner of my eye I thought I saw the soldier on the right give a slight nod to Kyal as he and I passed.

At the top of the stairs, a set of glass double doors sat open. Nobody was in sight. We passed thought them quickly and across a glass breezeway that hung dizzily over a busy street below. Through the windows I could see the golden tower looming high above.

I felt as if I was going to throw up.

I had no idea that we weren't already within its walls. All this time I thought that Emma and Kyal were trying to help me escape and yet here we were walking willingly back in. I stopped in my tracks, my mouth hanging open in silent protest.

"Woah Ash," said Kyal nearly bumping into me, sidestepping just in time. Emma noticed immediately and came to a quick halt, turning to see what was the matter.

"What's going on?"

I was still staring up at the building.

He followed my gaze quickly and turned back to me. "It's okay, you can do this."

My eyes stayed locked on the building. "I don't want to go back in there."

"You have to. We need you," Emma interjected.

"Why? What can I do?" I turned to look down at the street. "Let me go out there. They won't find me."

Kyal placed his hand on my shoulder. "We do need you. There are hundreds of scared, enslaved people in there—sex slaves, captives, employees, soldiers. If we succeed, we'll need all the help we can get to get them out of there."

"More than that," continued Emma, "You're Mr. Irvine's 'Golden Child'—his idea of perfection. Everyone has heard of you. If they see that you're free they will know without a doubt that Mr. Irvine is gone and that they are truly free. Without you beside us, people won't believe it. They'll be skeptical and less likely to help us fight against Mr. Irvine's few truly devoted followers."

I was shaking.

"I can't."

I felt like such a coward.

Kyal looked at me with empathy deep in his eyes. For the first time I could see that he too was afraid. "We have to do this."

"Think of Michael and Alina," said Emma eying me knowingly.

I looked up to the tower again. My whole body quivered. I knew they were right.

****

We were running again.

Another corner came up quickly. In fear of drawing attention to us, Emma didn't stop to survey who was in the next hall before crossing into it. She didn't have to. I could hear for myself that it was much busier than the others had been.

I was breathless with fear but I kept my head down and followed Emma around the turn.

People were everywhere.

Some were dragging a child behind, taking marvelling at the high ceiling and reflective architecture while others were carrying several plastic bags filled with food, but most seemed to be dressed in black or grey, carrying rectangular cases and talking rapidly into the little telephones in their hands, oblivious to the world racing around them. Ants, I thought. They're swarming like mindless ants.

I noticed several armed men standing near the exits, lazily observing the crowd. These men weren't dressed in the same manner as Mr. Irvine's soldiers. They wore simple brown short sleeved shirts and matching brown pants and seemed to only be carrying a radio. I knew right away that they were no threat to us.

Every fifty steps or so, the familiar black eye on the white mounting hung from the walls. Mr. Irvine's cameras.

We pushed our way through the crowd, walking quickly but not fast enough to attract attention. People bumped into me at every other step, making my sores screaming at me in pain each time, and it took every bit of restraint I had left to keep from yelling out.

Soon we reached a smaller side room lined with shiny elevator doors. Several people were in line waiting for one of the doors to open. Kyal stepped between the crowd and stuck a round key into the slot above the glowing yellow button. A moment later, the door to the elevator on the right slid open, revealing it's large, empty interior. The crowd surged forward to step in, but Kyal threw his arm across the opening before anyone could enter.

"Sorry, this is the service elevator," He announced. The crowd groaned and stepped back. I followed Kyal as he entered, and Emma quickly followed. I turned to face the door as it closed and noticed a dark haired woman staring at me in shock. The door closed and I saw my reflection on its inside panel. My blood had saturated the majority of my white dress shirt which now hung loose from my pants, my jacket wide open. Red spots of splattered blood dotted my pale cheek and neck.

I looked sickening.

My stomach lurched as the elevator jumped into motion.

"When we get to the top floor we have to move as fast as we can towards Mr. Irvine's private office." The urgency in Kyal's voice was palpable.

"That's where the master surveillance and system override panel is," continued Emma with equal seriousness. "We have to get in there to shut everything down, unlock all of the doors and access the PA system to notify everyone in the building that Mr. Irvine is dead."

"Why us?" I asked. "What about your contact in the control room? The one who shut down surveillance in the medical ward so we could speak openly there? Can't he do it?"

"She," clarified Kyal. "An no. A complete system shut down can only be done from Mr. Irvine's office. Any other attempt would lock down the whole building and put all the guards on alert."

I nodded slightly.

Emma looked me in the eye through the reflection in the steel door. Her voice was stern and foreboding. "Once we crash the system and make the announcement, prepare for conflict. There will still be a few people—mostly all soldiers—who follow Mr. Irvine as if he were a god."

"They're highly trained and heavily armed," said Kyal. "Stay low, keep your eyes open and keep away from them. You have no training—no chance in a fight."

"We'll protect you," finished Emma earnestly, though I caught a hint of doubt in her wavering tone.

The last square light in the row of above the door illuminated and the elevator came to a lurching halt. My stomach jumped into my throat. I wasn't sure if it were the sudden stop or a sudden surge of nervousness. My heart was already pounding violently but it now seemed to somehow speed up even more.

Kyal and Emma looked so calm and still as they stood behind me as if it were just an ordinary day of work for them. I admired their bravery while at the same time felt bad for them for lacking normal human emotions.

From somewhere within the walls a ding sounded and the doors began to open. I stepped forward nervously.

Suddenly an ear piercing siren cracked through the air, stinging my ears instantly—the vibration from its wail so abrasive that I could feel it stinging on my worst wounds. All around, alternating red and white flashing lights flickered in unison to the siren causing dizzying shadows on everything.

I instinctually backed away from the doors in surprise, bumping painfully into Kyal. The doors of the elevator froze in their place, open less than foot apart. Between them was a scene of complete chaos: People were running in every direction, bumping into one another, pulling and pushing their way through the crowds with dazed looks on their face, uncertain of what was happening. Some tried to run into side rooms, shocked to find the doors locked, while others disappeared or appeared around the corner at the end of the hall, unsure of where to go or what to do.

"Go! Go Go!" Yelled Emma above the noise of the sirens, pushing her way through the narrow gap in the door.

Kyal shoved me brutally in the back, sending shock waves of pain through my wounds. "MOVE!" he commanded.

It felt as if my skin was being ripped from my body as I pulled myself through the tight space and out of the elevator. I wanted to yell out in agony but the pain was so intense that only a muffled gasp passed my lips.

I stood behind Emma for a moment, breathing heavily with raging anxiety as Kyal came through the doors behind me. My head was spinning with all of the chaos. My pulse was thumping behind my eyes, my lungs burned, my hands were clammy and cold. I had never seen this much commotion before.

"This way!" Emma directed, taking off at a full sprint towards the end of the hall. I felt myself follow just a step or two behind despite a voice in my head that was screaming at me to curl up in a ball on the floor and hide.

We rounded the corner ahead of us and continued our race through the even more crowded hall. The corridor was long and wide and, just as before, dozens of people were moving in disorganized panic.

Yet again, people bumped into me from every angle and I winced with pain each time, but I somehow kept pace with Emma, only vaguely aware that Kyal was right behind me.

I could see the end of the hall ahead. We were probably fifty steps or so away.

That's when I noticed people start falling.

They seemed to be dropping for no reason—simply losing control of their limbs and crashing lifelessly to the floor.

"Down!" yelled Emma, falling to the floor herself just as the people in front of us had. Kyal and I followed suit, collapsing to the ground face first. "Lay still. Keep your eyes open but don't move a muscle."

Play dead, I thought. It had been one of my favourite childhood games. I hadn't realized the horrific reality of the activity until now.

A moment later several armed soldiers came crashing around the corner, their guns making muffled popping noises as the innocent people in front of them fell to the ground all around us—their screams just a whisper under the screech of the sirens.

I tensed my muscles as firmly as possible in an attempt to stay perfectly still. I even forced my eyes to stare blankly towards the wall without blinking despite the dryness and the fear.

Even though I couldn't turn to look at them I knew that the soldiers were quickly making their way through the hall—people were falling right behind us now. The armed men were only steps away. I could feel their heavy footsteps on the floor beneath me. I could hear the popping of their bullets just above my head.

A body fell across my legs. It took everything in me to keep from screaming out in agony and horror. My vision momentarily turned black and every inch of me throbbed, but somehow I still didn't move.

What seemed like an eternity later, the men were stepping past me and I could see their backs out of the corner of my eye. Another second or two and they vanished around the corner from which we came.

I let out a heavy breath and sucked in desperately for fresh air. My lids seemed to stick momentarily against my dry eyeballs as I allowed myself to blink a few times. I was just about to move when I turned my eyes towards Kyal. He was facing towards me, his eyes locked on mine wildly—a warning to stay still. Confused, I turned my eyes towards a glass window above Kyal's head. In its reflection I saw the cause of Kyal's alarm: a lone soldier was slowly making his way down the hall towards us, his weapon pointed downward as he kicked the bodies of the fallen, checking to see if any were still alive, shooting anyone who had survived.

I immediately stiffened my muscles again, my eyes locked on the reflection.

The soldier moved softly and silently under the hum of the alarm, stalking his prey like a patient snake about to strike on a mouse.

To my left I felt someone moving slightly. From my position I couldn't tell where Emma had fallen exactly, but I knew that she was somewhere in that area. I wanted to turn to warn her—or whoever it was that was moving—but I knew that it would mean certain death if I did. All I could do was lay still and hold my breath, hoping that Emma would be safe.

In the reflection I could see the soldier move closer and closer to me. The rustling on my left hadn't stopped, and I became aware of a faint whimper.

A small hand grabbed my bare ankle. It was cold and damp, and in its movement I could feel the stickiness of blood between our skin. The person was pulling gently at me, hard enough to move my leg slightly, but clearly weak and desperate. I strained my leg muscles to resist the pull and keep my own leg from moving.

With a pop the hand relaxed its grip on my ankle and lay still.

In the reflection I could see the soldier standing directly above me. The image was so clear that I could almost make out the colour of his eyes. His face was cold and dark—angry. I had never seen him before, but knew instantly that this was one of Mr. Irvine's devoted followers.

I felt a bead of sweat drip down my forehead.

With a brutal swing of his leg, the soldier kicked at the body that lay across my legs. The impact was so forceful that the dead person rolled almost completely off of me. Trapped blood rushed into the wounds on my calves causing them to sting intensely.

I felt myself twitch involuntarily.

In the reflection I saw the soldiers eyes dart from the dead person to my legs. I steeled myself as much as I possibly could but I knew it was futile—he had seen me twitch.

The soldier shifted his weight slightly and I closed my eyes.

Nothing I could have done would have braced me for that kick. I heard a rib crack as the wind was forced out of me and my head felt as if it had exploded off of my shoulders. The sound of the alarm was replaced by a dull, muffled ring that seemed to come from somewhere between my own ears.

I opened my eyes deliriously. The blow had rolled me over onto my back and the soldier was now standing over me straddling my torso. I knew that he was about to pull the trigger on his weapon which was now pointed directly at my forehead, and for a split second my pain was so intense that I wished he would, but then something in his face changed. A confusion. A recognition—a panic.

"You!" I saw him mouth, confoundedly.

I could tell right away what he was thinking: '*Do I kill him? Would I get in trouble if I did? Would I get in trouble if I didn't?*'

He suddenly looked so young. A teenager himself. Scared. Scarred.

I saw the flash of the blade only an instant before it pierced through his right eyeball.

He fell hard to the ground—another body among dozens.

Emma now stood in the soldier's place, holding her thin knife tightly in her hand, the fresh blood from the soldier glowing brightly against the browning stain on her shirt from the last soldier she had killed.

Kyal was immediately at her side pulling the soldiers weapon out of his dead hand and digging through other parts of his armour for other useful things.

"Can you move?" asked Emma.

It took a moment for me to snap back to reality.

"CAN YOU MOVE?" she asked louder.

I pulled myself up slightly. Every motion was grueling, but I forced myself to stand without complaint.

Kyal looked up at me and held his hand out. In it was a small weapon, similar in style to the larger one that he now held.

I looked down at it dumbfounded.

"Take it." It was a command, not a suggestion.

Bodies were everywhere. We ran through the hallways hopping over the limbs and torsos of all of the fallen, doing our best to avoid stepping on them as we passed, our shoes slipping on the glossy blood-covered floor.

The small gun in my hand felt incongruously heavy. It's smooth metal finish was hot in my cold hands and difficult to keep hold of without hooking my finger over the trigger for more support. I must have looked ridiculous holding it far away from my body in fear of it going off unintentionally while Kyal held his large weapon firmly and competently ahead of him.

Emma stopped in front of a large silver door and swiped Mr. Irvine's key card against the black panel off to the side. The door slid open quickly. Kyal didn't hesitate for a second before stepping in front of Emma and entering the room ahead with his gun still firmly aimed ahead.

I could see the look of surprise on his face an instant before I heard the first shot rang out. He had clearly expected the room to be vacant.

Emma fell first.

In the blink of an eye her shoulder exploded into a shower of splattering blood and jerked back as if it had been pulled by some unseen hand. Her body spun like a top and she dropped face first onto the floor.

Before I could even realize what had just happened, a staccato of pops erupted from Kyal's weapon as he knelt down low and sprayed the room ahead with bullets. I had fallen back against the wall beside the door and taken cover beside a small steel waste bin. I watched in petrified awe as Kyal swung left to right with his weapon, his mouth open in an inaudible battle cry beneath the sounds of the gun and siren.

Shards of glass and steel flew through the air in all directions around him, many slicing into the soft skin on Kyal's face and hands as he continued to fire unflinchingly. Behind him, lines of black holes burst through the crisp white wall as the enemies failed to hit their target.

I knew this couldn't go on much longer. Kyal's weapon would soon be out of ammunition. I looked down at the weapon in my shaking hand.

Across the entryway Emma rolled slightly, her face contorted with pain, her long blonde hair half red from her own blood. Her left shoulder hung unnaturally from her body. I could see her collar bone standing grotesquely upright through the ripped flesh above her heart.

Her eyes caught mine, I saw her mouth move but I couldn't hear what she was trying to say. She noted my confusion and looked down at the gun in my hand then back up to me imploringly.

Help him.

Just as I was about to move, two muffled thuds broke through all of the other noise around me.

I turned to see Kyal just as he slumped to the ground and fell onto his back. Two reddish holes perforated his abdomen, one above his naval and one below his right armpit. His eyelids flickered lightly before closing.

I looked up towards Emma, stunned. She was staring wide-eyed at Kyal, her mouth open in a silent scream.

Everything went numb. Cold. It was as if nothing were real. As if I were watching someone else's hands as they tightened their grip on the small weapon. As if it were someone else's legs pushing me off the floor. As if someone had pushed me from behind, directly into the open doorway.

I held the gun out in both hands at arm's reach as I stepped right into the room. Two men dressed in plain white clothing were in the process of standing from their protected positions behind a large desk, clearly not expecting another attacker.

My finger pulled the trigger all on its own as I raised the gun up to be in line with the first man's head. Four or five bullets ejected out of the chamber in a whirr of automatic fire, landing square in the middle of the man's throat before he had even noticed me enter the room.

Before his body hit the floor, my body was turning just enough to release another barrage of gunfire towards the second man. At least three bullets hit the wall behind him before making contact with his left arm, chest and abdomen. He looked up at me in utter surprise as the shots ripped through his flesh.

I realized I was screaming with the full force of my lungs as the man's body dropped to the floor.

****

Four other bodies laid in unnatural positions around the room. Not one of them moved. I felt as if I had been standing there for hours, my arms still outstretched, gripping tightly onto the empty gun that was still pointed at the wall ahead of me.

"Ash!" It was a yell, but barely audible beneath the noise of the alarm. "Ash! PLEASE!"

Something snapped in my mind and I felt like I had just entered the scene--as if all this had happened while I was elsewhere. I threw the weapon out of my hands like it were an animal that had bitten my hand and turned to see Kyal and Emma sprawled out on the floor behind me. Emma had dragged herself across the floor, leaving a crimson smear of her own blood from where she fell. She had now propped herself up beside Kyal and was pressing his hand against the worst of his wounds. His eyes were blinking slightly, staring blankly at the ceiling. She was looking up at me in desperation.

I nearly fell as I raced to their side.

"Oh shit oh shit!" I sputtered.

Emma said something that I couldn't make out.

"The gun!" She yelled, pointing to Kyal's weapon.

I hesitated slightly before picking it up, uncertain of what I was to do with it.

Emma shook her head impatiently, letting go of Kyal's hand and taking the weapon from me in one swift motion. Using her teeth, she slid a piece of metal backwards on the gun and pointed it up towards a box on the wall. With one shot she took out the speaker of the alarm, instantly silencing it's wail.

The room itself was now quiet, though the ringing continued in my ears for several minutes. Out in the hall I could hear that the alarm was still sounding throughout the building.

"We have to move quickly!" said Emma with urgency, pushing herself up from the floor with her one good arm. "Help me up!"

I looked down at Kyal in surprise. "What about him? We have to help him!"

292

"We can't worry about him right now. We have to finish this or else this has all been in vain!" It was a heartless command, completely devoid of emotion. I couldn't believe that Emma could be so cold when Kyal was the one person in this world who she seemed to have any sort of connection with.

"Now!" she barked, her voice raspy with aggression.

I stood as quickly as possible and pulled her to a standing position. Without letting go of my hand Emma yanked me into the room ahead of us, stepping over the fallen people on the floor.

The room was much larger than I had initially realized, housing a number of large desks, computer terminals and a wall of machines that I couldn't identify. Emma moved quickly passed all of it, stopping at the far wall. At first look it seemed like a solid and impervious panel of steel, but when Emma held up Mr. Irvine's key card to a tiny black square directly in the middle, a large rectangular section of the wall slid inward and swung open: a hidden door.

This was the entrance to Mr. Irvine's private office.

Directly ahead of the opening was a small seating area with dark wood panelling and a comfortable looking leather chair in front of a roaring wood fireplace. Above the fireplace, a life sized painting of a young toddler stared back at me, his tussled brown hair, dark brown eyes and innocent smile glowing as he held a tiny flower towards the painter. I knew that face immediately. It was me.

Emma moved by me quickly, breaking my stare. "Come on Ash!"

I followed her through the doorway. To the right, the room opened up in to a large space lined floor to ceiling with dozens of monitors and machines. Several of the monitors were cracked or damaged so badly that they were completely blank, but all of the others flickered automatically from one moving image to the next. In front of the wall of screens sat a large wooden desk, intricately carved with patterns of tiny flowers and vines, and feet that resembled powerful claws, each drawer the face of the winged child that Mr. Irvine had engraved onto his belt.

Somehow the desk seemed to glow from within itself.

On top of the desk stood a single computer monitor and a keyboard. Images flashed across its screen automatically as the computer cycled through a paired down version of the images shown on the wall of monitors.

I took a step closer.

Most of the images were scenes of places that I didn't recognize—offices of people working away robotically; cavernous spaces filled with dozens of sleeping people all laying quietly in a row; tiny rooms with a single bed, some empty, some containing several individuals engaged in all sorts of bizarre and disturbing activities—but the screens with the most activity were showing places that I recognized: Hallways filled with people, soldiers unscrupulously mowing down innocent, terrified people who scrambled desperately to get away. They were the hallways that we had just come from.

These images were being projected here straight from the black domed surveillance cameras that I had known all of my life. This was Mr. Irvine's personal control console. How many hours had he sat here watching me?

I stepped to the side so that Emma could sit at the desk, and looked back up at the wall of monitors.

"Why are they killing everyone?" I asked desperately.

Emma, who had begun pounding away on the keys the machine didn't look up as she answered.

"They know you've escaped. They're shooting first and looking for you after."

"All…" I stammered. "All of those people…. They're dying because… because of me?"

"Yes, that's why we have to act now," Emma answered coldly.

Tears were rolling from my eyes as I watched people continue to fall in front of the soldiers. Every one of them, dead because of me.

I forced my eyes away from the monitors and looked down at Emma. Her wounded shoulder hung lifeless from her body but her other hand flew across the keyboard in front of her in a blur.

Suddenly she turned to me, passing me a small white piece of plastic.

"It's got to be you," she said, her voice laden with a tone of desperation and importance. "Take it," she said, placing the stick into my hand and pushing it towards my face.

"What? What do I do with this?"

"Speak into it. Everyone in the building will be able to hear you. Tell them who you are. Tell them that Mr. Irvine is dead and that we're all free. Tell the soldiers to stop—tell the people to fight back!"

All of a sudden it felt as if a flock of birds had flown into my stomach.

"I—I can't!" I said, my voice shaking with nervousness. "You do it!"

Emma shook her head. "No it has to be you. Nobody will stop if they hear me. Most of them don't even know me, but the ones that do don't trust me and won't believe me. They all think that Kyal and I are enemies: We've had to do certain things that people will see as traitorous and cruel in order to get close to Mr. Irvine, and ultimately get to this point. It has to be you. You're an innocent. You're the epitome of innocent. If they see that you have actually escaped they will know that it's truly over."

I looked to the images of the people being gunned down, of the silent hallways littered with bodies, of the small dark room where a circle of naked old men surrounded the young, terrified girl that had been on the stage with me last night.

I swallowed hard and nodded. I knew that she was right. It had to be me and it had to be now. Every second wasted meant another second of torture, another life lost.

"Stand here," Emma directed, placing me in between the wall of monitors and Mr. Irvine's desk. I gripped the microphone tightly in both hands and held it to my lips. Emma skated her fingers over the keyboard again.

Out in the hallway the distant sound of the alarm went silent.

Behind me I could tell that the screens had flickered and I turned to look. I almost fell over when I saw that every other monitor was showing a live, moving image of me. My head was more than twice the size of real-life, and even though I could only see the back side of me, I immediately felt bewildered and disturbed at seeing myself in anything other than a mirror.

In several of the screens on the wall I could see people stopping in their place, looking more confused than ever--even the soldiers seemed puzzled—as my imaged popped up on screens around the building.

"Ash!" reminded Emma forcefully.

I turned back toward her and cleared my throat self-consciously. My ears and cheeks were burning in embarrassment and my mouth suddenly felt very dry.

"Hello? Um… Hi I'm, uh, my name is Ash." I looked up to Emma who was now watching me with nervous anxiety. "Am I doing it right?"

"Yes, keep going!" she said in a hushed voice.

"Um, yeah." I coughed. "You may know me: I'm the one Mr. Irvine.. uh… Apparently I was Mr. Irvine's… uh…"
I shook my whole body and took a deep breath. Be strong.

"Apparently you all know me and are well aware that he viewed me as his most prized possession.

A few minutes ago Mr. Irvine attacked me down in one of his cells in the basement. He beat and tortured me, but with the help of a secret rebel group that has been working for years to bring him down from power and free us all, I was able to escape--and kill-- Mr. Irvine."

I paused as my body shuddered, still deeply disturbed that I had actually murdered somcone.

"He's dead," I repeated. "It's over. We're free. All of us."

I wasn't used to having a one-way conversation. I turned to look at the screen for a reaction.

All over the building, people seemed to be having mixed reactions: in one hall groups of people were standing and cheering--even the guards--hugging one another joyously. In another corridor, a swarm of young kids were holding down and beating a now unarmed soldier who was clearly repenting for his actions.

Down in the dungeon area, adults were frantically scurrying from darkened rooms, disappearing out into the public areas of the building, leaving their scared victims where they lay.

I saw the little girl that I knew from the stage. She was alone, naked and crying uncontrollably. But her hands were free and she was pulling on her bright yellow dress.

My nervousness started to fade—the heat in my cheeks and ears now replaced by a calm tingling, while a lightness seemed to lift my shoulders and allow fresh air deep into my lungs. The coolness in my body began to warm like the first rays of sun after a harsh winter.

I turned to look at Emma. She too was staring wide-eyed at the monitors. Though she didn't turn to look at me, I could see a glimmer of happiness in her eyes and the slightest trace of a smile turning the corner of her mouth. She seemed to be holding her breath in disbelief.

I too couldn't believe it. I turned back to the monitors to absorb the full extent of the feeling.

My own words echoed in my head. *It's over. We're free.*

I watched closely as people continued to come to the realization that what I was saying was actually the truth. Many people continued to cheer, several broke down in tears, falling to the floor or into the arms of others in relief. Some ran immediately to the elevators, stairways and doors which were now unlocked thanks to some quick computer work by Emma.

Never in my life had I felt so good—so important.

In an instant the feeling vanished.

Emma noticed before I did.

One of the screens showed the doors to the elevator down the hall opening. A group of people scrambled towards them, racing to pack themselves in. A second before the first persons foot entered the door, bright red fluid exploded from his chest and back, spraying all over the crowd and throwing his lifeless body several feet behind him.

A flood of heavily armed men rushed out, mowing down any innocents that were in their way. Some stood bravely, some attacked the men with nothing more than their bare hands. Others scattered into corners and behind closed doors, screaming wildly as bullets rained over the crowd.

The soldiers raced through the hall.

I recognized their uniforms immediately: rigid, shiny black armor over gargantuan bodies, their faces hidden behind shiny black domed helmets with clear face-shields, long bulky white guns in their hands.

It was Mr. Irvine's personal military squad—the soldiers that had brought be here from the barn.

They were coming in our direction.

It was only seconds before I could hear them. Emma's eyes bulged from their sockets as she too noticed the noise.

Somehow despite her injuries, she flipped Mr. Irvine's heavy carved desk, letting the console crash to the floor, pulling me to the ground behind it to take cover. Just a few steps to the left, the hand of one of the dead men held a gun loosely but it was too risky to go for it.   Across the room, Kyal remained motionless on the floor, his eyes closed, a large weapon at his side.

The armed men stormed into the room like a boom of thunder. Emma and I kept our heads as low as possible. I could see their steel boots through a narrow space under the desk where it had fallen on a large book. There were at least six of the men.

We had no hope of fighting against them.

I was frozen with fear.

"Stand!" roared the familiar voice of Jack, the leader.

Emma nudged me softly, a warning to stay still.

"You have five seconds."

"Mr. Irvine is dead, Jack!" Emma called out. "There's no reason to do this anymore. "

"You murdered our leader! You'll pay for his blood with your own!" Jack growled.

"And then what?" countered Emma, grunting as she shifted her body to a less painful position against the desk.

"What happens after you kill us? You have no boss, no supreme leader! Look at the screens! Everyone is scrambling for the doors. Everyone! Even Mr. Irvine's highest operatives. The corporation has collapsed!"

"They're cowards! My team will hold this place together and you will all be held accountable for your actions!"

"For WHAT, Jack?" Emma called out in disbelief. "A paycheque? Oh wait, you've never had one of those! You've been a prisoner here just like everyone else!"

"Mr. Irvine saved each and every one of us!" he roared. "You should be grateful to him!"

"You know that's not true! He stole our lives from us! He took us all away from our homes, our families, our friends! You and your team—that's what your job is! You see it every day! You can't possibly think that we should praise him for it!"

"He rescued all of us from horrible situations and certain death! You people are all too stupid to understand the circumstances but that is a fact!"

"What circumstances? Did you ever ask? Did he ever tell you why he made you take children from their beds in the middle of the night or off the street in broad daylight? Did you ever ask why he beat and tortured so many of us and sold or discarded the ones he was unsatisfied by?"

"A good soldier never questions his leader! We're given our orders and follow them loyally knowing that he has his reasons for everything and knows more about the bigger picture than any of us!"

"No! You're wrong! You're a soldier because you're mindless! Stand down and think for yourself for just a second! Let me bring up your file on the computer—you have a family out there that is looking for you—that loves you! Everyone does!" Emma's voice cracked at the last part. I knew that her and Kyal were created by scientists in some lab somewhere and raised by a department of disconnected, uncaring staff. They had no parents, no family.

I realized now that everything that she was doing was for the good of others. She would fight to the death to ensure that people were returned to lives that she herself would never have. "Let me show you," she said softer.

Jack snickered sarcastically. "You're dumber than you look. Your five seconds is up."

Everything happened so quickly.

Through the gap under the desk I saw the soldiers advance towards us. I couldn't see above their knees, but I knew that all of the men had their weapons raised and poised to fire on us as soon as they got a clear shot. They were not here to take prisoners. This was the end.

Beyond the men's feet, Kyal lay lifeless on the floor, a weapon right at his side. His injuries had been substantial and I knew that he was either dead or close to it. I watched him for any movement—a flicker of an eyelid, a twitch of a finger. I willed him to move. I begged him inside my head hoping that he would hear me, pleading with him to jump up and blast the men down.

A heavy foot kicked at the chair that had fallen between the desk and the soldiers. I looked up as a large gun appeared overhead and turned down to point directly at my head.

"Kyal! NOW!" I heard myself yell.

The weapon above me immediately disappeared and all eight sets of boots in front of me spun in their spot to face Kyal.

I jumped with every last bit of strength towards the gun in the hand of the dead man to the left of me. I felt my shoulder hit the ground hard as I hooked my finger around the trigger and lifted the surprisingly light weapon.

Bullets rained from the end of the weapon like a violent lightning storm, showering the soldiers in their own blood as they pierced through the men's armour and into their soft flesh. I swung the machine back and forth as the soldiers fell forward and to the ground one after the other in quick succession.

Finally, with a hollow click, the gun fell silent.

I was afraid to put the it down. I knew it was empty but I was frozen with fear so intense that I kept hoping that the weapon would spring back to life and continue firing and firing. It was Emma who pulled the spent machine from my tight grasp.

"Ash," she whispered. "Ash let go. You did it. They're dead."

I blinked a few times to bring my mind back to reality.

"You did it," Emma repeated, turning my face towards her own. "You saved us."

Despite her injured arm, Emma helped me to my feet. Together we made our way over the bodies that littered the room and over to Kyal's side.

Emma knelt at his side with tears streaming from her eyes and touched his throat gently with her fingers. Electricity seemed to race through her suddenly.

"He's still alive!"

She pulled me down on the opposite side of Kyal.

"Put your hands here and push hard!" she said with desperation, placing my hands over two large holes in his chest.

"He's bad but he might pull through."

"Kyal!" she called loudly, just inches from his ear. "Kyal stay with me!"

Dabbing a pool of blood from his eyes with her sleeve she said again, this time gentler and more sombre, "Stay with me."

****

ah, Solomon, Florian—almost unrecognizable with buzzed hair, no makeup, plain black clothing--and Chiku flew into the room several minutes later. ah and Chiku fell immediately at Kyal's side and took over the efforts to keep h stable.

"od job," Florian said to me, a sad smile on his face as he shook my hand fily before pulling me in for a tight embrace. It was awkward at first, but soon Well into a warm, comforting hold that neither of us wanted to break. I knew W Florian was feeling: Relief. Disbelief. Elation. Sickening sadness. We had do the impossible, but a lot of people had been lost today.

Solomon too hugged me lightly. His eyes were damp with emotion but everything else about him remained as rigid and soldier-like as ever.

Together, the four of us pulled the bodies of the fallen towards the walls and away from Kyal so that Chiku and Sarah could continue working on him. As I was tugging on arms of the smallest of the soldiers, his eyes slowly opened.

"Wait! Stop!" I called to Solomon, who was lifting his legs, jumping back in surprise. "This one's still alive!"

Solomon instantly dropped the man's legs and raised his weapon in defense.

The man's eyes opened widely in fear and a garbled noise came out of his mouth. He looked like a frightened child.
His arms hung limply at his side, his weapon far across the room.

I knew he was no threat.

"Wait," I said urgently to Solomon, stepping closer to the man as he continued to mumble jumbled noises.

I leaned in close to him. His lips were quivering. Blood stained tears slid from his pleading eyes.

302

"Y… you," he muttered, his eyes turned towards Emma .

"Take a breath," I encouraged gently.

He breathed in sharply.

"You said….we have family."

Emma nodded compassionately and moved to set up Mr. Irvine's computer on another desk behind us.

"What's the number on his vest?" she called to me. I read it to her. The wall of monitors flickered and changed into one large image.

It was a child, maybe three or four years of age, standing obediently in front of a corn field, surrounded by three other children, all older, and two adults.

Words below the image stated : Russell Jenson, June 3rd 1985, Owen Sound, Ontario, Canada. Father: James Jenson. Mother: Rachel Jenson. Siblings: Tammy, Eric, Kara.

The soldier's eyes locked on the image as a smile spread across his lips.

A moment later I knew that he was dead.

****

We continued moving the bodies of the dead out of the way. Kyal was now conscious, but Sarah made it very clear that his condition was critical. She and Chiku decided that it was imperative to move him to the medical ward so that they could better treat his injuries and increase the risk of his survival. With the help of Florian, Solomon and Chiku, Sarah placed Kyal gently onto a folding table and the group rushed him from the room.

I looked at Emma, who was busily pounding away at the computer keyboard, seemingly unaware of what was going on.

"Emma, don't you want to go with him?"

"I can't do anything for him. They will notify me of his condition as time passes," she responded in her characteristic cool manner. "I have a lot of stuff to do here."

I touched her back gently. "He needs you there with him."

"He is in capable hands. These people need me more," she said, nodding to indicate the many people still scrambling throughout the building.

I watched her for several minutes as she created a program that automatically brought up name after name of people who had been held under Mr. Irvine's regime, uploading and sending their information to local and international authorities with the title 'FOUND'.

Once she was certain that the program was operating correctly, she turned to face me with a sigh.

"Okay, you need to come with me now."

I looked at her with confusion. "Where are going?"

"To get Michael."

****

It was all too eerie to be back down there. It felt like I had escaped only minutes ago, though in reality, it had been over two hours.

I kept my arms tightly wrapped around myself as I followed Emma. The memories of being trapped in that room, bound to the hard bed, feeling completely hopeless as Mr. Irvine's belt split through my skin; the musty, damp, uric smell in the air licking once again at the scars across my back and legs—it was almost too much to bear.

I felt myself falling behind Emma, slowing my pace to a near standstill, my body deciding for itself that it didn't want to go any further.

I reminded myself over and over that everything had changed since then.

Michael. I have to get to Michael.

The numbers on the doors were going down in numerical order as we walked through the darkened corridor. 41, 40, 39. Voices and moans echoed from the rooms—most doors now hanging open--but Emma moved past them without a moment's hesitation. I could feel my palms and armpits grow clammy with nervous perspiration.

32, 31, 30.

My throat struggled to swallow as we passed the open door of room number 28. I could smell the sour, stale scent of my old vomit, the bitterness of my urine, the salty smell of pooling blood. My mind begged me not to look as we passed the open door but I couldn't stop my head from turning.

The dead soldier lay still on the floor in the position that he had fallen. I shivered with the memory of seeing Emma thrust her metal spike up into his young chin.

My feet pulled me a step forward down the hall although the rest of my body seemed to be frozen.

Mr. Irvine's body came into view. Even though I knew he was dead, the fear and panic rolled in like waves and I fought against myself to stand and look. My ears began to ring loudly and my breath got trapped in my throat.

Someone, most likely one of the soldiers that I had just killed, had laid the body flat on the floor and had hastily covered it with Mr. Irvine's shirt and pants.

Memories of what he had done to me such a short time ago flashed through my mind in a high speed repeat that left me shaking violently.

I took a heavy breath and reminded myself that it was over now. That man could never hurt me again.

A ping of pride tickled my chest. For just a moment I allowed myself to be proud of the part I had played in setting so many people free from the horrors inflicted upon them because of this monster.

Things were different now. I was different. The quivering, insecure kid was already disappearing into the past like a bad dream that dims as the day goes on. I was no longer a powerless, meaningless victim, but a man who had affected change.

Someone who finally had a purpose in this life.

A step further and Mr. Irvine's body was out of view and completely out of mind.

I was about to see Michael again.

****

The door had been open when we got to the room, as many others in the hallway had been.

Number 21.

I had heard him. When Kyal and Emma had lead me down here the first time, I distinctly heard a moan from this room when we passed by. I had had no idea that he was that close. Only 7 doors away—three doors down and on the opposite side of the hall. I could have yelled to him—spoken to him! Let him know that I was here! Maybe it could have given him some hope, some solace to know that a friend was close by.

I steadied myself for a moment before walking through the doorway, preparing myself for the worst.

Emma stepped in first then stood aside, allowing me to pass. The stench was almost overpowering. Feces. Urine. Vomit. Sweat.

He barely flinched as we entered.

It was worse than I could have ever imagined. Cameras stood on tripods all around the room, their lights shining blindingly towards the opposite side of the room. On the floor, a variety of obscene tools, clothing and paraphernalia littered the room, some of which I could imagine their disturbing purposes, while others left me mystified.

My knees felt weak as I stepped further inwards.

There in the corner, naked and face down, stretched tightly across a narrow wooden bed, was Michael. Rusty, steel shackles bound his ankles, holding his legs firmly apart while his arms, as mine had been, were secured to a ring in the brick wall high above his head, which hung limply toward the wooden plank.

His body was streaked with blood and dripping with sweat. Whip marks, some shiny and white with age, others red and crusted around the edges, criss-crossed his back horrifically. He was disturbingly skinny and pale, a shadow of the boy that I knew.

"Michael," I whispered gently.

His head twitched almost imperceptibly.

I stepped quickly to his side and knelt down, putting my face close to his.

"Michael," I repeated softly. "It's me. It's Ash."

His eyelids fluttered weakly.

Emma came to the bedside and began inserting key after key into the lock on the shackles around Michael's ankles until they finally popped open.

Michael moaned painfully.

Quickly Emma sliced through the plastic restraints around Michaels wrists using her thin steel blade. I supported his arms as the ties snapped, lowering him gently to the bed. His wrists were black with dried blood and scabs, his hands purple from lack of circulation. I was surprised at how cold his skin was, considering how much he was sweating.

"I'm here," I said, rubbing my hand through his matted hair delicately. "It's over. We've killed him."

His eyes opened slightly. They were horribly blood shot and swollen, nearly eclipsing their characteristic blue-grey tone that I knew so well.

For only a moment I could see a glimmer of recognition, a look of salvation and relief. Tears welled in both of our eyes. At that moment he knew me. He knew that this was the end of his suffering.

Then, suddenly his gaze went blank. There was nothing. No indication that he knew me, no hint that he understood what I had said or what was happening. It was as if he were looking right through me—a blank stare searching for something far off in another land.

I fell into him, my head against his, my arms around his shoulders and neck away from his wounds, and cried.

****

The building was swarming with paramedics and police officers.

One by one they took out the injured, the sick and the dead from the building in a caravan of ambulances, cop cars and media trucks. Emma, Sarah, Solomon, Florian, Chiku and I stood on the balcony of the top floor staring down at the chaos below—a swarm of ants racing around as if their nest had just been stepped on.

The paramedics wouldn't let me go with Michael to the hospital. It was because I wasn't immediate family, they said, and with the number of injured and dead, they needed all the space in the ambulances that they could get.

They wanted to treat Emma and I as well, but with so many others who had more severe injuries than us, we declined, opting to be temporarily patched up by Sarah in her examination room, though we both knew that we would need more extensive care very soon.

We stood there in silence for several minutes before I realized that I no longer had that fear of looking down from such a height—vertigo. I was completely numb. I felt nothing. The world was continuing on around me like the background details of a dream. I was exhausted beyond anything I had felt before.

I kept seeing Michaels eyes, feeling the coolness of his skin, smelling the sourness of his body. I couldn't allow myself to picture what had been done to him. My insides were already icy with revulsion from the little bit that I had witnessed. I knew that even if he recovered, he would never again be the same happy, free-spirited kid that I had loved. Even though we had brought down Mr. Irvine's sick corporation, I couldn't help but feel absolutely devastated that I hadn't been able to get to Michael before this all happened to him.

Part 4

I woke up feeling cold and sore. The waves were particularly rough today and despite my best efforts to ignore the sound of their heavy crashes on the shore, I couldn't keep my eyes closed any longer.

The water was cool as I washed myself under the rusted tap, wiping the sleepy gunk from my tired eyes and rinsing the sand from my cheeks, arms and legs.

The others were already awake, heating water and cooking small chunks of yesterday's meat over the tiny fire in the middle of the sleeping area. Smoke blew wildly from the smouldering ashes, driven by the heavy winds that blew in through the large door which had remained open throughout the night.

We sat wordlessly while we chewed the tough strips of beef, nobody even acknowledging that I had joined the small circle of people. They were all tired, cold, miserable, and wished every moment to be away from this place. I wished that we would never have to leave.

It was a full six days later.

Emma had teamed up with the police and together it had taken them four days and nights to crack Mr. Irvine's computer codes. Every moment was agony: I knew that Alina had been sent back to the barn to either give birth or die and that the few remaining others—Nasha, Elin, Aaron, all of them—would be struggling to survive. I had no way of knowing how many days it had been since Mr. Irvine had last sent a supply of food, or whether the water tap was left on or shut off. At the very minimum, it had been five days since the group last had fresh food, and in my heart I knew that it had probably been much longer.

Emma and the police finally found the location of the barn. It had been seventh on a list of twenty-three other secret sites that were being actively used for similar purposes.

It took us a whole day to figure out transportation to the barn and nearly another whole day to get there.

Nothing could have prepared me for what we found.

The sun had just begun to set over the distant hills as we arrived. A dark storm loomed far out over the ocean, fronted by heavy winds. From my years of captivity in this place, I knew that the brunt of the storm would stay off shore, but that we were still in for some pretty nasty weather.

Solomon had thought ahead and brought a large pry-bar with him. It took four of us pushing on its sturdy handle to pop the electronic lock off of the exterior door that lead to the indoor parking area attached to the Entry Room.

Emma crossed the glossy space ahead of the rest of us, punching a 6 digit code into a panel on the inside wall. A moment later, the wall slid apart with a hiss.

I found myself rushing into the Entry Room before the door had fully opened, calling out to the people in the barn frantically--part of me overwhelmingly excited to see them all again, unable to wait any longer for their comforting hugs and familiar words, part of me afraid that we may have been too late.

The room was dark and my eyes had no time to adjust before I tripped and fell over the bodies.

I knew right away what I had fallen over. The smell was undeniable: rotting, bloating flesh—the kind of odour that comes from a dead fish washed up on the beach, or a decaying carcass of a bird high up in the rafters, though much, much stronger.

The back of my throat began to instantly water and I fought back dry heaves of vomit. I pushed myself like a crab away from the bodies, my eyes locked on the two dead people, so far into decomposition that they were almost unrecognizable. Had it not been for the immense size of the male body and the short brown hair of the young girl, I wouldn't have been able to guess that it was David and Kristy laid out carefully before me.

Florian, upon seeing my level of distress, ran to my side, blocking the view with his body.

"Shhh, shhh," he hushed, pulling my head to his chest in a surprisingly parental manner. "Don't look, Ash. Don't look. You don't need to see that."

As hard as I tried, I couldn't block out the image of the two of them lying there, rotting away, discarded like litter. I barely noticed as the others entered the room, smashing at the locking mechanism on the inside door that led into the main part of the barn, then helping Florian to guide me though.

The familiar musty scent of the barn snapped me out of my stupor like a slap to the face. I had never noticed how foul the barn smelled: Damp, still, smoky air, wet sand and soil, dry hay covered in mildew and mold, the pungent scent of human excrement and dried urine.

It was almost enough to mask the lingering scent of death that grew even stronger as we walked further into the barn.

I knew right then that no one had survived.

My legs felt weak and heavy as I walked slowly ahead holding tightly to Florian and Sarah. I was cold and hot at the same time, afraid to look ahead but knowing that it was inevitable.

A few steps ahead, part way between the Entry Door and the fire pit, a small mound of dirt rose from the otherwise flat ground. It was clearly a makeshift grave and from its size I could tell that there were more than a few bodies buried in its depths.

I shuddered as walked slowly passed, my eyes now locked on two curled up forms close to the empty, cold fire pit. From this angle I couldn't yet tell who's bodies they were, but I already felt overwhelmingly sad for them. They would have been the last two survivors. They would have had to watch as all the others slowly starved to death around them while they themselves faded and withered with insufferable weakness. They would have had to carry the lifeless bodies away, first into the Entry Room hoping that, as in the past, Mr. Irvine's men would come to dispose of the bodies in an appropriate manner. Then upon realizing that his men would not be coming, to scratch a hole in the earth with their bare hands and bury their friends one by one, knowing full well that there would be no one to do them the same service when their inevitable time came as well.

It was the long dark hair that had me breaking into tears before I even saw her face.

Wrapped loosely in the embrace of the other person, cradled on her back like an infant, Nasha's head hung unnaturally backwards, mouth open in a permanent plea to the heavens for salvation. Her closed eyes had sunken hauntingly into bony sockets on a skinny, almost unrecognizable face, her natural beauty and kindness still somehow discernable despite it all.

314

I crouched down at her side and touched her thin hand gently. She was so cold.

I could almost hear her voice, almost feel her hugs. I wanted to kiss her cheek and tell her that everything would be okay. To not be afraid. To finally go to a place where she would be safe and happy and comfortable. I wished I had been there in her final moments. I wish I had been there to save her. I wished that none of this had ever happened and that we could go back to our normal lives. I wished that she could hear me tell her that I love her just once. I had never said it to her before.

Turning my attention to the person who held Nasha's body, I found myself struggling to figure out who it was. I could tell that it was a female, but her head had drooped so low that her chin rested on Nasha's shoulder. She had gone to considerable lengths to wrap herself in many layers of clothing, even obscuring much of her face. Seeing this, I immediately flashed back to the many times when I too had been so deprived of food and water. Beyond the aches in the belly and all of the weakness and lethargy, the constant feeling of intense, bone shaking cold was one of the most intolerable sensations, and I understood why she had wrapped herself so tightly.

Gently, I began to unwrap the layers of cloth from her head and face. Her hair had been streaked with blonde and pink highlights and cut stylishly, but had obviously been left unmaintained for a long period before her death. The greying skin on her face seemed almost transparent and delicate, and hung unnaturally from her thin jowls. Scars lined every inch of her face.

It was the sweater that gave it away. As I removed the final scraps of blankets, I noticed immediately that the woman was holding the tattered, dirty, pink sweater that had once belonged to Julie; the one that Michael and I had used to keep Alina warm and comfortable as an infant.

Alina.

She looked nothing like her former self.

I had known her face so well; the shape of her youthful eyes, the slight curve of her tiny nose, her thin, nervous smile, the smooth, babyish cheeks that were always pink with timidity. I had spent every day of her life watching her with wonder as she grew, amazed almost daily with the small, subtle changes. When I saw her last, she had been a weak, nervous little child. This shell of a person in

315

front of me was a battle-worn, defeated person who looked more like someone in her twenties than someone who had not even made it to ten years old.

My heart felt like it were ripping in two. The young girl that I had helped Michael raise, that I had named, that we had protected and cared for and loved, was no longer.

I kissed her face and held her tightly, silently refusing to let go as the others placed David, Kristy and Nasha in a small hole beside the other grave. I could feel the small rise in her belly, reminding me sickeningly that she had been pregnant when she died. I drove away any thoughts about what she had been forced into. I couldn't allow myself to face it. All I could do was hold her and cry.

We buried her next to Nasha, interlocking their bony fingers together, forever to hold one another's hand. I ceremoniously threw the first handfuls of dirt over the bodies, but had to walk away and sit at the edge of the water as the others finished the job—the great door now open thanks to Solomon who had radioed back to headquarters, eager to clear the smell from the barn.

****

The sun hadn't yet risen over the horizon by the time I made my way down to the beach. I knew that this would be the last time that I ever watched this familiar charcoal morning sky change from the grey of dawn to the navy blue of early morning.

The night storm had left a thick swash of seaweed and ocean debris along the edge of the beach but I didn't hesitate to step to the edge of cool water and let the crashing waves flow over my feet.

I thought about everything that had happened. Nothing was left of my former life: Michael was in critical condition in some far away hospital, and even if he made a full recovery, he would never be the same. Alina, Nasha and everyone else that I had ever known and cared about were dead. From now on I would have to live in a unfamiliar and bewildering city, surrounded by strangers, forced to adapt to their bizarre and overwhelmingly elaborate lives. The quiet, slow, simple life that I had always led was gone, changed forever by the events of just a few days.

Changed forever, I thought. Just like me.

"Ash," said Florian, careful to speak softly enough to gently break me from my haze. I didn't realize that he had come down to join me.

"You alright?" He put his arm over my shoulder, knowing my answer without needing me to respond.

Together we stood and watched as the orange tip of the sun peeked up from the water's edge on the horizon and into the low, dark cloud the hung just above the surface.

"It's time to go," he said finally.

It struck me as we made our way back up into the core of the barn that this had been the first time in my life that I had ever gone to the water's edge without looking up to the cameras, worrying if this would be my last time that I would be allowed to do so.

The rest of the group was already standing beside the smouldering fire with their backpacks and supplies ready to leave. They all stood silently as I knelt down beside the large grave and wordlessly said my goodbyes. I knew I would never be back.

I led the way out of the barn, walking quickly, knowing that hesitating would make leaving all the more difficult.

After we had crammed all of our gear into the two jeeps that had carried us here I turned to the group:
"Wait, there's something I have to do."

They all observed me knowingly. Emma stepped forward and handed me a small, metal object. I had seen her use it when we arrived here and made our camp beside the fire pit: A lighter.

Walking back through the open door of the barn, I gathered a few small handfuls of hay and assembled neat pile against the wooden wall of the barn. Flipping open the lid, I noticed the familiar logo of Irvine Industries. There was a mild sense of satisfaction as I clicked the button on the side of the lighter and touched the flames to the small pile. It instantly ignited and the flames quickly leapt to the rough, hand cut, dried boards of building that had for so long been my jail cell. My prison. The only home I had ever known.

The flames grew violently. Soon the heat was so intense that Emma and Solomon pulled me from the room. We stood and watched for a few minutes as the flames began to sneak through the barn boards, but eventually even that was too hot to tolerate, and I found Emma once again pulling me away and strapping me into the passenger seat of the second vehicle.

I watched in the side mirror as the fire devoured the barn behind us while we drove up through the grassy, windy road and up into the hills. Eventually even the smoke disappeared behind the mountains and trees. Only then did I look away from the mirror and at the road ahead.

"Where do we go from here?" I said, breaking the silence.

Solomon, who was sitting in the driver's seat, cleared his throat uncomfortably. "Back to the tower for now. Our people are still working there with the authorities. There is a lot to be done."

I felt hot inside again. I didn't know what I had expected but the last place I wanted to go was back to Mr. Irvine's building.

"But before we do," Emma interjected, "we have one more stop."

****

It took another full day of travel.

We pulled up to the house slowly, cautious to avoid a group of children who were shooting balls at a makeshift net in the middle of the street.

The house was small compared to others on the street, its façade old and poorly maintained, overgrown with thick apple trees and weeds; An eyesore in an otherwise affluent and appealing neighborhood. There was something about it though--a sense of character or history hidden behind all of the neglect--that hinted that this home was once the star of the neighborhood.

There had been few words between us since we left the barn. We had traveled quietly, all of us finally processing our new realities within our own minds as the world flew past our windows.

Now, sitting in front of this strange house, curious as to why we were here, I had expected someone to speak, but no one did.

Beside me, Solomon was fidgeting with a screen built into the dash board that had just announced that we had arrived at our destination. In the far back row, Chiku and Sarah were unbuckling their seat belts and rummaging through the large purses that they had been carrying, looking for makeup to freshen up their tired looking faces. Behind me, Florian fumbled through a case full of papers. Emma sat perfectly still, staring out the side window.

Finally I spoke: "What are we doing here?"

Solomon sighed nervously, uncertain of how to start.
"We've done a little research," he said. "Or, well, I should say, Emma did some research." He looked up at her through the rear view mirror.

She caught his look and spoke: "This is where your family lives," she said mechanically.

It was the last thing I would have ever had expected. I didn't truly believe that I had a family. I wasn't sure if I even understood the concept. Mr. Irvine had told me a fantastical story of my mother bringing me to him in desperation, leaving me in his care to provide a better life, but I had found out that it had all been a lie. I hadn't had much time to think about it since, but somewhere deep down I had begun to believe that I was like Emma and Kyal—laboratory created, test-tube babies with no true mother, father or siblings.

Now, looking towards the dilapidated house, looking towards the flaking red door and the dirty, curtained windows, I felt a warmth in my chest, a pleasant flutter of nervousness in my heart, and I wondered if this could actually be true.

Florian stepped out of the vehicle first and opened my door for me, encouraging me out. My knees felt weak but I pulled myself from the seat and stepped onto the curb.

319

"Go knock on the door," said Sarah, now moving to my side and rubbing my back soothingly. "They're expecting you."

A torrent of thoughts raced through my mind: Who were they? What were they like? Do they want me? Why did they let Mr. Irvine take me? What would they look like? Would I stay with them? Do I have siblings?

Would they love me?

I took a deep breath and stepped onto the walkway leading towards the door. The house suddenly seemed to be looming over me and I felt my legs stop beneath me.

"Go on," encouraged Sarah. The others all looked on intently.

Putting one foot consciously in front of the other, I kept my eyes locked on the front door as I slowly passed a broken white picket fence overgrown with colourful vines, and a child's bike, rusting and almost concealed by long grass.

I must have stood in front of that red door for a full minute before I willed myself to raise my hand and knock.

It was only seconds before the door quickly swung open.

She was beautiful.

"Oh... m....," the woman stammered, tears instantly flooding from her eyes. She covered her mouth with both of her hands, visibly shaking.

I noticed immediately that she had the same dark eyes as me.

"Hello," I said nervously, uncertain of what to do. "Uh... my... my name is..."

Suddenly the woman, my mother, threw herself towards me, wrapping her arms tightly over my shoulders, burying her face in my neck as she broke down completely.

I held her awkwardly at first, unaccustomed to such a display of emotion, but soon finding a comfortable position and wrapping her tightly, my eyes now dripping with tears as well.

We held each other for what seemed like eternity, though it felt as if it ended too soon when she pulled herself slightly away to get a better look at me.

I could see myself in her features. We were certainly different in appearance—her face more round and feminine, her nose smaller and more pointy, her hair clearly dyed an artificial shade of yellow, but the similarity was undeniable.

"I can't believe it, I can't believe it," she sobbed. "My boy! Oh my God! We never stopped! We never stopped looking for you! We never stopped!"

She leaned in and hugged me again.

A young boy appeared behind her in the doorway, his body language closed and hesitant, his face red with emotion.
My face.

He was probably a year or so younger than me, but in every way we were the spitting image of one another: our mothers deep brown eyes, our wispy, thick brown hair, our wide shoulders and skinny limbs.

His mother, our mother, noticed his presence and pulled him into our hug. I could feel his body contracting as he attempted to hold back tears, but soon he too was weeping freely.

"Are you okay? Did they hurt you? Where were you?" my mother said desperately as she pulled slightly away again.

"I'm okay," I choked, wiping away my tears with my sleeve, unsure of how much she knew.

As if reading my thoughts, she interrupted before I could answer anything more.

"We just woke up one morning and you were gone! GONE! The window was open but the police couldn't find anything! We looked everywhere! We gave up everything! We devoted our whole lives to finding you! I hope you don't think we ever gave up! We *never* did. Your father died traveling the world looking for you. He never lost hope!"

Although I had never known him, never even knew of his existence, I suddenly felt an immense sense of loss, and fresh, new tears poured from my eyes at word of his death.

My brother looked up at me with desperation in his eyes. "What... what about..."

Our mother, seeming to realize that she had forgotten something important, looked up towards the group that I had come with, searching their faces with disappointment and concern.

"Where's your sister?"

I looked at her in stunned confusion.

"Pardon?"

"Your sister!" she said, her voice cracking with anxiety.

I looked to my brother. He too was looking at the others with confused anticipation.

"Your sister!" she repeated, stepping slightly towards the vehicle to get a better look. I could see the distress crush down on her as she turned back to me with panic in her eyes, frantic for an explanation. "Your sister! Your SISTER!" she yelled, "They took you both! They stole you *both*, right out from under us! They took you at the same time! She was with you! Tell me she's with you!"

I felt as if my heart was going to explode from my chest. It was a spark of a faint memory that I had long forgotten but I could see it clearly now: Two figures dressed completely in black, sneaking in through my bedroom window. The first man pounced on me before I was awake enough to scream. He covered my mouth with his hand, lifting me forcefully from my little race-car bed. The second man vanished silently into the hall, returning in just seconds, holding a tiny blonde infant, still deeply asleep, callously between his hands. My sister.

I looked now to my brother who stood blubbering in front of me, begging me with his eyes to give him good news.

I remembered his name now: Ryan.

The girl, his twin, I remembered her name now too. The realisation hit me like a punch to the gut. I'd always wondered where I got the name from. I had always thought that I just came up with it out of thin air on the day that Michael and I named the small girl that Julie had died giving birth to. All along it had been the name of a sister that I didn't know I had.

Alina.

My sister.

A shiver raced down my back.

She was still out there.

www.ingramcontent.com/pod-product-compliance
Lightning Source LLC
Chambersburg PA
CBHW062026170626
46813CB00001B/311